With a sudden laugh, he gripped Roger by the arm and said in a low voice, 'For months I've told everyone that I am dead. But I am not. And I've kept my secret well. I've not told even Pauline. You could not have joined me at a better time, Breuc. Tomorrow night we sail to reconquer France.'

BY DENNIS WHEATLEY

NOVELS

The Launching of Roger Brook
The Shadow of Tyburn Tree
The Rising Storm
The Man Who Killed the King
The Dark Secret of Josephine
The Rape of Venice
The Sultan's Daughter
The Wanton Princess
Evil in a Mask
The Ravishing of Lady Mary Ware
The Irish Witch

The Scarlet Imposter
Faked Passports
The Black Baroness
V for Vengeance
Come Into My Parlour
Traitors' Gate
They Used Dark Forces

The Prisoner in the Mask
The Second Seal
Vendetta in Spain
Three Inquisitive People
The Forbidden Territory
The Devil Rides Out
The Golden Spaniard
Strange Conflict
Codeword—Golden Fleece
Dangerous Inheritance

Gateway to Hell
The Quest of Julian Day
The Sword of Fate
Bill for the Use of a Body

Black August
Contraband
The Island Where Time Stands
Still
The White Witch of the South
Seas

To the Devil—a Daughter
The Satanist

The Eunuch of Stamboul
The Secret War
The Fabulous Valley
Sixty Days to Live
Such Power is Dangerous
Uncharted Seas
The Man Who Missed the War
The Haunting of Toby Jugg
Star of Ill-Omen
They Found Atlantis
The Ka of Gifford Hillary
Curtain of Fear
Mayhem in Greece
Unholy Crusade
The Strange Story of Linda Lee
The Irish Witch

SHORT STORIES

Mediterranean Nights

Gunmen, Gallants and Ghosts

HISTORICAL

A Private Life of Charles II (*Illustrated by Frank C. Pape*)
Red Eagle (*The Story of the Russian Revolution*)

AUTOBIOGRAPHICAL

Stranger than Fiction (*War Papers for the Joint Planning Staff*)
Saturdays with Bricks

SATANISM

The Devil and all his Works (*Illustrated in colour*)

Dennis Wheatley

DESPERATE MEASURES

ARROW BOOKS

Arrow Books Ltd
3 Fitzroy Square, London W1

An imprint of the Hutchinson Publishing Group

London Melbourne Sydney Auckland
Wellington Johannesburg and agencies
throughout the world

First published by Hutchinson & Co (Publishers) Ltd 1974
Arrow edition 1976
© Dennis Wheatley Ltd 1974

Made and printed in Great Britain
by The Anchor Press Ltd
Tiptree, Essex

ISBN 0 09 912850 0

Contents

In 1940 I dedicated a book to 'My soldier stepson, with deep affection and the wish that crossed swords and batons may one day grace the shoulders of his tunic'. Jack Younger had then just left Sandhurst and I watched him as an ensign in the Coldstream Guards march off from Chelsea Barracks to the war in North Africa. Now he wears those crossed swords of a Major General on the shoulders of his tunic and I am so happy to dedicate this book to him.

Publishers' Note

THE Roger Brook series covers every principal event in Europe between 1783 and 1815. During this brief period, initiated by the French Revolution, there occurred an upheaval which altered the way of life that the great majority of people had led for many centuries. Nothing had occurred to equal it since the fall of the Roman Empire. It is for that reason that these books are of special interest—and educational value. Historical novels are legion. But the story of Roger Brook stands alone, in that it conveys the whole picture, from start to finish, of those tremendous years.

At the age of fifteen, rather than be forced by his father, Admiral Brook, to become a midshipman, Roger ran away to France. After four years there, chance put him in possession of information which prevented a war between France and Britain. Subsequently he became Prime Minister Pitt's most resourceful secret agent.

He undertook missions to Sweden, Denmark and Russia. Having established a second identity as a Frenchman, he frequented Versailles before the Revolution as a Chevalier, and survived the Terror by getting himself made a member of the Commune. During those years he travelled to the Netherlands,

Italy and Spain. At the siege of Toulon he met young Bonaparte, then an unknown Captain of Artillery. Later he became one of Napoleon's A.D.C.s and accompanied him to Egypt and Syria. On his way to becoming the Governor of an island in the Caribbean, Roger was wrecked off Haiti and landed in the middle of the great Negro slave revolt. A duel in England resulted in his travelling to India. He served Wellington in the Peninsula, but was carried off with the Portuguese Royal Family to Brazil. In St. Petersburg he was involved in the assassination of the Czar Paul I. He went on missions to the Sultan of Turkey and the Shah of Persia. After the retreat from Moscow in 1812, he reached Sweden; but the ship he expected to take him home took him instead to New York, and the United States was then at war with Britain. With the help of Red Indians he escaped across the St. Lawrence to Canada. While secretly sending intelligence to England, Roger was present at nearly all Napoleon's great battles, from Marengo to Waterloo.

During these years he met all the most famous people of his time: Catherine the Great, Louis XVI and XVIII, George III and IV, the Emperor Francis, the Czar Alexander, and numerous other sovereigns; Marie Antoinette, the Empresses Josephine and Marie Louise, Talleyrand, Danton, Robespierre, Fouché, Nelson, Sir Sidney Smith, Sir John Moore, Fox, Castlereagh, Metternich, Blücher, all the Bonapartes and all Napoleon's Marshals.

Interwoven with true history there are murders, kidnappings, smuggling, blackmail, feats of great endurance, descriptions of Satanic rites and accounts of Roger's love affairs during the many years he spent abroad. But whenever he returned to England he renewed his lifelong devotion to Georgina—in turn Lady

Etheridge, the Countess of St. Ermins and the Duchess of Kew—who shared with him a passion that began when they were in their teens.

QUOTES

Howard Spring wrote of an early Roger Brook: 'I look forward with pleasure to the spectacle of Roger Brook turning the Scarlet Pimpernel pale pink.'

Perry Jones in *The Sunday Times*: 'Mr. Wheatley's historical detail is impeccable.'

George MacDonald Fraser (author of the Flashman books) in *The Glasgow Herald*: 'As a secret agent Roger Brook makes James Bond look like an infant gurgling in his play-pen.'

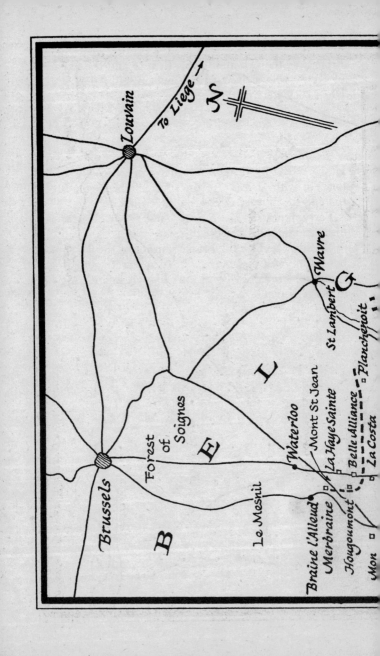

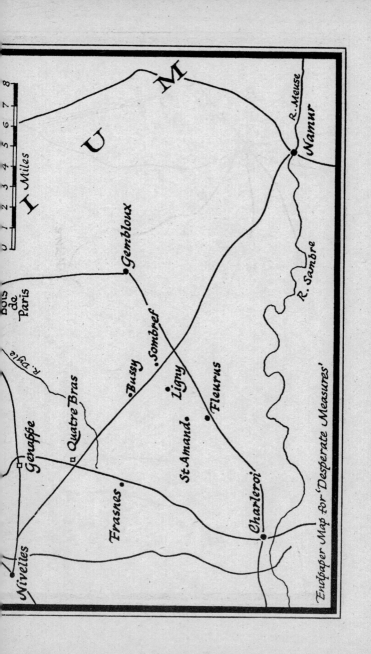

Endpaper Map for 'Desperate Measures'

1

Bedroom Scene

AT two o'clock in the morning on July 20th, 1814, Roger Brook—in whose favour his family's title, Earl of Kildonan, had recently been revived as a reward for many years of successful missions—and Georgina, Duchess of Kew, were lying naked side by side in bed.

They were both in their middle forties. Roger looked his age. The many dangers he had faced had caused his mouth to set grimly when in repose, and there were wrinkles round his bright blue eyes. His hair was grey, except for the wings above his ears, which were white and added a distinguished touch to his strong, regular features. His body was muscular and still slim, on account of the many thousands of miles he had ridden during Napoleon's wars.

Those wars had ceased only the previous April, on the Emperor's abdication. Roger had been lucky, for he had been wounded seriously only three times: a bullet through the chest at Marengo, a badly broken ankle when his horse had been shot under him at Eylau and, more recently, his left calf had been blown to ribbons by a German guerilla who had shot at him from a wood while he had been riding alone along a road near Dresden. This last injury he resented intensely, as he had been proud of his shapely legs when wearing silk stockings, and it had left him with a slight limp.

Georgina, on the other hand, looked as though she were still in her early thirties. The contours of her well-rounded figure had not increased since she was twenty, the ringlets of her abundant blue-black hair had not lost their lustre, the high colouring, smooth skin, full, ripe, naturally red mouth and flashing black eyes had long made her a reigning beauty. She was also blessed with an amusing wit and an exceptionally wide background of knowledge, for her highly-cultured father had educated her himself in many matters not even thought of in the Young Ladies Academies of that period. These many attractions had enabled her to enchant royalties, statesmen, ambassadors and poets whom her great wealth, inherited from three previous husbands, had made it possible for her to entertain lavishly.

From their teens Roger and Georgina had been lovers. When younger, he had many times pressed her to marry him, but she had always refused, on the grounds that his work as a secret agent kept him for such long periods abroad. Then, when he had at length decided to give up his adventurous career, she had agreed. But fate had dealt them a cruel blow. Roger had been unjustly accused in Berlin of murder, and condemned to death. Unknown to her, his sentence had been commuted to ten years in prison. After he had escaped and got home, he learned that Georgina, believing him dead, had mourned him desperately for several months; then, not caring what became of her, had married the old Duke of Kew. In consequence on the last day of 1812 Roger had married a girl he had first known as Lady Mary Ware.

The intimacy of Roger and Georgina had always

been sporadic, and there had been periods of even years when they had not seen each other. But always on his return to England, sometimes only for a week or so, at other times for several months, they had at once resumed their secret liaison; for, spiritually attuned as they had been from the time they were boy and girl, neither had ever found in any other member of the opposite sex such complete satisfaction as they derived from each other, both in bed and out of it.

This night had been no exception. After an epicurean supper, washed down with ample champagne, they had twice made most passionate love and, before dawn, would do so again. Yet, in one sense, it was an exception, because since Roger's marriage all their previous clandestine meetings had been carefully planned in advance. This one had not.

That day Roger's only daughter, Susan, had been married at St. George's, Hanover Square, to Georgina's only son, Charles, Earl of St. Ermins. At the reception, standing a little apart from the other guests, Roger and Georgina had been happily remarking on the joys that the newly-weds, who had long been in love, would experience that night. Roger had said with a sigh:

'If only you were in Susan's place and I could be in Charles's, what a night we'd make of it together.'

Georgina looked up at him with a wicked smile. 'What's to prevent us from pretending that is so? Let us put it from our minds that you have had me a thousand times. 'Twould make a delightful charade for me to play the part of the bashful bride, while you played that of bridegroom, gentle but desperate eager to see and explore my secret place and, there engulfed, experience the greatest of delights.'

'Dam'me, why not? 'Tis a marvellous idea!' Roger exclaimed with a laugh. Then his face suddenly became grave and he added, 'But what the devil shall I tell Mary?'

'Tell her that before leaving just now, my Lord Castlereagh asked you to wait upon him at the Foreign Office after a late Cabinet meeting this evening. She knows that he often consults you on matters concerning France.'

Roger needed no pressing. When the bride and bridegroom had been cheered away, he glibly told his wife that, much as he regretted it, he could not accompany her home to Richmond, giving the excuse that Georgina had provided.

Having seen Mary into their coach, he strolled along to White's, played several games of backgammon with a fellow member there, then made his way out to the studio-villa on the hillside overlooking Kensington village, where Georgina pursued her hobby of painting and, at times, spent the night with a beau who had won her favour.

They had been lying in silence for some minutes when Georgina enquired, 'How did Mary take your unexpected announcement that you were not returning home with her?'

Sitting up, Roger refilled their goblets with champagne, handed Georgina hers and replied, 'She pulled a face, but could hardly make in public the sort of scene she now treats me to each time I tell her that I mean to spend the night in town.'

Georgina sighed. 'What a bore the woman has become. Even if she does not believe the excuse you give her about attending men's dinners, or conferring with statesmen who value your advice on Continental affairs, why cannot she be sensible and reconcile herself to the idea of your having a mistress, as is the case with all but a small minority of men in your position?'

'I think it to be because she has never been accustomed to the ways of high society. Although her father was an Earl, he was as poor as a church mouse, and left her near penniless. Her only escape from the drudgery of becoming some old woman's companion was to marry that Baltic trader who went bankrupt and committed suicide shortly before I found her stranded in St. Petersburg.'

'I know! I know!' Georgina cut in, a little petulantly. 'While married into trade, she was naturally no longer eligible to be received by persons of quality. But, when you first met her, she was staying as the guest of our Minister's lady in Lisbon, and after you brought her back from the Americas as your wife we introduced her to numerous well-bred people.'

'True. But when in Portugal she had only recently put away her school books; then, between our return from Canada and my departure for the Continent in search of Charles, only a few months elapsed. Such brief periods were insufficient for her to become fully aware of the cynical customs of the aristocracy. During the time she was a merchant's wife, she would naturally have absorbed the outlook of the middle classes, who strongly condemn adultery. That, I doubt not, is why she resents my infidelity so intensely.'

'She does, then, believe that your nights in London are spent with another woman?'

'Yes, and to be frank, that woman to be yourself. I told you long since how, on my return from France, I found that she had taken to the bottle as a solace for my absence. What I refrained from telling you was that, knowing it was on your account that I had gone abroad, she declared, in a drunken outburst, that I had deserted her for all those months out of love for you. I admitted that we had been lovers in the past—for all the world knows that—but swore that our affair had ended when you married old Kew. I now fear it was stupid of me, but so that she should not think the less of you for marrying an old man of such ill reputation, I gave her an account of the pact that you made with him—that to gratify his vanity, you would become his Duchess and behave publicly like a model wife, on condition that, though he might gaze his fill at your exquisite body, he was not to lay a finger on it.'

Georgina laughed. 'That suited him well enough, since he was already impotent; but that is less than half the truth, since I also stipulated that I might take lovers, provided I did so with great discretion and allowed no breath of scandal to attach to me.'

'Exactly, and it was on account of your honouring your pact with him that we could meet only infrequently. Remember, too, that Mary did not meet you until after he had had his seizure. Knowing that he is confined to his bed—a living corpse, no longer even able to speak or conscious of what goes on round him—not unnaturally she refused to believe that you had not again become my mistress.'

'In her place I'd have assumed the same.'

'Well, there it is, and there is no avoiding the scenes she makes me. I would to God I'd never married her.'

'In that, alas, I am at least in part to blame, since on your return from Portugal I advised you to. During those months before you went there, you had become so mightily frustrated by the long intervals between our meetings, passed in idleness with naught to occupy your mind that, when you told me of her, I felt an excellent solution to your discontent would be to take a wife; and she sounded most suitable.'

'Dear one, your advice was sound, although I had

not the least intention of taking it at that time, for 'twas before your Duke had become paralysed. As he was already an old man, I still had hopes that in a few years he would die and we could then marry. Your suggestion was based on what I'd told you of Mary having developed a desperate passion for me. But, for my part, 'twas no more than an amusing flirtation. She was then only a pretty little chit of a girl, so I was able to salve her pride by telling her that I was much too old for her, and of such a roving disposition that I could never bring myself to settle down.

'It was those long months in Russia that changed my attitude toward her. The fact that during the retreat from Moscow I disguised her as my soldier servant made her no less a woman—physically weak compared to a man—yet she trudged through the mud and snow day after day, for hours on end at the same pace as the men. The fortitude she displayed was truly amazing. The cold was bitter beyond belief; the discomfort and nagging hunger almost unbearable, yet she never complained. Even when she was grievously wounded and nearly lost an eye she would not give up. And through it all she never lost her sense of humour. My admiration for her strength of character and courage grew from day to day.'

Georgina nodded. 'Yes, you have oft spoken of it. I can well understand how you came to love her, after she had become such a marvellous companion throughout your long ordeal during the retreat from Moscow.'

'All the same, I was a fool to marry her when we reached Stockholm. I should have realized that things would be very different here in England. She showed the same splendid spirit during our trials last year in the wilds of Canada; but, there again, we were entirely dependent on each other. Here she can give me nothing but love, and my only real love is forever yours.'

'I know it well, my own. But since she believes that we are still lovers, she should be grateful that we restrain ourselves to only occasional meetings, and that to remain at home with her you have denied yourself the many gay evenings it was your wont to spend with your men friends. I think her monstrous lucky to have your companionship nine days and nights out of ten.'

'Maybe she is, but I am not, for I now derive little enjoyment from her company. The root of the trouble is that, although born an aristocrat, poor Mary has the mentality of a bourgeoise. No sooner had I gone abroad in search of Charles than she ceased to associate with the pleasant people to whom I, and others like yourself, had introduced her. She feels an inferiority when in such company, and it is only with difficulty that I can, now and then, persuade her to accept invitations to social events. Moreover, she has no interest in international affairs and little knowledge of the wars in which I have been involved for the greater part of my life. So, living with her has become desperate dull for me.'

For a moment, while taking another drink of champagne, Georgina was silent, then she said, 'Dear one, since that is the case, methinks you should face the situation squarely. Tell her that, with or without her, you intend to resume your social life. And tell her about us, too. She may rage, then sulk for a while, but after a time she will become reconciled to her situation.'

Roger shook his head. 'No, that I will not do. As long as I continue to deny our intimacy, she has nothing definite to go on. Did I once admit it, she is capable of causing you the greatest embarrassment.

The odds are that she'll start drinking again, then one evening appear unannounced at some big function, and abuse you publicly as the cause of her unhappiness.'

'I had not thought of that, and 'twould be cursed unpleasant,' Georgina murmured. 'But deuce take the woman. Let us waste no more of our night talking of her. Make love to me again, then we'll snatch an hour or two of sleep.'

Nothing loath, Roger embraced her. For several minutes they savoured each other's kisses, then began to move in slow, rhythmic union. Georgina was already moaning with pleasure when Roger caught the sound of a creak, as though someone had stepped on a loose board; but he ignored it. Next moment there came, loud and clear, the rending of splintered wood. As he swiftly disengaged himself from Georgina and turned his head, bright moonlight flooded the room, dimming the light from the two candles.

The French windows, which gave on to a small garden, had been forced open. Framed in them, and silhouetted against the summer night sky, stood the figure of a hooded woman. Behind her, more indistinctly, lurked two men, one of them holding a jemmy. Turning, the woman thrust a purse into his free hand. He beckoned to the other man and they ran off together. The woman stepped into the bedroom, and threw back her hood, revealing herself to be Mary.

2

In Flagrante Delicto

In amazement and fury Roger stared at Mary, but it was Georgina who was the first to speak. Sitting up in bed and making no attempt to hide her splendid breasts, she asked in icy tones:

'To what, Madam, do we owe this unpardonable intrusion?'

Mary swallowed hard, then replied hoarsely, 'I had to know. I had to know for certain.'

'So you employed some roughs to break in here,' Roger snapped. 'How could you stoop so low?'

'For this you could be sent to gaol,' Georgina added calmly. 'And I've a mind to send for the Watch.'

' 'Tis an idle threat,' Mary retorted. 'You'd not dare face the scandal.'

'Would I not? Then you don't know me, girl. It has ever been my principle to defy all threats. I'd be praised for my courage, while you would be hounded from society as a vulgar, sneaking little bitch.'

'I care not a rap for society. My only interest is my husband, and you have stolen him from me. I've long suspected it, and by tracing him here have seen him with my own eyes disporting himself with you. That you show no shame brands you as a gilded whore.'

Georgina suddenly laughed. 'If "whore's" the word,

'tis you to whom it applies. I have "disported" myself, as you describe it, with a number of personable and distinguished men, but sought no gain other than my own pleasure from so doing; whereas you, my lady, sold yourself to a middle-aged man of no breeding, and so became a kept woman.'

'I was married to Mr. Wicklow,' Mary retorted angrily.

'What is the moral difference?' Georgina sneered. ' 'Tis mutual attraction alone that justifies a woman in giving herself. And I have loved Roger all my life.'

'Then by now you should have had your fill of him, and had the decency to refrain from pursuing him after he married me.'

'Mary, you are wrong,' Roger intervened. 'Georgina has not pursued me. Married or single, with the one exception of while she was St. Ermins' wife, by mutual assent we have continued discreetly to be lovers. To spare your feelings I have done my utmost to conceal from you this sole infidelity. But now that you have come upon us *in flagrante delicto*, you must reconcile yourself to Georgina and me occasionally gratifying our mutual passion.'

'I'll not condone it,' Mary burst out bitterly. 'Why should I allow you to wreck my life?'

'Fiddlesticks!' declared Georgina disdainfully. 'How can you have the face to say such a thing? Roger found you destitute in St. Petersburg, the widow of a common merchant. He married you, gave you a name you could be proud of, a delightful home, ample money and restored your status as acceptable in high society. Aye, and he has even since caused you to become a Countess. Wrecked your life indeed! From near the gutter he has raised you to be one of the most fortunate young women in England.'

'No matter. He gave me his love, and you have taken it from me.'

'I have taken nothing that has not been mine since before you were in your cradle.'

Again Roger intervened. 'Mary, I beg you to be sensible. I warn you now that, unless you accept the situation as it is, I'll have no alternative than to share a home with you no longer.'

'So be it, then!' Mary was trembling with rage. 'Desert me if you will. But I'll have my revenge. I'll ruin you. I swear it. And I'll put an end to your enjoying your sport with this lecherous witch.' Turning, she drew her hood over her head and fled from the room into the garden.

Roger got out of bed and closed the French windows. Georgina remained sitting up, with her hands clasped round her knees, until he came back and topped up their glasses of champagne. Taking hers, she said:

'What a little fool the girl is, cutting off her nose to spite her face like this. Still, one cannot help but feel sorry for her.'

He nodded. 'I agree, and I deeply regret having inspired in her this unbridled passion for me. If only she would be sensible and realise that nine-tenths of a loaf is better than no bread. Even so, this confrontation has its compensations for me. Much as I'll regret having to leave my home after having for so many years longed to settle down in it, I was getting little joy from her companionship, and at least we will be able to be together much more frequently.'

'You really mean, then, to make no attempt at reconciliation?'

'Yes. In threatening us in the way she did, she went too far. I'll make ample provision for her, but leave her now to stew in her own juice.'

'What will you do, and where will you live?'

'Dear Droopy Ned has always kept a room in Amesbury House at my disposal, against my unexpected returns from the Continent. No doubt he would willingly put me up, but I could not sponge on him indefinitely. I'll look round for a furnished apartment in the neighbourhood of St. James's. But what to do with myself is another matter. We had but one more rendezvous planned for Thursday next; then, with the season over, you'll be off to Newmarket, to maintain your show of being a good wife to old Kew. In August London will be as empty as a drum, and I know not where to go.'

She sighed. 'How I wish I could ask you to stay at Newmarket; but Kew's spinster sister, Lady Amelia, remains in permanent residence there, tending him. And you'll recall how damnably uncomfortable the old vixen made it for us at the time of your only visit.'

'Indeed I do. Realizing that we were lovers, she seized on every opportunity to make things awkward for us; and having her with us at every meal made our situation near intolerable. We were right to decide never to repeat that experience.'

After a moment Georgina's face brightened, and she exclaimed, 'I have it! Why should I not rent a small house nearby for you? She need not know of it, and I could leave the mansion every night by stealth, to come to you.'

Throwing his arms round her, Roger kissed her and cried, 'My love, you are a genius. What a prodigious fine idea. We could also rendezvous secretly in the daytime and ride together in the woods. August now bids to be a heavenly month for me.'

'For me, too,' laughed Georgina. 'And that we may the sooner be together, tomorrow—or today rather—

I'll cancel all my engagements. I'll give out that old
Kew has taken a turn for the worse, and may be
about to die; so I must leave at once for Newmarket.
In any case, I'm sick unto death of balls, banquets,
and command performances. I've never known such
an exhausting season.'

It was true enough that the past fortnight had taxed
even Georgina's seemingly inexhaustible vitality. As
the high spot of the peace celebrations, the Allied
Sovereigns had been invited on a State visit to London.
Old Francis of Austria, who hated having to make
public appearances, had excused himself, sending
Prince Metternich to represent him. But the Czar had
accepted, and so had his satellite, the weak-kneed
King Frederick William of Prussia, bringing with
them a host of Ministers and Generals, including the
rugged old Blücher, who was immensely popular.

Unfortunately, the Czar had behaved with great
tactlessness. In the first place, he had evaded the
Prince Regent, who had ridden out to Shooter's Hill,
and the thousands of people who had assembled there
to give him a tremendous welcome, by slipping past
them in a plain carriage. Then, instead of occupying
the royal accommodation prepared for him, he had
gone to stay with his widowed sister, the Grand
Duchess Catherine, who, from the previous March,
had taken over the Pultney Hotel in Piccadilly. The
Grand Duchess was a mischief-maker of the first order.
She had encouraged 'Prinny's' daughter to defy her
father, and make friends of the Whig leaders. She now
encouraged Alexander to act in ways offensive to the
Prince Regent. From the first dinner at Carlton House,
they took a dislike to one another, and on other State
occasions kept each other waiting, at times for as long
as an hour. But, in spite of their mutual animosity,

every day and night of the Sovereigns' visit had been one long succession of entertainments, at which people of Georgina's rank were expected to be present.

The following morning, after taking a loving farewell of Georgina, Roger went to Amesbury House in Arlington Street, arriving there shortly before midday.

On enquiring he learned that Lord Edward Fitz-Deverel—known to his friends as Droopy Ned from his myopia giving him a permanent stoop—was at home. He had, by his father's death, nine months earlier, become Earl of Amesbury. Roger was shown up to him in the same suite that, as a bachelor, Droopy had occupied during his father's lifetime.

That he had chosen to remain there, rather than move down to his late parent's more spacious rooms, was due to his reluctance to disarrange the strange assortment of items he had accumulated in his own suite. For a nobleman of his period he had unusual tastes, as he abhorred blood sports, and spent his time instead in experimenting with strange drugs, collecting antique jewellery and studying the religions of the past.

The walls of his rooms were decorated with Egyptian papyri, Roman mosaics and drawings from Greek vases. There was a side table on which stood a retort, surrounded by queerly shaped little bottles, another table with a glass top under which sparkled jewelled crucifixes and rosaries, a big bookcase holding scores of scrolls; in one corner stood a mummy in a sarcophagus, and in another was seated a large, stone Buddha. The Earl was dressed in a flowing, silk robe and his head was surmounted by an elaborate turban; but such a garb was still not unusual at that period as informal dress for men of his age.

He stood up as Roger came in, smiled at him, shook him warmly by the hand and said, 'Welcome, old friend. Sit you down and join me in a glass of Madeira wine.'

'That I'll gladly do.' Roger sat down and added, 'I'm much in need of sustenance after the night just past.' Then he gave an account of how Mary had broken in on him and Georgina, and all that had followed.

Droopy peered at him with his short-sighted eyes, shook his narrow, bird-like head, and said, ' 'Twas a shocking breach of the decencies; but are you really of a mind to leave Mary for good and all?'

'I am, indeed. Knowing how desperate jealous she is, I do not blame her overmuch for having me spied on to resolve her doubts; but to confront us naked in bed together was an act that I cannot forgive.'

As Droopy filled a glass for Roger, he said, 'I understand your outraged feelings at the moment. But, given time, I hope you will reconsider the matter. Remember, you are all that Mary has, and how she dotes upon you. Doubtless, she already repents her rash act, and as the price of your continuing to live at Richmond, will condone your occasional visits to Georgina.'

'Nay, Ned. My mind is made up. These past few months she's led me the very devil of a life, and I'll be damned if I'll submit to a renewal of it after a brief patching up of our differences. In fact, I'll not even see her again, and 'tis that which brings me here. I've come to ask you no small favour.'

Droopy smiled. 'In that case, name it, and I'll be your lordship's obedient servant.'

Not yet having become accustomed to being addressed as a lord caused Roger to give a sudden laugh. Then he said, 'I am greatly opposed to going down to Richmond and entering on an altercation with Mary. Do me the kindness, Ned, to go there in my stead. See my man Dan Izzard, and have him pack up such things as I am likely to need for the next few months, which I intend to spend with Georgina at Newmarket. Have him, too, pack all the rest and store them in the attics until I require them.'

'I'll certainly oblige you in that, and I'll order your room here to be prepared for you to occupy until you leave for the country. But in return I ask one thing. 'Tis that, on your return from Newmarket, you should go down to Richmond and see Mary.'

'I'll do that, since you wish it; though I doubt it will change my resolve to be done with her.'

For the week that followed, the two friends spent most of their evenings together, but Droopy was allergic to any form of exercise, while Roger disliked spending the best part of the day indoors; so he usually rode in Hyde Park in the mornings and spent several afternoons in long walks, often through parts of London rarely frequented by the gentry.

Except for the uneasy fourteen months' truce, in 1802–3, brought about by the Peace of Amiens, Britain and France had been at war for twenty-one years, and its effect on both countries had been devastating, particularly since Napoleon had initiated his 'Continental System' in 1806.

By his decrees in Berlin, and the following year in Milan, he had forbidden the import of British goods to all Continental ports; and he was then master of every country from the Baltic to the tip of Italy. The object of his 'System' was to ruin British commerce, and thus so deplete her vast wealth that she would no longer be able to subsidise coalitions of Continental countries with her gold, to pay their troops in attempts to throw off his yoke.

Britain had retaliated by a blockade that prevented
ships of neutral countries from landing cargoes in
Continental ports. In spite of an enormous increase in
smuggling, many cases of Napoleon's officials accepting
bribes to let goods through, and the reluctance of
several countries to enforce fully Napoleon's decrees,
the blockade had inflicted much grievous hardship on
the many millions of people then ruled by him. The
Industrial Revolution in Britain having occurred long
before that in other nations, she had supplied them
with the greater part of their agricultural implements
and other metal goods, woollens from Yorkshire,
cotton fabrics from Lancashire, china from the Pot-
teries, sugar and spices from the Indies and, most
resented of all, forced them to use ground acorns as a
substitute for their beloved coffee.

But the people of Britain had suffered almost as
severely. The loss of their principal markets had caused
hundreds of factories to close, and merchants great and
small to go bankrupt, resulting in an appalling degree
of unemployment. This had been still further increased
since 1812, when long-growing resentment by the
Americans because Britain prevented them from trading
freely with the Continental countries had caused them
at last to declare war, and thus also closed the markets
of the United States.

The situation had been greatly aggravated by the
shortage and high price of corn. A large proportion of
the Tory members in the House of Commons depended
for their seats on the farmers, and to protect their
interest there had long been a duty on imported wheat.
The Whigs, on the other hand, largely represented the
industrialists in the cities, whose interests lay in keeping
the price of corn down, so enabling them to pay
low wages to their workers. For several years previous

to 1813 there had been a series of bad harvests, which had led to a steep rise in the price of bread. The harvest of 1814 was better, but its effect was being countered by the cessation of shipments from America, with the result that the high price had had to be maintained. That spring a strenuous effort had been made by the Whigs, led by the fiery Whitbread, to introduce a Corn Law that would permit the import of corn free of duty. But it had failed, with the result that great numbers of the unemployed were starving from lack of the means to buy even bread.

Those walks through the poorer parts of London caused Roger great distress. In every street there were shuttered shops. On the corners stood idle groups of sullen, gaunt-faced men, clad in rags. The women were slovenly and haggard, slow-moving and having only a few potatoes or bits of offal in their shopping baskets, and the sad-eyed children were too listless even to play in the gutters. In the Midlands and the North, it was said to be even worse, with thousands of people, particularly children, dying from malnutrition every week. It was a terrible price to pay for victory, and it could not be wondered at that the government was so unpopular.

George III was now seventy-six, and no more than a cypher. In 1788 he had shown signs of a disordered mind, and the following year a Regency Bill had been passed by Parliament; but a few months later, to the delight of his people, the King had made an unexpected recovery. They admired him for his exemplary life, straightforward manner and for growing the biggest turnips in England—which had caused them to nickname him 'Farmer George'. But his recovery had not been permanent. By 1810 he had become unquestionably mad, and ever since, blind and often raving, had been confined to his rooms in Windsor Castle.

He had been most unfortunate in his sons, particularly the Prince of Wales, who had hated him and caused him endless trouble, not only by piling up mountainous debts and entering into a morganatic marriage with the actress Mrs. Fitzherbert, but also by openly encouraging the Whigs in their opposition to his father's Tory government. 'Prinny', as he was called, although known abroad as 'The First Gentleman of Europe', was a liar, a cheat and even bilked his friends out of money they had lent him. He was regarded as so despicable by many of the great nobles that they refused to know him. Moreover, he had been drunk when leading Caroline of Brunswick to the altar, and afterwards treated her abominably, a year after their marriage turning her out to live in a cottage near Blackheath which had formerly been occupied by Mrs. Fitzherbert. These many blackguardly acts had not only made him most unpopular with the people, but caused the government, when formulating the Regency Bill, to restrain his powers to such a degree that he, too, was no more than a cypher.

The control of the nation's affairs had therefore fallen into the hands of some one hundred noble families, many of whom held posts in the Tory government. Since 1812 Lord Liverpool had been Prime Minister, but his Cabinet was dominated by Lord Castlereagh who, as Foreign Minister, had long been extensively occupied with international relations. Yet, even had it been otherwise, it is doubtful if any Ministry could have greatly ameliorated the terrible state to which the people of Britain had been reduced by the Napoleonic wars.

On the last day of July Roger received a letter from

Georgina. She said that she had found a suitable house for him, no more than a mile from the Duke's mansion, and had arranged for him to take it on a yearly tenancy, in the name of Richard Barclay; as it was preferable that none of her people, who might have heard of her association with him should know him to be living in the neighbourhood. There followed particulars about the local solicitor and a middle-aged couple named Atkins which she had engaged to come in daily to 'do' for him.

On the next day Roger took the coach to Cambridge, and put up at an inn there for the night. Early on the following morning he hired a horse and, having left his main luggage at the inn, rode the fifteen miles to New-market. At the solicitor's a clerk was detailed to take him to the property and show him over it. He found it to be a pleasant little house, set well back from the road, beyond a small, neatly-kept garden. It was named Mellowmead and was the type of home to which a successful tradesman might have retired, having a sunny parlour, large kitchen and three bedrooms. Behind it there was stabling for two horses and a trap, and a small dairy. The furniture was country-made, the curtains worn but clean, and the linen of fair quality.

Happy at the thought that Georgina could hardly have found anything better suited to their purpose, he returned to the solicitor's, paid half a year's rent in advance, and completed the formalities. The lawyer promised to let Her Grace know that 'Mr. Barclay' had taken the house, have Roger's luggage brought from Cambridge by the local carrier and instruct the Atkins couple to report to him that afternoon. He also gave Roger the address of a man who had the reputation of an honest dealer among the many horse traders in Newmarket.

B

Having purchased a spirited piebald mare and hired
saddlery, Roger rode back to Mellowmead. There he
found the Atkinses awaiting him. The woman was
skinny, and Roger formed the opinion that, among her
equals, she might be somewhat shrewish; but her
husband, Jerry, was a cheerful ex-Dragoon. For a time,
before he had had his right knee smashed by a piece
of case-shot in the Peninsula, and been invalided out,
he had been an officer's servant, so he suited Roger
admirably.

Mrs. Atkins roasted a chicken and made pancakes
for Roger's supper, and her cooking more than offset
her forbidding manner, so Roger considered himself
in clover. As soon as they had gone, he settled down to
wait, hoping that Georgina would be able to pay him
a visit that night; although he knew that his wait would
be a long one, as it was high summer and she would
not dare come to him until well after dark.

To kill time, he made a more thorough inspection of
the house. Except for a Bible, there was not a book in
it; but in a cupboard he came upon a file of old news
sheets and amused himself by reading, mostly ill-
founded articles on the closing stages of Napoleon's
last campaign and abdication.

By midnight he was on the point of giving Georgina
up and going to bed. Then he heard knocking on the
back door. Jumping up, he ran to it and found Georgina
there, hooded and enveloped in a long, black cloak.
Joyfully, he took her in his arms and drew her inside.
She told him then that, as her sister-in-law normally
went to bed soon after supper, in future she could
come to him earlier; but, not expecting him so soon,
a few days before she had invited some neighbours in
to play whist, and they had not left until after eleven
o'clock.

Although the surroundings lacked the elegance and luxury to which they were accustomed, they found a new delight in this simple home where they could meet in secret. Georgina had told the local solicitor that she did not know Mr. Barclay, but had been asked by a friend, whose bailiff he had been, to enquire for a house in the neighbourhood suitable to his means. This was so that no-one would think it strange that he was not invited to dine with the Duchess.

However, to alleviate her boredom while keeping up appearances down there as a dutiful wife, she did invite friends in the district to dine and play cards two or three times a week. So it was decided that, on such nights, she should not come to Roger, but make up the sleep she would lose on those nights when she spent several hours with him. Nevertheless, they managed to see each other nearly every day, by making a rendezvous to meet and ride in the woods, since if anyone chanced to see them together it would be put down only to a casual encounter.

On all but a few days during early August, the weather was excellent, so they enjoyed their rides through the woodland glades dappled with sunshine, almost as much as the nights on which they had picnic suppers in the house, then spent happy hours in bed together until, well before dawn, Roger saw Georgina home.

But this blissful and carefree interlude was not destined to last. On the eleventh of the month, they were walking their horses down a broad ride bordered by large clumps of rhododendrons. Suddenly, only a few yards ahead of them, a figure emerged from the bushes. One glance was enough. Instinctively they pulled up their horses and stared in startled surprise at Mary.

Without a word she drew a pistol from under her
mantle. From those desperate days when she and
Roger had survived the retreat from Moscow he knew
that she had become a crack shot. Raising her pistol,
she pointed it at Georgina.

Appalled, Roger cried, 'Mary! Are you mad? For
God's sake, stop!'

Ignoring him, Mary took careful aim at Georgina's
face. Next moment she pressed the trigger. The silence
of the wood was shattered by the deafening report. At
the same second Roger hit out with all his force at
Georgina's left shoulder. The blow knocked her sideways, but did not save her. Hit by the bullet, she gave
a loud cry, lurched sideways, then fell from her saddle
to the ground.

3

'... or Else!'

ROGER'S heart seemed to rise up into his throat. For
a moment he was struck dumb, and paralysed by horror.
He knew that his swift blow on Georgina's shoulder
had saved her from a bullet in the face. But he had
heard too many men on battlefields give that same
sharp cry when shot not to be certain that Georgina
had been hit before falling from her horse. The bullet
might only have torn her ear, but it was just as possible
that it had penetrated her neck. If so, she might be
dead in a matter of minutes.

Both horses had taken fright at the sound of the
explosion. He had automatically held his in, but hers
had bolted. She was sprawled face down on the grass,
moaning. Flinging himself from his saddle, he ran to
her, knelt down and turned her over. Her eyes were
closed, and she was as white as a sheet. But, with
infinite relief, he saw that her face and neck were un-
harmed. Her right hand was clasped to her left shoulder, and blood was seeping from between her fingers.

Murmuring breathless endearments, he gently drew
her hand away. His blow on the upper arm had evidently caused her head to jerk to the right, automatically
raising her left shoulder, which had received the bullet.
Swiftly untying the stock she wore, he tore open the

neckline of her dress, exposing the wound. Opening her eyes, she lifted her arm, then gasped:

'Oh, Roger! For a moment I feared that wicked woman would kill me, or at least disfigure me for life. Her glaring eyes made her look as though she was possessed by a demon. 'Twas your presence of mind in thrusting me aside that saved me. It hurts, but I don't think my shoulder blade can be broken.'

'It's not,' he assured her quickly. 'Thank God, 'tis no more than a flesh wound, and the bullet seared through it. After your arm has been in a sling for a few days, you will be fully recovered. The bleeding is already easing.'

He had been staunching the blood with her stock and, after a moment, he added, 'Raise your arm again so that I can get this under it.' He had taken off his linen cravat and used it as a bandage.

Picking her up, he carried her to a nearby tree, so that she could lean against the trunk. Then he crossed the glade to fetch her horse, which was quietly grazing only fifty yards away. When he returned, he said with a frown:

'The problem now is to get you home. I fear one of your servants is sure to recognise me.'

She shook her head. 'Worry not, my love. If you see me to the edge of the wood, 'tis no distance from there, and I'm sure I can manage on my own. I cannot think, though, how I'll explain having come by my wound.'

After a moment's thought, he suggested, 'Why not say that a highwayman attempted to hold you up. To escape him you turned your horse and galloped off; then, hoping to bring you to a halt, he fired after you.'

Georgina smiled. 'Do you really think a highwayman would fire on a woman? The only one I ever met treated me very differently.'

Roger returned her smile. 'That handsome rogue, Captain Coignham, eh? He bartered the jewels he would have robbed you of for kisses, did he not; then shot not at but in you? I recall your telling me of it the day you seduced me.'

'Seduced you indeed! I did nothing of the kind. 'Twas pity for you that led me to let you have your way with me. The only difference 'twixt us was that I had already had experience, whereas you had not. As for Coignham, I admit to have been a willing victim when I let him have me on that mossy bank in the New Forest. 'Twas a most romantic way to lose one's maidenhead.'

'So you've often said, you sweet, shameless hussy. But, reverting to the present. In an attempt to stop you a highwayman might well have meant to fire over your head, but aimed too low, so that his bullet gashed your shoulder.'

She nodded. 'That's true, so 'tis the story I will tell. Blessings be, I have lost little blood, and on my way home there is no likelihood of my fainting. But the more speedily I can get my injury properly tended, the better. Help me up now on to my saddle.'

As she always rode astride and now held the reins in her right hand without pain, Roger felt confident that, after her quick recovery, there was no danger of her falling; so he raised her to her feet and mounted her. Then they walked their horses to a neck of the woods that adjoined the home farm of the mansion.

Before leaving the cover of the trees, they halted and Roger said, 'Dear one, I fear me we have not heard the last of that termagant of a wife of mine. Before she ran off into the bushes she may have realised that her dastardly attack on you had failed to achieve its object. In any case, she'll shortly learn of it. As soon as you are sufficiently recovered, we must discuss the situation fully, and decide what course we are to adopt for the future.'

Georgina nodded her dark head. 'You're right in that, so unless my wound becomes inflamed and I run a temperature, I'll come to you tonight.'

Having begged her not to take the risk if she felt the least groggy, they parted, and Roger watched her ride out from the trees along a track that led to the farm.

Soon after ten o'clock that evening he heard her now familiar knock on the back door of Mellowmead, and hastened to let her in. Her arm was in a sling, but she told him that her doctor had said the wound was only superficial, as no ligament had been cut and the salve he had applied had eased the ache that had at first nagged at her.

Her personal maid, Harriet, had long been in the secret of her affair with Roger, as she looked after them when he spent a night at the Kensington studio. In case Georgina's sister-in-law came up to see how she was, she had told Harriet to remain in her boudoir until eleven o'clock and say that she, Georgina, was not to be disturbed as she had taken a sleeping draught. She had then slipped down the back stairs and out of the house.

As she had had her supper in bed barely an hour earlier, she joined Roger in a bottle of wine, but would only nibble a piece of Mrs. Atkins's excellent shortcake while they settled down to talk.

Roger opened the subject by saying, 'From Mary's attack on you this morning, I can only conclude that jealousy has driven her out of her mind. She may be sane in other matters, but not so far as we are con-

cerned. 'Tis an appalling thought that, having brooded
on her grievance, the form of revenge she has decided
on is to shoot you down in my presence.'

'Given a mind crazed to the point of willingness to
commit murder, I think her plan was sound. She could
hardly have formulated one better calculated to strike
you also to the heart. What puzzles me, though, is how
she learned that you were at Newmarket.'

'Although I told no-one of it, that is easily explained.
Her mind would jump to it that, as I have no duties to
perform these days, wherever you were she would find
me not far off. I doubt not that, for the past week or
more, she has been lying at some small inn in the
vicinity and spying on you until this morning, when
she found the opportunity to make this dastardly
attempt. I have been worried near out of my wits
ever since that she may attack you again, and next time
with greater success.'

Georgina shook her head. 'To do so she would have
to continue to lurk about here. She would hardly dare
do that, from fear that I have already put the police
on to her.'

'You may be right; but that fear will restrain her
only for a while. Once she becomes reassured that no
steps are being taken to apprehend her, she will return
and again attempt to kill you.'

'Forewarned is forearmed. From now on I'll carry a
pistol. Then, should she spring out from some bushes,
I shall shoot her on sight.'

'Yes, 'twould be well to go armed. Though I think
it unlikely that she would attack you when alone. I
am convinced that, to satiate her hatred of us to the
full, she plans to kill you before my eyes. And, remember, she would not have to come out from behind a
bush to fire on you.'

'What, then are we to do?'

Roger sighed. 'I see only one thing for it. We must count this brief idyll of ours over. Since your life will not be safe as long as we remain together, I must leave you.'

'No! Oh, not for ever!' Georgina gasped. 'Roger, I could not bear it!'

'No! No! Nor I,' he swiftly reassured her. 'But until this menace is past, I'll return to London, see her as soon as possible, and endeavour to come to some arrangement with her.'

'Dost think she will listen to you?'

'Heaven knows! By the alternatives of the carrot and the stick, I may be able to induce her to cease from her vendetta.'

They talked on for another half-hour, but to protect Georgina's life no other course seemed open to them; so they agreed upon it. He then accompanied her as far as the stables of the mansion, and there they bade each other a tearful farewell.

On the following morning, as soon as the Atkinses arrived, Roger paid them off with a month's wages and arranged for them to send his valise up to London. Then he mounted his mare, and set off on the long ride to the capital.

He did not reach Amesbury House until a little after midnight. As it was mid-August, he had expected that Droopy Ned would be at Normanrood, his country seat, but learned that he had come up for a few nights on some legal business, and was out. Roger thought it probable that he would find him gambling at White's; but, being tired after his journey, he decided to go to bed, so they did not meet until the next morning at breakfast.

While they demolished some kedgeree, three cold quail apiece and a bottle of claret, Roger told his

friend of the shocking affair that had brought him back
to London.

Droopy sadly shook his narrow head. ''Tis almost
unbelievable, and I am desperate sorry for both you
and poor Georgina. As you well know, I have always
championed little Mary, maintaining that your troubles
have been due to her passionate attachment to yourself.
I hoped that she might in time condone your infidelity,
and that you would become reconciled. But it seems
now that that has become no more than one of my
Eastern pipe dreams.'

'It has,' Roger replied firmly. 'That I am to blame
for her unhappiness I do admit. And, although since
our return from Canada, owing to lack of common
interests we have grown apart, I would willingly have
continued to do my utmost to make her life a pleasant
one. She has now made that impossible. Nothing in
heaven or earth would induce me to give up Georgina,
and since Mary refuses to permit me the liberty usual
among men of my class, there is nothing for it but a
permanent severance of our relations.'

'I take it there is no possibility of your obtaining a
divorce?'

'None. I would wager any money that the most
searching inquiry would not reveal that she had been
unfaithful to me during the months I spent on the
Continent; otherwise 'tis most unlikely that she would
have consoled herself for my absence by taking to the
bottle.'

'Then the sooner you can come to some arrangement
with her about the future, the better.'

'You're right, Ned. Scared by her own act, 'tis
probable that she took the night coach back to London,
so is already at Richmond. I mean to ride out there this
afternoon.'

Having dined early, Roger reached Thatched House Lodge soon after seven o'clock. His devoted old ex-smuggler groom, Dan, informed him that, after being away from home for a week, 'her ladyship' had returned that midmorning, with no pleasant word for anyone, and looking far from well.

When he entered the house, Mrs. Muffet appeared, and he asked her Mary's whereabouts. As she dropped him a curtsey, looking distinctly uncomfortable, the housekeeper replied, 'May it please your lordship, milady is up in her room; but I fear you'll find her . . . er, not in the best of shape.'

Roger knew what that meant. Mary had been drinking again, and he would find her in the same state as when, earlier in the year, he had returned from France. In consequence, when he opened the door of their room, he was not surprised to see her in bed, propped up against the pillows and, beside her on a table, a half-empty decanter of port.

This time, instead of exploding with amazed rage, he only asked sternly, 'Well, Madam. What have you to say for yourself?'

She gave him a slow smile. 'Only that I am pleased to see that you have come to your senses.'

'What mean you by saying that?' he demanded, with a frown.

'Your presence here shows that I have succeeded in my object. As I saw matters, 'twas a case of kill or cure.'

'But for my prompt action, you would have killed Georgina. And by the act killed yourself, for they'd have hanged you on Tyburn Tree.'

'I'll not argue with your reasoning, my lord. Did I not say kill or cure? Had my bullet found its mark, your lecherous Duchess and I would both have lost our lives. But, as I vowed I'd do, I'd have ruined yours.

After I ran off into the bushes, I lingered long enough to see from under cover that I'd done no more than wound her slightly. I then made my way back here to await the outcome of the event. Your presence supplies it. You had the *nous* to realize that if you remained with her, at no distant date I would again attempt her life. As I thought probable, rather than chance my second attempt proving successful, you've thrown in your hand. From now on, you'll no longer dare sneak off and pay her the tribute that is rightly mine, so I'll be cured of the jealousy that has made my life a misery.'

Roger stared at her in silence for a moment. Although she had been drinking, she was not drunk, as she had been on that day the previous April when he had arrived back in England unexpectedly. Neither was she mad—at least, not completely so. She had thought matters out perfectly logically, then acted on her decision with fearless, ruthless determination.

'You have never lacked courage, Mary,' he said quietly, 'and your plan was skilfully designed. But there was one flaw in it. You failed to anticipate the consequences if your desperate bid to wreck my life ended as it has. By taking the law into your own hands and firing a pistol aimed at Georgina's head, you are guilty of attempted murder, so liable to be sentenced to spend the best years of your life in prison.'

Mary took a drink from her glass of port. 'The best years of my life are already gone. They were those when you truly loved me. And would you really dare have me prosecuted? Remember, when the full story was told in court, everyone's sympathy would be with me: the outraged wife driven to despair by the husband she adored. And what of Georgina? She'd be blamed and ostracized by all decent people.'

'On the contrary,' Roger retorted. 'The type of

person with whom Georgina consorts would be horrified to learn that her life had been placed in jeopardy because she had indulged in what they would consider a mere peccadillo. They would regard you as a mad-woman, too dangerous to be left at liberty, and probably you would end up chained to a wall in Bedlam.'

Mary's eyes narrowed. 'Do you then intend to prosecute me?'

'It is not I whom you attacked, but Georgina, so it is for her to decide. At the moment she so intends; for, resentment apart, it would provide her with the means of getting you out of her way for good. However, I think I could persuade her to refrain if you and I could come to terms.'

'And what would they be?'

'That I should allow you a thousand a year to live apart from me in some place not less than a day's journey from London, and that you should sign a confession about having attempted to murder Georgina. This could be used against you should you at any time transgress that undertaking.'

'I'll sign no confession, for without it you would find it difficult to prove anything against me. I at least had the sense to take such precautions I could against being convicted of killing her. It cannot be proved that I ever went to Newmarket. I made the journey dressed as a country wench, and took three days to get there by a roundabout route, sometimes by walking long dis-tances, at other times securing lifts in carts or wagons.'

'But you must have spent some days in the neigh-bourhood, spying on us, before you found the oppor-tunity to make your attack.'

Mary gave a low laugh. 'I did, but during that time I lived rough in the woods, off such food as I had brought with me, and fruit stolen by night from gardens. No-one saw me except yourself, and a husband cannot give evidence against his wife.'

Roger heard her out with a sinking heart. In spite of what he had said about Georgina's being indifferent to a scandal, that was far from being the truth, for she must come out of the business badly and they had not even considered bringing a case. Yet the threat of prosecution and prison was the big stick with which he had hoped to bring Mary to heel. Now it had transpired that it would be far from easy to prove her guilty. In a last effort to intimidate her, he said:

'You certainly went about the business with commendable caution, but your precautions will prove of no avail. Georgina, as you know, is immensely rich. Should you refuse my terms, she will offer big rewards for information concerning your movements during the past week. Wagoners and others who gave you lifts will come forward and identify you. The very fact that you used such devious methods to get to Newmarket will provide evidence of your malign intent. She will get you, Mary, even if it costs her thousands.'

'Let her try, then!' Mary cried defiantly. 'You have ruined my life, so I no longer care what becomes of me. Should I be condemned, I'll find a way to make an end of myself. Then my death, too, will be put at her door.'

For some moments Roger stared at her in silence. He could no longer think of anything to say. Taking another gulp of port, she went on more quietly:

'And now, my noble Earl, I'll tell you *my* terms. The first part of your proposition I will accept. You'll pay me a thousand a year to be rid of me. This house now holds too many unhappy memories for me to wish to remain on here, and I've a mind to take an apartment at Brighton. 'Tis you who are to be de-

prived of going to London, or, for that matter, even of
living in England. You've spent so much of your life
on the Continent, that 'twill be no great hardship for
you to return there permanently—except, of course,
that you'll be deprived of the company of your whore.
And 'tis that which I am determined to bring about.
Those are my terms, and you'll accept them. Otherwise, I swear to God I'll kill her.'

Only once before in his life had Roger been utterly
bested, and that was also by a woman. It had been when
Lissala da Pombal had tricked him into accompanying
her against his will to Brazil. Now it was again a
woman who had got the better of him. In his agreement to Mary's demands lay the only means of making
certain that Georgina should not be murdered.

Knowing himself defeated, he murmured sickly, 'So
be it, Mary. You have cornered me. There is naught
else to say.' Then, turning, he walked, stricken, from
the room.

4

Paris 1814

THAT evening Roger told Droopy Ned about the intolerable position in which Mary had placed him.

Droopy heard him out, then sadly shook his forward-thrust head. 'Dear friend, I see naught for it but for you to accede to Mary's demand that you go abroad. She has already shown that she'd have no scruples about killing Georgina, and in what way else can you prevent her from making a second attempt? Even were Georgina willing to face the scandal resulting from making the facts public, she could do no more than secure a magistrate's order that Mary may not molest her. And what difference would that make? A woman who is willing to risk being hanged for murder will not be deterred by a threat of imprisonment for contempt of court.'

Roger nodded. 'I agree. But the thought of idling for month after month on the Continent drives me to distraction.'

'No, no! You must secure some employment for yourself.'

' 'Tis well enough to say that, but I am fitted for nothing.'

'Nonsense. Your life-long acquaintance with international affairs and the several languages you speak qualify you for a variety of openings. You could perhaps secure a post with a banker or as adviser to some big merchant house. Better still, why not ask my Lord Castlereagh for an appointment at one of our embassies abroad?'

'The last is certainly a good idea,' replied Roger more cheerfully. So, the following morning, having been to Hoare's Bank to arrange for the allowance Mary had demanded, he went to the Foreign Office, arriving there at about midday. When he asked for his name to be sent up to the Minister, he was told that Castlereagh had already left his office and was unlikely to return there, since he was leaving for the Continent the next morning.

As Roger was well acquainted with him, and did not wish to lose the chance of the opening that Droopy had suggested, he walked round to No. 18. St. James's Square, the Minister's residence. After a wait of some ten minutes in the hall, he was shown into the library, where Castlereagh had just finished sorting some papers he meant to take with him.

He was a tall, slim man of imposing presence, with an oval face, fine forehead, strong, straight nose and good eyes under thick eyebrows. He was then forty-five, as were Napoleon, Wellington and Roger. The younger Pitt, to whom he had been devoted, had been his patron and he had served as that great Prime Minister's mouthpiece during the period he was out of office. Unlike Pitt, he was not particularly interested in financial affairs, but he had derived from him both his determination to bring about Napoleon's downfall and high ideals for the future of Europe. As Lord Lieutenant of Ireland, he had put down the rebellion there in 1788. As Chairman of the East India Board, he had formed a strong friendship with the Viceroy, the Marquess Wellesley and with the Marquess's younger brother, Wellington. It was largely due to him that, instead of the campaign in the Peninsula being abandoned, he had again and again insisted on the reinforcements being sent out that later enabled the Duke to achieve his great victories. He was suave in manner, but could be very obstinate; and, as Foreign Minister, he had dominated the Cabinet since Pitt's death.

As a secretary left the room with the bundle of papers, Castlereagh waved Roger to a chair and asked, 'To what do I owe this visit, my lord?'

Roger naturally had no intention of disclosing his real reason for going abroad, so he said, 'I fear that I have presented myself to your lordship at a most inconvenient time. But it was not until I called at the Foreign Office around midday that I learned that you were about to leave for the Continent tomorrow. Assuming that you may be out of England for some time, I was loath to lose the opportunity of making a request to your lordship before your departure.'

'Tell me, then, of this request.'

'As your lordship is aware, I have spent the greater part of my adult life on the Continent, engaged on affairs which have necessitated considerable concentration of mind. Since the cessation of hostilities, I have become increasingly bored with an utterly idle life. The possibility occurred to me that your lordship might see your way to giving me some quite minor post in one of our embassies abroad, where I would at least have duties to perform, and might be of some small service.'

Castlereagh smiled. 'My dear Kildonan, for a man with your record, this seems a very modest request. How well acquainted are you with the aspirations of ourselves and of our allies?'

'I am fairly well informed of our attitude and theirs, up to the spring of this year. For the three months preceding Napoleon's abdication I was Talleyrand's guest in Paris, and as we have been friends for many years, he confided freely in me. I am aware of Napoleon's insane belief that, after his disaster in Russia, he could still defeat the combined armies of Russia, Prussia and Austria; and at Frankfurt, by accepting the terms they offered, could have kept his throne. Then of the Conferences at Chatillon, where Caulaincourt tried so desperately hard at least to preserve the Bonaparte dynasty by having Marie Louise appointed Regent for her son, the King of Rome; and Napoleon sabotaging his Minister's efforts by refusing to give up Belgium. Naturally, Talleyrand told me also of the Czar's ambition to re-create Poland as a Kingdom, subject to himself, and his willingness to abolish Saxony so that it becomes part of Prussia. But, since my return from Paris shortly after the abdication, I know no more than is published in the news sheets.'

'You will at least know that the Peace of Paris was signed on May 30th; that by it France gave up all claims to Belgium, Holland, Germany, Switzerland and Italy and that in return, as a gesture of goodwill, we gave back the greater part of our conquests in the Indies to the French, Spaniards and Dutch, retaining only a few small islands and the Cape of Good Hope? Also, accepting Talleyrand's dictum that legitimacy should be our mentor, we agreed to the restoration of the Bourbons, in the person of Louis XVIII, and even allowed France to retain several minor territories which were not within her boundaries in 1792. Naught else of importance has been settled.'

Roger raised an eyebrow. 'Your lordship makes no mention of that ticklish question, the futures decided

for Poland and Saxony. I take it the time has not yet
come to make these matters public?'

'No,' Castlereagh replied. ' 'Tis not a matter of our
keeping it a secret. No decision has been reached as
yet. When the Czar first entered Paris as a liberator,
his reputation as a liberal who cared only for the welfare of the common people had preceded him. His
popularity was immense and Metternich and I would
have been put in a very poor light had we refused to
agree to anything he demanded. But, fortunately, he
lost his opportunity. He neglected to press us when he
had the chance, and has since ceased to dominate the
Alliance. He has failed his bootlicker, the King of
Prussia, been ill received by the new King of France,
has gravely offended the Prince Regent during his visit
here, and is more than ever at loggerheads with
Metternich.'

'Your lordship does not surprise me. Alexander's
dual nature causes him to give umbrage to the most
diverse people. Convinced of his own divine right, he
will tolerate no opposition from his subjects; yet,
equally convinced that he is the apostle of liberty, he
encourages the subjects of other monarchs to oppose
their ordinances. To me, though, he has always been
most gracious. He even conferred on me the Order of
St. Anne.'

'Indeed! You know him well then?'

'I have done so for several years, and he is aware of
my past secret activities.'

'Do you also know Frederick William of Prussia?'

'Only slightly. But the Czar presented me to him
when I was living in Talleyrand's mansion. Some years
ago I was falsely accused of a crime by Prince Haugwitz, condemned and imprisoned in Berlin. After a
few months I succeeded in escaping, but was liable to

have to serve the remainder of my sentence if caught by the Prussians. At my request, Alexander had Frederick William grant me a pardon.'

'And what of Metternich?'

'I met him first when he was Austrian Ambassador in Paris, and have since talked with him on numerous occasions. I have a considerable admiration for him, and he has accorded me his friendship.'

'Talleyrand I know to have long been your friend. With what other prominent statesmen are you acquainted?'

'Count Nesselrode, Hardenberg, the Baron de Vitrolles, Carnot, Fouché, Prince Schwarzenberg, the Duke de Dalberg, His Grace of Wellington, of course, and many lesser lights.'

Castlereagh smiled. 'And you are so modest as to ask of me some minor diplomatic post? In the hope that we may be able to settle the many still outstanding questions, and so bring permanent peace to Europe, the Powers are to hold a Congress in Vienna in September. There I shall have the assistance of Lord Cathcart, lately our Ambassador to St. Petersburg, and Lord Clancarty, who is an authority on affairs in the Low Countries; but the problems raised will be innumerable, and your wide knowledge of international affairs, my dear Kildonan, could prove invaluable. I should be most happy to have you join my staff.'

Roger could hardly conceal his delight. Being forced to leave Georgina was a sad blow, but he had had to do so many times during the past twenty years and hoped before many months that he would find a way to circumvent Mary. Meanwhile, instead of having to go into dreary exile, he was once again to be in the very heart of great affairs and privy to State secrets of the first magnitude. When he had accepted Castlereagh's offer, the Minister said:

'The Congress does not assemble until mid-September, but I intend first to spend a few days in Paris and I leave England tomorrow. It is very short notice to suggest that you should accompany me; so, if you prefer, you can take your time and join me in Vienna.'

'I thank your lordship, but 'twould intrigue me to see Paris under the new *régime*, so I'll accompany you. The bulk of my baggage can be sent on later to our embassy in Vienna.'

In high spirits at the outcome of this interview, Roger hurried round to Jermyn Street, to buy various items he wished to take with him, then returned to Amesbury House and told Droopy of his good fortune. Droopy promised to go out to Richmond, sort through the clothes with Dan and forward to Vienna such of them as he thought would prove useful. After they had dined, Roger sat down to write a long letter to Georgina.

Having given an account of his meeting with Mary, he said that only his conviction that she would carry out her threat unless he left England had induced him to give way to her; for, although he would have taken a chance with his own life, nothing would induce him to risk Georgina's. He went on to say that he had considered asking her to come up and spend a night at Amesbury House, in order that he could say good-bye to her; but even this would have entailed some risk, and circumstances had arisen that made it specially appropriate that he should leave London the following day. He added that, through Lord Castlereagh, he had been fortunate enough to secure work on the Continent, which would occupy him for some months and at least keep him from brooding over their enforced separation. Finally, he assured her that he would somehow find a way to render Mary powerless to prevent their being together in safety, and that his heart was hers forever, in this life and those to come.

A major question that Roger now had to decide was in which of his two identities he should return to France: as M. le Colonel le Comte de Breuc, lately A.D.C. to Napoleon and a Commander of the Legion of Honour, or as the Earl of Kildonan, until lately Mr. Roger Brook. During the many years, on and off, that he spent as one of the Emperor's entourage, he had met all the Marshals and Ministers and innumerable other officers and officials. On Napoleon's abdication the greater part of them had gone over to the Bourbons, so it was certain that he would again meet many of them who would greet him as Comte de Breuc. On the other hand, having for so many years been debarred from the Continent, immediately peace had been declared hundreds of the British upper classes had seized upon their right again to visit Paris, and inevitably, Roger would run into a number of them who knew him now as Lord Kildonan.

In the past, on occasions when he had unexpectedly encountered Englishmen abroad, or Frenchmen in London, he had bluffed his way out of the difficulty by pretending not to know them and, when questioned, stated that they had mistaken him for a mythical cousin near his own age, who chanced to resemble him as closely as an identical twin. But he must now definitely adopt one or other identity; so on their way to Dover he consulted Castlereagh.

After some thought, the Minister said, 'In Paris it is unlikely that you will be accosted by more than a handful of our compatriots as Lord Kildonan, whereas you are known to hundreds of people there as the Comte de Breuc. If you pretend you have never met any of them, it is certain that many will not believe the story that the Comte is your cousin. They will discuss it among themselves and decide that for many years you have imposed upon Napoleon. It is most undesirable for it to become generally believed that you have all the time been a British secret agent, and it could bring you into grave danger. You must therefore reappear in Paris as a Frenchman.'

'Your lordship's reasoning is indisputable. But how can we account for my being a member of your mission?'

'There is a way in which that can be overcome, because in Vienna you will meet few Frenchmen who know you as de Breuc. It would be well for you to remain in Paris for some weeks, in order to acquire a thorough knowledge of the present state of French affairs. Then, a few days before Talleyrand leaves to represent France at the Congress, you could precede him and enter Austria as Lord Kildonan. But you should secretly keep in touch with Talleyrand, as that would make you most valuable to me.'

As a result of this conversation Roger travelled direct to Paris and on his own, whereas Castlereagh—who took with him his portly, pleasant but not very intelligent wife—and the other members of his mission made short stays in Brussels and Antwerp, not arriving in the French capital until August 24th. Roger, meanwhile, on reaching Paris had gone straight to Talleyrand's mansion, as he had some trunks of clothes stored there. His old friend welcomed him most cordially, and again insisted that he should become his guest.

Private affairs had caused Roger to leave Paris in great haste on April 9th, two days before the ratification of the Treaty of Fontainebleau by the Allies. The treaty embodied the conditions of Napoleon's abdication; so Roger knew no more than the average, well-informed Englishman of the events which had followed.

It was reported that, on the evening of the 12th, Napoleon had attempted to commit suicide by taking a mixture of opium, belladonna and hellebore; but spasms had caused him to vomit and sick up the poison before it had done him any serious harm; that on the 20th his Old Guard had wept as he kissed the tricolour and took leave of them in the courtyard at Fontaine-bleau, then he had accompanied the Allied Com-missioners on his way into exile; that, on reaching the South of France, crowds of people who had lost husbands, fathers, sons and brothers in his wars, had stoned his coach and burnt him in effigy; that, to save himself from being lynched, he had disguised himself in an Austrian jacket and Russian *papenka*, then left the main road to reach Frejus by byways; that there he had been so frightened that French sailors would kill him that he had refused to go aboard the frigate waiting to transport him to Elba and, instead, sailed to the minute island kingdom allotted him by the Allies in H.M.S. *Undaunted*.

Knowing next to nothing of what had been occurring in France since the Restoration, Roger was naturally looking forward to a long talk with Talleyrand, and late on the night of his arrival, his wish was gratified. When the last guests of a reception had gone, the two old friends settled down to exchange confidences.

After Roger told Talleyrand of his new association with Castlereagh, the Prince was quick to realise how advantageous it would be to himself to have this secret link with the representative of Britain. Roger then asked to be briefed on the situation in France and the great statesman, elegant as ever in satin and powdered hair, replied:

'*Mon ami,* I regret to say it is very far from satisfactory. In the proper sense of the term, we have no government. As you will recall, while the Emperor was still at Fontainebleau, the Senate made me the head of a Committee of Five to negotiate the abdication. Having done so, when King Louis was well enough to travel from England, I offered my services to him. As a necessity, he retained me temporarily as his First Minister, but not for long. Instead, he gave me the Foreign Ministry, and thereafter placed himself in the hands of the Duc de Blacas, his favourite, who had shared his exile. Yet de Blacas is not Prime Minister. We have not one. Neither is there any Cabinet. Each Minister tells Blacas from time to time what measures he proposes to put before the Senate. Blacas informs the King of these intentions, and he scribbles his agreement or disapproval on little pieces of paper.'

'The Ministers never meet to formulate a common policy?'

'No. But I have no regrets about that, for discussions with such a collection of nonentities would be a waste of my time. Montesquiou, who has the Interior, is the only man both capable and honourable among them. He is, too, an admirable speaker, and valuable in the Chamber. The others are most ill chosen. For example, Dupont, who is Minister of War. Could you conceivably think of a more unpopular man with the Army? It has never forgiven him for surrendering with twenty thousand men at Baylen when he had only a rabble of Spanish irregulars against him.'

'The King must be out of his wits.'

'No. He is, of course, much handicapped physically, as he suffers greatly from the gout and, being so monstrous fat, finds difficulty even in rising from his special cradle-chair; but he has read omnivorously, so has a

well-stocked mind, is gentle, shrewd and wise enough
to know that to keep his throne he must pursue a policy
of moderation and conciliate those who made France
great under the Emperor. It was that which caused him
to confirm most of the Marshals in their rank and titles,
and allow them to retain their great estates. Incident-
ally, I am no longer Prince de Benevento, as my Princi-
pality no longer belongs to France. I am now Prince
Talleyrand. The King's great curse is his laziness, and
the difficulty he has in restraining his brother, d'Artois,
and the other returned *émigrés* from taking revenge for
having been forced to spend twenty years in exile.'

'While in England, I heard it said that they were
crazily set in restoring conditions as they were under the
ancien régime.'

'You have heard aright. It was agreed that lands
confiscated during the Revolution from the nobility
and the Church should be retained by those who
bought them from the State. One cannot be surprised
at these nobles wanting to get back their estates, but
they should have the sense to know that, were they
given their way, it would result in another revolution.
Under the Liberal Constitution to which our Louis
XVIII had to say he would subscribe to ascend the
throne, the liberties of the subject, secured by the people
between '89 and '92, were fully recognized, and their
equality; but these Royalist Marquises and Counts
intensely resent now having to pay taxes in the same
way as the middle and lower classes. The Church, too,
is as greedy as ever it was for both land and the restoration of tithes free of tax which it used to enjoy.'

Talleyrand had been the Abbé de Perigord when
Roger first met him, and later Bishop of Autun. He
had defied Rome to become the first Bishop of the
newly-created French National Church, and shortly

afterwards abandoned the priesthood altogether. Recalling this, Roger remarked with a smile, 'I take it these avaricious black crows receive scant sympathy from Your Highness?'

Chuckling, Talleyrand replied, '*Parbleu!* My past makes me anathema to them. They'd sooner deal with the Devil. The *émigré* nobility, too, barely bother to disguise their hatred of me. They have not forgotten that, although of a lineage as old as the Bourbons, I was one of the leading Liberals who forced Louis XVI to grant his people a constitution.'

'I should have thought that having later to go into exile yourself, to escape the Terror, would have led them to condone your earlier activities.'

'By no means. When the passport you secured for me saved me from the guillotine and enabled me to leave France, I was received by them in England as a pariah; and you may recall that I was forced to seek asylum in the United States. Even after twenty years of exile, these people have learnt nothing, forgotten nothing and forgiven nothing. D'Artois, his son the Duc de Berry, and the Duc d'Angoulême, all openly encourage them in their pretensions, and the latter's wife, the Princess Marie Thérèse, is the most virulent of them all.'

Roger shrugged. 'In her case that is hardly to be wondered at, when one recalls what she must have suffered as a prisoner in the Temple. For a young girl to see first her father, then her mother, dragged off to be guillotined would have left her with an indelible hatred for the masses.'

'True. Yet it makes her a major menace to stable government. She is fanatically pious, malicious, strong-willed and has the ear of her uncle, the King. It is even said of her that she is the only man in the family. Her reception of myself, when she arrived in Paris, was positively frigid, and our old associate, Fouché, was given the *coup de grâce*, at her insistence.'

'Fouché!' exclaimed Roger. 'Did he then reappear after his years of exile?'

Talleyrand took a pinch of snuff. 'Indeed, yes. That unspeakable rogue had the impudence to arrive at the Tuileries, and offer his services as Minister of Police. In his old post he would have been invaluable, but the Duchess has the name of every regicide engraved indelibly on her mind. White with fury she demanded that he be instantly debarred the Court, and the King submissively obliged her. She has also made the Court near unbearable to attend. Naturally, the Marshals and Ministers who came over to the new *régime* are obliged to attend the State functions with their wives. The Duchess is the accepted leader of the ex-*émigré* ladies. She incites them to boycott the lower-class women of the Bonapartist nobility, and loses no opportunity of showing contempt for them. As you can imagine, Ney, Marmont, Augereau, Macdonald and others become intensely angry on seeing their wives insulted, so there is not a smile to be seen at these receptions.'

'Things are then in a far more parlous state than I had imagined,' Roger commented. 'But I pray your Highness be good enough to tell me how matters now stand between France and the Allies.'

The Prince smiled. 'Ah, there I can flatter myself that I have done well for my country. Largely owing to the overbearing attitude of the Czar, who still insists that he will have the whole of Poland, and Prussia's demand that she should have all Saxony. These claims caused dissension among the Allies and enabled me to gain the support of Metternich and Castlereagh, both of whom wish to thwart Russia and Prussia, and desire to give France liberal terms.

'We wrangled for a month, then on May 30th signed the Peace of Paris. The thorny questions of the future of Poland and Saxony have yet to be decided when we all meet in Vienna. But Britain was most generous, returning to us many of our old colonies in the West Indies and, in spite of the millions she had poured out in the war, forewent any indemnity, as the price of being given a free hand in Belgium and Holland. Austria hopes to receive compensation in Italy and Illyria for any concessions she may have to make in the north, and we have renounced all claims to territories in Germany and Switzerland. But I succeeded in retaining some minor territories on our borders, which have a population of near half a million people. Surprisingly, too, I even succeeded in keeping for France all the works of art that Napoleon looted from the countries he conquered. I did so on the pretext that if they were returned to Italy and other countries, the hazards of the roads might seriously damage them.

'Of course, there are many questions yet to be settled, among them the future of numerous small, previously independent principalities on the far side of the Rhine. But the great thing is that I secured peace for France. We are no longer at war with anyone, and have no demands to make; which will place me in a very strong position at the Congress.'

Having congratulated his friend on this extraordinary diplomatic triumph, Roger said, 'Since Your Highness has no further concessions to resist or benefits to ask for, I am somewhat at a loss to understand why the Allies should wish you to attend the Congress.'

Taking another pinch of snuff and gracefully flicking the fallen grains from his lace cravat, the Prince smiled and said, '*Mon cher ami*. There you have a point; and at first the others were reluctant to have me with them in Vienna. At that I showed great surprise, exclaiming, "But we are no longer enemies! We are all friends, and as one of the five great nations of Europe it is only reasonable that France should be permitted to hold a watching brief over the deliberations which will affect the future of us all." '

'A watching brief!' Roger echoed with a laugh. 'I'll wager it will prove much more than that. Your Highness will have a finger in every pie.'

'No, no!' the great statesman protested amiably. 'A quiet word here and there perhaps, just to forward matters a little in the right direction. But no more I assure you. And now 'tis time for us to get some sleep.'

When Castlereagh arrived in Paris, he stayed there for only three days, then left to travel on by easy stages to Vienna. Roger saw him only once, when he called on Talleyrand, and remained in the French capital for the better part of three weeks. During that time he renewed his acquaintance with many of his old French friends and ran into only four English people who took him for the Earl of Kildonan. By using an atrocious English accent and the evidence of French friends who were present on these occasions, he succeeded in convincing these compatriots that they were mistaken.

In July the Duke of Wellington had been appointed British Ambassador to France, and had arrived there on August 22nd to install himself in the magnificent Palais de Charost, in the Rue Faubourg St. Honoré. It had belonged to Pauline Bonaparte, from whom the British Government had bought it as an embassy.

As Roger's past secret activities were known to the Duke, he took an early opportunity of calling on His Grace and informing him that he would be going to Vienna as a member of Castlereagh's mission. Being old acquaintances, they reminisced pleasantly for a while about India, where they had first met, the Peninsular campaign, and discussed the present deplorable state of things in Paris.

As Roger went about the city and talked with all sorts of people he became ever more convinced of the unpopularity of the Restoration. The middle classes were content enough, as the peace at last enabled commerce and industry to be carried on in tranquillity. But there was much discontent among the lower classes, and among the upper, constant friction between the returned émigré nobility and that created by Napoleon. By the Treaty of Paris the streets of the capital had been freed from Cossacks, Uhlans, Hanoverian Hussars and white-uniformed Austrians; but there were swarms of beggars who had been wounded in Napoleon's wars, then dismissed from the Army, and now received either no pension at all or hopelessly inadequate ones.

It was the Army which had suffered the most from the Restoration. It had been greatly reduced and thousands of officers were now living idle and disgruntled on half-pay. Great offence had been given by the down-grading of the Imperial Guard, which had been sent to the provinces. Instead, the King had agreed to the restoration of the old *Maison du Roi*. To form it, at enormous expense, no fewer than six thousand young émigré gentlemen, the majority of whom had never seen a shot fired in anger, had been embodied and provided with gorgeous uniforms. The act most deeply resented by both the troops and the people had been the change in the national emblems. Against Talleyrand's most earnest advice, the tricolour, under which the French armies had won such glory, had, with the eagles, been abolished. Instead, the Bourbon lilies on their white ground again fluttered from standards and

C .

flagstaffs, and every soldier had perforce to wear the white cockade.

The return of the priests, once more to batten on a people who had mostly been atheists for nearly a quarter of a century, was intensely unpopular; and a measure more deeply resented than any other was one that had been instigated by the grimly austere Duchess d'Angoulême: that all cafés should be closed on Sundays.

Soon after Roger's arrival Talleyrand took him to the Tuileries and presented him to the grossly corpulent King, assuring the indolent monarch that the Comte de Breuc was one of the men who had seen the light and was now a staunch supporter of the Bourbons. Roger was also able to state that, in the old days, as the young Chevalier de Breuc, he had been presented to his gracious Majesty, then Comte de Provence, at Versailles. On learning that he was not just another of Bonaparte's jumped-up adventurers, the old man became quite gracious, and promised to have his title of Count confirmed.

But as Roger afterwards moved round the great salon, and talked with numerous old acquaintances, he was profoundly shocked at the appalling rudeness of the old aristocracy toward friends of his who had been ennobled by Napoleon.

Between 1786, when he was still in his teens, and now, 1814, Roger had visited Paris many times, often staying there for months at a stretch, and he decided that, except for the years of the Terror, he had never known it to be such an unhappy city. So he had no regrets when, in mid-September, he left for Vienna, to be present at the remaking and rolling up of the map of Europe.

5

Pastures New

OCTOBER 1st had been decided upon as the official date for the opening of the Congress, but for many weeks prior to that innumerable discussions had taken place between the diplomats of various nations. A secret clause, No. XXXII in the Treaty of Paris, had stipulated that the Congress should be held in Vienna, and that invitations to attend it should be sent to all the nations who had participated in the war on either side; but all questions regarding the future of Europe should be decided between themselves by the four great Allied Powers: Russia, Austria, Great Britain and Prussia.

Talleyrand was quick to see that by this last stipulation the Big Four had put themselves in an untenable position. On his arrival in Vienna, he asked them who, having signed a peace with France, were they now allied against? He further enquired what was the point of having invited all the other nations to send representatives, if they were to be denied any say in the deliberations, and how could they be expected to abide by decisions regarding their territories, without having been consulted?

By this skilful manoeuvre he got himself accepted to represent France and, after much argument, it was decided to increase the Grand Council from four to eight by the additional admission of Spain, Portugal and Sweden. Ultimately the outstanding personalities at the Congress were Metternich, Castlereagh, Nesselrode, Hardenberg and, intriguing separately with them all, Talleyrand.

As the Peace of Paris stated only the bare outlines of the major claims of the Big Four, these had to be agreed in detail. In addition the future of many minor states had to be discussed and settled; so the work to be undertaken was immense, and on the majority of issues bitterly disputed. It was to the tact and determination of Metternich, strongly supported by Castlereagh, that agreement was finally achieved on the lines they both desired: namely, that all Republican tendencies should be thwarted and the re-establishment throughout Europe of rule by an educated aristocracy. This brought peace to the Continent for forty years.

Metternich was then forty-one: a handsome, pale-faced man with bright blue eyes, an aquiline nose, humorous mouth and, above a broad brow, prematurely white, curly hair. His person was elegant, his manner gracious, and he was as attractive to women as they were to him.

By birth he was not an Austrian, but a Rhinelander, and his estate at Schloss Johannisberg produced one of the finest wines in the world. His father, a pompous, old-world courtier, had represented the Elector of Trier at the Court of Vienna, and it was from his mother, born Countess Beatrice Kagenegg, that Clement Metternich had inherited his brains.

He had been a student at Strasbourg University, and there witnessed a revolutionary mob burn down the Town Hall. It was this that had given him his life-long addiction to the maintenance of law and order, and opposition to rule by the people. After moving for a time to the University of Mainz, he had been sent, at the age of twenty, for six months to England. Having been a spectator of sittings in the House of Commons and watched with great admiration a review of the British Fleet, he had become a fervid Anglophile. The invasion by Napoleon of the Low Countries and resulting loss of them to Austria, had further stimulated his antipathy to the French.

In 1795 he had married Eleanor von Kaunitz, the grand-daughter of the powerful Chancellor of the patriarchal Emperor Francis II of Austria, and entered the diplomatic service under the most favourable auspices. His first post was Dresden, and it was there, at the Saxon Court, that he met Frederick von Gentz, a converted ex-revolutionary who, many years later, acted as Secretary General at the Congress of Vienna, and supported him most ably. They agreed that revolution imperilled the whole of Europe, and that Napoleon's suppression of it could prove only temporary. Metternich was moved to Berlin in the hope that he might bring about a united German opposition to it; but the weak Prussian King shillied and shallied until it was too late and his country was overrun.

Talleyrand, who had always wanted a strong and friendly Austria, had heard good reports of young Metternich. With his extraordinary flair for picking promising men, he succeeded in getting him made Ambassador to France, and it was in Paris, where Metternich thoroughly enjoyed himself, that, in 1806, he had first emerged as a great diplomat. It led, after Austria's defeat at Wagram in 1809, to his Imperial Master recalling him to Vienna, and placing him in charge of Austria's foreign affairs, which he continued to control for very nearly forty years.

Every afternoon during the Congress, the three monarchs of Austria, Russia and Prussia met to discuss the morning's deliberations of the Grand Council; but, apart from its members and their staffs, whose minds were almost exclusively occupied with diplomatic fencing, there were hundreds of other visitors to Vienna, who had little or nothing to do.

Among the Emperor Francis's guests for the Congress there were no fewer than thirty-two minor German royalties, envoys from Holland, Bavaria, Switzerland, Denmark, Saxony, Naples, the Pope, the Sultan and numerous representatives from smaller territories. In order to occupy this horde of Kings, Princes, Landgraves, Counts, Barons and the wives and mistresses they had brought with them, the Emperor ordered an unceasing succession of entertainments to be arranged for them, regardless of the colossal cost. There were balls and banquets, water parties on the Danube, horse races in the Prater, excursions up to Grinzing to drink the musk of the new vintage, gala nights at the opera, concerts, command performances at the theatres and of the ballet. In addition to this regal hospitality, between the evening assemblies at the Hofburg there were receptions, dinners and dances, given at all the principal embassies.

As was to be expected, this glittering assembly of men in colourful uniforms and lovely women wearing satins and jewels led to many love affairs. The Austrian Court had never been dissolute so, in deference to the Sovereigns, the affairs had to be conducted circumspectly; but the gossip was endless and at one point it was even rumoured that the far from cordial relations between the Czar and Metternich had been exacerbated by their rivalry for the favour of the same obliging lady.

From the time that Roger had returned from his first years in France, to find Georgina married, there had never been any jealousy between them. He had since been absent so many times from England for long periods that it had been tacitly agreed between them that, while apart, both of them should freely indulge their passions with members of the opposite sex who attracted them. As Georgina rarely knew even where Roger was, there had been few occasions when they had been able to exchange letters, and then it was only on urgent matters, with no mention of their peccadilloes. However, when they were reunited they always told each other about their recent affairs, and laughed over the idiosyncrasies of their conquests.

In consequence, from long-formed habit, soon after Roger arrived in Vienna he began to look about him for a charmer who might for a while console him for being separated from his life-long love. Unhurriedly, he took stock of numerous beauties and, having danced a few times with a lovely Swede, he decided to pay his court to her. She was a tall, willowy blonde, with very fair hair, big blue eyes, a slightly retroussé nose, and a full-lipped mouth which suggested a passionate nature. He judged her age to be about twenty-four.

Her name was Selma Thorwaldsen, and she was the wife of an elderly diplomat. After partnering her one evening in a cotillion, Roger had his first opportunity to talk with her. They used French as a common language, in which they were both fluent, and he opened the conversation by remarking, 'I was at the Court of Stockholm for several months two years ago, but I did not have the pleasure of seeing you there.'

With charming frankness she replied, 'You would not have, for I am not nobly born, and was not then married. My father made a big fortune as a timber merchant. He was ambitious for me, and my husband's family had fallen on hard times.'

Roger smiled. 'I find it truly amazing that a big dowry should have been necessary to find a husband for anyone as lovely as yourself.'

'Oh, I had many offers, but from men of my own class. I, too, was ambitious, and the Swedish nobility are most averse to marrying into trade; so, when the opportunity occurred, I took it willingly.'

'I imagine, though, that having achieved your desire, you were somewhat disappointed with life at the Swedish Court. I have been *persona grata* at many, and have never had to mix with a duller set of people.'

She laughed. 'You are right in that. They are deep sunk in ancient ceremonial and shocked by any display of levity. That awful draughty castle, too, with its miles of gloomy passages. It cannot be wondered at that Prince Bernadotte's wife refused to stay there, and after a few months returned to France. But I am not discontented with my lot, as my husband is a diplomat, and for most of the time we shall live abroad. I have never been away from Sweden before, and Vienna has proved a revelation to me.'

During the week that followed, Roger danced with and talked to her on three other occasions, then casually let it drop that he had travelled as far afield as Turkey, Persia, India, the West Indies, America and Brazil. Her blue eyes opened wide with interest, and after that she could not hear enough of his accounts of distant lands.

Talleyrand was not only the astutest of diplomats, he was also an extremely accomplished lover and said to have enjoyed more beautiful women than any other prominent man of his time. On arriving in Vienna, he had taken the Kaunitz Palace in the Johannesgasse, and brought with him, to act as his hostess, his niece, the Countess Edmond de Perigord, who later, as

Duchess de Dino, became his mistress in his old age. To aid his intrigues, he kept himself remarkably well informed about the love affairs of all the important men at the Congress: so Roger decided to ask him what he knew of Selma Thorwaldsen.

As Roger was the secret link between Castlereagh and the Prince they kept in touch by passing notes when they met at evening receptions and, when urgent matters required it, Roger would go to the Kaunitz Palace very early in the morning, going in, shabbily dressed, by the garden entrance. At a back door he would ask for the Prince's valet, who knew him, and took him up to his master. It was on the next such occasion that Roger inquired about Selma.

The Prince of roués replied with a smile, 'Thorwaldsen, although only in his late thirties, appears to be well on in middle age. That is owing to a shooting accident a year or so ago. At close range a blast of shot caught him in the groin and lower stomach. 'Tis said that it rendered the poor fellow impotent. In any case, it resulted in internal troubles that made him a semi-invalid; so, although he attends most of the important functions, he always leaves early to get to his bed. But he does not appear to mind leaving his young wife to dance till dawn.

'As you may know, Admiral Sir Sidney Smith has long been a friend of the Swedish Royal Family, and although Thorwaldsen represents Sweden, Sir Sidney has unofficially attached himself to the mission as protector of the interests of the House of Vasa. He accompanies the Thorwaldsens to all the principal entertainments here. Thorwaldsen, pleading indifferent health, bows himself out early and I suppose he relies on Sir Sidney to see that his wife does not get into mischief. But the Admiral is a hare-brained eccentric, and I doubt if he bothers himself much about what she gets up to.'

Roger nodded. 'Yes, the odds are he is too fully occupied with forwarding the numerous wild schemes he is always evolving. He is, though, a great man in his way, and at times succeeds with his schemes. For example, when he defied Nelson's orders and, by sending his sailors ashore with the guns from his ships, defeated Napoleon at the siege of Acre. It forced the Emperor to retire to Egypt, instead of advancing on Constantinople as he had intended, and so changed the whole course of the war. I was with him there, and will never forget the fanatical energy he displayed during that operation. '

With a smile, Talleyrand replied, 'I remember now; and it was I who had you packed off to the Near East, to prevent you from continuing your secret communications with London. But, reverting to the lady, although she is more or less free to do as she pleases after her husband has retired to his bed, I doubt if you will find her an easy conquest, and she certainly has no acknowledged lover. I have a shrewd suspicion, though, that she is having an affair with the Archduke John. In fact I am almost certain of it, but they are naturally being very discreet, otherwise the Archduke would get into hot water with his puritanical brother, the Emperor.'

The mention of the Archduke was of special interest to Roger, as he knew of an affair that he had had a few years earlier. Under the pseudonym of Count Stulich he had chartered a yacht and gone for a holiday up the Rhine. The yacht had fouled a rock just below Schloss Langenstein, and damaged her rudder so badly that a new one had had to be sent for and made in Mainz. This had necessitated the yacht lying disabled for a week. In search of pleasant company, the Archduke had made his way up to the Schloss, which was owned by the Baron von Haugwitz, and presented himself. The Baron happened to be away from home and, at that time, the Baroness had been Georgina. She had naturally entertained the Archduke, and it was not surprising that two such charming people should spontaneously have been attracted to each other. Lonely, bored and by then hating her husband, Georgina had willingly allowed herself to be seduced and, later, told Roger how greatly she had enjoyed a most hectic week with the Emperor's youngest brother.

Talleyrand's information had the effect of redoubling Roger's inclination to seduce Selma, as it now had the additional attraction that to make her his mistress would be a piquant return for the Archduke having had Georgina. He then said to the Prince:

'I find Selma enchanting, but my problem is to get her on her own in some place where I can make love to her. Here in Vienna, where conventions are, at least openly, strictly observed, it is by no means easy to arrange such a rendezvous.'

'The reception I am giving here on Thursday,' replied the Prince, 'could afford you an opportunity, as she has accepted for it. My private cabinet will, of course, be locked, but I will give you the key. If you can persuade her to enter it with you, your luck may be in.'

Having thanked his friend, Roger hurried back to his quarters at the British Mission. Unlike Talleyrand, who for the greater part of his life had lived in splendour, Castlereagh had taken quite a modest apartment in Im Auge Gottes Street, and Roger found life there anything but amusing. Not only had he to attend morning prayers every day but later, as the Castlereaghs were taking dancing lessons, he had been selected to act as partner to Lady Castlereagh's portly sister, whom she had brought to Vienna with her.

Two days after Roger had consulted Talleyrand he met Selma again at an evening reception, and got her on her own for long enough to enquire if she was going to Talleyrand's on Thursday. As he expected she replied that she was. He then asked her to save at least three dances for him, but she laughed and shook her head:

'No, no! Two is the most I can promise. My husband, as you know, is a semi-invalid, so I have to be especially careful of my reputation. If we are seen too much together there will be gossip about us and, being a faithful wife, that I should strongly resent.' However, she agreed to give him the supper dance and save another waltz for him.

When Thursday came, having arranged matters with Talleyrand, a bottle of champagne, some lobster patties, foie gras sandwiches and a bowl of fruit were put in the statesman's cabinet; then, in due course, Roger claimed the supper dance with Selma. Halfway through it, he guided her to the edge of the floor, released her and said:

'Come, don't let us wait for the crowd. There are a few special tables set in the conservatory, and I want to show you a most beautiful flower.'

Suspecting nothing, she took his arm and accompanied him downstairs. In the conservatory there were some tables, as yet unoccupied. Instead of seating her at one, he led her through a door at the far end. Beyond it, across a narrow corridor, lay Talleyrand's cabinet.

'Where are you taking me?' she asked in surprise.

'To see the flower,' he replied, quickly unlocking the door and drawing her inside.

With a frown, she exclaimed, 'There is no flower here! What . . . ?'

Cutting her short, he gave a laugh. 'Oh, yes, there is. Look now in that big mirror.'

Instinctively she turned, to see herself reflected in a gilt-framed panel of Venetian glass, as he cried, 'Behold! The most beautiful flower in all Christendom!'

'Oh, you wicked trickster! How dare you lure me in here in this fashion!' Her rebuke came swiftly, but she could not forbear to smile, although she added, 'I vow your intentions are dishonourable. Take me from here at once.'

'Nay,' he protested. 'I brought you here only that we might finish our dance.' The door was still a little open and the strains of the waltz came faintly to them from above. Before she could say anything further, his arm was about her waist, and he whirled her round.

'You crazy fellow,' she laughed. 'Very well, then; for two minutes, but no more.'

In the early days of the waltz, partners always danced most decorously, with a space of not less than six inches between their bodies. But Roger's right hand pressed swiftly and hard low down on Selma's spine, bringing them firmly pressed together from their breasts down to their thighs. She gave a gasp and endeavoured to draw away, but he was much too strong for her to succeed, and after a moment she found herself circling with him to the haunting music.

In the fashion of the time she was wearing a high-waisted dress that showed off her small, firm breasts to perfection. The skirt was long and fell gracefully to her feet; the material was so thin as to be very nearly transparent, and Roger knew that she had very little on beneath it.

As he clasped her to him, his satin breeches at once grew tighter, and he was well aware that she knew the reason. She flushed, but made no further effort to break away from him. Instead, she dug her fingers into his shoulder and herself increased the pressure of her lower body against his. Her big blue eyes grew moist, her lips redder and her breathing quicker.

Against one wall of the spacious room there was a long, wide sofa that Talleyrand had installed to accommodate the lovelier of his lady visitors, if he could persuade them to lie down upon it. Roger knew that he now had only to carry Selma to it and she would not resist him. But he was no callow youth, to deprive himself of delightful preliminaries by rushing his fences. Just in time to check his own pulsing passion, he gave her a swift kiss on the mouth, then put her from him.

While she stood there, panting and half dazed, he crossed swiftly to the door, took the key from it, shut it and locked it on the inside. Then, plucking the bottle of champagne from the ice bucket, he smiled at her and said gaily, 'Now for some supper.'

For a moment she swayed dizzily, then quickly sat down at a small table on which the food had been set out. Regaining her breath, she cried, 'How dare you! How dare you treat me as though I were some Viennese street-walker you had taken to a dance hall! I have told you, too, that I am faithful to my husband.'

As he opened the champagne, he replied quietly, 'My beautiful Selma, you are not the first lovely lady I have heard declare that, when I know it to be to the contrary. You have had at least one lover since coming to Vienna.'

Her eyes grew round. 'What do you mean? I . . . How did . . .?'

He laughed. 'Far from regarding you as a *demi-mondaine*, I greatly admire you for having set your sights so high, yet succeeded in retaining your reputation and that of your august lover.'

She stared at him in frightened distress. 'You know then . . . know about . . .?'

'The Archduke John? Yes. But I pray you have no apprehensions that I will tell others of it. Your secret is as safe with me as if it were a parchment buried in a tomb.'

'But others must know of it already. Someone must have told you. How else could you have found out?'

'I have an unusual gift,' he lied glibly. 'I am psychic. As you must have realized, from the moment I first saw you, your beauty overwhelmed me. Naturally, I resorted to my crystal, to find out all I could about you. I have watched you in it many times.'

Selma flushed scarlet. 'Do you mean that you've actually seen me with John in . . . in bed?'

'Nay. That would have been indelicate. I'll admit that I was tempted to. I saw only enough to be certain that he was your lover, then returned my crystal to its velvet bag.'

Taking the glass of champagne he was holding out to her, she gave a sigh of relief and quickly gulped the wine down. As she did so, he took the other chair at the table and offered her the plate of lobster patties. Automatically she took one, then another. For some minutes they ate and drank in silence. Having given her time to recover, he said:

'All's fair in love and war, and I adore you. Please tell me that you forgive me for seizing this chance to have you to myself for a while tonight.'

With a faint smile, she shook her head. 'You are the veriest of rogues. Yet how can I say "No"? I cannot think that any woman resents being wooed with audacity by a man for whom she has already shown her liking, or would not be flattered by the resource you have displayed in catching me in your snare.'

As they began on the foie gras sandwiches, he said, 'Tell me about your Archduke. I have, of course, met him several times, but talked with him only for a few minutes on each occasion. I have a natural eagerness to know the qualities in him that appeal to you.'

'I find him very sympathetic. He is kind, gentle and amusing, extremely well informed, and has proved himself to be an able General. Besides, I think any woman of my background would find it hard to resist the attentions of a man both good-looking and the brother of an Emperor.'

'Apart from not being of royal blood, would you say that I, too, possess most of those qualities?'

She laughed. 'You are asking to be flattered. But I can't deny you your due. To be honest, you are more handsome, and although you spoke of them with modesty, some of your exploits on your travels filled me with admiration for your resource and courage.'

'I am indeed flattered that you should have formed such a good opinion of me. But you have said naught of your Archduke as a lover.'

Selma looked thoughtful, then replied. 'That is difficult to answer, because my experience is so limited. I imagine him to be of average ability, but from what I have learned from other women when talking of their affairs, by no means so insatiable as, for instance, the Prince de Talleyrand is reported to be.'

Standing up, Roger took her by the elbow, and said, 'Come, let us continue our conversation in greater comfort.'

She hesitated only for a moment, then let him lead her over to the sofa. As they sat down, he put his arm about her, drew her to him and gave her a long kiss. She did not resist and let him slide his tongue between her full, soft lips until it met and toyed with hers. As they broke their kiss to draw breath, he smiled down at her, slipped his fingers under the fichu of her corsage and cupped them round her small, firm breast. Their mouths met again and again in lingering kisses. Withdrawing his hand, he reached down, lifted the hem of her flowing dress and began to stroke her long, beautifully-shaped legs. Six inches above her knees her silk stockings ended, and his probing hand came into contact with her smooth, tender flesh.

At his touch she quickly drew back her head and cried, 'No, no! No further, please. I beg you to desist.'

Ignoring her protest, with the touch of an expert his fingers continued to caress her. After a few moments she gave a little moan, lay back and murmured:

'Oh, Rojé, you have defeated me. I am yours. Take me! For God's sake, take me.'

Releasing her, he came swiftly to his feet and, with trembling hands, undid his breeches. His brief preparations over, with fast-beating heart he strove to fight down the urgency of his desire. Ready and willing as she now was, he meant to give her all the enjoyment of which he was capable, and he had long trained himself to exercise stern control.

When they had recovered and he was pouring the last of the champagne for them, he said, 'Selma, my love, that was positive heaven. But when and where can we meet to enjoy this bliss again?'

Still adjusting her dress, she shook her head. 'I know not, dearest Rojé. As a lover you are magnificent. Far better than my Archduke. But you pose a most difficult problem.'

'I know it. For your reputation's sake, I cannot take you to a hotel, and it may be weeks before Talleyrand gives another entertainment so that we could again use this room.'

She had stood up to tidy her hair in the Venetian mirror. Turning, she threw him a startled glance. 'These preparations, the supper and wine! The Prince must know that you meant to bring me here.'

He shook his head. 'You have no need to trouble yourself on that score, my love. Our supper was set here, of course, with his conniving, so that I might use the room with some fair one. But who she was to be I did not tell him.'

Reassured by this prevarication, Selma finished re-doing her hair while they continued to endeavour to think of a safe rendezvous where he might enjoy all her beauties when nude and in bed together; but in vain. At length they had to leave the questions until both of them had had further time for thought and they met again. Then, after further kisses, Roger unlocked the door, and they returned to the ballroom.

6

Caught Out

DURING Roger's pursuit of Selma, the Grand Council of the Congress had continued its frequently acrimonious discussions and appointed ten Committees to advise it on special questions. Several of them concerned themselves with special areas of Europe, others with the international rivers, diplomatic precedence, statistics and the slave trade.

The last question was never resolved satisfactorily by the Congress. Britain and most other countries had abolished the trade several years before, and Castlereagh had promised Wilberforce, the determined leader of this humane movement, to do his utmost to secure unanimity on it. But Castlereagh's efforts were thwarted by the Spanish member of the Council, Don Pedro Labrador—a most tiresome and long-winded man— who, supported by Portugal, insisted that their countries could not possibly agree to Abolition for at least another eight years.

Another personality who made a great nuisance of himself was a Corsican named Pozzo de Borgo. He was one of the foreign advisers to whom the Czar lent a ready ear, and an old enemy of Napoleon's, so he lost no opportunity of carrying on his vendetta against the Bonapartes.

Naples had sent two deputations, one from Napoleon's brother-in-law, King Murat, to urge that he should be allowed to retain his throne, the other from Ferdinand, the Bourbon King of the two Sicilies—who had escaped from the French to his island—to urge that he should be given back the mainland half of his kingdom. Talleyrand, on the orders of Louis XVIII, who naturally wished to see his relative restored, pressed the case for the Bourbons. But Metternich, having been Queen Caroline's lover, supported her husband, Murat, and the matter was further complicated by Lord Aberdeen, when Ambassador to Austria, having committed Britain, without consulting Castlereagh, to giving Austria a free hand in Italy.

The Swedes succeeded in getting confirmed their claim to Norway, which Bernadotte had recently annexed; and Castlereagh achieved one of his major objects in establishing William of Orange as King of both Holland and Belgium. Count Capo d'Istria, the representative of Corfu, pulled off an excellent coup. He feared that his neighbours, the Turks, who then ruled Greece, might invade his island, so he persuaded Castlereagh to take it over as a British colony; thus ensuring its protection for many years until the Greeks gained their independence, and Britain voluntarily handed it over to them.

But there remained many questions upon which agreement could not yet be reached. The behaviour of Lord William Bentinck, Britain's Ambassador to King Ferdinand of Sicily, caused grave concern. Without consulting anyone, he had forced the King to give his subjects a constitution; but, as the Sicilians were extremely backward, democracy failed to work with them and resulted in hopeless confusion. He then dashed off to Genoa and, again without authority,

published a declaration restoring the independence of
that ancient, and once powerful, Republic. This directly
conflicted with Castlereagh's understanding with
Metternich that, when Austria and Murat between
them had defeated and driven out the French Army of
Italy, commanded by Eugène de Beauharnais, the
whole of northern Italy should again become part of the
Austrian Empire.

A prime cause for acrimonious discussion in the
Grand Council was the future of Germany. Unlike
Sicily, the conglomeration of small principalities,
ecclesiastical enclaves and Free Cities on the far side
of the Rhine, Hanover, Westphalia, Mecklenberg and
Saxony had all been overrun by Napoleon, and the
French had brought with them the doctrines of the
Revolution. The German lower orders had gleefully
accepted their liberation from serfdom and, naturally,
now wished for democratic government. To that both
Castlereagh and Metternich, in accordance with their
principles, were most strongly opposed, whereas the
Czar, in his idealistic conception of himself as the
great Christian Liberator, championed the demand for
government by the people, and he was supported by
Frederick William of Prussia, who had already introduced many reforms in his kingdom.

Even more violent disagreements concerned the
boundaries of territories. For centuries the Holy Roman
Empire had been the one great power in Central
Europe. All the many potentates, great and small, in
southern Germany, as far south as Tuscany and as far
west as Belgium—although certain of them were
represented by a Diet—owed allegiance to the Emperor.
But Napoleon had torn to shreds this loosely-knit
Confederation, and Francis had wisely assumed the
lesser title of Emperor of Austria.

In the meantime, although Prussia had also been overrun by Napoleon, her great military contribution to his defeat and the backing of the Czar made her a potential rival for the overlordship of the lesser German states and leadership of the Germanic peoples. She claimed not only Saxony but a great part of the Rhineland; and, if given them, would become as powerful as Austria.

Castlereagh was by no means averse to that, for his grand objective was to achieve in Europe a balance of power by which, together with Austria, a strong Prussia would be capable of restraining either Russia or a resurgent France from launching a new war of conquest. By these means he aimed to save Britain from becoming involved in another European conflict.

Talleyrand, too, wished to create a balance of power, and for many years that had been his secret ambition. But the two statesmen differed on the way in which it was to be brought about. Castlereagh knew that, owing to Napoleon's wholesale slaughter of French manhood, several generations must elapse before France was again strong enough to launch a war of aggression; but Russia could do so at any time, and, military glory now having gone to the ill-balanced Czar's head, might well do so. His overriding fear was therefore of Russia.

On the other hand Talleyrand, who was far more long-sighted, thought that a triple alliance between a strong Austria, France and Britain could not only keep Russia in check, but also Prussia; and it was Prussia he feared. With extraordinary acumen he visualized a future in which Prussia, given large areas of territory in several parts of Germany, all connected by main roads, and an industry which would make the smaller states largely dependent on her would, sooner or later, dominate and probably absorb them all. That would give her a manpower in Europe equal to Russia's, but with a higher degree of intelligence and led by such ruthless, determined generals as Blücher. Then the day would come when a huge German army would be launched against her weaker neighbours.

Only the alliance he planned could prevent that, so he intrigued unceasingly to prevent Prussia getting all that she demanded. His skilful efforts were eventually successful to a large degree; and it was due to this that for one hundred years there was no further international conflict in Europe.

Two evenings after Talleyrand's ball, a concert was given by Freiherr von und zu Stein, another of the great men at the Congress. He had been responsible for many of the liberal measures that, in a few years, had converted Prussia from a backward autocracy into very nearly a democracy; so that even the freed serfs felt they had a stake in their country and later fought with fanatical patriotism to drive out the French. During Prussia's occupation, his writings had stirred up such furious animosity against the French that Napoleon had forced the weak-willed Frederick William to exile Stein, who had then gone to Russia. The Czar thought very highly of him and made him his principal adviser on foreign affairs. He still held that position, which was why he was in Vienna, and it was said that he had even greater influence with Alexander than had Count Nesselrode.

Roger painted a little when he had the time, although by no means so well as Georgina; but classical music had no appeal for him, so he had gone to the concert solely in the hope of seeing Selma, and his hope was realized. They exchanged covert glances, but sat some distance from each other, while Beethoven, now almost blind, conducted several of his renowned symphonies. It was not until the guests mingled at a buffet supper that Roger succeeded in detaching Selma from a group of her admirers, on the excuse of showing her a famous painting in one of the anterooms. There, in a window embrasure, they held a swift conversation in lowered voices.

'Have you any ideas?' she asked.

'Alas, no,' he replied ruefully. 'I've racked my brains every moment of the past two days, yet can think of no place where we could be alone together without risking your reputation.'

'Would you be willing to chance being ordered to leave Vienna, or perhaps even sent to prison?'

Wondering what was coming, he looked at her in surprise, but replied without a moment's hesitation, 'Yes. I'd take any risk to hold you in my arms again.'

She smiled. 'You are very gallant, and very sweet. In fairness I had to ask you, but I would not make the suggestion I am about to, did I believe there was any serious risk of our being caught. Now listen, for we must not linger here for long.

'Under another name, the Archduke John owns a small chalet only a few miles away, in the Wienerwald. It is there that we have taken our pleasure. No servants live in the chalet, but a couple occupy a cottage several hundred yards away. Their duties are to clean the chalet daily, light fires there every evening and leave ready an excellent cold supper. They are under orders not to be within sight of the chalet between seven o'clock in the evening and ten o'clock next morning, so they never see either John or any lady he may entertain there, either arrive or leave. Whether he has used the place or not is known to them only by its state when they come to clean it.'

Roger smiled slowly. 'And your idea is that we

should occupy it one evening when the Archduke is known to be fully engaged?'

She nodded. 'We have met there only once or twice a week, because his position compels him to attend so many functions, and he cannot, like other men, slip away from them unnoticed. He gave me a key to the chalet, so that I could let myself in should I arrive earlier than he does; and I have my own coach, so we could drive there in it.'

'You count your coachman trustworthy, then?'

'Yes. I pay him handsomely to keep secret these visits of mine to the chalet.'

'Marvellous! Oh, marvellous!' Roger's eyes were shining. 'But when, when, can we make this expedition to Paradise? Wait! I have it. On Monday there is a Court ball at the Hofburg. The Archduke will have to remain in attendance on the Emperor until all the principal guests have left. That will provide a perfect opportunity for us.'

'I, too, had thought of that. I will feign illness and send my excuses. Having made your bow, you could quietly leave at, say, ten o'clock. Go straight to the west door of the Stephen's Kirke and I will pick you up there. But we must not linger here longer now. You had best take me back to the buffet.'

Over the weekend the hours seemed to drag interminably for Roger. But, at last, the Monday evening came, and everything went according to plan. Selma picked him up outside the Stephen's Kirke and they drove out to the chalet in the woods.

He found it to be a delightful retreat, and everything had been prepared in accordance with the Archduke's standing orders. Thick curtains were drawn across the windows, so that no poacher or casual passer-by should glimpse even the candlelight that lit the interior. The walls of the main room were decorated with hunting trophies, on the floor there were bearskin rugs, a tempting supper had been set out on a small, oval table, and beside it stood an ice bucket holding a magnum of champagne. The fire had burned down, but Roger quickly made it up. The bedroom had been designed like a large tent, so that folds of pink silk hid the walls and ceiling. The only furniture in it was a huge bed. The satin sheets were already turned back, and two big mounds in the centre showed the bed-warmers had been put in.

During their drive, the lovers had delighted in a score of kisses and, as soon as Roger had relieved Selma of her wraps, they embraced again. Soon they were laughing gaily together as they fed each other with titbits from the supper table, and shared a big goblet of the sparkling wine. But both were too eager for other pleasures to linger long over the meal.

In the bedroom Roger persuaded Selma to strip for him, so that he could revel in the sight of her long legs, small pouting breasts and blonde cendré hair falling upon her nude shoulders. But she made no secret of it that she was eager to be done with these preliminaries. The moment he had got his clothes off, she flung herself backwards on to the bed and pulled him down on top of her.

For four hours, with only languorous rests in between, they excited each other to new frenzies of passion; then, with great reluctance, dressed so that she might be home by four o'clock in the morning, which was about the time she would otherwise have returned from the ball.

Throughout November the Congress continued its wrangles. Numerous minor problems were settled, but agreement on the major one of Poland's future was postponed, because the Czar demanded the whole of that country. Austria refused to give up her part of it and Prussia hers, except as the price of receiving the whole of Saxony; and Austria was opposed to that, while the wily Talleyrand continued to put forward one reason after another why Saxony should be preserved as an independent Kingdom.

During these weeks Roger thoroughly enjoyed himself. From a variety of sources he kept himself informed of nearly everything that was going on behind the scenes. As had been foreseen by Castlereagh, he proved a most valuable go-between, enlisting Talleyrand's support for policies favoured by Britain, and Castlereagh's for settlements favourable to France. The Czar spoke pleasantly to him on several occasions and, being in the secret of his past close association with Napoleon, listened amiably to what he had to say. Metternich, having been informed that he was in Castlereagh's confidence, frequently sent for him to learn the British statesman's views, or to convey his own prior to meetings of the Grand Council.

Meanwhile, he had acquired a lovely, passionate and laughter-loving mistress. Twice a week he and Selma enjoyed hectic sessions at the Archduke's chalet. For that there was a price to pay as, had she not continued to go there now and again with her Imperial lover, he might have taken another mistress, and they would have had much more difficulty in ascertaining the nights when they were confident he would not go there himself.

As Selma had fallen desperately in love with Roger, she now resented having to give herself to the Archduke also, so Roger had to pretend that he was desperately jealous. But past experience with lovely ladies who had, from time to time, had to oblige their husbands, had taught him that to insist on fidelity was to cut off one's nose to spite one's face. Wisely, as far as he could, he put her affair with the Archduke out of his mind and, having developed a genuine depth of feeling for her, quite apart from her physical attraction, revelled in the joys he experienced with her during their secret meetings.

It was on the last day of November that there occurred the *contretemps* which they had, from the beginning, believed most unlikely to overtake them. Two nights before, the Archduke had told Selma that the following morning affairs connected with his military duties necessitated his setting out for Linz. As the city was the better part of a hundred miles away, it had seemed certain that he would be absent for, at the very least, three days.

On the evening of the 29th, Selma was giving a dinner party, so it had been impossible for her to take advantage of the Archduke's absence; but on the 30th she and Roger followed the evasive tactics concerning social engagements which they had by then developed to a fine art, and happily drove out together to the chalet. They reached it shortly before eleven o'clock, indulged in mutual caresses for some minutes, then sat down to supper.

Roger had only just begun to shell for Selma some of the delicious *écrevisses* from the Danube when he heard the front door slam, and footsteps in the little hall.

Dropping the baby lobster, he came swiftly to his feet. At that moment the door of the room was thrown open, and the Archduke, dressed in a plain, civilian suit, strode in. He was followed by a woman, wearing a hood that, in the candlelight, made her features indistinct.

As the Archduke stared angrily at Roger, the woman

threw back her hood, and cried with a laugh, ' 'Tis clear, John, that you have been properly *trompé* by this lovely lady. And dam'me if the cuckoo in your nest is no other than my old friend, Lord Kildonan.'

The woman was Georgina.

7

Ruined

THE atmosphere was electric. At the sight of the Archduke, Selma had given a startled cry, jumped up from
the table and, to hide her scarlet cheeks, sank in a deep
curtsey. Roger was staring at Georgina, wondering
how ever she came to be in Vienna. Momentarily,
seeing her so unexpectedly had robbed him of his wits,
but her amused exclamation had also checked the
Archduke's immediate impulse to demand an explanation.

Roger knew that there was no possible excuse he
could offer for his presence in the Archduke's chalet,
supping with his mistress. He and Selma had been
fairly caught, and the inference that they had later
intended to make an appropriate use of the bedroom
was obvious to anyone. Yet the idea of slinking guiltily
away was insupportable. Those few seconds of silence
enabled him to recover his resourcefulness. Stepping
forward, he made only a slight bow, and said pleasantly:

'Sir, your arrival is, admittedly, ill-timed, but nevertheless I bid you welcome.'

At this impertinence, the Archduke almost choked.
'*Teufel Nochmals!*' he exclaimed. 'Knowing who I am
and that this chalet is my property, how dare you
address me in such a manner!'

Roger had first met him some years before, and recently on several occasions since the opening of the Congress. But he pretended not to recognize him. With a lift of his eyebrows, he replied in apparent surprise, 'Sir, it strikes me that you bear some resemblance to His Imperial Highness the Archduke John, but I was given to suppose that this property belongs to a private gentleman.'

'You know full well . . .' the Archduke burst out angrily. But Georgina swiftly laid a hand on his arm. She had instantly realized that the line Roger had taken was designed to discourage her companion from taking any action that might endanger his reputation. Having checked the Archduke, she said quickly:

'You are right, my lord. And I am certain that His Highness would manifest the greatest displeasure should his name become associated with this matter.'

Her intervention gave the Archduke pause. As Selma had warned Roger on first suggesting that they should make use of the chalet, discovery might lead to his being expelled from Vienna, or even imprisonment; and thoughts of giving Roger reason to regret his temerity had been coursing swiftly through His Highness's angry mind. Now, having scowled at Selma, he muttered:

'No matter my identity. I am of royal blood, so cannot duel with an inferior. But I am a close friend of the Archduke, and could request him to send one of his gentlemen to demand an explanation of your presence here with Madame Thorwaldsen.'

Roger bowed. 'I should be happy, Sir, to meet him at any time.'

Again Georgina intervened, saying quickly to the Archduke, 'I pray you, put any such idea from your mind. The prowess of my Lord Kildonan has long been known to me. In a duel he fought when barely twenty he killed the Comte de Caylus, who was then accounted the finest swordsman in France. The odds are that it would go hard with any unfortunate gentleman sent to measure blades with him.'

The Archduke frowned. 'If that is so, my conscience would not permit me to expose some gentleman not concerned in this to such a dangerous antagonist. But there are other means by which I could cause him to regret this intolerable intrusion. A nominee of mine could declare this chalet to be his property, call in the police and bring a charge of trespass and theft against the interloper. That would get him a prison sentence.'

'To trespass I would admit,' Roger gave a little shrug. 'As to theft, surely little value could be set on two glasses of wine and an *écrevisse*? It must then be that you were referring to my taking from you the lady in the case.'

'No, please!' Selma cried. 'It would prove my ruin.' Then, covering her face with her hands, she burst into tears.

'It would be no more than you deserve.' The Archduke's voice was harsh. 'But no gentleman could resort to avenge himself in such a manner on a lady for her infidelity.'

'Exactly,' Roger remarked with a cynical little smile. 'But you cannot have me charged without involving Madame Thorwaldsen. Come, Sir, I beg you to be magnanimous. Accept my sincerest apologies and let matters rest at that.'

For a moment the Archduke considered, then he said with a return to the graciousness that was usual in him, 'To find you here naturally caused me great annoyance, and had my companion been a lady other than the Duchess of Kew, whose past association with me, she

has told me, is known to you, it would have proved
most embarrassing to her. But, all things considered, I
deem you right. I accept your apology and we will
forget this regrettable encounter.'

Placing his hand on his heart, Roger made a deep
bow. 'For that, Sir, I am truly grateful and if I can at
any time be of service to you, I beg you not to hesitate
to call on me. And now, Sir, we will relieve you of our
presence.'

With a sigh of relief, Selma came to her feet. Picking
up her wraps, Roger swiftly draped them round her and
offered her his arm. They exchanged polite bows with
Georgina, left the chalet and walked through the cold,
silent wood to the clearing in which they had left
Selma's coach. Her coachman was walking the horses
up and down to keep their circulation going. Five
minutes later, they were on their way back to
Vienna.

It was a far from happy drive. Selma broke down and
cried again. Roger took her in his arms and strove to
comfort her, but she was inconsolable at the thought
that they had been deprived of the love-nest in which
they had spent many happy hours, and would have
great difficulty in finding another place where they
could meet in secret. His mind was mainly occupied
with thoughts of Georgina. She had helped materially
in getting him out of a very unpleasant situation; but
the knowledge that she was now supping with the
Archduke, and that they would shortly be in bed together, caused him far more concern than a possible
ending to his affair with Selma.

When Selma dropped him outside the Stephen's
Kirke, he told her that, when they next met in public,
he hoped that he would have thought of some solution
to their problem. He then promptly dismissed her from

D

his mind, and walked home to Castlereagh's house, disgruntled and angry.

Discreet enquiries of a number of people next day failed to inform him whereabouts in Vienna Georgina had taken up residence, and it was not until midday on the 2nd that, through Talleyrand's ubiquitous legion of spies, he learned that she was living at the Villa Rosen, a pleasant house overlooking the park, out at Schönbrunn. That afternoon, he drove out there and the front door was opened by one of her footmen whom he had known in London.

Smiling recognition, the man took up Roger's card and returned to say that Her Grace would receive him. Upstairs in a boudoir, handsomely furnished in the *Louis Quinze* fashion, he found Georgina alone, seated on a sofa. As he entered, she rose, swept him a low curtsey; then, raising her beautifully curved eyebrows, asked coldly:

'To what do I owe the honour of Your Lordship's visit?'

Taken aback, he automatically made a leg, then exclaimed, 'Georgina, my love, what the devil has got into you? Surely it cannot be that you have taken offence at finding me with that pretty Swede the other night?'

She waved him to a chair. 'Certainly not. We have always agreed that, when apart, we should amuse ourselves with any other of the opposite sex who took our fancy. On the contrary, I congratulate you on her. Although her breasts leave something to be desired, if her legs are as shapely as they are long, she must be a pleasant sight when in the nude, and a finer pair of eyes it would be difficult to find. Presumably she performs well in bed, or you would not bother with her.'

'She does,' Roger replied curtly. 'And is altogether a charming young creature. But you have never before displayed jealousy of women with whom I have pleasured myself when abroad, so why now?'

'Jealous!' Georgina laughed, but not gaily. 'Lud, no! I'm not in the least.'

'Then why this frigid reception of me?'

'I should have thought you would have guessed that. I care not a snap of my fingers whom you go to bed with when I am not available. It is your neglect of me that I resent.'

'But, dam'me, I had not the faintest idea that you were in Vienna.'

'No. Nor I that you were here. You told me in your letter only that Castlereagh had found some employment for you abroad. For all I knew, you might have been in Paris, or in any other city on the Continent. While Britain was at war, and you abroad, obviously you could not write to me. But now there is peace, what was there to prevent your letting me know your whereabouts?'

'I'm truly sorry,' Roger said contritely. 'The only excuse I can offer is the habit of years. I never . . .'

Georgina's black eyes flashed angrily. 'Never gave me a thought. You were quite content to disport yourself here with that Swedish wench.'

'Nay, I protest! I think of you often, and bitterly deplore the fact that I had to leave England for fear that Mary would murder you.'

'Is England the only place in which two people can make love? Surely your mind has not become so dense that it failed to occur to you that you could ask me to join you here? Not permanently, of course, in view of my obligations. But there was naught to prevent my coming over for a few weeks, and a perfect excuse for such a visit was provided by the Congress, with its many entertainments.'

'My dearest love, you are right in that my wits must be failing me. I swear to you that, had such a thought entered my mind, I'd have been overjoyed and lost not a moment in begging you to come to Vienna.'

'Well, 'tis clear that someone else has more lasting memories of happy times with me, and values my company more than yourself.'

'The Archduke John?'

'Yes. He has never forgotten that joyous week we spent together in my castle on the Rhine. He implored me then to leave von Haugwitz and come to Vienna. I confess that I was tempted, but that was before his wife died. Owing to the war, I was then unable to get any of my money out of England, so I could not have set up my own establishment. To live here and be looked on by everybody as his kept woman was more than my pride could stomach. But now things are very different. When he wrote, imploring me to renew our happy association, I rented this house through an agent and brought several of my own servants with me. I am just one of the innumerable visitors who have come from all quarters to enjoy the society of this international gathering of notables. John now has no wife, and should it leak out that we are having an affair no-one can possibly regard me as a whore. And, to be honest, my reunion with him has brought me great happiness.'

Roger gave a gasp. 'Can this possibly mean, Georgina, that my having failed to ask you to join me here has filled you with such bitterness towards me that, after all these years, you mean to cast me aside in favour of him?'

The expression on his face was so desperately distressed and pathetic that she gently shook her head.

'Nay, Roger. That could never be. The bond we've forged between us is so strong that it will last all our lives and into our many lives to come.'

At that his relief was so overwhelming that he threw himself at her feet, grasped her hands and cried, 'Thank God! Oh, thank God. Then, now we are again united, you'll forgive me my stupidity and sacrifice your Archduke for me.'

She smiled a little wistfully. 'Dear one, that is too much to expect. It was John who asked me here, and with obvious expectations. I'm fond of him, Roger. He is kind, generous and this is no sudden passion of his. For years he has treasured the remembrance of our brief idyll. Having agreed to come to Vienna at his behest, how could I now be so cruel as to deny myself to him? But you are in my life a being apart, so on certain nights I would be happy for you to come to me here.'

'What!' exclaimed Roger angrily. 'And share you with him?'

'Why not?' Georgina laughed. 'You have been sharing that pretty young Swede with him.'

'That is quite different. She and I were attracted by physical passion; no more. And, whenever I have returned to England, you have willingly terminated your current affair with some other lover to be mine alone.'

'True, but in two cases there were husbands whom I could not cast off, and you had to share me with them.'

'I know it, but the Archduke is not your husband.'

Georgina sighed. 'Roger, my love, I pray you be sensible. What, after all, is a slice off a cut cake? And mine has been cut I know not how many times. Aye, and it was cut yet again only two nights since, after you left John and me alone in the chalet. My heart and soul are yours, but with my body I'll do as I will.'

'I have never claimed any rights upon it, nor you on mine. But, whenever we have been able to resume our life-long joy in being together, neither of us has given a thought to any other. Yet now you refuse to give up the Archduke for me. For that there can be only one explanation. You are in love with him.'

'You are right. I am,' she replied calmly.

'What!' Roger's face went white and his cry of anguish came from the heart. 'You admit it?'

'I do. I've never lied to you, and I'll not do so now. But I did not say I loved him more than I do you. Love is not indivisible. 'Tis not an unbreakable iron bar or a precious stone that one gives to one person, then takes away and gives to another. All of us have minor loves. Many give a part of their love to pets; dogs, horses, even monkeys. Given kind parents, we love them. That is so, too, with brothers, sisters, friends whom we find sympathetic. I have loved many men for a while, and all my husbands, except old Kew—at least to begin with. For a woman to love two men at the same time is by no means unusual. Yet, while loving others, I have always placed you first. Even in the case of Charles's father, whom I loved very dearly, when you were in such great distress about Amanda's conduct I offered to deceive my husband in order to comfort you. Since you were his friend, you most honourably refused my offer. But I made it as I make it now, for you to share me with John, but more I will not do.'

Roger could not contest her reasoning. Although Georgina had ever remained paramount in his heart, he had loved many women and some, as in the case of Susan's mother, Amanda, at the same time as he had her. He felt certain that had he asked Georgina to come to Vienna, however much she was attracted to the Archduke she would not have allowed him to become her lover. But since he had neglected the opportunity to invite her over himself, he could not blame her for offering him only a share in all but her mental fidelity. She made no demand that he should give up Selma, so how could he complain that she was acting selfishly?

Reluctantly he admitted that everyone had many loves, and they ran concurrently, differing only in degree. Realizing that to argue the matter further was futile, he changed the subject and asked her how it was that, although the Archduke had been believed to be in Linz, he had arrived so unexpectedly with her at the chalet.

' 'Twas pure chance, and good weather,' she replied. 'Knowing that I was on the way, his eagerness to join me was such that he rode out to meet me at a castle he has not far from Linz. But I and my people had lain there the night before, so we encountered each other halfway to Vienna. Hence his return a day earlier than expected, and that same night I agreed to accompany him to his little house in the woods.'

They talked on for half an hour, but only about the Congress and forthcoming social events; then Lady Castlereagh was announced, with her sister who was staying with her. Having learned that Georgina was in Vienna, the two ladies had come to pay a formal call, so when Roger took his leave he had to do so as no more than an acquaintance of the lovely Duchess.

The arrival of Georgina's visitors had prevented her and Roger from coming to any agreement regarding the future and he was by no means sorry about that. He knew that he had no grounds that justified his quarrelling with her on the attitude she had taken up, yet he was deeply distressed by it, and wanted time to decide whether to show his resentment by refusing her offer that he should share her with the Archduke, or eat humble pie by accepting it.

That night, at a reception given by Prince Metternich, he saw Selma, and they were able to have a short talk, sitting on a settee in a corner, partially hidden by potted palms. Since their meeting at the chalet she had been ignored by the Archduke, and had no regrets about that, but she was most anxious to continue her affair with Roger.

As had been their trouble to start with, since Roger was not living in an apartment of his own and he could not take her to a hotel, they were again at a loss to think of any safe rendezvous.

However, an idea occurred to Roger. The Marquis de la Tour du Pin, a member of Talleyrand's mission, who was a good friend of his, had taken an apartment for himself, and during the following week was returning to Paris for consultation with King Louis. It was possible that the Marquis might be willing to allow his quarters to be used as a rendezvous during his absence. This hope did much to dispel Selma's gloom, and Roger promised to let her know as soon as he could if the Marquis was agreeable. They then parted to mix again with the company.

Two mornings later, on going into a bank in the Kärutner Strasse to change some money, Roger ran into an old acquaintance of his, Nathan Rothschild. He was not surprised, as among the many missions attending the Congress there was one representing the Jews of Frankfurt. Until Napoleon had conquered Germany, the Jews in all the German cities had been confined to ghettoes. In accordance with the principles of the Revolution, the Emperor had freed them from all restrictions and given them equal rights as citizens. Now that the Kings and petty Princes were again about to rule their old territories, the Jews naturally feared they would once more be deprived of their freedom, so had come to plead for the protection of their interests by Britain and other democratic powers.

It transpired, however, that Nathan, who was the head of the English branch of the amazing family that, in a quarter of a century, had become the greatest banking house in Europe, had come from London to Vienna only on a brief visit. Drawing Roger aside, he said:

'I trust Your Lordship will not think it impertinent in me. I take the libery of asking this only because we have known each other for many years, and it was largely due to your recommendation of me to the British Treasury when I first went to England that I met with such success there. Are you in any difficulty with regard to funds?'

'Why, no,' Roger replied in surprise. 'My fortune is not great, but with the money I inherited from my father and what I have put by, I have ample to see me through a comfortable old age.'

Rothschild shook his head gloomily. 'I fear, my lord, that may be so no longer. That is, unless you have some other banker beside Hoare's.'

'No. Hoare's hold all my securities.'

'And they have your order that at any time your current account becomes too low to meet demands upon it they should sell securities to put it in funds again. Is that not so?'

Roger frowned. 'Yes, but how you should be aware of it I am at a loss to know.'

'My lord, I beg you not to ask the source of my information. It is, I admit, unorthodox; but I have no doubt of its reliability. During the past two months many thousands of pounds of your securities have been sold, and the proceeds used to pay drafts presented by jewellers, antiquarians, picture dealers and for the purchase of a house at Brighton.'

'My God!' Roger exclaimed. 'Are you . . . are you certain of this?'

'Quite certain, my lord. Knowing you to be here in Vienna, and the unostentatious life you usually lead, this sudden inroad on your fortune struck me as most strange. I feared that you might already have found yourself in difficulties. Hence my question, since for old times' sake, I would have been happy to see if I could not straighten out your affairs for you.'

'I am deeply grateful to you, both for the information you have brought me and for your generous offer; but for the moment I'll not avail myself of it.' Roger grasped the banker's hand, shook it firmly, then, still dazed by the news of this terrible misfortune that had overtaken him, walked out into the street.

Had he had any doubt about what had happened, Rothschild's mention of the purchase of a house at Brighton would have settled it. Mary had been forging his signature.

While at the Academy for Young Ladies she had attended she had made a hobby of calligraphy. With exquisite penmanship she could write Elizabethan script or copy poems, the lettering of which was in ancient Greek. He well remembered how skilfully, when they had been in the United States, she had forged the document which had enabled them to get through the war zone to the Canadian frontier.

On getting back to his quarters, he told Castlereagh that an urgent private matter necessitated his setting out post haste to London. Having sent a note to Talleyrand to the same effect, he wrote two others.

One was to Georgina, simply saying that he was

compelled to leave Vienna for a week or two; and, all
his rancour at her treatment now blotted from his mind
by this catastrophe, adding that he would not be living,
only breathing, until he could hold her in his arms
again.

The other was to Selma. Fearing that if his missive
to her showed any evidence of affection it might get
her into trouble if it fell into wrong hands, he used the
fact that she was giving a rout at the Swedish Mission
on the following Tuesday. He had already received an
invitation, and had accepted it. Now he sent another
formal note, regretting that he would not, after all, be
able to be present, as he had to leave Vienna on important diplomatic business, and would not be returning
for some weeks.

He left Vienna that night. The average time taken
by fast couriers to reach London was eight days, but
Roger was lucky with the weather, and did the journey
in seven, arriving on December 11th. At Amesbury
House he learned that Droopy, like many other wealthy
English people, had gone on a visit to Brussels. Feeling
much too unsociable to walk round to White's, he
spent an anxious, lonely evening in Droopy's suite, then
went to bed in the room on the floor above, which was
always kept for him.

Next morning found him in the Strand, waiting impatiently until the doors of Hoare's Bank were opened.
He then had to kick his heels for a further half an hour
until one of the younger partners arrived. In a private
room upstairs, they went into his account. It emerged
that the disaster was even worse than Roger expected.
While he had been in Vienna, Mary had robbed him of
all but a ninth of his small fortune.

8

The Final Blow

ROGER was aghast at this terrible blow Mary had
struck him. In less than four months she had succeeded
in getting hold of the best part of eighty thousand
pounds. Presumably she had sold the jewels, pictures
and *objets d'art* she had bought, and purchased stock
with the money, or put it into an account she had
opened somewhere under another name. But there was
the house in Brighton. He might be able to take that
from her.

Young Mr. Hoare was most helpful. The forgeries
were so perfect that the bank was clearly in no way to
blame, and the only question now was how to best
protect what remained of Roger's investments. There
were probably other orders on his account not yet
presented. To refuse payment he would have to prove
that his signatures on them were forgeries. To do that
would result in a number of actions entailing heavy
legal costs. It also meant that he must bring disgrace on
his name by publicly accusing his wife of being a
criminal. He decided that they must be honoured, and
could only pray they would not be for large sums.

It was then suggested by Mr. Hoare that a notice
should be published in *The Times* that, as from a certain
date, no draft bearing Roger's signature would be
honoured unless it was countersigned with a second

signature; and that, from that date, he would no longer be responsible for his wife's debts. To guard against the second signature also being forged, the name of the person signing would not be disclosed.

December 16th, four days hence, was the date Mr. Hoare proposed, as that should give sufficient time for people who already had drafts to present them, yet not give Mary long enough warning of what was afoot for her to issue more forged drafts before a second signature became necessary to cash them.

Roger agreed to these sound suggestions, and said he would arrange for all his future drafts to be countersigned either by his son-in-law, the Earl of St. Ermins, or his friend, the Earl of Amesbury; but, as Droopy was abroad and he was uncertain of Charles's present whereabouts, he drew one thousand pounds in notes, so that he would not have to bother either of them for several months to come.

In a mood of black depression he left the bank, resolved next to confront Mary. But he did not know her address in Brighton, so he decided to drive out to Richmond, in the hope that she had left with their housekeeper an address to which letters could be forwarded.

At Thatched House Lodge he found the faithful Dan and Mrs. Muffet the only occupants. Since Mary had gone, close on four months earlier, no wages had been paid to the servants, so all of them had left, except for Mrs. Muffet and Dan. Gratefully, he paid what was owing to them and said that, as he was shortly going abroad again, he would arrange for his bank to pay them in future. To his relief he learned that Mary had written to Mrs. Muffet only three weeks earlier, giving as her new address 25 Marine Parade.

As it was by then too late to reach Brighton that evening, he returned to London, booked a seat on the coach that left at midnight, and then drove to the St. Ermins mansion in Berkeley Square, to see if his daughter, Susan, and Charles were there.

They were, and both of them were delighted to see him. When he had told them of Georgina's safe arrival in Vienna, he learned that they had been going out to a musical evening; but Susan insisted on sending a running footman with their excuses, so that they could spend the next few hours with her father.

The newly-weds—Susan with her mother's abundant auburn hair and Roger's bright blue eyes, and Charles with his dark good looks inherited from his ancestor, King Charles II—made a handsome couple. They had been in love all through their teens, and there could be no doubt that the marriage was a happy one. Both of them were bubbling over with cheerfulness and vitality, and bursting to tell him about the joys of their three-month honeymoon.

The war being over, Charles had obtained in-definite leave without pay from his regiment, on the plea that he must administer his estates. But he had first taken Susan up the Rhine in the lovely summer sunshine, to see the now untenanted Schloss Langen-stein where he had spent part of his boyhood. In Frankfurt he had shown her the inn where Roger had been under arrest and from which he had rescued him. Travelling north to Hanover, they had visited Schloss Bergdorff, where Charles had been held as a prisoner of war, and would have been hanged had not Roger arrived in time to prevent his execution. From Hamburg they had taken a ship down the coast to Antwerp, spent a week in Brussels, then gone on to Paris. By then the autumn was setting in, so they had made a slow progress through France to warmer climes. Bordeaux, where Charles had been when the war ended, then to Bayonne and across the Pyrenees to the château which had been Wellington's last headquarters before he launched his final offensive. Travelling on through northern Spain as far as Bilbao, from there they had taken a ship for home.

Back in England the shooting season was in full swing; and, while Charles and his neighbours went after the pheasants, Susan had played hostess and joyfully settled in as the mistress of his splendid seat, White Knights Park in Northamptonshire. They were in London only for a short spell, so that she might order the latest fashions in dress materials to be made up for her to wear during the coming winter season, and they meant to return north at the end of the week in good time to prepare for the Christmas festivities.

In any case Roger would not have depressed them by giving an account of the terrible misfortune that had befallen him and, for a while at least, their gay chatter took his mind off his unhappy situation. Over an excellent supper he even found himself giving them an amusing account of the Congress, the royal entertainments, the outstanding personalities, and laughing with them over absurd episodes which had occurred owing to *faux pas* made by people who knew little of the language of those to whom they were speaking.

At a quarter past eleven, much heartened by the past few hours and well fortified by good food and wine, he took a fond farewell of them; then, having collected his valise from Amesbury House, made his way to the coach station. He had booked an inside seat and managed to sleep fitfully during the greater part of the fifty-mile journey. On arriving, he took a room at the Ship Inn, shaved and tidied himself up. In the coffee room he ate a leisurely, hearty breakfast and then spent an hour perusing the day's news sheets. By then it was half past ten, and he decided that was a not unreasonable hour to make his call on Mary.

Until toward the end of the past century, Bath had been the most fashionable resort for society desiring a change from London; but, owing to the Prince Regent's patronage, Brighton had now superseded it. He had had an exotic Pavilion built for him, designed on the lines of an Indian Maharajah's palace, and he frequently came down to it for a few nights. Many of the nobility now owned houses in Brighton and scores of young bucks, who termed themselves 'Corinthians', competed in making the fastest journey from London in their racing curricles. The town had spread in all directions, and several new terraces of elegant houses had sprung up.

Roger found the Marine Parade to be one of these, and knocked loudly on the door of No. 25. It was opened by a footman in a baize apron. Announcing himself, Roger demanded in harsh tones to be taken straight up to her ladyship. With a scared look, the man mumbled that he was not certain if she was yet about, but he would see. As he turned toward the stairs, Roger followed him up. Apart from the landing, the first floor was one large room. A door to it was open and, glancing in, Roger saw that it contained a dozen or more card tables of varying sizes. Some had already been cleared by another footman who was working there, but there were still used glasses on others, scattered cards and spilt snuff. He swiftly decided that the party held there the previous night had not been a social gathering, but an assembly of gamblers in a public gaming house. Frowning, he followed the footman up the second flight of stairs. There the man threw open a door and stood aside for Roger to walk past him.

The room was a small boudoir, looking out from the front of the house on to a paved way, on which a few people were already promenading, and the sea. There was no-one in the room, but Roger noted two empty glasses, and the remains of a decanter of port on a small table in front of a settee, and on the settee a colourful wrap which Mary had brought back with her from Canada.

After a few minutes a door opposite the window opened, and Mary came through it. She was wearing a hastily-donned chamber robe over her nightdress and her bare feet were in slovenly mules. In the prevailing fashion, her hair was bunched in a bun on top of her head and corkscrew curls dangled on either side, covering her ears. She had obviously not done her hair since the previous evening, and her face was blowsy; but her eyes were bright with a malicious glitter as she said:

'So you've had the audacity to return, in spite of my warning that if you did not stay abroad I'd kill your whore, the Duchess?'

'No, you will not,' he replied coldly, 'for she is no longer in England. I am here to demand an explanation from you.'

'About what?'

'About the way you have played ducks and drakes with my money, of course, you filthy little forger.'

'Oh, that,' she laughed. 'I wondered how soon you would learn of it.'

'You admit it, then?'

'Why not? There is naught you can do about it.'

'Oh yes, there is. I can have you sent to prison.'

'Don't talk like a fool. In the first place you'd not find it easy to prove that it is I who have been forging your name.'

'You are wrong there. How otherwise could you

have found the money to buy this house, jewels, furniture and God knows what beside?'

She shrugged. 'But you would have to take me to court, and you are far too proud of your name to have it dragged in the mud.'

Roger knew that she had him there, and had called the bluff by which he had hoped to make her return a good part of his money. After a moment he asked in a milder tone, 'Why have you done this to me, Mary?'

Her reply was prompt. 'Because I vowed that to pay you out for your treatment of me I would ruin you.'

'You have by no means succeeded in that,' he retorted. 'You forget that, under English law, a wife's property belongs to her husband. I've come here to let you know that I mean to close down the gambling den into which you have apparently turned this house, sequester and sell it with all its contents, and so get back at least part of my money.'

With a mock sigh of distress, she shook her head. 'Poor, stupid Roger. Do you take me for such a nitwit that it had not occurred to me that, sooner or later, you would attempt to do as you suggest? No. This house belongs to a Mrs. Emily Vidall. In my loneliness I found gambling a pleasant way to pass the time. Mrs. Vidall had had a run of bad luck, so was in need of funds. I bought this house from her and we became partners. But, later, to scotch any claim you might make to it, I sold it back to her. She owns the place and everything in it. Take so much as a candle-snuffer, and we'll have the law on you.'

Finding himself outwitted, Roger seethed with rage. Thrusting out a hand, he grabbed the bun of hair on Mary's head and shook her, while shouting, 'You bitch! You filthy little trickster!'

She screamed. The door by which she had come into

the room was flung open. Turning his head, Roger saw a middle-aged woman, who had evidently been listening at the keyhole, come dashing toward him. As she grasped his arm, he let go of Mary's hair and turned to face the newcomer. She, too, was in *déshabillé*. Unsupported by stays, her paunch hung down to her crotch, her hips were thick and her legs short, her mouth thin-lipped and hard; there were heavy bags under her sharp, shrewd eyes. White-faced, Roger stared at her, then said:

'I take it you are Mrs. Vidall?'

'I am,' she acknowledged, still puffing after her effort. 'And you may be a lord, but that's no way to treat a lady.'

'My wife was born one,' Roger snapped, 'but by her conduct has forfeited any right to be regarded as other than belonging to the criminal classes. And you, I gather, have aided and abetted her.'

'Best mind your ps and qs, my fine gentleman, or you'll find yourself in trouble,' the woman retorted. 'I run a respectable house and no-one can say aught to the contrary.'

'Yet you must be aware of how my wife obtained the money to buy this property, and other things.'

'That's neither here nor there. And, as she's told you, the house again belongs to me. Now, get out and stay out.'

There was nothing more to be said. Roger strode toward the door, but as he reached it he turned and had the last word by remarking to Mary, 'You have been monstrous clever in tricking me, but have a care that you are not yourself tricked by your charming friend, Mrs. Vidall.'

As he walked downstairs he was followed by a spate of filthy abuse from the gaming-house keeper.

On his way back to the Ship Inn, he ruefully contemplated the fact that the two women had got the better of him, and he might have saved himself the journey to Brighton, as it had failed to get him back one penny of his money.

He tried to understand the intensity of Mary's bitterness, and thought it might be partly accounted for by the life she had led in her teens. Although well born, she had become an orphan when very young and had had no close relatives to care for her. Having to forgo every luxury, dress very cheaply and constantly sponge on her friends was calculated to make any girl secretly bitter. His had been the fairy wand that had changed her life, and she had not only loved him physically but given him her absolute devotion. Georgina had argued that love was not indivisible, and in general she was right, but Mary's case was an exception.

When they had returned to England after their long travels, during which they had had no permanent companions, she had no friends, nor even pets to absorb a part of her affections. Then, when she had discovered that Georgina was his real love, the bottom had dropped out of her world. The sour, hidden resentment of her youth had returned, but she no longer kept it secret. Instead, her disillusion and grief had unbalanced her mind, and with regard to himself and Georgina it was as if she were possessed by a demon.

The trouble had started, of course, a year and a half ago, when he had left Mary to go to the Continent in search of Charles. He had expected to be away from England for no more than a few weeks but one unforeseen happening after another had prolonged his absence for eight months. And as time had gone on Mary's resentment must have festered from the knowledge that it was his search for Georgina's son that kept her husband from her. It was then she had first taken to drink to solace her loneliness; and many hours of half-drunken brooding on her situation must have prepared the way for her present implacable determination to revenge herself by putting an end to Roger's association with Georgina and ruining him.

Mary's appearance had shocked him deeply. When he had returned to England the previous April, to find her drunk in bed, although never a great beauty, she had still been attractive and, at least, clean. But now she had degenerated into a dirty, bedraggled trollop; her face puffy, her complexion muddied, her hair uncared for, and she was still in her early twenties. The only explanation was that drink and jealousy had rotted poor Mary's brain so, in spite of the awful tribulations she was inflicting on him, Roger could not help feeling sorry for her and reproached himself for being in part responsible.

That morning the notice Mr. Hoare had suggested would be published in *The Times*, and three days had yet to elapse before Roger would know the full extent of his misfortune. In London on the previous day it had been foggy, whereas there was pleasant winter sunshine at Brighton; so he decided to stay on there for the next two days.

However, with nothing to think of except his worries, he was by evening reduced to a state in which he could bear his idleness no longer. It then occurred to him that he might occupy himself by visiting his old home, Grove Place, at Lymington. It was a medium-sized mansion, with some twenty acres of garden and farmland round it, and looked out over the Solent to the Isle of Wight, so it was quite a valuable property, and a consoling thought that, now the bulk of his investments had gone, he could sell it. On the death of his father, the Admiral, he had leased it to a Mr. Drummond who, as a member of the banking family, was very well-off and might like to buy the freehold.

With this in mind Roger went next morning to the post house, picked out a chestnut mare and set off on the fifty-five-mile ride along the coast to Southampton. There he spent the night, then rode on to Lymington on the following morning. Having thought over the matter, he was of the opinion that, with luck, he might get ten thousand pounds for the property, but would be prepared to sell for eight thousand.

When he called at the house a little before midday, he was told, to his annoyance, that Mr. Drummond was in London; but his handsome, middle-aged wife received Roger, as an old friend, most kindly and insisted that he must stay to dinner. As the meal was not until three o'clock, when they had settled down in the drawing room she sent for Madeira and biscuits. While Roger was taking his first sip of the wine, she asked conversationally:

'How are you enjoying living at Brighton?'

Roger looked at her in swift surprise. Struck with an awful premonition, he nearly dropped his glass. Then, after a moment, he murmured, 'I . . . I'm not living there.'

'Oh, you've moved, then,' she smiled at him. 'At least I feel sure it was to an address in Brighton that my husband sent those bearer bonds when he bought the freehold here from you last month. I recall his wondering at the time why you should prefer bearer bonds to a draft on his bank.'

It was horribly obvious to Roger that Mary had struck him another dreadful blow by forging a correspondence with Mr. Drummond, then signing the contract of saie. It was also obvious to him why she had asked for bearer bonds. She could cash them at any time, whereas a draft would have had to go into his account at Hoare's, and then the money got out again by forged cheques for all sorts of purchases.

Having swallowed his Madeira at a gulp, endeavouring to keep his voice steady, he replied, 'I was going abroad almost at once, and it was more convenient to have bonds, so that I could take them with me.'

How he managed to get through the next few hours he could never afterwards remember. Years of concealing his emotions and practice in maintaining a casual manner when in difficult situations had, he supposed, enabled him to carry on an intelligent conversation with his hostess; but his relief had been overwhelming when, at last, he could take his leave of her.

That night he again slept at an inn in Southampton. At five o'clock on the following morning, again riding post, he set out for London, arriving in ample time to go to Hoare's Bank before it closed. There young Mr. Hoare informed him that the notice in *The Times* had, in the past three days, brought in four more drafts forged by Mary. In all she had robbed him of over eighty thousand pounds, and he was left with a balance of only four thousand three hundred. Had he not returned to England when he had, that would also have gone, and yet more forged drafts continued to come in until Hoare's would have had to refuse to honour them. Then, in due course, he would have been made bankrupt. To have escaped that was some consolation, also that he still had his home and, Thatched Lodge being a grace and favour residence, by no possible means could Mary dispose of it.

As on his first visit to Hoare's he had drawn a thousand pounds, he decided against writing to either Charles or Droopy to let them know what had hap-

pened, and ask them to countersign his future drafts.
There would be time enough for that when he was
again in need of money. Since there was no point in his
remaining in London, after supping alone at Amesbury
House he took the night coach to Dover.

Snow had fallen in Kent and on the other side of the
Channel, but two days later a mild spell set in, so he
was able to make better going, and arrived back in
Vienna late on the evening of the 24th.

When he woke the next morning, he realized that it
was Christmas Day; and, as far as his future prospects
were concerned, he had never known a bleaker one. At
the rate at which he was used to living, the income on
four thousand pounds would go nowhere; Napoleon's
war chest, from which for years he had drawn all the
money he needed, no longer existed. Although confirmed as a Count by Louis XVIII, the generous
allowances made by the Emperor to all the nobles he
had created, in order that they might suitably maintain their rank, were no longer being paid. It was now
several years since he had ceased to be a secret agent, so
he no longer received the handsome payments from the
British Treasury which had enabled him to build up
his respectable fortune; Castlereagh, believing him to
be a rich nobleman, had not offered him any remuneration for these few months' attendance at the
Congress; and Talleyrand was under no obligation to
pay him anything.

Georgina was very rich and would, he knew, happily
provide him with a handsome income. Charles, too,
could easily afford to give him a couple of thousand a
year, and a home into the bargain. Droopy, like many
other noblemen of the period, often gave house room
for months at a stretch to impecunious authors, artists
and others, and would gladly have him as a permanent

guest. But the very idea of sponging on his friends indefinitely was abhorrent to Roger.

Besides, he dared not even stay with them for a while from time to time, because Georgina was not likely to remain for more than a few weeks in Vienna, and if he returned to England, it was as good as certain that Mary would make another attempt to kill her. It seemed that the only course open to him was to do as he had done when first the threat had been made—go to Castlereagh and ask him for some minor appointment at an embassy abroad; but such a post held no attractions now that he would have such a small private income.

Despondently he dressed and went out. It was snowing, but nearly every window was brightly lit, and Vienna gay with Christmas festivities. Outside the Hofburg a huge crowd had gathered and he soon learned the reason. In the Imperial chapel, Mass was being celebrated. He had often been there, for it was a beautiful example of baroque architecture. It was too small to hold more than perhaps two hundred people, so only the most important persons at the Congress would have been allotted seats, and the great crowd was waiting to see them come out.

. He could imagine the magnificence of the scene inside: the walls and ceiling covered with gilded carving, the colourful saints and cherub-angels, the hundreds of candles, the Cardinal Nuncio in scarlet and other high prelates wearing rich robes and embroidered surplices, kneeling, rising, bowing to one another before the altar; their young attendants swinging silver censers which would fill the atmosphere with incense, the boy choristers with their sweet treble chanting, the surging music from the organ; the Emperor, his family, the Czar, and the King of Prussia would be in the big, curved balcony, below them would be row upon row of lesser monarchs,

Princes, Generals, Ambassadors and Court officials, all
wearing their most brilliant uniforms, sashes of many
Orders of Chivalry, stars and medals and, with them,
their ladies, silk and fur-clad, and sparkling with
precious jewels.

When the Mass ended, he watched those who had
attended it being driven away in their great, gilded,
state coaches. Then, disinclined to talk to anyone, he
dined early and alone at Die Drei Huzzaren. The food
was the best to be had in any restaurant in Vienna,
but he hardly noticed what he was eating. After his
meal he returned to Castlereagh's and spent the rest
of the afternoon lying on his bed.

During the day he had made up his mind to attend
the reception that was being given that night at the
Hofburg. Not from any intention of joining in the
festivities, but in order to see Georgina, whom he felt
certain would have received an invitation.

After much thought he had decided that he had
behaved like a fool about her. He had had to share her
with both her first and third husbands, so it was absurd
to refrain from sharing her with the Archduke. It had
troubled him that she seemed to have a much deeper
feeling for this royal lover than for any other of whom
she had told him in the past. Nevertheless, he would
have staked his life that he still stood and would always
stand far ahead of any other man in her affections. And
now her company was, above all things, what he needed. At tonight's gathering the Archduke would have to
remain until the last royalties had gone; so when he
told Georgina that he was in trouble, he felt sure she
would make some excuse to leave early and take him
with her out to her villa at Schönbrunn.

In due course he went to the Palace and made his
way among the slowly-moving throng up the grand

staircase. For nearly two hours he wandered through the great mirrored salons, talking for a few minutes to Talleyrand, Castlereagh and numerous other gentlemen and ladies he knew, while becoming inwardly more and more impatient. Three times he caught sight of Selma in the distance, but succeeded in avoiding her.

It was just after midnight when he found himself face to face with the Archduke. As Georgina had still failed to put in an appearance, he bowed and said amiably, 'Your Imperial Highness's humble servant. Are we not to have the pleasure of seeing our mutual friend, the Duchess of Kew, tonight?'

The Archduke returned his greeting politely, then raising his eyebrows, replied, 'Did you not know? She left Vienna three days ago. The news reached her that her husband died early this month, and she had to return to settle various matters with his heir.'

For Roger it was the final blow. Georgina had married her Duke only because she believed Roger to be dead. And he had married Mary only because the doctors had said that the paralysed Duke had such a healthy body that he might live on like a vegetable well into his nineties.

And now Georgina was free again. What a hideous, scurvy trick Fate had played them. If only he had not married Mary, he and Georgina might at last have wed, as they had planned to before he had been sentenced to death in Berlin. But now, as long as he remained tied to the demon-possessed Mary, he and the love of his life must still live apart.

9

An Enemy from the Past

IT seemed to Roger the cruellest of all the misfortunes that, like a series of avalanches, had overwhelmed him during the past few weeks that Georgina should again be free and he himself tied to Mary. Yet at that moment he was even more distressed that his hope of seeing her that night was now completely dashed. Had the Archduke simply said that she was not coming to the ball, he had meant to go out to her at Schönbrunn. But she was no longer there. She was on her way back to England, where he dared not follow her. Yet from her alone could he draw the strength to face his uncertain future with new courage.

Pulling himself together, he bowed himself away from the Archduke, to find himself almost face to face with Selma. He pretended not to see her, and moved quickly across the room as though someone had beckoned to him. Greatly as he had enjoyed making love to her, no passionate embraces of a lovely lady could at this juncture have given him any comfort; only the sympathy that Georgina, owing to their life-long spiritual attachment, would have poured out to him.

Half an hour later he was back in his bedroom. There he drank the whole contents of a flask of good French cognac which he always kept by him, then flopped into bed. When he woke in the morning, he lay thinking for a while. The outcome of his cogitations was the decision that, while he remained in Vienna, he must allow no-one to learn of his misfortunes, but again conduct himself as he had formerly. That meant continuing to live extravagantly, but the great world had no use for the poverty-stricken, and his chances of obtaining some profitable employment lay in leading everyone to suppose that he was still the wealthy Lord Kildonan.

Later in the day he gave Castlereagh an account of the little he had learned of the political situation in England; but he felt so averse to mixing in company that, for the next week, he attended none of the parties to which he was invited, and it was not until January 4th that, at a ball given by the Czar, he saw Selma again.

She was dancing with a tall, fair-haired young man, and appeared to be greatly enjoying herself. As the music ceased and the young man led her from the floor, Roger intercepted her, bowed and said, 'Your servant, Madame Thorwaldsen. Could you spare me a dance?'

Glancing at her programme, she replied, 'I fear I am engaged for every one; but it is a long time since we have met and I would much like a word with you.' Smiling first at Roger, then at her partner, she introduced the two men, then added, 'As I have another dance later with Monsieur Kielland, I feel sure he will excuse me now.'

Having exchanged bows with young Monsieur Kielland, Roger led Selma away to a settee in a quiet corner. When they were seated, her pleased smile gave place to a frown and she demanded:

'Are you not ashamed of the way in which you have treated me.'

As he answered her, he looked contrite. 'Indeed I am. The only excuse I have to offer is that I had to go at such short notice to England, and have been greatly upset by family matters.'

'But you were back by Christmas. I saw you at the Hofburg ball. To my utter amazement you cut me dead there. What possible excuse have you for that?'

'None, except, as I have told you, my mind has been distraught by happenings in my family, and I felt utterly incapable of giving you the attention that you had a right to expect from me.'

'Is this why I have not seen you at any entertainment during the past ten days?'

He nodded. 'I could not bring myself to mingle with gay society. And I am still so preoccupied by my troubles that I fear that for some time to come I shall prove a most morbid companion.'

For a moment she was silent, then she asked, 'Does this mean that you no longer wish to be my lover?'

As he looked at her he was very conscious of her fair loveliness, but he no longer felt any desire for her, and knew that he would be unable to enter with his usual gay lightheartedness on an affair with any other woman until he had, in some way, solved the problem of his own future. Sadly he said:

'Selma, the gods indeed favoured me when they blessed me with your affection. But, alas, I am no longer worthy of it. My mind being in such an unsettled state, 'twould not be possible for me to renew with you the joys we experienced together up till a month or more ago.'

She sighed. 'From your recent conduct I feared as much. And, sorry as I am about your troubles, I deeply regret that they should have brought an end to our affair.' Then, behind her fan, she whispered, 'I have never concealed my sensual nature from you, and you aroused in me a greater degree of passion than I have ever known before. In this past month I have suffered acutely from lack of satisfaction, and now I'll have to appease my cravings elsewhere.'

'The Archduke,' he ventured hesitantly. 'I take it that, after surprising us at the chalet, he ceased to seek your favours?'

'Yes. He regards me now only coldly, which was to be expected. However, I have another string to my bow should I choose to use it.'

Roger raised a faint smile. 'For your sake I am glad of that; although it does not in the least surprise me. There must be scores of attractive men in Vienna who would jump at the chance of becoming your lover.'

She returned his smile. 'This one would, I feel sure, play that role most satisfactorily. It is young Juhani Kielland, with whom I was dancing just now. He was sent from Sweden as an attaché to our mission shortly before you left Vienna. He at once became most attentive to me, and several times since has, when we have been alone together, expressed his passionate devotion. I find him charming, amusing and I am attracted to him physically. But I have refrained from giving him any encouragement up till now, because I hoped you would return to me. As he also lives in the house, we shall not be faced with the problem of finding some place outside, where we can meet in secret without endangering my reputation.'

'How overjoyed he will be when he learns of his good fortune,' Roger said, 'whereas I at this time seem to be the victim of some awful curse.'

At that moment a Hungarian Hussar approached to claim Selma for the next dance. Roger rose, kissed her hand and bowed himself away. He was, at one and the same time, torn with regret at abandoning this beautiful, passionate and sweet-natured mistress, and relieved at having disembarrassed himself of an entanglement which would call for a light-hearted gaiety which he could no longer feel.

In the meantime the Foreign Ministers had been greatly worried, for matters at the Grand Council of the Congress were going from bad to worse. The Czar and Metternich were no longer on speaking terms, and the former was the cause of all their troubles.

He had persuaded himself that he alone had been responsible for the defeat of Napoleon—the greatest general Europe had produced since Julius Caesar—so now looked upon himself as another Alexander the Great. With the most powerful of all the Allied armies behind him, he claimed it as his right to dictate all the new boundaries that were to remake the map of Europe.

In vain his representative on the Council, Count Nesselrode, agreed concessions to his colleagues at their morning meetings. In violent outbursts Alexander repudiated them when the three monarchs met in the afternoons.

The major cause for dissension among the Powers was the future of Poland. Up to the middle of the past century Poland had been an enormous country, but her government was chaotic, her frontiers indefinable, and her neighbours aggressive. In the seventies, Russia, Prussia and Austria had all grabbed great areas of her territory; then, by the final partition of 1796, they divided all that remained of her between them. In 1807 a tiny, new Poland had been created by Napoleon, who named it the Duchy of Warsaw, and gave sovereignty over it, theoretically, to his ally, the King of Saxony. Shortly after the retreat from Moscow the French had been driven from the whole country, and the question now was how should it again be divided or, alternatively, re-created as an independent state.

The Czar's dual mentality led him, for two reasons, to insist on Poland being given independence. In one aspect because, as 'The Great Conqueror', he intended to make it subservient to himself as a new reservoir of manpower for his army. From the other because, as 'The Great Christian Liberator', he intended to give the Polish people a greater degree of liberty than had been enjoyed by any other people on the Continent until the coming of the French Revolution.

His own nobility were far from happy about this last project, because they foresaw that if the serfs in Poland were freed by the Czar that could provoke endless trouble with their own serfs in Russia—who, in turn, would demand to be freed.

The serfs in Austria would also agitate for their freedom, which would have meant trouble for Metternich; but he was even more opposed to the Czar's plan because it would have meant giving up Austrian Poland and, above all, increasing the might of Russia by an additional population of over ten million.

For Britain, the future of remote Poland seemed a comparatively minor matter, so Castlereagh held no very strong views on it. He would naturally have liked to see Poland given a liberal constitution; but backed Metternich, because he was opposed to increasing the power of Russia.

The King of Prussia had no reason to be concerned about the question of serfdom, because he had already freed his serfs. But he was very much concerned about what he could get out of the deal. In those days it was generally accepted that, if one country gave up an area of territory, it must be compensated by receiving a territory of more or less equal value somewhere else. Frederick William was quite willing to give up Prussian Poland to his friend and patron the Czar, provided that

E

he was given instead the Kingdom of Saxony, which Alexander had promised him he should have.

But the future of Saxony was another bone of contention.

Castlereagh favoured a strong Prussia as a counterpoise to a resurgent France and, as Austria was to be given compensation in Italy for ceding her Polish territories, he tried to persuade Metternich to let Prussia have Saxony. But Metternich showed determined opposition to the plan. For hundreds of years the Germanic Princes had looked to the Austrian Habsburg sovereigns for leadership, and he wanted no jumped-up Hohenzollern as a rival to his Emperor. Talleyrand, foreseeing the danger to all Europe that a powerful Prussia might become, worked tirelessly to save Frederick Augustus of Saxony from losing his kingdom, arguing stoutly that the paramount consideration of 'legitimacy' applied to Saxony just as much as it had to France.

During the first weeks of January, the wrangles in the Council became ever more acrimonious, and the Czar ever more impossible; at one moment possessed of a religious mysticism, declaring that his only ambition was to ensure peace, liberty and happiness to all the peoples of Europe, and the next threatening that if he was refused his just demands he would make war on Austria.

While their wrangles went on, the leading statesmen at the Congress were overworked and intensely worried, but the horde of visitors continued to enjoy a great variety of entertainments, at tremendous cost to the Austrian exchequer. There were in Vienna the heads of no fewer than two hundred and fifteen princely families. At the Hofburg the Emperor had staying with him fifteen of the principal royalties, each with a crowd of

courtiers and servants in attendance. Forty tables were
laid every evening for dinner, and in the stables one
thousand four hundred horses had to be fed. The balls,
banquets and receptions were unceasing. There were
sleighing expeditions, amateur theatricals, ballet, concerts, *tableaux vivants,* shooting parties, tombolas, routs
and skating competitions on the lakes in the parks.
Candles by the ton burned away nightly to light the
splendidly decorative throngs of noble idlers.

The tall, austere figure of Castlereagh, almost alone
being dressed in plain civilian clothes, moved among
the revellers at the evening assemblies. Yet such was
his prestige as the representative of Britain that, at
the Christmas ball, it was Lady Castlereagh whom the
Emperor Francis had led out to open the first quadrille.

Occasionally, early in the morning, Roger rode with
Castlereagh in the Prater, and it was on January 15th
that they had a lengthy talk when riding alone together.
The Foreign Minister confided in Roger that, so
alarmed by the Czar's threats had his opponents become that a secret treaty had been signed between Great
Britain, Austria and France, binding the three Powers
to support one another in the event of one of them being
attacked, and each to put one hundred and fifty
thousand men in the field.

He went on to say that, in view of the urgency of the
matter, he had signed the agreement without waiting to
consult the Cabinet, although he was aware that Parliament had passed a resolution to the effect that,
however unsatisfactory the results of the Congress
might prove, Britain would not again become involved
in a Continental war. In consequence he now felt it
imperative to return to London, to clarify the position;
so he had arranged for the Duke of Wellington to leave
Paris and replace him at the Congress.

As they were riding home, Castlereagh said, 'When we talked in London of your accompanying me on this mission, I recall your mention that you were on good terms with the Czar. Is that still so?'

'I've no reason to believe otherwise,' Roger replied. 'When I was taken prisoner by the Russians after the battle of Eylau, he saved my life, and on my confiding to him that I was in fact an Englishman supplying information about the French to London, he had me exchanged so that I could continue to assist the Allied cause. I was of some use to him at the Conference of Erfurt, and it was I who brought him together with Bernadotte. That resulted in the pact by which Sweden agreed not to attempt to regain Finland when Napoleon invaded Russia, and so secured Alexander's left flank. Lastly, it was I who was sent just before the surrender of Paris to offer him Talleyrand's mansion during the occupation; which invitation, you will recall, he accepted.'

'Then your association with him has been a long and valuable one. Have you held any conversation with him during the Congress?'

'No, my lord. But whenever we have met at one of the entertainments, he has always spoken to me very pleasantly.'

'Then I pray you, ask an audience of him tomorrow. If he grants you one, any pretext for talking to him will serve. You may leak it to him if you wish about this new alliance. Do not say that it is already signed, but that you have reason to believe that Britain, Austria and France will combine against him should he endeavour to secure his demands by force of arms; and stress the dangers of starting a new war. His nobility are set against it, and they might well prevent it by assassinating him, as they did his father. A man as well known to him as you are could say things to him in private that we members of the Council could not. It may prove futile; but there is a chance that you might influence him to cease his sabre-rattling, so it is worth a try.'

Roger agreed to do what he could, and the following morning, through Nesselrode, secured an audience with His Imperial Majesty. The Czar extended his hand for Roger to kiss and, with a quirk of a smile, said:

'So, as the English say, that "bad penny" Mr. Brook, turns up again. But, forgive us, you are now the Lord Kildonan, are you not? And what have you up your sleeve this time? Has that sly rogue, Talleyrand, sent you to offer us the use of his mansion again, when we once more lead our victorious armies across France to occupy Paris?'

'Nay, Sire.' Roger returned the smile. 'I feel confident that so kind-hearted and enlightened a monarch as Your Imperial Majesty will not do that. God knows, the common people who have no say in the making of wars have suffered enough in the past twenty years, without having another war thrust upon them.'

'Ah, the people!' The tall, handsome Czar turned his eyes heavenward. 'How right you are. 'Tis they who bear the brunt of war. No splendid uniforms or loot for them, but crushing taxes, their young men conscripted to die in foreign fields, burned homes, their women raped and their little treasures stolen. But God sent us to be their protector, to free them from tyranny, to give them a voice in how they should be governed, to lead them back from the atheism spread by the accursed Revolution to a true Christian way of life. Each morning when we read our Bible, we become more convinced where our duty lies, and of our great destiny as the Liberator.'

Roger bowed. 'How it rejoices me, Sire, to hear you speak in such a vein. It puts my mind at rest on a matter I thought it my duty to inform you of, on account of your past graciousness to me. I have good reason to believe that Austria, France and Britain are plotting, not to wage war against Your Imperial Majesty, but to combine and put an army of half a million men in the field should you attack any one of them, as it has been rumoured you contemplate doing. My relief at knowing these rumours to be false . . . '

Suddenly Alexander's manner changed completely. His blue eyes flashing, he cried, 'They are not false. Unless our just demands are met, Metternich shall rue the day he dared thwart us. And your friend, Talleyrand, too. Austria could not now raise a hundred thousand men, and France lies exhausted. They would be mad to oppose the combined might of Russia and Prussia. Austria has not a general worthy of the name. We had nearly to use a knout on that craven fellow, Schwarzenberg, before we could induce him last year to advance on Paris. Before the Prussian Generals Blücher, Gneisenau and von Bülow, he would go down like a ninepin. Ah, and even without them we could eat him up. Who but ourselves conquered the great Napoleon? Vienna would be ours in a matter of weeks, and Paris a month later.'

'Sire, I beg you . . . ' Roger pleaded, as Alexander paused for breath, then, ignoring him, continued his violent diatribe.

'We see the hand of Talleyrand in this. In Paris, we thought his advice sound, and allowed him to persuade us to restore the Bourbons. And what thanks did we get? Dost know how we were treated when we visited that stupid mountain of flesh, Louis XVIII, in his château at Compiègne? We were led through a fine suite of rooms. They were occupied by that vain reactionary, the King's brother, d'Artois. Through another fine suite. It was the Duc de Berry's. Through yet a third, reserved for the gloomy, puritanical Duchess d'Angoulême. At length, beyond them all lay three miserable little rooms—for us! For us, can you believe it! For us, the Czar of all the Russias, who had put Louis back on his throne.'

Roger shook his head, as though shocked beyond belief. His face distorted by anger, Alexander raved on. 'And dinner that evening! Naturally, we were seated next to him. Some ill-trained lout brought the first dish, then hesitated whether to first serve us or the King. Louis looked round, saw the fellow's dilemma and piped up querulously in that squeaky voice of his, "Me first! Me first!" Any of our serfs would have had better manners.'

In silence Roger listened as the tirade continued:

'And this after all we had done to save France from the greed of the Prussians! They would have despoiled her to the last silver fork. We insisted on terms of generosity to a fallen foe having no precedent. We made Louis grant them a liberal constitution, forewent any indemnity, even allowed them to retain the countless works of art they had stolen from other nations. But it will be different next time. Very different. We will make them give up their ill-gotten treasures. We will saddle them with a bill which will take them fifty years to pay. We will teach the French a lesson they will never forget.'

'Sire, Sire,' Roger pleaded. 'I implore you not to allow there to be a next time. If only Your Imperial Majesty will be reasonable, I am confident that . . . '

'We are reasonable,' came the haughty retort. 'We ask only that Poland should be restored as an inde-

pendent state. That entails Austria withdrawing and
contenting herself with the restoration of her territories in the Tyrol, Illyria, Venezia, Lombardy and
Tuscany. The King of Prussia has already agreed to
give Warsaw up to us and withdraw to the Elbe;
and we intend to insist on his being given Saxony as
compensation. Now, you have our leave to withdraw.
We thank you for informing us of this projected combination to challenge our supremacy should it come
to war. But war we will make should it prove necessary.'

Deciding that it would be most unwise to suggest
to Alexander that, rather than take up arms again,
his own nobles might assassinate him, Roger bowed
himself backwards out of the room.

On returning to the large house in the Minoritenplatz—to which Castlereagh had moved on finding
his first choice of residence too small for the entertaining necessitated by his position—Roger described
his abortive audience with the Czar to the Foreign
Minister.

Having heard him, Castlereagh said gloomily,
'I am not surprised at what you tell me. These past
few weeks he has become impossible. Even his own
people confess to having no idea which way he will
jump. One moment he is the inspired Evangelist,
vowed to bettering the lot of all Europe's people;
the next a mighty war lord prepared to drench its
soil in blood again. But there is another matter on
which, since no Englishman was closer to Napoleon
than yourself, I would value your opinion. Think
you he may attempt to escape from Elba?'

' 'Tis a question I hesitate to answer,' Roger replied.
'His mind is extraordinarily active, and he carries
out his decisions with great speed. According to report,
he has found much to occupy him in his tiny island

kingdom. If that is true, and continues to be so, he may well be content to remain there. But should he become bored, there will then be danger of him planning some lightning stroke in the hope of reasserting himself. And Elba, being so near the mainland, should not be difficult to escape from.'

Castlereagh nodded. 'That is true, and I now think it a mistake that he was sent there. When we discussed it, I favoured keeping him a prisoner in England, or possibly Gibraltar, though that would have been far from popular with our countrymen. When they learnt of the proposal, *The Times* wrote of it: *No British possession should be polluted by such a wretch. He would be a disgrace to Botany Bay.* Metternich, too, would have preferred to see him sent further afield, and suggested the Azores. Fouché proposed sending him to learn about democracy in the United States. The Prussians, of course, wanted to hang him, but the Czar favoured treating him with chivalry, and it was the Emperor of Austria who had the last word. Against Metternich's advice, he insisted on his son-in-law's being given a small kingdom. Sardinia and Corfu were talked of, but Elba finally decided upon.'

Shuffling through some papers on his desk, Castlereagh picked one up and went on, 'I have here a report sent on to me from London. It is by Colonel Neil Campbell, who keeps a watch on Napoleon for us, and Lord John Russell, who visited the island. They drew it up on December 28th. In it they state that the Emperor was in good health and excellent spirits. That he is very well informed about affairs in France, and expressed the opinion that there will be a violent outbreak there, similar to the Revolution, in consequence of the humiliation of the French at having been robbed of their frontier on the Rhine, and of the feebleness of the Bourbons. He added that to recover their rights they should make war as soon as possible, and that it should not be difficult to drive the Dutch out of Belgium.'

Roger sighed. 'Truly, that man is an appalling menace.'

'He would be, were he free. Campbell and Russell warned our Cabinet that they believe him to be plotting some great move, and are of the opinion that he will attempt to land in Italy.'

'I disagree, my lord. His only chance of powerful support lies in the old soldiers of his own army, whom he led so many times to victory, and who loathe the Bourbon *fleur-de-lys*. If he lands on the Continent at all, it will be in France.'

This brief discussion over, Roger took his leave. As he marched out into the anteroom, he came to a sudden halt. Seated there was a broad-chested, red-faced soldier in the uniform of a British Brigadier. His name was George Gunston. At that moment he glanced up. Recognition was mutual and instantaneous. They had been schoolboys at Sherborne together, and had hated each other ever since.

Gunston was a few years older than Roger, and in their schooldays had bullied him unmercifully. Over the years they had met on a number of occasions: in Martinique, India, Portugal and many times in England. These meetings had all resulted in violent quarrels. They had fought two duels and their hatred had been intensified by their relationships with three different women. In India Gunston's tardiness in bringing up his troops had led to the death of lovely young Clarissa, then Roger's mistress. Later he had attempted to rape Georgina. In the drunken brawl that had ensued, a sword-thrust by Roger, intended for Gunston, had killed Georgina's husband. Roger had been tried for manslaughter, and spent several months in Guildford prison. Still later, in Lisbon, Gunston had deliberately led Roger to believe that Mary, who was his cousin, was easy game, when she was actually still a virgin. The consequences had been so painful that Roger had sworn that, when they next met, he would kill Gunston. And now they were again face to face.

With a slow smile, the Brigadier came to his feet and said, 'Why, dam'me if 'tis not my old friend, Bookworm Brook.'

Roger glared at him. 'The nickname you gave me at Sherborne is now a little stale. And I am not your friend. For that filthy trick you played me in Lisbon, had you not been lying in hospital, I would have sent you to the devil with a sword-thrust.'

A grin spread over Gunston's face, stretching nearly to his reddish side-whiskers. 'Instead, you delivered your thrust into little Mary, or so I guessed from your hasty departure for England and her woebegone appearance afterwards. As a pauper the poor girl had naught else than her virginity to offer a husband, and I'll wager she screamed "Murder" when you robbed her of it.'

'I'll not deny that. But 'twas your vile lies to me which brought such grief upon her. You swore to me that her demure manner was no more than a mask for her passionate nature, that she had been tumbled by a dozen men. Ay, and that you had had her yourself.'

' 'Tis true enough that she was a passionate young piece. I dam'ne near had her, too. She fought me off only at the last moment. How fares she now?'

'Her present state has no bearing on the past, and 'tis for that I mean to call you to account.'

'Am I to take that as a challenge?'

'You are. Where are you living in Vienna?'

'No doubt Lord Castlereagh will offer me hospitality here for the next few days. I have just arrived, sent ahead for His Grace of Wellington to whose staff I have recently been attached, to find suitable quarters for him.'

'God help us! The Duke must have gone out of his mind to take an oaf like yourself into his military family.'

'Hard words break no bones, my lord.'

'Nay, but a sword thrust through your big belly will cause you to squeal louder than would any fracture. And I mean to give you one.'

Gunston knew Roger to be a far better swordsman than he was, and had no intention of exposing himself in a duel. Shaking the mop of coarse red curls that grew low down on his forehead, he retorted:

'Oh no, you won't. Times have changed these past few years. The powers that be have become more than ever harsh on those who ignore the edict against duelling. To army officers it is strictly forbidden, and I've no mind to risk being cashiered for a chance to stick you in the gizzard.'

White to the lips, Roger roared, 'Edicts be damned, you filthy coward! Do you refuse to meet me, I'll take the first chance that offers to slap your fat face in public.'

Attracted by the sound of angry voices, Castlereagh had opened the door of his room, and stood there staring at them. After a moment he asked in a stern voice, 'What goes on here? Did I hear you, Lord Kildonan, challenge Brigadier Gunston to a duel?'

'You did, my lord,' Roger replied promptly. 'I have a long-standing matter to settle with this oaf, who has more than once disgraced the uniform he wears.'

'Surely you know that duelling is most strictly forbidden?'

'That did not prevent you, my lord, from settling a dispute with Mr. Canning with pistols one morning on Wimbledon Common.'

Castlereagh paused. 'I admit it. But that was years ago. Since then the laws against duelling have been enforced much more rigorously. While you remain on my staff I strictly forbid you to fight Brigadier Gunston. Moreover, should you insult him in public, as you threatened, you will incur my utmost displeasure, and I'll instantly dismiss you. Now you may go.'

Beckoning to Gunston to follow him into his sanctum, he turned away, leaving Roger standing there still white-faced and furious.

Upstairs in his room Roger gradually regained his calm and considered whether he should pursue his quarrel with George Gunston or, for the time being, let the matter rest. He was strongly beset by the inclination to force George into a duel, or cause him to be publicly branded as a coward, and here on the Continent the British laws against duelling did not apply, so he would have had nothing to fear from the authorities. But there was a special consideration that did, in his case. If he pursued his vendetta against George openly, Castlereagh would dismiss him. A month ago that would not have caused him great concern. But now things were very different. With his fortune gone, he was counting on Castlereagh, after the Congress ended, to appoint him to a post in some embassy, which would at least provide him with a living. He dared not defy the Foreign Minister and forfeit his goodwill.

In consequence Roger decided to stifle his antagonism and eat out as long as Gunston remained a guest at the house in the Minoritenplatz and, as far as possible, avoid coming into contact with his *bête noir*. Fortunately he did not have to do so for long, since the accommodation for visitors was limited and, two days later, Gunston was moved out to an hotel. After that they saw each other only occasionally, at entertainments, and on such occasions kept well out of one another's way.

On February 3rd Wellington arrived. He was received with great honour, even by the Czar, and everyone found his genial personality a pleasant change from the dour austerity of Castlereagh, who remained on for the better part of a fortnight to run in his successor.

Within a week of his arrival the Duke had taken over such matters as Roger was involved in, and on the evening of the 11th, Wellington said to him:

'My lord, as you may be aware, under the Treaty of Paris, it was agreed that Napoleon was to receive two million francs a year from the French Government, to support himself in his kingdom of Elba, and other Bonapartes were to receive substantial lesser sums. So far the Bourbons have not paid out a single penny to any of them. It is a disgraceful neglect of an obligation freely entered into, and King Louis ought to be ashamed of himself. I should be grateful if you would see Talleyrand and raise the matter with him. Tell him that if his master continues this mean obduracy, it may affect badly French interests at the Congress.'

Accordingly, early next morning, in a scruffy old cloak that he kept for such occasions, Roger made his way through the garden of the Kaunitz Palace to the

back entrance and was taken up by Talleyrand's
valet to his master's bedroom.

When he had delivered the Duke's protest which,
without stigmatizing the King of France, could not
have been made openly, Talleyrand agreed that his
Sovereign's meanness was despicable, and said he
would raise the matter in his next despatch.

Opposite the garden of the palace, and partly overlooking it, stood a big house. Just as Roger came out of
the garden gate, he saw a figure emerge from a side
entrance of the mansion. Next moment he realized
that it was Gunston. Head down, he quickly turned
away, and walked off at a smart pace, but he feared
that Gunston had recognized him.

Gunston's swagger and muscular limbs held an
attraction for certain types of women, and he was a
born womanizer, so Roger had little doubt about why
he happened to be about at that early hour of the
morning. It was a pretty safe bet that he had spent
the night with the lady of the mansion or, equally
probable, with some pretty serving wench who lived
there.

Owing to the Duke's numerous engagements that
day, it was not until evening that Roger had a chance
to report to him. When he had done so, Wellington
said, 'I regret to have to tell you that you were seen
leaving the Kaunitz Palace early this morning. It was
Brigadier Gunston who saw you, and he hastened
here to tell me of it.'

Roger frowned. 'I have known him for many years,
and feared that he had recognized me. He is a black-
guard of the first order and, if I may make so bold, it
surprises me that Your Grace should have taken him
into your military family.'

'I did not, although he has a fine record as a cavalry

officer. He was sent here direct from London by my lords and masters at the Horse Guards, to secure suitable accommodation for me. But that is beside the point. The devil of it is that he jumped to the conclusion that you are a spy in the pay of Talleyrand.'

'Dam'me, Sir! That will make things mighty awkward. He is my personal enemy. By now he will have seized on the chance to blazon it all over Vienna that I am a traitor. There's only one thing for it. I must repudiate the charge, call him out and kill him.'

Wellington shook his head. 'Nay, that would be no remedy. To kill a man does not prove him to be a liar. Besides, I could not permit it. You must be aware of the anti-duelling laws and, on your return to England, you would find yourself in prison for having forced a duel on a British officer.'

'But, Your Grace, we cannot ignore the accusation. I'll not submit to continuing on here with everyone in the city believing me to have sold information to a foreign Power. Neither can you afford to have it thought that, by taking no action on Gunston's report, you have allowed me to pull the wool over your eyes.'

'I agree on both counts. Later, I will take some step to clear your reputation. But to admit that you acted for me as a secret agent is unthinkable. It would deprive you of your future usefulness. For the time being, much to my regret, I must dispense with your services here, and have it put about that you are leaving Vienna for personal reasons after having voluntarily resigned.'

'I can only bow to Your Grace's decision,' replied Roger unhappily.

The Duke gave his high-pitched laugh. 'Look not

so miserable, my lord. I have already thought of a most interesting employment for you.'

Roger brightened. 'If that is so, Your Grace, I am all eagerness to hear it.'

'This morning I sent you to Talleyrand to protest at King Louis's having neglected to pay the monies due to the Bonapartes. This must cause Napoleon considerable umbrage. His mental attitude has now become of great importance to us. As you know, the Czar is threatening to bring about a new war against Austria. Should he do so, all Europe will again go up in flames. Britain and France are pledged to support Austria. By that, of course, I mean Bourbon France. But what if Napoleon suddenly returned, and the French rallied to him? In such circumstances he might offer to renew the alliance he made with the Czar at Tilsit. What then? Austria annihilated, and Britain once more involved in a war to which one can see no end, against a combination of Continental Powers. You will see, then, how imperative it is that we should have some idea of which course Napoleon would be likely to adopt. Is he tired of war and content to remain at ease in his island kingdom? Or does he still secretly nurture the ambition to seize on any chance that might again make him arbiter of Europe? As Colonel Comte de Breuc, you were, my lord, for many years in his confidence. I wish you to go to Elba and probe his mind.'

10

The Bonapartes

ROGER smiled. 'It will be an interesting mission, Your Grace. And I'll confess I'll not be sorry to have a change of scene from Vienna. I wonder a little, though, about your anxiety concerning Napoleon. At the beginning of the month it would have been very understandable; but I gather that these past ten days the likelihood of Russia going to war with Austria has greatly decreased.'

Thoughtfully stroking his high beak of a nose, Wellington replied, 'They have. Metternich put forward a proposal that Austria should retain the province of Galicia and Prussia that of Posen, while the Duchy of Warsaw and the remainder of Poland should be established as a kingdom for the Czar. Under pressure from all sides, the Czar assented to an agreement on those lines being drawn up. But who can guarantee that he will not change his mind, and when the time comes refuse to sign it?'

Impressed by the Duke's fears that the Czar might yet resort to war and Napoleon's attitude become of great importance, Roger nodded, then remarked, 'Being allowed to retain Posen should reduce Prussia's claim to Saxony.'

'It has. Frederick Augustus is to be robbed only

of two-fifths of his kingdom, and will remain an independent monarch. But those greedy Prussians have no grounds for grumbling. They are to be given the fortresses on the Elbe, Swedish Pomerania, Westphalia and extensive territories on the east bank of the Rhine.'

'I am surprised that Metternich agreed to that, since it will mean Austria surrendering to Prussia her dominance over the Germanic states.'

The Duke shrugged. 'It will not be popular with Metternich's own people, but his prime consideration is to have Prussia as a powerful counterpoise against Russia. Only Talleyrand vigorously opposed this proposed settlement, and he can speak only for a greatly weakened France.'

'I appreciate that; although, Your Grace, I think there is much to be said for his attitude. I must let him know that I am leaving Vienna, but, of course, shall not disclose the reason. I will be on my way tomorrow morning.'

It was agreed that Roger should take one of the British Mission's travelling coaches for the first part of the journey; then he took leave of the Duke and set about his preparations for departure.

On studying the map he saw that there was a choice of two ways from Vienna to Elba. In any case, he would go south to Gratz. He could then go down to Zagreb, thence to Zara and cross the Adriatic to Ancona, which lay on the east coast of Italy almost opposite Elba off its west. The alternative was to go from Gratz to Trieste, cross the gulf to Venice and from there proceed to Leghorn, from which he could get a ship down to Elba.

The distance either way was about six hundred miles; but to go via Zagreb meant worse roads, more mountainous country and a much greater risk of encountering brigands; so, although the Trieste–Leghorn route meant longer passages by sea, with possibly unfavourable winds, he decided it was the better choice.

As it was still February, the weather was cold, with intermittent snow; but sleeping under a pile of rugs in the coach as it continued on its way during the nights, Roger did not find the first two hundred miles, through Gratz and Maribor to Celje, particularly unpleasant. From there on, by way of Ljubljana to Trieste, which meant travelling through the foothills of the Alps, he suffered severely and, when he arrived at the port, had rarely found more welcome a well-warmed bed at an inn. In Venice it was raining, but the climate was much milder, and as he travelled south from Mestre in a hired coach, the weather improved. At Leghorn he was fortunate in finding a felucca about to sail for Portoferraio with a cargo of wheat, and it landed him at the capital of Elba on the afternoon of February 24th.

During his eleven-day journey, Roger had had ample time to review in his mind all he had heard of Napoleon since his abdication. At Fontainebleau, on April 20th, he had bade his Old Guard a touching farewell; then, escorted by four Commissioners, each representing one of the Allies, set out on his journey.

On his way south he had met Augereau, who had commanded the army based on Lyons, and prematurely surrendered to the Austrians. Instead of reproaching this old friend, Napoleon had left his carriage to embrace him. But the Marshal had roughly addressed him as 'thou', a familiarity never used to him since he had become Emperor, then told him that he cared not a fig for either his cause or that

of the Bourbons, and had brought the battle to an end
only for the good of France.

The nearer he came to the Mediterranean the more
hostile had become the crowds in the towns through
which he passed; until, fearing for his life, he had
disguised himself.

His favourite sister, Pauline, had then been living at
the Château de Bouilledou, near St. Maxime. He
stopped off there to say good-bye to her. So shocked
had she been at seeing him clad in pieces of various
enemy uniforms that she would not embrace him.
From Frejus, fearing that the French sailors would
throw him overboard, he had sailed to Elba in an
English frigate.

The respect and courtesy he had met with in the
British ship had impressed him immensely; and it was
reported that he frequently spoke with great admiration of the British people, declaring that, with the
exception of the French, their troops were the finest
in the world. Blissfully ignorant that, for the past two
decades, nurses in England had scared naughty
children with the awful threat that 'Boney would get
them', he believed that if he were allowed to live
there he would be given a warm reception.

The people of Elba, flattered that their little island
had been chosen as the residence of the once mighty
Emperor, had given him a tremendous welcome, and
his presence there was said to have attracted many
wealthy tourists. Those who were received by him
had formed the opinion that he was fully resigned to
living in his miniature kingdom, and happy in busying
himself with improvements to it. But about one matter
he complained unceasingly—namely, that his wife and
son had not come to live with him.

When Marie Louise fled from Paris to Rambouillet,

Napoleon had sent her a letter from Fontainebleau, asking her to join him. She had not only ignored his request, but refused to send him the greater part of his money which she had taken with her from the capital.

By the Treaty of Fontainebleau she had been awarded the Duchy of Parma in Italy, which was no great distance from Elba. But she did not go there. Instead, she returned to her father in Vienna, and was given apartments for herself and her son in the palace at Schönbrunn. Napoleon wrote to her repeatedly and, at first, her replies led him to hope that she would come to Elba. But the Emperor Francis was determined that she should not do so. He could never forget that he had given her as a wife to an upstart Corsican adventurer, and now that mighty man had fallen, he grasped eagerly at this chance to terminate what his guilty conscience told him was a degrading relationship.

Curiously enough, one of Napoleon's most deadly enemies, Marie Antionette's now elderly sister, Queen Caroline, whom he had driven from her throne at Naples, urged Marie Louise to defy her father. The old lady instanced how both the Princesses Augusta of Bavaria and Caroline of Württemberg had resisted the pressure of their fathers and refused to leave their husbands, Eugène de Beauharnais, Napoleon's stepson, and his brother Jerome. She even incited Marie Louise to evade the people her father had set about her by tying her bed-sheets together and lowering herself from her window. But Marie Louise was not of the stuff of which heroines are made.

On the contrary, she was a spineless, sensual creature, slow-witted, lazy and selfish. Napoleon had gained her shallow affections by a tempestuous wooing, his boundless generosity and by making her, as his Empress, the first lady in Europe. But once he had fallen from his great estate she hardly gave him a thought. So self-centred was she that she could not even be bothered to take an interest in her son. The Comtesse de Montesquiou, who was in charge of the little King of Rome, and adored him, as he did her, wrote of Marie Louise; '*She is more indifferent to her child's lot than the most careless of the strangers who wait upon him.*'

To have left France with two million francs of her husband's money and refused to join him in his exile was not the full extent of her perfidy. Her father had appointed General Count Neipperg to be her Chamberlain, with instructions to do his utmost to prevent her thinking about Napoleon. The Count was a great man with the ladies, who seem to have been particularly attracted owing to his good looks being partially obscured by a black silk scarf worn over one blinded eye and a forehead wound, which gave him the appearance of a handsome pirate. He carried out his instructions with such zeal that, within six months of leaving Napoleon, Marie Louise made no protest at all when the Count got into bed with her. In September they had gone off to Switzerland on an unofficial honeymoon and, being too lazy to conceal this shameless adultery, she became known to the cynical Viennese as 'Mrs. Neipperg'.

How differently, Roger thought, would the former Empress, Josephine, have behaved. He had known her long and intimately, having saved her from the results of a youthful indiscretion which, had it come out, could have prevented Napoleon from marrying her. She had later saved Roger's life and brought him into the favoured circle that frequented the beautiful home she had created at Malmaison. After the royal

divorce, Roger had lived there for a while as the Comp-
troller of her Household. Everyone loved and sympathized with her, so it had been no lonely retirement.
She was always either entertaining visitors or happily
busying herself with her garden and wonderful collection of tropical plants. When Paris fell, all three of the
Allied monarchs had driven out to pay their respects
to her and assure her of their protection. It was with
deep feeling that Roger had learned of her death the
previous May after a brief illness of less than a week.
Although put aside by Napoleon in order that he might
beget a son by a Princess of ancient lineage, she had
never ceased to be devoted to him, and no torture
would have induced her to disgrace his name after he
had been sent into exile.

While in Vienna, Roger had kept himself informed
about the doings of the other Bonapartes.

Napoleon's eldest sister, Eliza, had, when young,
been married off by her mother to a Corsican land-
owner named Bacciochi. He was a stupid oaf who,
when Napoleon made him a General, proved hopelessly incompetent as either a soldier or administrator.
What he lacked in brains and ambition Eliza more
than made up for. Like all the Bonapartes, she was both
lecherous and avaricious. But collecting erotica and an
assortment of lovers had not prevented her, as Grand
Duchess of Tuscany, from ruling this territory given to
her by her brother with considerable ability and
amassing a great fortune from it.

On the Emperor's fall, her brother-in-law Murat,
King of Naples, who had already gone over to the
enemy, drove her out of Florence. She, too, then
repudiated Napoleon, so the Austrians had permitted
her to settle in Bologna.

Murat's wife, Caroline, was still Queen of Naples.

But the situation of the Murats had become precarious, because King Ferdinand and his Queen, the other Caroline, were pressing the Congress to restore Naples, from which they had been driven to their island of Sicily. And they had powerful backing for their claim, for Caroline had been an Austrian princess. Ferdinand was a Bourbon and, since they had been reduced to living in Sicily, Britain had acted as their protector.

Three of Napoleon's brothers: Louis, King of Holland, Jerome, King of Westphalia, and Joseph, King of Spain, had all sought refuge in Switzerland. The last had even succeeded in getting out of France his magnificent art collection.

Lucien—the fanatical Republican—who in the days of the Revolution had changed his name to Brutus, having stolen enormous sums from Napoleon's government and blackmailed the wives of numerous officials into sleeping with him, had denounced his brother years earlier as a reactionary and had taken himself off to Italy. More recently he had spent some time as a voluntary prisoner in England. Freed after Napoleon's abdication, he returned to Rome and, contrary to all revolutionary principles, persuaded His Holiness to give him the Papal title of Prince de Canio.

Josephine's daughter, Hortense, Queen of Holland, had bravely remained on in Paris to save what she could from the wreck. Her brother, Eugène de Beauharnais, a man respected by all, had with equal boldness, arrived for the Congress in Vienna.

Napoleon's mother, who had refused all titles and was known as *Madame Mère*, had gone with her half-brother, Cardinal Fesch, to Rome. During the Revolution Fesch had abandoned the priesthood to become an army contractor. That had laid the foundation of his fortune and, during the supremacy of Napoleon, he had seized on every opportunity to increase it, cannily investing the bulk of his money abroad; so he was still immensely rich and quite content to live a lazy life in the Papal States.

But *Madame Mère,* indomitably courageous, upright, pious, shrewd and parsimonious, had always made it a principle to support whichever of her children, right or wrong, was in trouble; so she had soon left Rome to go and live with Napoleon on Elba.

There remained the gay and beautiful Pauline. There was little that Roger did not know about her character, as on her return from the West Indies, where she had lost her first husband, General Leclerc, he had become her lover. She had even wanted him to marry her, and pushed him into asking the Emperor for her hand. Napoleon had aimed much higher as the next husband for his favourite sister, so played a most scurvy trick on Roger. He had told him that, if he was to become a Prince of the Imperial Family, he must first become a General, and packed him off for special training at Ghent, under that terribly strict disciplinarian, Marshal Davout. Bored by Roger's absence, lovely Pauline had been tempted into marrying Prince Borghese, because she could not resist the idea of decking herself out in the fabulous Borghese emeralds. But the Prince had proved a poor bedfellow, so Roger had again become her lover—only to discover, to his fury, that his licentious charmer was, at the same time, having midnight romps with three other gentlemen.

Apart from Napoleon's mother, Pauline was the only one of the Bonapartes who had remained loyal to him. Late in May Murat had sent a frigate to fetch her from the South of France to Naples. On the way she made a brief stop at Elba, and promised the Emperor to return and spend the winter with him. In November

she had arrived to fulfil her promise and Roger wondered, a little uneasily, if she might expect him to
resume their old relationship, should she still be
there.

He had set off from Vienna happily enough, but
during his journey a worrying thought had come into
his mind more than once. He had counted on Napoleon being delighted to see him, but that might not
prove the case. Provided the Emperor knew nothing of
how he had spent the past few months, he could expect
a warm welcome; but it would be taken for granted
that Napoleon had many sources of information. He
could not know that Roger was in the service of
Castlereagh and Wellington, but might know that he
had been in Vienna. If he did, he would naturally
assume that he had been attached to the French Mission. For years past Napoleon had distrusted Talleyrand and, at the time of the abdication, the Prince had
come out in his true colours; so now, as the representative of Louis XVIII, he was openly an enemy and a
very powerful one. Therefore, should the Emperor
believe Roger to be associated with him, not only
would he be given little chance to assess the situation
on Elba, but might, as a potential spy, find himself in
a very unpleasant situation.

He was thinking about this when, under a light wind,
the felucca approached the island. Geologically, Elba
was a mountain on a spur running out from the Tuscan
mainland, only a few miles distant. The town of
Portoferraio was situated on the western side of a great
bay facing north. In the February sunshine, its white-
and lemon-coloured houses, stretching along the harbour and rising steeply to a fortress-crowned height,
looked sleepily attractive. But as the felucca came nearer,
Roger could see that most of the buildings were small

and shoddy in appearance, and that the streets consisted of stone steps up narrow alleyways.

When he went ashore, much to his surprise he was
told that only English visitors were allowed to land,
unless they had obtained special permission. He had,
of course, travelled from Leghorn as Colonel Comte de
Breuc, and now sent in that name a message by the
port official to General Count Bertrand who, on the
death of Duroc, had succeeded him as Marshal of
Palaces and Camps.

Duroc had been a dear friend of Roger's for many
years, whereas he knew Bertrand only slightly and little
about him. Although he had served in most of Napoleon's campaigns, he was not considered a very able
General and, it was said, had accompanied the Emperor
to Elba not out of affection but from an obsessive
sense of duty.

About an hour later, Bertrand arrived and greeted
Roger in a courteous but noncommittal way, saying
that he had been ordered to take charge of him, and
that they had to be very careful whom they allowed on
the island, as only the English could be trusted. People of
other races might attempt to assassinate his master. He
added that, during their first weeks there, they had
greatly feared that the Emperor might be killed or
kidnapped by Barbary corsairs, as these Algerian
pirates sailed quite frequently right into the Gulf of
Genoa, and Elba then had only a small French garrison under General Dalesme, who had become subject
to Louis XVIII.

On their way along the quay, Bertrand said that
Dalesme had received the Imperial exiles with due
honours and done everything in his power to make
them welcome. But they had not felt even relatively
safe until, towards the end of May, Dalesme and his

men had been replaced by seven hundred of the Old
Guard, one hundred Polish Lancers and the three-
hundred-ton, sixteen-gun brig *Inconstant*—all of which
had been allotted to Napoleon under the Treaty of
Fontainebleau. Moreover, the British Commissioner,
Colonel Neil Campbell, whom the Emperor found most
courteous and obliging, had arranged that the British
Mediterranean Fleet should take Elba under its protection; so they were now much less nervous of Portoferraio's being raided.

Side by side they covered the few hundred yards to
the Hôtel de Ville. It was there, with happy shouts of
'*Viva il Imperatore! Viva nostro sovrano!*' that the Elbans
had installed the Emperor on his arrival; but he had
not liked it and shortly afterwards moved up the hill to
a house called The Mills—since then known as the
Mulini Palace.

Bertrand, as Chief Administrator of the island, had
then taken over a part of the Hôtel de Ville and lived
there with his wife and children. Roger was presented
to Madame Bertrand—a well-bred but sour woman
who had recently lost her third child. She told him at
once how much she hated Elba, and resented her
husband's absurdly conscientious scruples in refusing
to leave the Emperor who, she was happy to say, they
had to dine with only occasionally. She added that, as
a relief from the down-at-heel society at Portoferraio,
Roger would prove a welcome guest, and had him
shown up to an ill-furnished room with bare walls, no
curtains and a truckle bed.

While Roger unpacked and spruced himself up, a
messenger arrived from the palace, to say that His
Imperial Majesty commanded the Comte de Breuc to
present himself. Accompanied by Bertrand, he was
driven up to the Mulini in a carriage and four, by a

road that the General told him had been cut through the little town, because the Emperor disliked having to walk up hundreds of steps.

The 'palace' proved to be a two-storey building, with a frontage of not much more than one hundred feet. The hall, newly decorated in the Egyptian style, also served as a reception room. It was quite crowded, and Roger was somewhat surprised to find that Napoleon maintained the same formal etiquette as that he had insisted on when living at the Tuileries. Bertrand introduced him to the principal officials present, and he soon learned a certain amount about them.

General Drouot, Bertrand's No. 2, was Military Governor of the island. A typical old soldier of the revolutionary wars, he had fought under Kellermann at Fleurus, under Moreau at Hohenlinden and through many of Napoleon's campaigns. He was a rough, jovial bachelor, who cared little for his comfort. Extremely pious, he looked upon the Emperor as second only to God, and had followed him into exile, not from any sense of duty, but extreme devotion. He had even refused one hundred thousand francs which Napoleon had offered him.

The Chevalier de Peyrusse was the Treasurer. In 1800 he had left active service in the Army to become a Paymaster and on numerous occasions Roger had drawn money from him. He, too, had volunteered to accompany his master into exile, and he was a valuable addition to the party, for he was not only highly competent but a *bon viveur* and an eternal optimist, always cheerful, always laughing.

Roger also recognized 'Purge' Fourreau, in the old days surgeon of the Imperial Stables, but now rejoicing in the title of Physician-in-Chief, presumably because no-one more competent was available. Fortunately, apart from his bladder trouble, Napoleon was in excellent health.

In addition there were four Chamberlains, recruited from the local *bourgeoisie*, six officers wearing sky-blue uniforms with silver piping, two secretaries and numerous footmen.

Bertrand had gone into the Emperor's cabinet, and Roger was talking to Signor Lapi, one of the Corsican Chamberlains, whom Napoleon had made Director of Domains and Forests, when *Madame Mère* and Pauline came down the stairs. The courtiers at once formed into two lines and bowed low.

Napoleon's mother was as upright and sprightly as ever. Most people dreaded her for her caustic tongue, but she liked people who stood up to her and had always been pleasant to Roger. Her quick, black eyes picked him out at once and, stopping in front of him, she asked him where he had come from.

'France, Madame,' he replied promptly. 'But it is much changed and I do not care to reside there any longer.'

Pauline was now in her middle thirties and still very beautiful, although she had suffered from ill-health for a long time. It was an internal trouble, probably the result of an infection she had contracted while in the West Indies. At the sight of Roger, her fine eyes lit up and as he kissed her hand she gave it a quick squeeze.

'So far, so good,' Roger thought. It was evident that neither of the ladies nor any of the other people realized that he had been in Vienna. Otherwise they would have questioned him about the Congress. He could only hope that Napoleon had not heard from someone that he had been there, but kept it to himself.

At that moment Traditi, the Mayor of Portoferraio, another of the Chamberlains, rapped sharply three times on the floor with his wand of office. The courtiers again formed two lines, a door on the left was thrown open and, followed by Bertrand, the Emperor emerged.

He was, as always, wearing the familiar green and white uniform of the Guides. For a minute he stood quite still, looking directly at Roger who, not being a member of the Court, had taken up a position at the far end of one of the lines, but his face remained quite expressionless.

When the dozen courtiers straightened up after their bow, the Emperor walked slowly down the avenue they formed, stopping for a moment before each of them and saying a few words, mostly questions about the various duties on which they were engaged.

As he approached, Roger had ample time to note the alteration in his appearance. In the past ten months his girth had increased considerably. From a small paunch his stomach had become an outstanding protuberance, and his thighs were much thicker. His face seemed paler than ever, and he now wore his hair quite short, with one black lock descending in the middle of his forehead.

At last he halted opposite Roger, whose anxiety had been greatly increased by seeing no warmth in the first glance Napoleon had given him. After staring at him in silence for a moment, the Emperor asked in his harshest voice:

'Well! How is your friend, that despicable rogue, Talleyrand?'

11

The Imperial Exile

ALTHOUGH not the question Roger had feared he might be asked, for it had included no mention of Vienna, it was highly disconcerting. As though extremely surprised, he took a quick step backwards and exclaimed:

'Talleyrand, Sire? Like Your Majesty, I have known him for many years; but why you should assume him to be my friend . . .'

'Associate; cat's-paw, then!' the Emperor burst out. 'You stayed with him, lived in his mansion in Paris at the time of the occupation. Dare you deny it?'

'No, I do not, Sire.'

'Very well, then; you were among that nest of traitors, conspiring to bring about my abdication. Caulaincourt saw you there, and told me of it. Talleyrand was the arch traitor. He had shown his hand before. I should have had him shot then, instead of only calling him to his face "shit in a silk stocking". But there were others, lesser traitors, Dalberg and yourself among them.'

Inspiration suddenly came to Roger, and he said boldly, 'You wrong me, Sire. I was only one of many living in Talleyrand's mansion at that time, and the Czar Alexander was among them.'

F

'I am aware of that. What of it?'

'Why, surely Your Majesty has not forgotten that I have long enjoyed the Czar's confidence. You yourself sent me from Moscow to St. Petersburg to negotiate with him. It was not as Talleyrand's guest that I was staying in the Rue de St. Florentine. Hoping to influence the Czar in your favour, I contacted him the day before he entered Paris. He made me a member of his suite, and when Talleyrand invited him to use his mansion as his headquarters, he took Nesselrode, myself and others there with him.'

This was a distortion of the truth, as Roger had been responsible for the Czar's occupying Talleyrand's house, but the account he had given of the matter was perfectly plausible. Napoleon's expression changed. The muscles of his exceptionally broad jaw, which had been thrust out aggressively, relaxed.

'I see,' he muttered. 'Yes, I see. And at that time Alexander was not ill-disposed toward me. It was good of you to endeavour to do your best for me with him when so many others were deserting me. I appreciate it. Welcome to Elba, Breuc. Whence have you come?'

'From France, Sire. I could not bring myself to live there longer under those hateful Bourbons.'

The Emperor smiled and, making his old familiar gesture of approval, tweaked Roger's ear. 'You are thrice welcome then. And I'll find plenty to occupy you. Meanwhile, you must stay to dinner.'

Shortly afterwards Bertrand was given leave to withdraw and most of the others left with him. There remained Pauline, who lived in the house, Drouot and Peyrusse, who always dined with their master, and *Madame Mère,* who did so frequently but, as Roger learned, occupied a house nearby which she had taken over from the Vantini family.

They walked from the hall through to the dining room at the back of the house. It looked out on a pleasant garden, at the end of which, in the failing light of the February afternoon, Roger could make out a balustraded terrace overlooking the town and bay.

During the meal, while bolting his food as usual, the Emperor did most of the talking. He dwelt at length, for Roger's benefit, on the blessings he had bestowed on the Elbans. When he had arrived, the towns and villages had been indescribably filthy; he had promptly impressed scores of men to go round with the big baskets which they carried on their backs when harvesting the grapes, and the inhabitants had been ordered to shovel into them the refuse accumulated through the years, with the result that he had delivered the place from its swarms of flies. Another of his sanitary measures had been to decree that, for the future, no more than five people should sleep in one bed. By imposing the *corvée* system of the *ancien régime*, he had built roads all over the island. It was mostly barren rock, with pockets of poor soil here and there, so Elba had never been self-supporting in wheat. To rectify this he had sown grain on the previously uninhabited nearby islet of Pianosa, where the soil was much richer. He had also brought potatoes, onions, cauliflower, lettuces and radishes to Elba, previously not grown there. He had planted a great number of trees, mainly chestnuts for flour, and mulberries, the leaves of which would in due course bring in revenue as food for silkworms. In many of the vineyards he had found that fig trees gave so much shade that the grapes did not ripen properly, so he had made the farmers cut them down and plant olive trees instead. In fact, there seemed no end to his activities, which Roger, knowing his restless nature, did not find at all surprising, and regarded as a good indication that he really meant to stay there.

Toward the end of dinner Napoleon remarked that they usually spent the evening playing cards, but that night he did not wish to do so A quarter of an hour later *Madame Mère* was escorted to her house, and Pauline went upstairs to a suite that Napoleon had had prepared for her. As she wished Roger good night, she said:

'Although I live here most of the time to keep His Majesty company, I also have a house of my own about three miles away, up on the slope of San Martini. You must come and visit me there.' The invitation was accompanied by an almost imperceptible wink, and Roger smiled his thanks, although inwardly not too happy about the possible results of being on his own with her.

Napoleon then showed Roger round the 'palace'. On the ground floor, his study and bedroom, like the dining room, looked out from the back of the house into the garden; there were two other rooms, his library and bathroom, which faced the drive. All of them were quite small and plainly furnished. Upstairs Pauline's suite occupied the north-west end of the house. The centre of the upper floor had been a jumble of rooms. Napoleon had pulled down the walls and raised the roof to make one large room where he could hold receptions for up to two hundred people. He was quite proud of his reconstruction, and spoke with enthusiasm of two more 'palaces' in other parts of the island which he was having rebuilt to suit his convenience.

As they came downstairs, Peyrusse caught the Emperor's eye. Napoleon stepped aside to him, and the Treasurer whispered a few words in his ear. Turning abruptly to Roger, Napoleon said:

'Breuc, I have work to do. But I am most pleased that you have come here, and we shall, I hope, give you an interesting time. You must see the island. Yes, tomorrow come up here and you can ride one of my horses over to our iron mines at Rio. Pons will show you over them.' Turning to Peyrusse, he added, 'See de Breuc back to the Bertrands, otherwise he may lose his way.'

As the cheerful Peyrusse accompanied Roger down the steep streets of steps to the waterfront, he explained that the open-cast iron mines at the east end of the island were its principal source of revenue, and that André Pons had been the administrator for several years. The island was only about eighteen miles by twelve, so the mines were no great distance away. Peyrusse said that ten o'clock would be quite early enough for Roger to start, and that he would arrange about a mount and guide for him. He then invited Roger to dine with him on his return.

Next morning, when Roger came down to breakfast, he found that Bertrand had already gone out, so he had a long conversation alone with his hostess. She was a tall, dignified woman and came from a good family. Her father, a General, had been guillotined and her mother had been a cousin of the Empress Josephine. As she was still under thirty, she greatly disliked being deprived of civilized society, owing to her husband's unshakeable determination to remain with the Emperor.

Roger sympathized with her in that, and the discomfort in which she was compelled to live. The floors were of bare brick, the rooms draughty and, to make a sofa, she had had to arrange a horsehair mattress on two chairs. After condoling with her, he remarked:

'I imagine *Madame Mère* and the Princess Pauline also find life very dull here.'

'On the contrary,' came the quick reply. 'The old woman could not be happier. It is almost as good for her as being back in her beloved Corsica. She can even see it from the south side of the island, and the Elbans and Corsicans are of the same stock—miserable Italian peasantry. She never cared for the grandeur of the Court and is in her element here, as she does not even have to bother to speak French any more. Her only vice, if you can call it one, is cards, and on most nights up at the Mulini they play *vingt-et-un* or *reversé*, also chess and dominoes. As ever, the Emperor always cheats, and she delights in catching him out. He retaliates by making her pay up, which she is very loath to do, whenever she loses. During the day she goes for drives or does her tapestry and listens to gossip. As for Pauline . . .' Madame Bertrand gave an eloquent shrug, 'she enjoys parading her ill-health and has herself carted about everywhere in a carrying chair, but forgets it as soon as a personable man appears on the scene.'

For stables the Emperor had commandeered the salt warehouses, which were far larger than the palace, and when Peyrusse took Roger there he was surprised to find that Napoleon had a score or more carriages, and at least half a hundred horses, among which were eight of his famous greys which he had ridden in his campaigns. All of them had to be exercised, and Roger was given Tauris, a Persian with a white mane which the Czar had presented to the Emperor at the Congress of Erfurt. His guide was a lanky youth who spoke a little French, with a strong Italian accent.

To get to Rio they had to ride right round the great bay, so they did not reach the little town which was the

centre of the mining industry until close on midday.
The surroundings were dreary and depressing, as the
land was barren and a red dust covered everything.
The only house of any size was the residence of André
Pons, the superintendent of the mines. He was in his
early forties, and had known Napoleon for many
years. Earlier in the day he had been notified of
Roger's visit and, soon after he received his guest, it
emerged that they had both been present twenty years
before at the siege of Toulon, memories of which
created a common bond between them.

In those far-off days, Pons had been a rabid revolutionary and he was still a Jacobin at heart. He strongly
disapproved of the Empire, but had conceived a great
admiration for Napoleon as a genius. Having told
Roger this, he added that, while he had happily continued in his post under Elba's new Sovereign, he
stood no nonsense from the 'little Corporal', and often
had rows with him. They had had a fine scene when the
Emperor, on the grounds of economy, had ordered the
dismissal of the crews of the two guard boats that
patrolled the coast to prevent the ore from being
smuggled out to the mainland; and on several other
occasions Pons had defied the Emperor.

After inspecting the mines they enjoyed a midday
meal of *bouillabaisse*, for which Pons's cook was famous.
But when Roger remarked that Napoleon's coming to
Elba must have been a blessing to the inhabitants, as
he had done so much for them, Pons removed his
spectacles and burst out:

'Had you been here more than twenty-four hours,
Count, you would think very differently. When he
arrived, everyone expected him to turn Elba into an
earthly paradise. But now they loathe him. He regards the island and all that is in it as his personal

property. He commandeers anything he takes a fancy to, and if he pays for it at all, at only a quarter of its value. He closed the peninsula of Insola in order to raise boar and deer there, and Capo di Stella he has had walled in as a shooting preserve. Everything he does is solely for his own benefit or pleasure. By forced labour he has made major additions to three houses that he calls "palaces". The miles and miles of roads he has constructed, also by forced labour, are of no use to the people. They were perfectly content to use their mules along the old mountain tracks. He made the roads only so that he could drive from one place to another in his carriages. He regards the revenues from the mines here and the tunny fisheries as his personal income, and spends nothing on useful projects. Then there are the receptions he is always holding. Everyone of any substance is expected to attend and dress up for the occasion. The women feel that they must have new clothes and falderals every month or so, and I know a score of honest citizens who have been brought near to ruin by this extravagance. Before he came the townsfolk were poor but contented, and free to do as they would. But that is so no longer. He still thinks of himself as the Emperor and issues, through Bertrand, Drouot and Peyrusse, a dozen edicts a day, each of which means further hardship for the people. I tell you, they could not be more put upon and worse off were they living under the tyranny of one of the great nobles of the *ancien régime.*'

This gave Roger much food for thought as he rode back early in the afternoon to Portoferraio. He was now sorry for the Elbans, but decided that, as Napoleon was so absorbed with every form of activity in his small kingdom, it was a clear indication that he had no intention of leaving it.

On Roger's return he went to dine with Peyrusse. The Treasurer had taken as a lodging for himself a small but pleasant house that belonged to a very pretty young widow, and it soon became clear that she was his mistress. They enjoyed an excellent meal, accompanied by much laughter; but, toward the end of it, when Roger enquired if his host found his duties onerous, the cheerful Peyrusse made a wry grimace:

'The work would not worry me, if only we had enough money. Those miserable Bourbons have not sent us one single sou of the two million a year they undertook to pay the Emperor. At his orders I have sold nearly everything that is saleable—even a store of provisions that was in the fort at Longone. He has taken over the forests and we are selling the timber. His personal funds are now at such a low ebb that he is cutting down the salaries of all his people, and the revenue from the mines, fisheries and salt are hopelessly inadequate to meet the expenses of the state he considers it his right to maintain. Soon after we arrived here he sent out the tax collectors to get in all dues that were in arrears from the previous year, although he had no right to them. Many Elbans refused to pay, so he sent in his Guards to live free upon them until they did. That caused some unpleasant scenes, I can tell you. There were even revolts in some of the country places. Led by their priests, the villagers stoned the tax gatherers and drove them off. He has become terribly mean and rapacious, even charging his mother and sister for alterations to their residences. He has robbed his old veterans, too. The revenue of the Rio mines were given by him years ago to the pensioners of the Legion of Honour. Monsieur Pons had fifty thousand francs he was holding for the Legion, but the Emperor insisted on it being handed over to him.

Hundreds of citizens have just claims against him, and I have the unpleasant task of constantly putting them off.'

'Then I certainly don't envy you,' Roger remarked sympathetically. 'I realized, of course, that the Bourbons' refusal to pay must be making things difficult for him, but not that they were as bad as this. Have you any idea of his total indebtedness?'

Peyrusse gave a grim smile. 'There must be many claims that have not yet come in, but if I give you the approximate figure of our annual budget, you can make a rough guess for yourself. His military establishment—the Guard, his squadron of Polish Lancers, gunners, sailors and the Elban militia—costs one and a half million; his household one million two hundred and sixty thousand; civil administration a hundred and fifty thousand. That is near enough three million. Against that, our total revenue is only six hundred and six thousand.'

'Then you are on the wrong side by well over two million.'

'You have said it, Count. But no doubt God will provide; so let us open another bottle of wine and talk of more pleasant things.'

However, they were not destined to enjoy this further bottle. Peyrusse had only just uncorked it when a running footman arrived with a message from the Emperor, requiring Roger's presence.

Having warmly thanked the ever-optimistic Treasurer and his charming mistress for their hospitality, Roger went out and in the early February sunset slowly climbed the streets of steps up to the Mulini. Peyrusse's revelations about the state of the Emperor's finances had given him food for much thought. Contented as the Imperial exile appeared to be in having created a miniature Court that paid him as much deference as though he were still at the Tuileries, and with his innumerable projects for occupying himself at the expense of his twelve thousand subjects, this state of things could not go on indefinitely. He was obviously bankrupt, had few resources left and no amount of cheese-paring was going to alter his situation materially.

There could be only one remedy for it. He had at his disposal something over a thousand troops. They were in strength—compared with the armies of six hundred thousand and more that he had commanded—as a two-foot-high sapling to a hundred-year-old oak. But the man himself was incredibly potent. If he were desperate, as he must soon become, he would gamble everything on a return to the Continent.

When Roger reached the Mulini Palace, the major-domo informed him that His Majesty was in conference with Generals Bertrand and Drouot, and had given orders that he was not to be disturbed. From years spent as one of the Emperor's A.D.C.s Roger was well aware that people sent for hurriedly often had to wait for hours before they were actually called in; so he settled himself with a week-old Italian news sheet in the hall, on a well-worn settee.

He had been there only a few minutes when Pauline came down the stairs. She greeted him with her sweetest smile, and when she learned that he was waiting to see her brother, said, 'It may be ages yet before he has finished with his dreary old Generals. In the meantime, come up to my boudoir and sit with me. They will send up and let you know immediately he is free.'

On the upper floor she led him into a pleasant little room, much more elegantly furnished than those downstairs. When he commented on it, she replied with a shrug, 'Poor Napoleon, he has to make do with a lot of old, worn-out stuff that was all Eliza would send him from Tuscany. I had these few things shipped from my palace in Rome. I also managed to get out of France over a hundred cases of *objets d'art* from my Hôtel de Charost.'

As she spoke, she put her hands on his shoulders, smiled into his eyes and went on, 'But surely you have more pleasant things to say to me than just remarking on my furniture?'

He smiled back at her. 'I have. It is that you look more ravishing than ever.' Then he put his arms round her and kissed her on the mouth. She returned his kiss with interest and pressed herself against him. As her lips grew warmer under his, he put a hand up to her breast, but she quickly drew back, exclaiming:

'No, no! Not here. Not now. A footman may come up for you at any minute.' Turning away, she sat down on her *chaise-longue*, swung up her legs and reclined gracefully upon it. He took a chair beside her and said:

'I think it very gallant of you to come and live in this God-forsaken island when you might be enjoying yourself in Rome or Naples.'

She shrugged. 'As you know, I have my share of vices, but ingratitude is not one of them. Napoleon has become monstrous mean of late. He even made me pay for the curtains in my rooms here. But when he had his millions he never grudged any of us anything, and 'tis to him I owe the carefree life of luxury that I enjoyed for so many years. The least I could do was to give him the benefit of my company now that he has fallen from his great estate.'

'I fear, though, you must find it monstrous dull here.'

'I did for a while. Would you believe it, one of our

evening entertainments was listening to that pious fool, Drouot, reading passages from the Bible? But I soon introduced many innovations. I persuaded Napoleon to turn the abandoned church of the Carmelites into a theatre, and I had made a smaller one in an outhouse here, in which we perform amateur theatricals. I took the lead myself in both *Les Fausses Infidélités* and *Les Folies Amoureuses*. We have dances and masked balls. Then there is sailing in the bay and I have my own house at San Marino. I am dying to show it to you.'

'I should love to see it when you next go there.'

Pauline raised her tapering eyebrows. 'Why not tomorrow? It is Sunday, and you could drive up there with me after Mass. We shall have to be very careful here, because 'tis certain that Napoleon will remember our old attachment. But up at San Marino we can do as we please. You could come up ostensibly to dine with me, and stay the night.'

'You open again the gates of heaven for me,' Roger cried, taking her hand and kissing it.

Nevertheless, her frank offer once more to become his mistress did not fill him with the delight it would have a few months earlier. In order to spare her feelings, he felt he could not decently refuse her overture, but was unhappily doubtful whether he would be able to play the role of her lover wholeheartedly.

Ever since he had learned how Mary had stolen his fortune, that had preyed on his mind. The future seemed to hold nothing for him other than a diplomatic post on the Continent and, as he was not a professional diplomat, he could not expect a post of any importance. It would mean running errands for some Minister with far less experience of courts and camps than himself. This would not have been insupportable had he still had a large income, could afford his own coach, had the money to entertain and make handsome presents to women who attracted him. But with a paltry salary of only two or three hundred a year, he would be unable to do any of those things or even, as he had for so long, dress elegantly in expensive clothes. He would become a dowdy, middle-aged clerk, with only the lesser fry of other embassies for companions. Having no heart to express further false adoration for the vain and coquettish Pauline, he put the thought of the coming weekend from his mind and said to her:

'Tell me about the Emperor. He seems happy enough here. Do you think he really is?'

'Oh, yes. There are so many activities in which he is interested. Quite often he says that, as far as the world outside Elba is concerned, he is now dead.'

'It seems, though, that he is devilish short of money.'

'That is so. Those miserable Bourbons would gladly see us all starve to death. But, in spite of the indifference to his misfortunes that most of his own family have so far shown, at a pinch I am sure they will help him. And, between us, we have succeeded in saving many millions from the wreck. The only thing that really grieves him is the behaviour of the Empress. She was given the Duchy of Parma. To begin with, she wrote, promising to live there and pay him frequent visits here; but for months now she has not even replied to his letters.'

Roger nodded. 'From what I have heard she is completely dominated by her father, who means to keep her in Vienna and bring up the little King of Rome as an Austrian Archduke.'

'Oh, that horrid man!' Pauline exclaimed. 'He can have no heart at all. He must know how Napoleon adores his son, and to deprive him of the joy of even seeing the boy from time to time is positively inhuman.'

'I agree; and I think that spineless woman, Marie Louise, has behaved abominably. But what of other women? In the old days, much as it pained poor Josephine, he was always pulling her maids of honour or the ladies of the Opera into his bed. Has he not found some charmer here to console him?'

'Not to my knowledge.' Pauline shook her head. 'He says that in Paris one can do more or less what one pleases, without the public becoming aware of it; but on this little island any liaison would provoke a scandal. And he will not have it. That is why we must be so circumspect. 'Tis common knowledge that he has loved few people so greatly as he did the Walewska. Yet, when she came here and wished to remain with him, he would not let her.'

The Countess Walewska had been the young, lovely and virtuous wife of an old man of seventy when Napoleon had first met her in 1807. He had fallen desperately in love with her, but had great difficulty in overcoming her scruples about becoming his mistress, succeeding only after the Polish nobles had persuaded her that her influence with him would prove invaluable to her country. She had then come to return his love, bore him a son and had gone to live in Paris, where he had frequently relaxed in her company.

Roger had not known of her visit to Elba and enquired about it.

'Poor dear,' Pauline sighed. 'He requited her ill for the adoration she lavished on him. She drove out to Fontainebleau just before the abdication, but he was so overwrought that he refused even to see her. Then, at the end of August, when she proposed to visit him here, he ordered her to come ashore on the far side of the bay, and had her spirited by night up to

a four-roomed hermitage called Marciana Alta, near
the peak of Monte Giove, that he visits from time to
time. With her little son she stayed there only a few
days, and they were kept indoors all the time, in
case some peasant saw him with her. He enjoyed
playing with the boy, but packed them off after
telling her that, had *Madame Mère* learned that she
was living on the island, she would have taken great
exception to it. As this visit by a lady could not be
altogether concealed, he gave out that she was Marie
Louise who had come to see him in secret, and . . .'

A soft knock on the door caused Pauline to break
off. On her call to enter, a footman appeared and
announced that Roger's presence was required by the
Emperor. Having kissed Pauline's hand, he hurried
downstairs, to find Napoleon impatiently walking
up and down the hall. With a scowl, he said:

'So you've lost no time in renewing your attentions
to the Princess Borghese, eh?'

Pretending innocent surprise, Roger exclaimed,
'Attentions? No, Sire. Your Majesty cured me of that
long ago. But I would be sadly lacking in good manners
did I fail to pay my respects to Her Highness.'

'So you say,' the Emperor grunted. 'But I know you
both, so you'd best have a care or 'twill be the worse
for you. The Elbans set high store on correct behaviour
and I insist that the members of my Court should set
a good example. I'll tolerate no tittle-tattle about any
member of it. Now, I wish for some fresh air. Put on
your cloak and accompany me into the garden. I
will talk with you there.'

Napoleon led the way along paved paths between
the orange and lemon trees and oleanders, above
which rose a few palms, to the balustraded terrace.
There were two alabaster vases there, through which

the light of oil lamps glowed. Although it was now fully dark, the houses of the town, clustered on the hundred-foot slope below, could be easily made out by the lights coming from many of the windows, and in the big bay beyond, the lanterns in several fishing boats made paths across the gently-rippling water.

'Well, what have you to tell me about France?' the Emperor asked, as they began to walk up and down the terrace.

It was the question that Roger had been expecting, and he had considered carefully how he should answer it. The last thing he wanted to do was to give Napoleon the impression that the whole country was seething with discontent, and so encourage any thoughts the ex-Sovereign might have of returning there. On the other hand, ships from both large and small ports all round the Gulf of Genoa must constantly be putting in to Portoferraio, so it was certain that Napoleon would have a very shrewd idea of the state of things in France. In a quiet voice, he replied:

'The majority of the people are far from happy. Although France is now a constitutional monarchy, the life led by the masses has been put back to 1790, when for centuries they had been used to living under an autocracy. All bills have to be passed through the Chambers, but many ordinances are simply issued by the Ministers, and have to be carried out. There is no cohesion in the government, no Cabinet to agree a common policy. Each Minister takes his orders from the King, and many of them cause hardship and discontent.'

'From a fool like that sack of flour, Louis XVIII, what else could they expect?'

'Nay, Sire. He is not a fool. He is shrewd, cautious, and might even make a good ruler were it not for the people by whom he is surrounded. His brother, d'Artois, is the root of the trouble. He leads a pack of greedy *émigré* nobles who have not the sense to put behind them the inconveniences they have suffered for the past twenty years. They and the clergy never cease to put pressure on the King to restore their lands and privileges and, as he is too lazy to argue with them, in most cases they get their way.'

'Think you there is any likelihood of a revolt?'

Roger shook his head. 'I think that very unlikely. The bourgeoisie are prospering, so would be against it; and they are far more numerous and powerful than they were before the Revolution.'

'The Army does not prosper, though. The treatment of my old soldiers is disgraceful. I hear that thousands of officers have been sent back to civilian life with only miserable pensions, and my Guard has been insulted, deprived of the honour that was its due and degraded to a regiment of the line.'

'That is true, Sire. But, as far as the Army as a whole is concerned, it must be remembered that many of your troops were weary of marching and fighting. Although they may be short of money, they are happier to be free of discipline and safely settled in their homes.'

'You are wrong, Breuc; quite wrong. They gloried in the victories to which I led them, and they would have fought on for me to the last man had I not been persuaded to abdicate. It was the Marshals who betrayed me. They had no more stomach for battle. All they wanted was to enjoy the wealth and the great estates I had bestowed upon them. My big mistake was not to have got rid of them and appointed younger, more ambitious men to lead my corps and divisions.'

'That may be so, Sire. But, however brave and devoted such men might have proved, they could not have won the last battles for you. The Army that remained to you was hopelessly outnumbered.'

'Again you are wrong. Had the Marshals stood by me I could still have triumphed. Twice I wrote urgently to Augereau, telling him to march north so that our armies could present a united front to the enemy, but he ignored my order. Even if he had remained at Lyons he could have held off the Austrians had he a mind to do so; but he surrendered. Marmont, by calling the National Guard to his assistance, could have held Paris for another week; but he threw in his hand. Even Ney and Macdonald declared at Fontainebleau that my case had become hopeless. But it had not. My garrisons in the east were still holding out. I could have bypassed Paris, joined up with Augereau to defend Lyons while Soult and Suchet brought their armies up from the south to join us. I'd again have had a quarter of a million men, and with them could have driven that craven Schwarzenberg out of France.'

Halting, the Emperor pointed over the terrace to a small, open space a little way down the slope. There was a bonfire there, round which a dozen men in uniform were doing a wild dance. 'Look at them,' he said. 'They are some of my Polish Lancers. Poor devils, they would have been better off to return to their homes than follow me here. So would the men of my Old Guard. They have naught to do, so have become bored and discontented. One can hardly wonder that a few of them have even deserted in fishing craft to the mainland. And things could go from bad to worse, now that I have had to cut their pay. But they will not.'

With a sudden laugh, he gripped Roger by the arm

and said in a low voice, 'For months I've told everyone that I am dead. But I am not. And I've kept my secret well. I've not told even Pauline. You could not have joined me at a better time, Breuc. Tomorrow night we sail to reconquer France.'

12

The Great Gamble

ROGER was so nonplussed that for a moment he
could not speak. Had he been sent to Elba a fortnight
or even a week earlier, he could hardly have failed
to become aware of Napoleon's intentions, for he was
not the man to undertake any enterprise, let alone
such a desperate one, without making the most careful
preparations. Many of them must have been obvious
to anyone of Roger's astuteness spending a few days
in Portoferraio, and it flashed into his mind that it
was to guard against the chance of his doing so that
the Emperor had packed him off to spend most of
that day on his trip to the iron mines at Rio.

The thought of Napoleon as once again master of
France appalled him. It must inevitably lead to a
reopening of the interminable war that had almost
ruined Europe and killed or mutilated millions of her
young manhood. Neither Britain nor Austria would
ever consent to Napoleon again becoming Emperor
of the French. But the Czar had become such a weather-
cock that no-one could predict what attitude he
would take up. Out of hatred for Austria he might,
as he had at Tilsit, enter on a *rapprochement* with
Napoleon; and Prussia, gorged with her newly-
acquired territories, would probably remain neutral.
If such a situation arose, the Emperor's insatiable

ambition might lead to further ghastly battles, with no foreseeable end to them.

Roger's immediate instinct was to use every possible argument which might dissuade Napoleon from undertaking this rash adventure. While still General Bonaparte, he might have listened to the very real odds against its success, but since he had crowned himself in Notre-Dame, he had increasingly ignored the warnings and advice of his Marshals and others he had previously trusted. After his elevation to son-in-law of the Habsburg Emperor, his meglomania had become such that he would not even tolerate the expression of an opinion contrary to his own and, military genius though he was, it was a fact that in every campaign he had waged since marrying Marie Louise he had been defeated.

Realizing the futility of any comment other than a favourable one, Roger exclaimed, after a moment of apparently breathless surprise:

'*Mon Dieu!* But this is marvellous! What fantastic good fortune for me, Sire, that I should have arrived here in time to accompany you.'

'My star brought you to me,' Napoleon replied complacently. 'My present A.D.C.s, picked from the officers of the Guard, are good fellows but have no experience of staff work. You, on the contrary, have spent years as a member of my personal entourage. Your knowledge of how I require things to be done will prove most valuable. You will, of course, be my A.D.C.-in-Chief, and I shall make you a General.'

Roger bowed. 'Your Majesty is most generous. I am truly grateful. May I enquire when you took this momentous decision?'

'I have been meditating on it for some time. It came to my ears that my enemies in Vienna were uneasy at leaving me here so close to the Continent. Both Metternich and Talleyrand have been urging that I should be removed either to the Azores or St. Helena. They would have found that easier said than done for, soon after I arrived here, I put Elba in a state of defence. I've mounted cannon with small garrisons on Pianosa and Palmajola, a smaller offshore island, and have a force of over a thousand devoted troops, who would fight desperately to prevent me from being carried off. But I could not have resisted a full-scale invasion by several divisions supported by a fleet.'

'Your Majesty is really confident, though, that with the small force at your disposal you could reconquer France?'

'Yes. Those idiot Bourbons have made a hopeless mess of things. As you remarked yourself a while ago, the Army has been treated most shamefully, and the small proprietors who purchased the lands of the *émigrés* dread being dispossessed. The reimposition of tithes, owing to the influence of that pious old bitch the Duchess d'Angoulême and her horde of greedy priests, has caused intense resentment. So you were wrong about France not being ripe for revolution. I know it, and my last doubts were removed by a letter I received a fortnight since, brought to me by Fleury de Chaboulon from Marat, the Duke de Bassano. You will remember him?'

'Of course, Sire. He was your Foreign Minister before you gave the post to Caulaincourt.'

'Yes, and he wrote urging me to return. He was always a cautious man, yet he states that the overthrow of the Bourbons is certain and imminent. But I must lose no time in reclaiming my throne, for a new threat to my regaining it has arisen. The Czar was persuaded, against his better judgement, to assent to the return of the Bourbons, and the English are disappointed in them because they have failed to govern democratically. Since Louis XVIII has proved so inept, it is now suggested that he should be replaced by the head of the younger branch of the Bourbons.'

'What! The Duc d'Orléans? But, Sire, his father was a regicide. He voted in the Assembly for the death of his cousin, Louis XVI.'

'Exactly.' Napoleon gave a cynical laugh. 'And was later guillotined himself, in spite of having endeavoured to curry favour with the mob by calling himself *Philippe Egalité*. But that is the whole point. Since Louis XVIII is doomed, it would suit the Powers much better to have him replaced by a King who has inherited Liberal principles, than to have the people rise in another revolution.'

Roger had heard nothing of this plot by the Orléanists to secure the throne for their leader, but he agreed that if the move succeeded it would put an end to the hopes of the Bonapartists. Napoleon then went on:

'But I have a much larger following in Paris. As you know, my symbol is the violet. I am told that scores of men there regularly wear buttonholes of that flower, and violet is now the most fashionable colour for women's dresses. They also wear rings of violet enamel with the words *"Il reparaîtra au printemps"* inscribed on them, showing that they expect me to return in the spring. There is a catch phrase, too, which refers to me. One says, *"Do you believe in Christ?"*, and the other replies, *"Yes and in the Resurrection"*. But, having just come from France, you must know all this.'

As Roger had not been in Paris since his stay with Talleyrand before going on to Vienna, he did not; but it did not greatly surprise him in view of all he had

heard during the past six months. The Legion of
Honour had been degraded by being bestowed on
hundreds of civil servants, and an Archbishop made
Chancellor of the Order; the Duc de Berry had torn
off an officer's epaulettes and described the wars of
the Empire as 'twenty-five years of brigandage';
the Duc d'Angoulême had strutted about Paris
wearing an English uniform; the pensions for invalided veterans had been reduced; the many thousands
of prisoners of war returned from England, Russia,
Austria and Germany had been left to starve; the free
schools for the daughters of dead heroes abolished and
the military college of St. Cyr suppressed. It could
not be wondered at that vast numbers of people who
had prospered under, or been cared for by Napoleon,
were now longing for his return.

'My problem,' the Emperor continued, 'was to
reach France before Colonel Campbell, the British
Commissioner here, could report that I had left Elba
and have me intercepted. He is a pleasant man, most
courteous and helpful, but he has an English brig, the
Partridge, at his disposal, and I doubt if my *Inconstant*
could have proved a match for her. But my star is
again in the ascendant. Campbell has been suffering
from increasing deafness, and the very day after I
received Marat's letter, my nice bulldog said he was
sailing in the *Partridge* for Leghorn, to see an ear
doctor, and would be away for ten days. The ship was
hardly below the horizon before I gave orders for
Inconstant to be careened, repainted like an English
ship and provisioned for three months.'

'Three months?' Roger repeated in a puzzled voice.

Napoleon laughed. 'One of my deception plans. It
was to make those who were working on her think
that I mean to go to America. By the 22nd she was

ready for sea, and two small merchant ships I hired, the *Etoile* and the *Saint Esprit*, have been loaded with extra cases of cartridges, saddlery for my Poles and a few of my carriages. All this has been done out of sight of the town. To deceive the inhabitants, instead of having my Grenadiers drilled, I've employed them in remaking the gardens, and every day I have continued to issue a dozen or more orders about future projects; so, although a lot of people must have guessed that there is something in the wind, they cannot possibly suspect that I mean to depart almost immediately.'

After a moment he went on, 'We had a nasty scare the night before you arrived, though. The *Partridge* unexpectedly appeared and put into harbour. I feared that Campbell had returned two days earlier than he had meant to. But it proved a false alarm. Captain Adye came ashore and we learned that he was only on a routine cruise. He will not be picking up Campbell from Leghorn until tomorrow.'

'Your Majesty is once more a favourite of Fortune,' Roger smiled. 'How I should laugh if I could see the faces of the great men at the Congress when the news of your having landed in France reaches Vienna.'

'Oh, the Congress.' Napoleon shrugged. 'Did you not know? It ended a week ago, with nothing settled, and the Czar setting off in a huff for Russia.'

This was news to Roger, and his heart sank. Had the Congress still been in session when it was learned that Napoleon had left Elba, the ex-Allies might have temporarily sunk their differences to combine and crush him; but if the Czar had already left Vienna, the chances of reviving the Alliance were slight.

'We will go in now,' said the Emperor, turning toward the house. 'It is my custom to play cards most evenings for an hour or so, and we must adhere to routine, otherwise the servants may suspect that my departure is imminent. Yesterday I placed an embargo on all shipping leaving the island until further notice, but someone might slip away in a fishing smack, and every hour we can preserve our secret counts. You will speak of this to no-one, Breuc, not even Bertrand or Drouot. The former was glad when I told him of my intention, the latter urged me to change my mind. He is a good man, but a fool.'

Round the card table there were already assembled *Madame Mère*, Pauline, Drouot and Lieutenant Taillade, who commanded the *Inconstant* and had been asked to dine that evening. They were playing *vingt-et-un*, and Napoleon and Roger joined them. But after only half a dozen hands the clock struck nine, the Emperor rose from the table and played a few bars on the piano. Apparently it was his usual practice at that hour, and a signal for everyone to go to bed. *Madame Mère* was ceremoniously seen off in a sedan chair to the nearby Vantini house; then, when about to go upstairs, Pauline gave her hand to Roger to kiss, smiled at him and said:

'Until tomorrow, Count. After Mass we will drive up in my little carriage drawn by a pair of ponies to San Martino.'

'No, you will not,' interjected Napoleon abruptly. 'Breuc is again entering my service. I wish to introduce him to the officers of the Guard as my A.D.C.-in-Chief.'

Pauline made a little *moue* of annoyance and said to Roger, 'We must make it another day then—Monday perhaps.'

He was relieved rather than disappointed, as in his depressed state he had felt no pleasurable anticipation about this chance to renew the amorous encounters with Pauline that had once filled him with delight. No sooner had he left the house than his mind turned to the momentous project of which Napoleon had told him an hour earlier.

Had he arrived in Elba only a week sooner, he felt certain that within a few days the many preparations going forward would have revealed the Emperor's intentions to him. He could then have hired a fishing smack in which to slip away by night to the mainland, warn the British Consul at Leghorn what was afoot, and have warships in the vicinity alerted to intercept Napoleon's small flotilla. But it was too late. And an embargo had now been placed on all ships leaving the island. As he walked down the steep street of steps, it crossed his mind that he might be able to bribe a fisherman to defy the order and take him off that night. But he at once dismissed it. The risk that the man might refuse the bribe and report the attempt to suborn him was too great. The Emperor would have him arrested and leave him behind, imprisoned there. His only course now was once more to play the part of a devoted A.D.C., and so be certain of retaining his freedom.

On his truckle bed in the dingy little bedroom at the Bertrands' apartment he lay long awake, speculating on the outcome of the Emperor's decision to attempt to regain his throne. Everything, he decided, would depend on the attitude of the Army. The rank-and-file would welcome Napoleon's return, but the majority of the officers would not risk their commissions, and possibly being shot as traitors, for going over to him. Would the men dare defy their officers? And even a single division loyal to King Louis could overwhelm with ease the small force Napoleon would have at his disposal. To invade France with only one thousand men seemed the height of madness. But their leader was a man apart. With his imagination, tirelessness, swiftness of decision, courage, determination and personal magnetism, there was just a chance that he might achieve the seemingly impossible.

The following morning, Sunday, February 26th, Roger accompanied the Bertrands to nine o'clock Mass, at which Napoleon, his mother, sister and all the notables were present. Afterwards a procession of the Imperial carriages took the leading personalities, including Roger, up the hill to the Mulini and everyone else of any importance in Portoferraio followed on foot. The whole company was then received by the Emperor in the big room he had made on the first floor of the palace.

Three proclamations that had been printed during the night were read by Signor Traditi, the Mayor. They announced Napoleon's immediate departure and promised that he would ever have the well-being of his loyal Elbans at heart. Very few of those present had been made privy to his intentions, so the announcement met with some cheers to encourage him and other cries of lamentation—largely hypocritical—that they were to be deprived of his presence.

Wine was taken round, healths were drunk, then the civilians departed, leaving the officers of the Guard and other formations. Roger was presented by Bertrand to General Cambronne, the Commandant of Portoferraio, Colonel Mallet, who commanded the Guards, Colonel Jersmanowski, who commanded the Polish Lancers, Captain Paoli, who commanded the Elban gendarmerie, and a number of other senior officers; then the Emperor gave his orders to each of them.

The troops had not yet been let into the secret. They were at that moment partaking of their main Sunday meal. Afterwards they were to be told to prepare for immediate embarkation. In the event, it proved that a number of them, suspecting nothing, had already gone off with Elban wenches to picnic in the countryside, so had to be left behind.

The invasion flotilla had, meanwhile, assembled in Portoferraio harbour. The guns of the *Inconstant* had been increased from eighteen to twenty-six, the *Etoile* and *Saint Esprit* each had six. In addition, there were four large feluccas. At five o'clock the embarkation began. There were six hundred of the Old Guard, one hundred Poles with saddles but no horses, three hundred and fifty Elban militia and gendarmes and about one hundred others of various categories— roughly one thousand one hundred and fifty in all.

At seven o'clock Napoleon said an emotional farewell to *Madame Mère* and Pauline who, with the affection she had always shown her brother, on learning what was about to happen had swept all her jewels into a black leather box, and now gave them to him.

He then drove down to the harbour in her little low-wheeled pony carriage, at walking pace. Bertrand, Drouot, Peyrusse, Pons, Roger and the rest of the household marched behind. On the quay a small crowd of townsfolk had gathered. There were faint cheers as they went aboard the felucca *Caroline*, which took them out to *Inconstant*. She and the other six ships of the flotilla were all flying the flag Napoleon had designed for himself soon after arriving in Elba. It was an adaptation of the ancient standard of the Medici, with a stripe down the middle, and the initial N in wreaths, eagles and bees on it. As dusk fell, the expedition put to sea.

The night was fine, with bright moonlight, but windless; so the Emperor ordered the sweeps to be got out, and these were used until the ships were clear of the bay. Then, at about midnight a slight breeze sprang up, coming from the south, which enabled them to make better headway.

By eight o'clock the next morning they were south-east of the island of Capraia. H.M.S. *Partridge*, with Captain Campbell on board, was, they learned later, at that time lying becalmed off Leghorn, so they were in no danger from her. But the day was one of constant anxiety. Two French frigates, *Fleur-de-Lys* and *Malpomène*, were cruising off Capraia. They sighted both, and the frigates must have sighted them, but neither turned in their direction and challenged them.

Then, at four o'clock in the afternoon, they sighted a French brig sailing in a direction that would bring her right across *Inconstant*'s bows. Taillade recognized her as the *Zephyr*, and knew her to be commanded by a friend of his, Captain Andrieux. Hurriedly Napoleon ordered all his officers and the Guard to go below, then took cover himself beneath the poop, so that he could still tell Taillade what he wished done.

As the ships closed, they hailed each other. Andrieux said he was bound for Leghorn. At Napoleon's prompting, Taillade replied that he was making for Genoa. Had Andrieux seen the troops aboard, he would at once have jumped to the conclusion that Napoleon was escaping from Elba and would have gone into action. As it was, he assumed that *Inconstant* was on one of her frequent short voyages to the mainland, to pick up stores, so he only shouted through his loud-hailer, 'How is your great man?' To which Napoleon told Taillade to shout back, 'He is wonderfully well.'

Roger had been with the Emperor when, many
years before, as General Bonaparte, he had abandoned
his army in Egypt and run the gauntlet of the British
fleet in order to get back to France. In these very
waters they had sighted a British squadron, but it had
failed to take notice of them. Now he had again been
extremely lucky, as Captain Andrieux's suspicions
had obviously not been aroused by the fact that
Inconstant had been repainted to resemble a ship of
the Royal Navy and, owing to her greater speed, she
had left the six smaller ships of the flotilla far behind
below the horizon; for, had they been with her,
Andrieux could not have failed to realize that *Inconstant* was not making one of her normal, innocent
trips.

In order to give the smaller ships time to reach the
rendezvous on the French coast within a few hours of
Inconstant, the Emperor ordered a detour to be made in
the direction of Genoa. While on that course they
again suffered acute anxiety on sighting a French 74
ship-of-the-line, but once more fortune favoured
Napoleon. Presumably, taking *Inconstant* for a British
ship, the 74 ignored her.

On the morning of the 28th they sighted the Alps
inland from Savona; whereupon the Emperor conferred the Legion of Honour on Taillade and on every
man of the Guard who had seen four years' service,
and accompanied him to Elba. Poor Peyrusse had been
very seasick during the voyage and, in a high good
humour, Napoleon said to him, 'A glass of Seine
water will put you right, Monsieur le Trésorier,'
and added with superb confidence, 'We shall be in
Paris on March 20th, the King of Rome's birthday.'

That evening *Inconstant* was rejoined by the other
ships of the flotilla. Early next day they were off

Antibes. Instead of the Elban flag, the Emperor ordered the tricolour to be hoisted, and came on deck with a tricolour cockade in his hat. Another proclamation which had been secretly printed in Elba was then read to the troops. There were cheers and shouts of '*Vive l'Empereur*', but afterwards some of the officers expressed doubts about the possibility of conquering France with only one thousand men.

Napoleon replied to them, 'I can count on the whole Army. I have received addresses of welcome from many regiments. A revolution has already broken out in Paris, and a provisional government has been established.' All of which, Roger felt sure, was a tissue of lies. But it stilled the murmurings of the doubters. At one o'clock on March 1st, the vessels were all at anchor in Gulf Juan, and the debarkation began.

The Emperor's first act was to despatch Captain Lamouret with twenty-five Grenadiers to take over Antibes. They entered the town, but the Colonel commanding the garrison there proved loyal to King Louis. He promptly ordered the gates to be locked, so that the detachment could not escape from the town, confronted it with superior force and compelled Lamouret and his men to surrender.

When news of this initial setback reached Napoleon's staff there was general consternation. The Generals took it for granted that the Emperor would at once order a much larger force to attack Antibes and rescue Lamouret's contingent. But the town was walled, so considerable time and effort would have been required to force an entrance. In consequence, the Emperor overrode all protests, declaring that time meant everything. To achieve success not a moment must be lost in advancing on Paris, so Lamouret and his men were left to their fate.

G

Their abandonment gave Roger furiously to think.
Up to six months ago he had, for the greater part of
many years, led a dangerous but mainly enjoyable
life. He was still leading a dangerous life, but the
future, as a middle-aged man with little money and
dependant for most of that on someone else's goodwill,
held little prospect of enjoyment. In his worst periods
of depression he had felt that, rather than face such
a dreary existence, he would be better dead. Pain he
had always dreaded, but never death, because he
and Georgina had often discussed the subject of survival, and both were convinced believers in reincarnation. Therefore, for him, to die meant starting a new
life in due course, in a different body but with the
same personality, so might well be preferable to
living on, perhaps for many years, a prey to semi-
poverty and frustration.

Nevertheless, he had the normal man's instinct to
preserve his life. There was also always the chance that
some turn of fortune might better his situation and
provide him with a sufficient income to enjoy his
recently acquired earldom. In any case, he had no
intention of throwing away his life uselessly. Yet now,
it was borne in upon him that such a fate might well
overtake him.

Willy-nilly he had become involved in what, regarded logically, was a forlorn hope. If other commanders reacted to Napoleon's reappearance in France in
the same way as the Commandant of the Antibes
garrison had done, he would be killed or captured
within a matter of days, and there would not be an
earthly hope of his remounting the throne in Paris.
One thing seemed certain. The Marshals who had been
confirmed in their rank, honours and estates by King
Louis would side with him; for, if they did not and

the Emperor triumphed, he would have them court-martialled and shot as traitors.

That applied equally to Napoleon's adherents. If he was defeated, they could expect no mercy from the Bourbons. There was also the possibility that he might send Roger off on some mission and, if he was captured, abandon him as he had Lamouret. In such a case it would be useless for Roger to protest that it was only through force of circumstances that he had joined Napoleon, that he was in fact an Englishman and in the service of the Duke of Wellington. In France he had for so long been known as *le brave Breuc* that no-one would believe him. Weeks before the Duke in distant Vienna could confirm his story and secure his release he would have been put up against a brick wall and shot by a firing squad.

So when, at five o'clock that afternoon, Roger accompanied the Emperor ashore, it was with most gloomy forebodings.

13

The Road to Paris

TENTS were erected outside Antibes in a grove of
olive trees, but Napoleon did not allow his troops to
rest there for long. He needed no reminding of the
abuse and ill-treatment he had met with in the South
of France eleven months earlier, on his way into
exile; and, apart from being anxious to get away from
this hostile territory, he was determined to reach
Paris as soon as possible. In the early hours of the morning they were on the march along the coast, and a
few hours later entered the little township of Cannes.
From there the column turned inland up the winding
road to Grasse.

There, in the foothills of the Alps, it was bitterly
cold, snow still lay on the ground and the road ended.
Napoleon had expected it to continue, as plans to
extend it had been approved by him before his abdication; but, like many other matters, the Bourbons
had neglected to have the work carried out. To his
annoyance, this necessitated his having to abandon
his carriage and four cannon he had landed from
Inconstant. Throughout the day the Quartermaster had
been buying up all the horses they came upon, and a
number of the Poles were now mounted, providing
the Emperor with a small escort of cavalry, but ahead

lay only mountain paths. Pressing on along the icy, rock-strewn tracks for another fifteen miles they reached the village of Séranon. At last, after the terrible twenty-four hours' forced march, Napoleon ordered camp to be made and the exhausted troops were allowed a few hours' sleep.

There followed another two days' march up and down precipitous slopes and over passes, at times having an altitude of three thousand five hundred feet. With their heads bowed and their bearskins pulled right down over their ears the men tramped doggedly through blizzards. On the 4th they entered the little town of Digne. Here the Emperor received his first encouragement. The amazed inhabitants welcomed him with cheers. Elated by this reception, he produced his third proclamation, calling on the French army to join him.

By then the startling news that Napoleon had landed at Antibes was spreading through France like a prairie fire. It reached Paris on the 5th. The government there was not perturbed, as it seemed that so small a force could be dealt with easily. King Louis, as was his custom, shrugged off personal responsibility and sent a message to his Minister of War, now Marshal Soult, simply telling him to do whatever he might think necessary.

General Cambronne, with an advance guard, was some way ahead of Napoleon's main body. Early on the morning of the 7th the Emperor was wakened from a brief sleep in the village of Gap by a message from the General, to say that a battalion of the 5th Regiment of the Line was assembled, ready to attack them a few miles further north. Napoleon set off there at once. Having observed the position of the battalion, he sent an officer ahead to parley with its commander, a Major Delessart. The officer asked, 'Do you intend to oppose us?' The Major shouted back, 'Yes. I shall do my duty.'

The battalion was about seven hundred strong, whereas the Emperor had over one thousand men, the majority of whom were his 'old moustaches'; so, had this confrontation led to a conflict, there can be little doubt that Napoleon could have forced his way through the defile. But the last thing he wanted was bloodshed, for, almost certainly, it would have been the first spark to ignite civil war. In fact, such was his abhorrence of it that in the aftermath of the Revolution, when only a junior general, he had risked his whole career by evading an order to take command of an army despatched to La Vendée to suppress a rising there by the Royalist peasants under their Chouan leaders.

A matter that had caused him intense annoyance while in Elba had been reports reaching him from France that his surrender and ignominious journey into exile had been due to cowardice—a failing he had never been accused of in the field. To show that he was not a coward was, he claimed, one of his main reasons for invading France with all the odds against him. Now he performed an act that demonstrated forever that he possessed supreme bravery.

Having drawn up his Guards, he ordered the tricolour to be unfurled and their band to play the *Marseillaise*, that immortal marching song of the Revolution and the Empire, sung by the French troops on their way to victory from one end of Europe to the other, yet forbidden by the Bourbons since the Restoration. He then rode forward, dismounted and walked to within fifty feet of the soldiers from Grenoble. Their muskets were raised and trained on him. A young Captain named Randon gave the order to his men, 'Fire.'

For a moment there was utter silence in the valley. Every man on both sides held his breath. Roger was no exception, and was torn by conflicting emotions. He had spent so many years in Napoleon's company, witnessed so many acts of kindness, forbearance and generosity by him that he could not bear the thought of seeing him fall, riddled by bullets, never again to laugh, exercise his quick wit and receive homage for his genius. Yet he knew that he deserved death for the countless thousands of other men he had sent to their deaths, solely for the gratification of his own insatiable self-glorification; and that, if he survived, thousands more would surely die in battles yet to come.

As the order to fire rang out, Napoleon halted, grasped the lapels of his grey greatcoat, threw it open to reveal his white waistcoat and cried in a loud voice:

'If you wish to kill your Emperor, here I am!'

Instantly a soldier in the front rank threw down his musket; others followed suit and there rang out a great shout, '*Vive l'Empereur! Vive l'Empereur!*'

There followed a scene of joyous confusion. The soldiers from Grenoble broke ranks and rushed forward, cheering madly, to embrace Napoleon and fraternize with the Guard, waving their shakos, firing their muskets in the air, tearing off the white cockades they wore to trample them underfoot and replacing them with the old tricolour ones which they had long treasured in their haversacks.

At last order was restored and the march resumed. That evening a vedette of the Polish Lancers galloped back to the Emperor, to tell him they had sighted a strong column of troops approaching. Napoleon deployed his men in battle formation. With bated breath they waited to learn whether this would prove the end, or if the sight of the Emperor would again have the magical effect of bringing another formation of King Louis's army over to him.

Again there came the confrontation. These troops from Grenoble were the 7th Regiment of the Line, commanded by Colonel de Labédoyère. Halting his men, he advanced alone, carrying a drum, toward Napoleon. He then smashed in the top of the drum as a sign of surrender, and handed the regimental colours to Napoleon. Again there were deafening shouts of 'Vive l'Empereur' from the troops, and joyous fraternization.

Now, with nearly four thousand men devoted to his cause, the Emperor advanced on the walled city of Grenoble, arriving before it at nine o'clock that evening.

Inside there was a strong garrison and a considerable number of cannon. As Napoleon had no artillery, it is doubtful if he could have taken it had a determined resistance been put up; but here it was the farmers and townsfolk who came to his aid. News of his approach had gone before him. Two thousand of them went up on to the ramparts, restrained the soldiers from firing, waved torches and greeted him with shouts of welcome. He called on the Commander of the garrison to open the gates, but the officer refused. The people then smashed down a gate from inside and, to wild cheers, Napoleon rode through the streets to the Trois Dauphins hostelry, where the excited citizens carried him upstairs to the best bedroom.

The next obstacle to be overcome was the great city of Lyons. By this time intelligence had come in about the situation in Paris. King Louis and his Court were still not seriously worried. Every Marshal, with the one exception of Davout, had gone over to the Bourbons, and had been awarded the Grand Cross of the Order of St. Louis. A few had gone into retirement, but Marmont, Berthier, Ney, Macdonald, Augereau, Suchet, St. Cyr, Masséna, Oudinot, Mortier and Soult were all still on the active list. At the time of the abdication several of them had endorsed Ney's statement that the troops would no longer take orders from the Emperor, only from their officers. How then, argued the Bourbons, could the Corsican usurper, with only a few battalions behind him, possibly defeat the armies commanded by these paladins?

Soult, as Minister of War, directed all the readily available artillery to be concentrated in the neighbourhood of Lyons, and *Monsieur,* the King's brother, Charles d'Artois, was given command of a considerable army, to kill or capture Napoleon and his handful of troops. D'Artois was accompanied by Marshal Macdonald, to advise him, and they reached Lyons with three regiments of the line, plus one thousand five hundred National Guards.

On March 10th, Napoleon arrived before the city. That morning Macdonald had assembled his troops in the Place Bellecour. After addressing them in a rousing speech, he called on them to show their loyalty by shouting *'Vive le Roi!'* Not a single man complied. Glumly, in the pouring rain, d'Artois inspected the troops. As he did so, catcalls and abuse were hurled at him by citizens looking on from the windows round the big square. Napoleon had always been popular in Lyons, because it was he who had started the silk industry there that had made the city so prosperous. The silence of the troops and the hostility of the people proved too much for d'Artois. A quarter of an hour later he had jumped into his travelling berlin and was being driven hell for leather back to Paris.

That night, after receiving a great ovation, Napoleon slept in the Archepiscopal palace which, before his abdication, had been the official residence of his mother's half-brother, Cardinal Fesch. But, as Roger moved about among the excited crowds celebrating in the streets, he had reason to take an ominous view of future possibilities. There were frequent shouts of 'To the guillotine with the Bourbons,' and 'Let's burn those fat pigs of priests!'—

This put a new aspect on the reception given to Napoleon by the people of Grenoble and Lyons. They were not welcoming back the Emperor as a person, much less the war lord who had deluged Europe in blood. Their cheers were for a symbol about which to rally, in order that they might drive out the Bourbons who, in less than a year, had made themselves so hated by reviving the oppression of the *ancien régime*. It was from the Revolution that Napoleon had emerged, and they were envisaging another, in which in the name of freedom they could despoil the rich, desecrate the churches and murder masters whom they felt had ill-used them.

Napoleon also soon realized this, and became acutely aware that if he allowed himself to be carried back to power as the figurehead of anarchist mobs, that power would be short-lived. He would find himself subservient to a committee of Jacobins. To counteract that possibility, he promptly issued a series of proclamations, calculated to assert himself and reassure the upper classes, yet retain the support of the workers. He declared himself Emperor, but appeased the democrats by summoning the 'electoral colleges', abolished feudal titles and confiscated the estates of the Bourbon Princes. Then he again set off for Paris, now at the head of fourteen thousand men.

Meanwhile, Marshal Ney, Prince de la Moskwa and Duc d'Elchingen, had assembled an army at Besançon, and had boasted to the King that he would 'bring Napoleon back to Paris in an iron cage'.

During the retreat from Moscow, Ney had made his name immortal by performing prodigies of valour. Yet, as a result of that terrible campaign, his mentality had undergone a change. Previously he had cared nothing for honours, titles, money and displayed no interest in politics. His sole desire had been to acquire glory. Since then his mind had become more and more concerned about the damage that unending war was inflicting on the French people. It was he who had led the other Marshals at Fontainebleau the previous April to defy the Emperor, refuse to fight further, and insist on Napoleon's abdication. Now, it seemed, it was his conviction that Napoleon's return would lead to further war that made him fanatically determined to oppose him.

On the night of March 13th Ney was staying at the Sign of the Golden Apple in Lons-le-Saunier. For several days past he had been exhorting his troops to remain loyal to the King and pay no heed to the peasant proprietors along the wayside, who openly displayed their joy at the news that Napoleon had returned to France. He had need to do so, for one of his regiments had already deserted and there were many men among the others who took little trouble to conceal that at heart they had always remained Bonapartists.

During this night in March, Ney suffered an appalling mental conflict. Should he keep the solemn oath of allegiance he had sworn to Louis XVIII, or should he return to the service of the usurper under whom he had won so much glory?

Only the previous day he had declared, 'Bonaparte is a wild beast, a mad dog upon whom one must throw oneself in order to avoid its bite.' Later it was said that, during the night, an officer had secretly brought him a letter from General Bertrand, written by the order of Napoleon, appealing to him to abandon the cause of the King. Be that as it may, his second-in-command, General Bourmont, had brought to him Baron Cappelle, the Prefect of the Ain, who came with the news that Lyons had gone over to the Emperor. He then talked for two hours with Generals Bourmont and Lecourbe, both devoted Loyalists.

Everyone knew that Ney's attitude would almost certainly prove decisive. If he ordered his men to fire upon Napoleon and they did so, it would be the signal for civil war, and the Emperor's few thousand men would be overwhelmed by the tens of thousands under officers who had taken the oath of loyalty to the Bourbons. But, if Ney abjured his oath, who else would dare oppose the advance of the Corsican?

On the morning of the 14th Ney assembled his men, called his senior officers round him and took a paper from his pocket. Sitting his horse, in his brilliant uniform, he made a splendid figure. Among the men he was called *le Rougeaud*, on account of the mass of copper-red curls which crowned his head, the side-whiskers coming right down his cheeks and his red face, now sadly haggard. Lifting the paper, he read in the clarion voice that had rallied thousands of men on the battlefield:

'Officers, non-commissioned officers and men. The Bourbon cause is lost for ever . . . '

His next words were drowned in a storm of frantic

cheering. The troops broke ranks, tore the white cockade from their hats and surged round him, yelling their unbounded joy at his declaration. It was many minutes before he could continue to read out the speech he had written in the early hours of that morning:

'*The legitimate dynasty which the French nation has adopted is about to reascend the throne. It is the Emperor Napoleon alone to whom the duty belongs of ruling over our fair land.*

'*Whether the Bourbons and their nobility exile themselves or consent to live in our midst, of what matter to us? The sacred cause of our liberty and our independence will suffer no longer from their baneful influence. They have sought to debase, to wipe out our military glory, but they have been unable to do so. . . .*'

These were the sentiments enshrined in the hearts of ninety-nine out of every hundred men in the Army. Only a small group of senior officers stood about the Marshal, silent, thunderstruck and appalled by this sudden *volte-face* from Ney's boasts that he would bring Napoleon to Paris in an iron cage. One old Colonel, the Comte de Grivel, broke his sword across his knee, others refused to break their oath and asked to be relieved of their commands. Ney accepted their resignations.

The parade dissolved, the people of Lons mingled with the troops, delirious with joy, shouting '*Vive l'Empereur*', and toasting him in gulps of brandy poured freely from the casks carried by the *vivandières*. Ney had thrown himself from his horse, embraced the nearest of his men and danced with them in wild abandon.

That evening at the Golden Apple he entertained his senior officers and staff to a magnificent supper.

The choicest dishes and the finest wines were served to his fifteen guests. From outside the hotel could be heard the drunken shouts of the soldiers and poorer citizens, celebrating in a saturnalia the anticipated downfall of the hated Bourbons; but inside there was no laughter and only halting conversation. The Prefect of the Jura had bluntly told Ney that he held his office from the King, and could not serve two masters. When the Marshal, his face drawn and blotched, proposed the health of the Emperor, his supper guests rose out of courtesy and drank the toast, but without enthusiasm. His favourite A.D.C., Levavasseur, bitterly reproached him and warned him that, in spite of what he had done, Napoleon would never forgive him for his conduct at Fontainebleau. He replied that he had had no alternative, since to have attacked Napoleon would have started a civil war. He then added a sentence that revealed all the pent-up bitterness felt by the Bonapartist nobility for the slights put upon them by the ancient aristocracy of France. His wife was a lovely creature, but the daughter of a chamber-maid.

'I can no longer bear,' he snapped, 'to see my wife return home in tears from the insults put upon her by those *émigré* women at the Tuileries.' And that perhaps discloses the fundamental reason why Ney had that afternoon sent his submission to his old master.

By that day, the 14th, Napoleon was in Mâcon. A number of his adherents had gone ahead of him. Over posters issued by the government, calling upon the people to remain loyal to the King, they had pasted copies of the Emperor's proclamation issued on the 1st at Golf Juan. It read:

Frenchmen, in my exile I heard your laments and your prayers; you demanded the government of your choice, which

alone is legitimate. You blamed my long sleep, you re-
proached me for sacrificing to my repose the great concerns
of our motherland. I have crossed the seas amid perils of
every kind. I arrive among you to resume my rights, which
are your own.

The wind was cold, patches of snow still lay on the
fields and there were gusts of chilly rain; but that did
not prevent the citizens of Mâcon from giving the
returned exile a tremendous welcome. Five regiments
of infantry and the 5th Hussars, coming from Moulins
and Bourg, had mutinied and were pouring into
Mâcon to fight for him. There were also scores of small
groups or single junior officers and N.C.O.s who had
deserted from other units there displaying their passionate devotion to Napoleon.

Leaving the bulk of his now considerable force
behind, he pressed on through Tournus to the big town
of Chalon. When approaching the gates, he saw a
line of vehicles along one side of the road. As he came
nearer, he realized that they were guns and limbers,
and was told by soldiers who had run out of the town
to greet him that this was the artillery sent to be used
against his men, but they had confiscated it and it was
now his.

At Chalon he slept for a few hours at the Hôtel du
Parc, but was up again before dawn on March 15th
and off in his carriage, with only a small escort. As
protection in front of him he had now only General
Brayer, with the 13th Regiment of Dragoons. Brayer
had come over to him at Lyons and, as a reward, had
been given the advance guard. When Napoleon
reached Autun, he found that the General had already
taken it. There, as in other towns, he cynically accepted
the homage of the Royalist-appointed Mayor; then he
received from Baron Passings a despatch written by

Ney, declaring his adherence. Overjoyed, the Emperor sent the Baron back with the message:

'My friend, keep your command. Set all your troops on the march right away, and come and join me at Auxerre. I shall receive you as on the morrow of Elchingen and Moscow.'

On the 16th he sped on to Avallon, along roads beside which there were cheering groups of small landowners who had come many miles to see him pass. From there, having covered fifty miles in a day, he reached Auxerre. In the town that morning a General Ameil, who commanded the light cavalry, had declared for the Emperor, but the Royalist General, Boudin de Roville, promptly had him arrested. By evening the picture had changed. The Prefect, Monsieur Gamot, read a proclamation to General Boudin which he had just written, heartily welcoming the Emperor. Jeered by his troops, the unhappy Boudin mounted his horse and, abandoning his wife and children, galloped off along the road to Paris, while Ameil was released and fêted.

The plaudits of the troops and people in the towns through which Napoleon had ridden would have turned most men's heads; but, having arrived in Auxerre, he took serious stock of his situation, based on the information he was now receiving from many quarters.

He had made a triumphant progress through southwestern France, but Marshal Masséna, who commanded in Marseilles, had now closed the whole coast of Provence, making retreat impossible, and had also sent an army in pursuit of him. Bordeaux had always been a Royalist city and, at this moment, the troops there were virtually commanded by that bitter, pious woman, the Duchess d'Angoulême, who would cheerfully have seen him crucified. Her husband was in Nîmes, organizing an army for the reconquest of the towns that had welcomed the invader. In central France the Duc de Bourbon commanded a strong force at Angers, and in Normandy there was another army commanded by Marshal Augereau, whom he had denounced as a traitor for surrendering Lyons to the Austrians. In addition, Marshals Marmont and Macdonald, now his inveterate enemies, were both in Paris mustering yet another army to bar his way to the capital. With amazing rapidity he had succeeded in being accepted by a considerable part of the population, and some twenty thousand troops had rallied to his colours; but he still had four-fifths of France to subdue.

The almost unceasing shouts of *'Vive l'Empereur'* along the way had greatly heartened him, and he continued to declare, with unshakeable optimism, that he would be master of Paris by the 20th; but he had yet either to suborn or defeat the army gathering outside it, which would be officered by the hard core of the Royalists. He believed he would succeed in that, but another matter was causing him far greater concern.

In every town through which he had passed, he had been received by country people, workers and troops as a 'liberator'; but that had not proved at all the case with the officials. Many of them had fled on his approach, or come reluctantly to him with hypo-critical excuses for having accepted from the Bourbons posts as Prefects or Mayors. It had been the same with most of the senior officers. And the better-off citizens in the towns had not joined the cheering mobs. Many of them were National Guards, and they had remained in their houses.

He had for too long been the all-powerful Emperor to enjoy having rough soldiers and toil-stained workers shake him vigorously by the hand, pat him on the back and embrace him. From long habit he had become fastidiously clean. The smell of stale sweat revolted him, and he had never had any liking for the common people. Yet it was they, not the educated and well-to-do, who looked upon him as their champion. Again and again he had heard them yelling, 'Death to the aristos! Burn the priests! Throw out the Bourbons! Down with the rich! Long live the people!'

The majority of them had lived through the Revolution. It was he who had restored law and order and, by his skilful measures, gradually forced them again into servitude as the underdogs who provided cannon fodder and paid heavy taxes. By bringing glory to France he had duped them into accepting him as a despot. Yet they had clearly forgotten that, and now hailed him again as the young Revolutionary general. It was not to play that role that he had returned, but once more to sit on his throne in the Tuileries, surrounded by pomp and splendour.

Now his problem was to control the mobs, prevent them from starting a new Terror and protect the wealthy and the middle classes upon whom the prosperity of France depended. The answer lay in Paris. Somehow he must secure the support of men there who had held office under him in the past, and had influence with the people.

It was at Auxerre that he called Roger into his room and said to him:

'Breuc, so far things have gone excellently. Not a shot fired, and now that Ney has come over to us I greatly doubt if there will be. The troops who have acclaimed me come from every part of France, so they are a fair sample of the feeling throughout the whole army. I am told that the Bourbons are massing many formations to bar my path to the capital. The attempt will prove futile. The troops will either lay down their arms, or turn them on those young *émigré* popinjays who have been made officers.'

'You are right, Sire,' Roger agreed. 'While you reigned, any private could hope to end his days as a Duke and a Marshal of the Empire; but under the Bourbons, however brave, he could not hope to become even a Second Lieutenant. And, under them no junior officer can hope to reach high command unless he comes from a noble family. This insane return to pre-revolutionary custom has given you back the Army—lock, stock and barrel.'

'It has. And the workers and small proprietors are for me, too. But the fools seem to think that I shall abolish all taxes. They haven't the sense to realize that one cannot run a country without money.

'Now, to come to the point. I am most averse to entering Paris as King of the Mob. In no time I should find myself reduced to chairman of a revived Committee of Public Safety, and we'd have the guillotine at work again. Most regrettably, judging by the towns through which we have passed, the middle classes are opposed to me. They fear I shall start new wars which will end by our enemies again invading France; and, as happened last year, Cossacks and Prussians being billeted on them, getting drunk, smashing up their furniture, stealing their valuables and raping their women.

'But I have done with war. I intend to reign henceforth as a liberal monarch, giving equal opportunity to all, but protecting those who have money from lawlessness and disorder. This must be made known, and proclamations are not enough. It is necessary to convince a dozen or so really influential people. To do so I need your help.'

Roger raised his eyebrows. 'Willing as I am to give it, Sire, I fail to see how I could influence anyone.'

'Oh yes, you can. You know everyone of importance in Paris, and I wish you to go there. Although you have not served the Bourbons, you have a clean slate with them because, at the time of my abdication, you were one of the Czar's people, and living in Talleyrand's mansion. You will not, of course, let it be known that you came to Elba. You can tell the truth about having spent the last eleven months in retirement, at that little château of yours near St. Maxime. You could easily have been noticed there by some of my people, and felt that discretion was the better part of valour, so decided to join me temporarily. Naturally, as one of my old A.D.C.s, during the past fortnight we should have had many talks together. Say that, having arrived within easy distance of Paris, you made up your mind to leave me and find out how things were going there. You will give the impression that you still have an open mind on the question of my restoration, as must be the case with hundreds of other men there who served me in the past. But your position will differ from theirs, because you have had the opportunity of learning my intentions. Without committing yourself, you can reassure them. Tell them that I mean to issue an amnesty to all who went over to the Bourbons, so they have nothing to fear; that I will make war no more and, given the support of the Chambers, will be in a position to prevent the Jacobins from initiating another reign of terror.'

Smiling, Roger willingly agreed to do as he had been

asked, said he would set off at once, and bowed his way from the room.

Nothing could have suited him better than this mission which he had so unexpectedly been given. In the early days of the landing he had several times contemplated deserting; but the extraordinary enthusiasm with which Napoleon's arrival had been greeted in town after town had led him to believe the Corsican's mad venture would succeed, and that if it did his own future prospects would be immeasurably better than they had been when he left Vienna. He would again be high in favour and in receipt of a handsome income. In Paris only Talleyrand's intimates knew that he had been to Vienna. To others he could tell the story he had told Napoleon—that he had been living in retirement at St. Maxime. This was a marvellous chance to hedge his bet. Should Napoleon's bid to regain his throne fail after all, the Comte de Breuc would appear only to have played a part in it until he had an opportunity to desert; so at least he would escape the vengeance of the Bourbons.

By riding hard and stopping only to eat and rest at Sens and Melun, he reached Paris early on the following afternoon. Along the road and in the towns, he had encountered small bodies of troops, but it was not until he came to Melun that he met with any large formations, so it was evidently in that neighbourhood that the Royalists meant to make their stand in defence of the capital. As he was still wearing the civilian clothes in which he had left Vienna, no-one halted him, and to those who eagerly questioned him in the inns where he stopped, he replied that he had come from Chinon—which was far to the south of the route being taken by Napoleon—so he knew nothing of the movements of the invaders.

The attitude of the troops through which he had ridden that morning had convinced him that the chances of their standing and fighting for the Bourbons were almost non-existent; so he had decided to carry out Napoleon's instructions and reap the benefit of gaining a few important adherents for him.

In Paris he rode straight to Talleyrand's mansion and asked for the Marquis de Jaucourt, one of the Prince's cronies and deputy Foreign Minister, whom he had left in charge of his office and establishment there. Within a few minutes he was shown into the Marquis's cabinet, where he was working on some papers. He rose at once, welcomed Roger as an old friend, and asked, 'What news from Vienna and of our Prince?'

Tired and dusty, Roger sank into a chair, then replied, 'I do not come from there, but from Bonaparte, whom I left last night in Auxerre.'

'The devil you did,' exclaimed de Jaucourt. 'Whatever were you doing . . . ? But that can wait. Is it really true that in every town he enters, the mob goes mad with joy at the sight of him, and that the troops are deserting to him by the thousand?'

'It is. So far not a shot has been fired, and from the coast it has been one long triumphant progress. Now that Ney has defected and gone over . . .'

'What!' The Marquis gave a gasp of amazement and consternation. 'Ney defected! And the King set such high hopes on him. This is indeed a setback.'

'It trebles Bonaparte's chances. As I was about to say, he vows he'll be in Paris by the 20th and, short of a miracle, I believe he will.'

'God help us! I had no idea things were as bad as this. But tell me, how comes it that you were in the South of France when he landed?'

'I was at my little château there, near St. Maxime. But how I got caught up in this affair is a long story, and must wait till later. I have ridden all night, so am desperate fatigued. I've taken our Prince at his word, that there is always a bed for me here, and am eager to get to it.'

'Of course. You are most welcome. I'll order one to be prepared for you without delay.' The Marquis took up the bell on the desk and rang it for a footman. Then he added, 'I would to God Bonaparte had broken his neck in Elba or drowned on the way over. His return could be worse than a visitation of the plague; for, if he does get to Paris, it will result in the death of thousands more soldiers.'

Roger shook his head. 'I judge you wrong there. I had several long talks with him and, believe me, he is a changed man. His only wish now is to regain his throne, rule as a liberal monarch and work to preserve a lasting peace for the people. Soon after I met him, he told me that the Congress of Vienna had broken up and the Czar, having quarrelled with the others, gone off in a huff; so there is no likelihood of their again combining against him. With Marie Louise as his Empress, the Austrians will give him no trouble, and he plans to adopt the policy that our Prince has favoured in secret for so many years—an alliance with England.'

With a little laugh, de Jaucourt said, 'Luckily for us all, this is naught but moonshine. He was wrongly informed about the Congress. 'Tis true that Russia and Prussia were at daggers drawn with Austria and England when the news that Bonaparte had left Elba reached Vienna on March 7th. But the Congress had not broken up. The news was received with the utmost consternation. They thought he had gone to

Italy, but by now will know that he is in France. In any case, the Allies at once agreed that, in the face of this new menace, they must continue in conference and devise measures to meet it. I had a despatch from our Prince only yesterday. It was he who persuaded them to sink their differences, and he now has every hope of renewing the Grand Alliance. Have no illusions, Breuc. If Bonaparte does succeed in reaching Paris, he'll not have regained his throne for long. Whether you are right or not about his pacific intentions, the Allies will drive him from it by unremitting war.'

14

Of Hedging Bets

DE JAUCOURT was a dyed-in-the wool Royalist, so
Roger's account of Napoleon's good prospects and intentions had not been given with the least thought of
changing his outlook; but the news that the Congress
of Vienna was still in session came to him as a great
surprise. On the road from the coast he had, on several
occasions, heard the Emperor tell officers and func-
tionaries who had come over to him that the English
had connived at his escape from Elba and that he had
been secretly in communication with his father-in-
law, the Emperor of Austria, who favoured his return.

Having long known Napoleon to be the most unscrupulous of liars whenever his own interests were concerned, Roger had had grave doubts about both asser-
tions; but he had taken it for granted that the Emperor
had reliable agents in Vienna, so it had not even
occurred to him to question the statement that the
Congress had broken up, and he had personal knowledge that the four Great Powers had split into two
bitterly hostile camps.

With a puzzled frown, he said, 'When I left Vienna,
Metternich and the Czar were hardly even on speaking
terms, although some progress had been made on the
Polish and Saxon questions. That they should have
buried the hatchet overnight and are about to enter

into a new alliance positively amazes me.'

The Marquis smiled. 'Yet it is so; and, of course, 'tis due to the brilliant handling of this new situation by our Prince. To have allowed Bonaparte again to occupy the throne of France would have brought to naught all he has laboured for so consistently these many years.'

Roger needed no telling what Talleyrand's attitude would have been nor of his extraordinary powers of persuasion. Thoughtfully, he said, 'If the Alliance holds, it must lead to Bonaparte's inevitable defeat. But there is no guarantee that it will. The Czar has become a dual personality. He will agree to a thing one day, and violently repudiate it the next. Bonaparte's intentions are now pacific, and all the other nations are heartily sickened of war, so once he is back on the throne, he may well succeed in splitting the alliance and preventing a renewal of hostilities. And I'll wager any money that, within the week, he will be issuing his orders from the Tuileries. Tell me, now, how are things going there?'

'At first they were entirely complacent and felt sure they had nothing to fear. Then, as news came in that Bonaparte was meeting with no opposition and that Lyons had opened its gates to him, they did become quite concerned. But, as you know, the King is incurably lazy and quite incapable of personal leadership. He leaves everything to his favourites: that fool de Blacas, who does his utmost to prevent anyone speaking to the King unless he is present, the reactionary de Vitrolles, who acts as the highly persuasive mouthpiece of the Comte d'Artois, and the Abbé Montesquiou, who is not content with his job of Minister of the Interior and would really like to be the leader of a Liberal Government.

'As you can imagine, they all quarrel like a gaggle of old washerwomen, and give contrary advice, to which that monstrously fat King of ours listens while reclining with his feet on a gout stool. But all he does is to nod his head without agreeing to take the advice of any of them. He treats our veterans, Berthier and Marmont in the same way, and the other night when Marshal Macdonald paid a surreptitious visit to the Tuileries, he fared no better. As he had just come hotfoot with d'Artois from having abandoned Lyons to Bonaparte, he went there in civilian clothes, so as to be less readily recognized. When he asked the monarch where he wished to retire should we have to abandon Paris, all the reply he got was "My dear Duc de Taranto, we have not come to that yet." '

With a slight shrug, Roger remarked, 'What you tell me confirms my impression that Bonaparte will meet with little organized resistance before he is again master of Paris.'

'I would not be too certain about that. Yesterday morning, the twelve legions of the National Guard were paraded in the Place Vendôme, and inspected by their Colonel-in-Chief, d'Artois. They gave him a really rousing reception and, although they are under no obligation to leave the city, at his appeal many of them volunteered to form special companies which would march out and assist in repelling Bonaparte.'

'Oh come, Monsieur le Marquis! What use as soldiers are the National Guard? They are honest bourgeoisie, the majority of whom are middle-aged and incapable of marching five miles carrying full war equipment, let alone forming square and resisting a cavalry charge.'

'You forget that nearly all of them are old soldiers who fought in Bonaparte's campaigns, and I am sure you underestimate the opposition he will meet from the people as a whole. Futile as the King is, they recognize his goodness, and that as long as he reigns there will be no war. I assure you the great majority of the Parisians are loyal to him. Had you been here yesterday afternoon, you would have had ample proof of that from their behaviour.'

'What took place then?'

'His Majesty crossed the Seine to the Palais Bourbon, and there addressed the combined Assemblies. In spite of the fact that it was pouring with rain, the streets were lined with people and although, contrary to his custom, he was an hour late, they gave him a tremendous ovation. The ceremony, too, was most impressive. Twenty Peers and twenty Deputies received him at the doors of the palace. His two best friends, de Blacas and the Duc du Duras, supported him to the throne, and he made a truly touching speech. Afterwards d'Artois, d'Orléans and the other Princes ran forward, fell on their knees before him and kissed his hands. To a man the Peers and Deputies renewed their oaths of allegiance to him. Some of them even burst into tears and, remember, many of them were Senators who had been the leaders of the people in the old days of the Revolution.'

Again Roger shrugged. 'You do not surprise me, in view of all that these people stand for. Many of the Peers are *émigrés* and have everything to lose. The majority, whatever their pasts, are now solid citizens with wealth and property, who fear that Bonaparte's hope of restoration is based on the power of the mob and that his coming will bring about a return to anarchy. Yet I'll wager that most of them will alter their tune when they realize that he is a changed man and wishes only to right the wrongs that many sections of the community have suffered at the hands of the Bourbons. I'll also wager that there are many officials in the present government who served Napoleon in the past, and are still Bonapartists at heart.'

'That may be so. But measures have been taken to render the most important of them harmless. The King can be credited with at least one shrewd gesture. On the 13th he decided to re-create the office of Prefect of Police, and fill it with a man well acquainted with such influential people who would support Bonaparte. For the post he selected Bourrienne, and he could hardly have made a better choice.'

Roger's expression remained unchanged, but this unexpected news came as a most welcome surprise to him. For many years Fauvelet de Bourrienne had been one of his closest friends. He felt confident that he could get from him in his new post more accurate information than by talking to a score of other acquaintances. After a moment he said:

'You are right. Few people have better cause to hate Bonaparte, or know more about his old friends who deserted him only to save their own necks.'

De Jaucourt smiled, 'And you may be sure he is losing no time in arresting them.'

Smothering a yawn, Roger stood up. 'I see now that you have good reason for your belief that, on arriving here, Bonaparte will not receive the support he expects. But, Monsieur le Marquis, I am dog-tired. I pray you to excuse me so that I can get a few hours' sleep.'

'By all means.' The Marquis, too, stood up. 'I am sorry not to have your company for dinner, but we'll talk again tomorrow. In the meantime, pray do not hesitate to ask for anything you want.'

In the room that had been prepared for him, Roger went straight to bed, well satisfied with his situation.

He had come to Paris on the Emperor's orders, so anything he might do or say there could later be attributed to his having been secretly working in Napoleon's interests. As against that, having taken advantage of Talleyrand's standing invitation to stay at his mansion whenever he was in Paris, he had reaffirmed de Jaucourt's belief that he was in the Royalist camp. This meant that, if Napoleon did triumph, Roger would be able to live honoured and wealthy in France; but, should he fail, Roger would be covered for accompanying Napoleon on the first part of his journey as he had gone to Elba by Wellington's order, and de Jaucourt would vouch for his activities in Paris.

Freed from all worry by having hedged his bets so satisfactorily, Roger slept solidly for six hours. When he woke he ordered some sandwiches and a bottle of wine to be sent up to him, then made a picnic meal while he shaved and dressed. Soon after ten o'clock, he went out and made his way to the Ministry of Police.

De Bourrienne's career was common knowledge. He had been one of the very few friends Bonaparte had made when they were cadets together in the Military College at Brienne. But, instead of going into the Army, Bourrienne had become a diplomat. When the Revolution had developed into the Terror, he had been *en poste* in Stuttgart. The Committee of Public Safety had recalled him. As an aristocrat he had known that, if he returned to Paris, he would be sent to the guillotine, so he had resigned his post and remained in Germany.

In 1797, after Napoleon's first triumphant campaign in Italy, he had recalled this clever friend of his youth, and written offering him the post of *Chef de Cabinet* on his staff, with immunity as an *émigré*. Bourrienne had accepted, and had more than proved his worth. In addition to having a much wider knowledge of international affairs than his master, he spoke six languages and could write a type of shorthand with such speed that, even in a coach travelling fast over rough roads, he could take down despatches as fast as Napoleon could talk.

For eight years he had been constantly with Napoleon, and his right-hand man. Then, in 1805, it had emerged that he had been unsuccessfully speculating with public funds. Napoleon had dismissed him, but later relented to the extent of appointing him Governor of Hamburg. In 1813 it had come to the Emperor's knowledge that he had made a great fortune by selling licences to import goods from abroad to the detriment of the blockade imposed by the Continental System. He had then been recalled and finally disgraced.

During the years that Bourrienne had been Napoleon's *Chef de Cabinet*, Roger had, on many occasions, been deputed to act as his assistant, so he knew the inside story of Bourrienne's offences. He had received no regular salary, but been told by Napoleon to draw what he required from the cash in hand and, in view of the fact that the Marshals and Generals were making immense fortunes by looting half the cities in Europe, he could not be greatly blamed for seeking to acquire sufficient capital to ensure a comfortable old age. Regarding Hamburg, in spite of the Emperor's fanatical desire to ruin Britain's trade by his Continental System, he had found himself compelled to allow the issue of licences to import certain essentials, and Bourrienne was only one of many officials who had made fortunes by also granting licences for non-essentials. So, while Bourrienne was unquestionably guilty of fraudulent transactions, Roger regarded him as no more culpable than hundreds of other civilians

or soldiers, who had consistently acquired illicit wealth
while serving Napoleon. Moreover, when Roger had
escaped from prison in Berlin and reached Hamburg,
it was Bourrienne who had got him out of Germany by
secretly arranging a safe passage to England for him.

In consequence, when he was shown up to the private
apartments of the Prefect of Police, he was received with
surprise and delight. The two old friends embraced
affectionately, Bourrienne produced a bottle of fine
sillery and glasses, and they happily sat down to talk.

Apart from the fact that Roger had always been a
British agent, he had no secrets from Bourrienne and
Bourrienne had none at all from him, so they discussed
the situation with complete frankness. Having told
Bourrienne how he had come with Napoleon from the
South of France, Roger ended by saying:

'And now, *cher ami*, to the first purpose of my visit.
In spite of what some people here appear to think, I've
not the least doubt that, within the next few days, the
little Corsican will again be back in the Tuileries. He
already counts you among his enemies, and having
become old Louis's Prefect of Police could cost you
your head. So, if you wish to save it, the sooner you
quit Paris, the better.'

Bourrienne laughed. 'Believe me, I'm most grateful
for your warning, but it was unnecessary. My bags are
packed and I'm ready to go at whatever I judge to be
the right moment.'

'When do you reckon that will be?'

'Perhaps tomorrow, when it will become generally
known that Ney has defected. If not, when the King
takes fright. But I must not be seen to run away before
Louis and the rest of them take to their heels. You see,
in view of the Allies having again become united in
Vienna, I regard it as certain that within a few months

Napoleon will again be defeated, and Louis put back on his throne. That is why I accepted this post. From Napoleon I can expect nothing; but, by having openly sided with the Bourbons, I shall stand well with them on their return.'

'I congratulate you on your foresight,' Roger smiled. 'But, *mon ami*, it is quite possible that Napoleon will succeed in dividing the Allies and be accepted by them in his new guise of a peaceful, constitutional monarch. The patronage of the Bourbons will be of little value to you then. Still, by playing your cards as you have, you have nothing to lose. Meanwhile, I take it you are busying yourself putting our old colleagues into prison?'

Bourrienne returned the smile. 'I was handed a list of twenty-odd people to arrest, among them Davout, Fouché, Savary, Marat, Lavalette, Syèyes and Excelmans. As you have remarked, there is always the possibility that Napoleon may succeed in coming to terms with the Powers who threaten to crush him. If that occurred, it might prove of value if I had some of his best friends under an obligation to me. So I pulled in only a few of the less important ones and gave the others a chance to go to earth; although, of course, I had to make a show of endeavouring to secure them. The King was particularly anxious to have Fouché behind bars, but I was equally anxious not to put him there, so I evaded the issue by a rather skilful little ruse.

'My appointment was made late at night, and during the Restoration the office had been allowed to lapse; so I made out the warrant to the effect that 'the person of the Duke of Otranto is to be secured on the order of the Prefect of Police'. When my men presented the warrant on the following morning, my appointment had not yet been announced, so Fouché—as I felt sure he would

H

have the wit to do—refused to surrender himself, on the grounds that there was no such person as a Prefect of Police. Then, while my men were seeking further instructions, he slipped out of his house, mounted a ladder he had set ready against his garden wall, in case of such an emergency, crossed into the garden next door, at the back of Queen Hortense's house, and from there drove off in a coach to the country.'

After laughing at this clever trick, Roger asked, 'How have the people reacted to the startling news of Napoleon's return?'

'It was hardly startling, at least not to those who remained Bonapartists at heart. From the fall of Paris last year they have looked on his abdication as only temporary. Many were convinced that he would wait only until the spring to leave Elba. Hence the adoption of the colour violet as a symbol, and in conversation between Bonapartists, he is often referred to as *"Père Violette"*.'

'However, as no precautions seem to have been taken to prevent his landing, it must have come as a surprise to the government and the Court?'

'Indeed it did. But what else could one expect from such a collection of ostriches? The *émigrés* have been far too busy enjoying the fruits of the Restoration to think of looking ahead. Had they done so, even such fools could hardly have failed to realize that if Napoleon did not return in the spring, by summer the people would have risen and again driven them into exile.'

Roger raised an eyebrow. 'The people seemed reasonably contented when I was here for a short time in the autumn, so I find so swift a change of feeling surprising.'

'It needed those six months for the yeast to ferment the mixture. Then they were still cock-a-hoop with having been let off so lightly by the Allies, and Louis was the wise, kind old man who would not drag them from their homes to fight more wars. Although he wriggled out of actually signing the undertaking that he would maintain the liberties they had won by the Revolution, at least he was, unlike Napoleon, no despot. But since then they've realized the price they are having to pay for the return of the Bourbons.'

Having taken a pinch of snuff, Bourrienne went on, 'You have seen for yourself how many regiments of the Army have already welcomed Napoleon. Others may resist, but if they do it will be only from loyalty to their Marshals. For twenty years France was inspired by the glory won by her soldiers. That is so no more. The Army itself has been humiliated. Many regiments have been disbanded, a whole host of junior officers have been retired, theoretically on half pay. I say "theoretically" because their pensions are not sent to them. The Legion of Honour has been dragged in the mud by giving it to hundreds of civil servants. The money that should go to ex-soldiers goes instead to the Church. The priests have swarmed back, and again tax the peasantry by demanding tithes. Still worse, the Church and the *émigré* nobility will not rest content until they get back the lands they owned before the Revolution. As you must know, the Convention con-fiscated those great estates, and they were sold by the State in small lots to the peasantry. The purchasers became known collectively as the "Proprietors". There are thousands of them, and now they all live in dread that any day they may hear that a new law has been passed, depriving them of their holdings. Naturally, Napoleon's return is to them the coming of a Saviour. And had he not returned within three months there would have been a revolution.'

'There may yet be one, from what I saw of the mobs in Grenoble, Lyons and other places.'

Bourrienne nodded gravely. 'That is what is most to be feared. Already there is open unrest in the Faubourgs. In the slums there today there were scenes reminiscent of '93. Gangs of *sans culottes* parading the streets, shouting *"A bas les aristos"*, and burning the Comte d'Artois in effigy.

'It is what Napoleon himself fears. We can only pray that when he gets here he will succeed in controlling that hydra-headed monster.'

For a further half-hour the two old friends continued their talk; then Bourrienne invited Roger to come to see him again on the following night and learn how matters were going at Court. After which they parted.

Next morning Roger breakfasted with de Jaucourt and several of Talleyrand's other intimates, who had come there to discuss the news, then he went out to see for himself the state of Paris. Having learned from Bourrienne the previous night that Davout, Savary, Lavalette and other leading men whom Napoleon counted on for support had gone into hiding, he realized that it was impossible for him to carry out the mission on which he had been sent; so he wandered the streets, now and then going into a café and getting into conversation with men at neighbouring tables.

An atmosphere of dread mingled with suppressed excitement permeated the city. The bourgeoisie had flourished under the Bourbons, so were anti-Bonapartist. They clearly feared that Napoleon's coming would disrupt their secure and prosperous lives, and in the cafés they frequented there were many uneasy references to the rowdy gatherings in the Faubourgs which, if not suppressed, might lead to bloodshed and looting.

In other cafés regularly patronised by ex-officers, not even a mention was made of that. They had just learned of Ney's defection and the talk was joyfully of Napoleon's advance, or rumours of happenings in parts of the country to which he had not yet penetrated. Although the divisions there were commanded by Marshals loyal to the Bourbons, in certain areas there had been risings in favour of Napoleon.

On March 8th General Count Drouet d'Erlon had declared for the Emperor and led his enthusiastic garrison at Lille out to march on Paris. In the north, too, General Lefebvre-Desnöettes, accompanied by two other Generals, Henri and François Lallemond, had set out with the cavalry of the Guard to seize the arsenal at Le Fère. But it was now said that Marshal Mortier had suppressed the mutiny at Lille and arrested d'Erlon; while at Le Fère, General Aboville had proved loyal to the King, with the result that Lefebvre-Desnöettes and the Lallemond brothers had been repulsed, deserted by their men and taken to flight.

From such happenings Roger formed the conclusion that only the actual sight of the Emperor was sufficient to inflame the troops to a degree at which they would defy their officers; so, although he might reach Paris, that would by no means make him again the master of France.

Late in the day, Roger dined with de Jaucourt and learned that although the King flatly refused to make any plans for abandoning the capital, numerous precautions against his having to do so were being taken. The banker Baron Louis, who was dining there, described a violent scene which had taken place between de Blacas and de Vitrolles. The former was still blandly confident that Napoleon could be checked at

Melun, but the other expressed doubts and urged that
the crown jewels and the contents of the treasury
should be got out of Paris without delay.

Vitrolles had had his way, and the diamonds were
entrusted to the King's chief valet, M. Hue, to take to
Calais. But the problem of moving twenty-five million
francs was a very different matter. It was proposed that
they be loaded on to ammunition wagons, and sent to
the Belgian frontier. Baron Louis had then pointed out
that there were not enough ammunition wagons in
Paris to transport such a tremendous weight in coin,
so efforts were now being made to exchange them for
bills on London.

After having dined, Roger went for another walk and
he saw indications of panic setting in. Quite a number
of wealthy people appeared to think that Paris could
not be held, and there was much more traffic than
usual at that hour on roads leading to the north:
coaches with armorial bearings, wagons and barouches,
some loaded with pictures, fine carpets and packing
cases.

At ten o'clock he went to the Prefecture of Police.
There he was told that Bourrienne was at the Tuileries,
so he sat down to await his return. The wait proved a
long one. It was not until past two o'clock in the morning
that the Prefect appeared, took Roger up to his cabinet
and told him what had been happening at the Palace.

The King never slept in his state bedroom, but had
a narrow iron bedstead erected for him every night in a
small room adjacent to his cabinet. There, his vast bulk
overflowing the narrow cot, he had lain listening to an
hour-long wrangle between his favourites. De Blacas's
mind appeared to have become paralysed, and he
refused to take the responsibility of ordering any action
in the King's name. Others urged flight, one to La

Rochelle, a second to La Vendée, and a third to Belgium. De Vitrolles implored Louis to remain and fight. So did Lafayette. The Marquis who had played a leading role early in the liberal revolution, had deserted in '92 and for seven years been held prisoner by the Austrians. Later he had been allowed to live in retirement in France, but on the Restoration returned to Paris as a supporter of the Bourbons. Both he and de Vitrolles argued that the only means of keeping the troops loyal was for the King to show himself and that he must join his army at Melun, even if he had to be carried there in a litter. The monarch had listened to them with apparent indifference, but he did agree that he would encourage the resistance of the National Guard by inspecting them next morning in the Champs de Mars.

When Bourrienne had finished his account, Roger asked, 'What news have you of the Emperor?'

'He is bringing his troops downriver in barges and on rafts, which is much quicker than having them march; but, even so, he won't wait for them. You know how impatient he is, and he's now so positive of success that he is driving on miles ahead of his advance guard, with only a few Lancers as escort. He is on his way to Fontainebleau and my agents tell me that, when he arrives there, not only will he be received with the usual rejoicing, but the old servants at the Palace have brought up from the cellars everything he had left there when he abdicated, and have the whole place ready for him to occupy.'

Roger laughed. 'Then he'll make good his boast and be here by Sunday. Last night you expressed the opinion that, although he would get to Paris, the Allied armies would put an end to him before many months were past, and you would return in triumph with the

Bourbons. But there is no certainly that things will go like that. He may succeed in dividing them, as he has done several times before, and be allowed to remain on here as a constitutional monarch. If that does happen, you would be left high and dry. It occurred to me this morning that you might care to hedge your bet.'

Bourrienne's eyes narrowed. 'Only a fool fails to do that if it is possible; but I don't see how I can, apart from having given a few Bonapartists time to avoid arrest.'

'I think I could manage it for you, if you are in a position to give me certain information. As you know, having got away from him, I am not committed to either side. But I have decided not to break permanently with him yet; so I shall remain on in Paris. If I can prove that you and I conspired to help him, we will both be back in favour should he come out on top. If he does not, as you will be leaving with the Bourbons, you will still be in their good books.'

'Your reasoning is sound enough, *cher ami*. But what is this information you require?'

'I wish to know where Lavalette has gone to earth.'

'I cannot tell you at the moment. But, given a few hours, I don't doubt I could find out.'

'Excellent,' Roger smiled. 'Then I will come to see you again tomorrow at midday.' Well satisfied at this propitious opening to a plan he had thought up with a view to satisfying Napoleon that he had not remained idle while in Paris, he returned to Talleyrand's mansion, and so to bed.

Next morning Chateaubriand was among those who breakfasted with de Jaucourt. The famous writer, with his big head of untidy hair and small, pox-pitted face, was a fervent Royalist and had urged that the King must remain in Paris, asserting that if he did so every-

one would support him. Tall, red-haired Benjamin
Constant, dressed in a yellow suit, was also there. He
agreed with Chateaubriand that the King could hold
Paris, as his twenty-five thousand National Guards
were devoted to him, and all the regular troops who
were unreliable and might have gone over to Bonaparte, had now been sent out of the capital to Villejuif and other places.

During the past week the King had issued a number
of proclamations denouncing Bonaparte and calling on
his people to remain loyal to him. Another had been
circulated that morning, and he had announced his
intention of reviewing his National Guard in the
Champs de Mars.

Marshal Macdonald saw him off in his carriage, surrounded by a glittering escort including Marshals
Berthier and Marmont. But, to Macdonald's surprise,
the splendid cortège returned half an hour later. In
spite of deafening shouts of '*Vive le Roi*' from the
National Guards, there had been such massive silent
crowds lining the route that the King had become
frightened, and, cutting short the review, turned back.

At midday Roger was again at the Prefecture of
Police. Bourrienne gave him the address of a house in
the suburb of Neuilly and said, 'It belongs to a widow
who at one time was Lavalette's mistress. I have good
reason to believe you will find him there.'

Having thanked him, Roger set off in a coach for
Neuilly.

During the past few days he had given much thought
to his future. He dared not return to England for fear
that Mary would carry out her threat to kill Georgina;
moreover, apart from the contents of Thatched House
Lodge, he now had practically no resources there. On
the other hand, in France he still had his little château

near St. Maxime, and if Napoleon did succeed in persuading the Allies to let him rule France as a constitutional monarch he, Roger, could continue to live
there as General Count de Breuc, in honourable retirement and in receipt of one of those truly handsome
annuities that the Emperor paid out both to his
nobility and to those officers who had distinguished
themselves in his service.

In any case, his opinion was that nothing could now
stop Napoleon from arriving in Paris, so anyone who
could make it easier for him to maintain law and order
when he had installed himself in the Tuileries had
nothing to lose and everything to gain. Hence this
decision to seek out Lavalette and propose a daring
coup to him.

When he reached the house in Neuilly he sent in his
name to the lady who owned it. A few minutes later she
received him in her salon, and asked the purpose of his
visit. With a smile he asked, '*Madame, aimez-vous la
violette?*'

Returning his smile, she replied, '*Il reviendra au
printemps.*'

These Bonapartist passwords having been exchanged,
he handed his visiting card to her and said, 'Madame,
I will not enquire of you the whereabouts of M. le
Comte de Lavalette, but should you know it I pray
you give him this. We were at one time brother
A.D.C.s, so are old friends. Tell him I come from
Père Violette and am anxious to disclose a certain pro-
ject to him.'

After a moment's hesitation, she replied, 'I might be
able to oblige you, Monsieur. But caution is required in
such matters. Return in an hour. If I succeed and
Monsieur de Lavalette is willing to meet you, he will
be waiting for you here.'

Returning to his coach Roger had himself driven half a mile down to the Marne, where it is joined by the canal, and sat there on the bank for the better part of an hour, idly watching the river traffic. He then drove back to the house, again had himself announced and, on entering the salon, found his handsome friend waiting for him.

After exchanging hearty greetings, Roger told Lavalette how he had accompanied Napoleon from Elba, then from Auxerre had been sent ahead to make contact with leading Bonapartists in the capital. After listening eagerly, Lavalette said:

'Having been proscribed, I and many of our other friends had to go into hiding. But, from all I hear, within a few days now the Emperor should be here, and we will be able to rally round him.'

'I've not a doubt of it,' Roger smiled. 'I am staying with de Jaucourt at Talleyrand's, so I get all the news. Everyone at breakfast there this morning was packed and ready to get out of Paris—that is, except Chateaubriand. He means to remain, but only because he is desperately enamoured of Juliette Récamier, and cannot persuade her to leave. 'Tis said the King intends to stay and fight, but I'd wager he won't. He's too scared of a rising by the mob. The Faubourgs are seething and many cities are reported now to be agitating in favour of the Emperor: Cherbourg, Brest, Strasbourg, Troyes, Rouen—and in Orléans the troops have already mutinied and driven out General Dupont.'

'What splendid news! If there is any way in which I could help, you have only to let me know it.'

'Can you raise a dozen brave officers who would be prepared to risk death for the Emperor with you?'

'Yes, fifty if need be.'

'A score should be enough. When the Emperor reached Lyons, he decided whom he would appoint as his Ministers. Davout is to have the War Office, Cambacérès the Ministry of Justice, Carnot the Interior . . .'

'Carnot! Can you be serious? He is still a Jacobin and would oppose the Emperor on everything.'

'No. He has matured with age and is no longer a revolutionary. The Emperor has realized that the people will not again submit to a dictatorship. But he must control the mob. He can do that only by ruling through the Assembly. By making Carnot a Minister he will secure the support of the Liberals, and so be able to maintain law and order. But, to continue— you are to be restored to your old office as Minister of Posts.'

Lavalette smacked his hands down on his knees. 'But this is marvellous! How happy it makes me now to think that I never succumbed to the temptation to go over to the Bourbons.'

'And I take it you would like to show your gratitude to our old master for having remembered you so handsomely,' Roger smiled.

'I would indeed.'

'There is a way in which you could do so. The Ministry of Posts controls all communications. If, instead of it being in its present hands, it was in those of one of the Emperor's adherents, messages by semaphore telegraph from the Ministry of War to all army commands throughout the country could be either suppressed or altered. So, too, could Royal proclamations and orders to Prefects of Departments to take various steps to maintain the Royal authority. If you took over the Ministry before the Emperor arrived in Paris, you would be able to render him an immense service.'

'*Mon Dieu,* de Breuc, you are right!' Lavalette exclaimed excitedly. 'But the National Guard are all loyal to the King, so 'twould be a hazardous business.'

'A risk, yes, but no really great one. I give those fools at the Tuileries twenty-four hours. They are already scared to death that the mob will storm the palace. Tomorrow, Sunday, the streets will be even fuller than they are today. If you and your friends appeared outside the Ministry tomorrow morning, shouting *Vive l'Empereur* at the top of your voices, the people would be with you to a man. The National Guard sentries outside the building would not dare fire on you for fear that the mob would tear them to pieces. Now, what say you?'

Lavalette stood up and held out his hand. 'You are a genius, *mon vieux*. I'll do it. I'll go out tonight and collect a score or more of the Emperor's diehards. If need be, we'll hold the place against all comers until he arrives. And I'll not forget to tell him that it was you who inspired me to the deed.'

As they shook hands, Roger said, 'That is good of you. But tell him also that, but for an old servant whom he has treated harshly I would not have been able to suggest this to you. I speak of Bourrienne. You were among those whom he had orders to arrest, but he deliberately let most of them slip out of his net. At my request he traced you, in order that we might meet.'

'Then, I pray you, thank him for me. I always thought him a good fellow, and that the Emperor made a mountain out of a molehill about his speculations. Look at the fortunes he let others make without even a reprimand.'

Roger smiled. 'That was because they were robbing foreigners, whereas poor Bourrienne made the mistake of robbing the French exchequer. But I must be off now. Good luck with your venture. We'll meet next in the Tuileries.'

On his way back into central Paris, he saw many more conveyances of one kind and another leaving the city than he had the previous evening and, on several street corners, little crowds of poorly clad people had congregated for no apparent purpose. Back at Talleyrand's he found that his host had gone to the Tuileries, so he supped early, then went to bed; but he was not destined to sleep the night through.

In the early hours of Sunday morning he was roused by de Jaucourt's coming into the room and slamming the door behind him. By the light of a shaded candle the Deputy Foreign Minister was carrying, Roger saw that he had on only a chamber robe and was in a furious temper. In a harsh voice de Jaucourt cried:

'Get up, Breuc! Get up and dress at once. We are leaving as soon as the grooms can get the horses harnessed to the coaches.'

'What . . . what has happened?' Roger asked in swift surprise.

'I've just been woken by a friend who came from the palace. The King has betrayed us. After letting everyone suppose that he meant to stay here and face things out, he left the Tuileries secretly at two o'clock this morning, accompanied only by de Blacas and a few of his other cronies. That bladder of lard had himself carried to a coach, then sneaked out of Paris. Not one word of warning did he give to any of us who were with him this evening, and he hasn't even let anyone know where he is going.'

15
Tumult in Paris

ROGER swung his legs over the edge of the bed and asked cynically, 'Did you really expect him to stay?'

'Yes,' snapped de Jaucourt. 'Vitrolles and Lafayette had persuaded him to. Lafayette told me so himself before I left the palace last night.'

'That inefficient windbag!' Roger's voice was contemptuous. 'What faith could anyone put in him at a time of crisis? Surely you recall his cowardly conduct in '89 when, as Commander of the National Guard at Versailles, he had sworn to protect Louis XVI and Marie Antoinette, then let the mob carry them off forcibly to Paris?'

'True, true! But in this instance there would still have been some hope for the monarchy had the King given an example to his people by defying Bonaparte.'

'*Mon cher Marquis,* would you expect a chicken to stand up to a mastiff?'

'This is no time to argue the matter. We must leave with the least possible delay.'

'You would be wise to do so,' Roger remarked calmly, putting his legs back under the sheets. 'But I shall remain.'

'What! And risk that fiendish Corsican having you shot?'

'He'll do me no harm. As I accompanied him from
the coast, he regards me as his man. That I left him
at Auxerre I'll explain by saying that I went ahead to
contact his friends in Paris. I've a mind to see how
things go here. When it suits my book, I'll slip away
and join Talleyrand wherever he may be.'

De Jaucourt nodded. 'Just as you wish. By staying
you will be able to bring us helpful information later.'
Turning, he hurried from the room.

Roger remained in bed for another hour, then slowly
dressed and went downstairs. Everything there was
bustle and confusion. Servants were loading coaches
and secretaries burning papers. Finding the dining
room empty, he went through to the kitchen, helped
himself to coffee from a big pot bubbling on the stove
and, in the larder, cut some slices of ham for his breakfast.

On re-entering the hall he found de Jaucourt and his
aides just about to leave. The Marquis said to him,
'We have now heard that he drove off towards St.
Denis.'

Roger laughed. 'How appropriate, as it is there that
all the Kings of France are buried. I'll wager, though,
that by this time he'll be well away from Paris.'

'Yes. But the route he takes will be easy to follow. By
nightfall we should catch up with him.'

With a quick handshake they parted. Daylight had
now come, and Roger stood on the steps of the mansion
to wave the cavalcade away as it drove out of the
courtyard. A fine rain was falling, so he collected his
cloak, then went out. The streets were almost empty,
with the usual quiet of an early Sunday morning. He
had not gone far when two horsemen came trotting
toward him. He recognized one of them as the Duke de
Richelieu, who pulled up and called to him:

'The King's gone. He left the Tuileries in secret at two o'clock this morning.'

Roger was about to reply that he already knew, but the Duke hurried on, 'Would you believe it? As his First Gentleman of the Bedchamber, I spent half an hour with him last night, yet he said not a word to me of his intention. He's just bolted and left us all to be butchered. Get to horse as quickly as you can, and head for the Belgian frontier.' Setting spurs to his mount, the angry Duke and his companion trotted on again.

As Roger passed a row of arches he saw groups of tattered figures in them, some still sleeping, others cooking bits and pieces over charcoal fires. He had noticed them before, and many other groups like them who made their homes in any available shelter the city offered. They were ex-prisoners of war who, from the time of the peace of the previous year, had returned from Russia, Austria, Prussia and England. Every city in France had its quota and it was said that from Russia alone a hundred thousand of these skeletons, with many seriously crippled among them, had straggled back. The majority had families to support them, but many were homeless and the government had done nothing for them, so they lived as best they could, by begging and stealing.

Roger could imagine the tremendous welcome they would give Napoleon. They would not still be apathetically lounging about if they had any idea that he was so near; but very few people were yet aware of that. From the beginning, the Press had been entirely subservient to the Bourbon government. It had even published a flagrantly false account of d'Artois's having defeated Napoleon at Lyons and driven him back. More recently, the columns had been full of statements about the great army the King was forming outside Paris, and of how he was prepared to shed his own blood in defence of his throne.

It was Palm Sunday, and in the streets there were many middle-class people on their way to attend early Mass. They, too, had no idea that Napoleon must by now be at Fontainebleau, much less that the King had fled. Their only worry was that, during the past few days, the mob had shown its ugly head and the government might not prove strong enough to restrain it.

Eager to see what was going on at the Tuileries, Roger had been making his way toward it. When he reached the palace he saw that the great iron gates were shut, and through them he glimpsed the court-yard filled with National Guards. Knots of people had formed round the Place du Carousel. Most of them looked well-to-do, and as they exchanged rumours, their faces were anxious. Soon it became known that the King had fled, and many of them hurried away to their homes. At about ten o'clock those who remained had good reason for their anxiety. Several columns of ragged marchers entered the square. They were *sans culottes* from the Faubourgs, where many thousands of poor lived in squalid hovels, and they were singing the songs of the Revolution: the *Ça ira,* the *Carmagnole* and the *Marseillaise,* interspersed with occasional shouts of '*Vive l'Empereur*'. They made a half-hearted attempt to force the gates of the palace, in order to loot it; but a threat from the bourgeois National Guard to fire on them caused them to desist.

Roger turned off down a side street. On a corner a hundred yards along it, he came to a café, and it was open. The proprietor had defied the hated law, brought in at the Restoration, that all cafés should remain closed on Sundays, and it was doing good business.

Sitting at a table, he ordered café-cognac, and was soon in conversation with his neighbours.

One of them was a well-dressed man with a high forehead, who might have been a lawyer. A priest was hurrying, head down, along the pavement opposite. Pointing to him, Roger's neighbour remarked, 'I've nothing against those black beetles, but what fools they are. They have asked for what's coming to them.'

'In what way?' Roger enquired. 'I have no use for them myself, but they do only what they have been taught is right.'

'No, no,' the other protested. 'Nine-tenths of them are harsh bigots who wilfully cause much unhappiness. Look at the case of Mademoiselle Rancour.'

'You mean the famous actress who used to play at the Théâtre Français? She must be quite old now. What have they done to her?'

'She is dead. You must have been away from Paris for some time, Monsieur, or you would have heard about it. She was of a most respectable character, and her funeral was attended by a great concourse of people of all degrees, but the priests of St. Roche refused her Christian burial.

'Why did they do that?'

'Because that bitter woman, the Duchesse d'Angoulême, made them revive the old pre-Revolution custom that, on account of their profession, all actors and actresses were automatically excommunicated. Imagine the grief caused to Mademoiselle Rancour's relations and friends.'

'I can, indeed. What a shameful attitude to adopt.'

'That was what all Paris thought, and riots ensued until the priests gave way. But to maintain such hateful, mediaeval practices is typical of them. They will be the first targets of the people's anger if real trouble

breaks out. Now that the King has deserted us, we can
only pray that Bonaparte will soon enter Paris, for he
alone can save us from another blood bath.'

Those sentiments, Roger soon found, were shared by
nearly everyone else in the café. None of them expressed admiration for Napoleon, or joy at his imminent return. They wanted him back now; but only
because they felt confident that he would promptly take
strong measures to suppress disorder, and be a change
from the Bourbon government that all classes, except
émigrés, had come to detest.

The fear of outbreaks by the mob decided Roger that
he ought to return to Talleyrand's mansion, in order to
organize the servants remaining there for its protection,
should an attempt be made to loot it.

On his way back, he saw that all the other cafés he
passed were open. In some ex-officers were noisily
carousing, and drinking the health of the Emperor; in
others groups of well-dressed men sat talking anxiously
in low voices. It was still raining which, he felt, explained the fact that such groups of marchers as he saw
were not numerous; but at the head of each column a
man carried the tricolour flag, and many people now
had tricolour cockades pinned either to their hats or
buttonholes.

In the Rue St. Florentin there were no signs of
trouble, and he found that Talleyrand's *maître d'hôtel*
had already taken precautions against a mob attempting to wreck the Bourbon Foreign Minister's residence.
The great gates of the courtyard had been shut, and
he was let through only after being inspected through a
grille. He saw then that the shutters of all the ground
floor windows had been closed, and when he was let
into the hall by a footman, there were two others there
armed with muskets.

Supposing that Roger had left with M. de Jaucourt and his staff, the *maître d'hôtel* was surprised and pleased to see him. He assured Roger that the Prince was such a good master that his staff could be relied on to defend his property and would serve his guest as readily as if he were there in person.

Thanking him, Roger said that, having been up so early, he would rest in his room for two hours, then take a meal before going out again.

While lying on his bed, he once more considered his own future. There was now no longer the least doubt that Napoleon would soon be in Paris, and very little that, once master in the capital, the whole country would follow in again acclaiming him as Emperor. For some time past it had been obvious to Roger that, for him, Napoleon's success would mean that, although he had been robbed of his fortune in England, he would be rich and honoured in France. But for how long would such a situation last? Only for as long as Napoleon remained Emperor. If he succeeded in con-ciliating his ex-enemies, or detaching Austria and England from the other two allies, he might retain his throne for many years; but if he failed in that, his second reign might come to an end within a matter of months, and the benefits Roger would derive by sup-porting him end with it. Then, as a known Bonapartist, he would have sacrificed the possibility of making a new career for himself, either in France or in any of the Allied countries. And now was the moment of decision.

Napoleon had no doubt of his loyalty, so he could stay on in Paris, reap the rewards of serving him and risk his restoration being only temporary. Talleyrand believed him to be devoted to the Allied cause, so he could play safe by leaving Paris that night, and re-joining him wherever he might be; but, in that case, he could hope for no more than some minor diplomatic post, while living on a shoestring.

His thoughts turned to Georgina, as they had at some time nearly every day since he had last seen her, and with ever-increasing resentment that they were separated by Mary's insane, murderous jealousy. Supposing Napoleon did succeed in retaining his throne, their situation would remain the same as far as his return to England was concerned. But Georgina's old Duke was now dead, so she was free again and there was nothing to prevent her coming to France and living with him at his little château near St. Maxime.

That glorious possibility decided him. He would stay on in Paris and gamble everything on Napoleon's cleverness and luck.

At half past one he went out and made his way to the Hôtel des Postes. The National Guard sentries outside it were wearing tricolour cockades. Taking this as a sign that Lavalette had succeeded in the coup they had planned, Roger went in and boldly asked for his friend. His name was taken up and, a few minutes later, the handsome Lavalette threw his arms about him in a bear-like embrace, then told him what had occurred there that morning.

At ten o'clock he and his friends had arrived outside the Ministry, shouting '*Vive l'Empereur*', which at once attracted a crowd, many of whom had supported them. He had demanded to see the Minister, Count Ferrand, who had come downstairs and, on realizing the situation, had made no protest but, in a quite friendly manner, handed over his office. All but a few of Ferrand's staff had cheerfully accepted Lavalette's orders. Working with a will, they had prevented all despatches from other Ministries being sent out, suppressed that morning's issue of the *Moniteur*, which contained a proclamation from the King intended to rally his supporters in the provinces, and sent messages to all the Prefects of the Departments announcing the restoration of the Emperor.

Roger was still congratulating his friend when Lavalette broke in:

'But that is not all. I have just had news from Essonnes that the Emperor will be in Paris before nightfall. You know how the road from Fontainebleau slopes down, so that from the edge of the forest one can see right across the valley in which Melun lies? The Royalist army was drawn up in the valley, barring the road to Paris. As the Emperor emerged from the forest, he had a clear view of it. With him, in an open carriage, he had Bertrand and Drouot and, as escort, he had only a single troop of cavalry, yet he drove straight on down the hill. When he was within fifty yards of the nearest infantry, he gave a signal to his escort. They pulled up, dismounted, cast away their arms and ran forward. Instead of firing on them, Macdonald's men threw down their muskets and ran forward to embrace them. The Emperor drove right into the middle of the troops, until his carriage was stopped by sheer pressure of numbers, while regiment after regiment took up the cry, "*Vive l'Empereur*".'

'What a triumph!' Roger exclaimed. 'Complete victory, and not so much as a blow struck.'

'Yes. The Generals fled, the whole army turned about and is now escorting the Emperor to Paris. The courier I sent to let him know that I had taken over here met him at Essonnes, but the road is blocked there by scores of vehicles and thousands of troops delirious with excitement, so it will be hours yet before he can cover the remaining miles to the capital.'

'It is still possible that the troops at Villejuif may put up a resistance.'

Lavalette shook his head. 'Nay, they are already dealt with. Sebastiani rode out there early this morning. All on his own he charged up to the 2nd Regiment of the Line, waving his sabre and shouting *"Vive l'Empereur"*. The men had already been disputing which side they should take and the sight of the famous General settled the matter. They all went over to the Emperor.'

As Lavalette was overwhelmed with work, having heard all this good news Roger left him and proceeded to the Tuileries. There he found the gates still locked and the courtyard still crowded with National Guards; but, on looking up, he saw that, instead of the Bourbon white flag embroidered with golden *fleurs-de-lys*, a huge tricolour was now flying from the clock tower of the palace. Through the railings he asked an officer how it came to be there, and received the reply:

'At about two o'clock, General Excelmans, leading a body of Bonapartist officers, marched up to the gates and demanded to be let through. He had that great flag wrapped round his body and said that, if we refused to open the gates, he would blow them in. As the King has gone, we are not now here to defend him but to prevent the palace from being looted, and we didn't want bloodshed, so we let him and his friends in. He entered the palace and hoisted the flag himself. It was then agreed by our commander, Adjutant Major de Laborde, that some of General Excelmans' friends should remain in possession of the palace, while we stayed here in the courtyard to protect it from the mob.'

Although it was drizzling again, there were still many groups standing about the Place du Carousel, and Roger mingled with some of them. From an *agent de ville* to whom he spoke, he learned that General Savary,

Duc de Rovigo, had that morning taken over the Ministry of Police and that, having hoisted the tricolour on the Tuileries, Excelmans had set off hell-for-leather for St. Denis, hoping to win over the troops there and, with them, pursue the King in an attempt to capture him.

As the news spread that Napoleon had met with no opposition at Melun, more and more people took tri-coloured cockades from their pockets and pinned them on. Here and there squabbles broke out, but there was no serious disturbance. By mid-afternoon it had become generally believed that Napoleon could be expected within a few hours.

To kill time Roger took a walk along the Rue St. Honoré and back to the Palais Royal. As it was Sunday the shops were shut, but many of the shopkeepers had come down from their lodgings on the upper floors and were very busy. Perched on ladders they were hard at work taking down the signs showing that they had appointments to supply the King or Bourbon Princes, and replacing them with Napoleonic eagles retrieved from their cellars.

On returning to the Tuileries, Roger saw that a long line of carriages was now drawn up in front of it, and that the gates had been opened. The courtyard was still full of National Guards, but they had all donned tri-colour cockades, and when he walked through the gates none of them attempted to stop him.

Going up the grand staircase, as he had so often done to attend brilliant receptions, he entered the long series of lofty salons that led to the throne room. A number of other gentlemen were there, and they were all looking on at a strange sight, which explained the line of carriages, in which, led by Napoleon's step-daughter, Hortense, ex-Queen of Holland, some fifty or more Bonapartist ladies had arrived. They were now either

kneeling on the floor or standing on chairs to reach
curtains, at work with pairs of scissors. When Napoleon
had lived in the Tuileries, he had refurnished all the
main rooms with specially woven Aubusson carpets
and heavy silk hangings from Lyons. The patterns of
all these consisted of wreaths encircling his emblems,
the eagle and the bee. At the restoration the previous
year, the Bourbons had decided against getting rid of
those costly furnishings. Instead, they had a number of
fleurs-de-lys made in various materials, and sewn over the
bees and eagles. Now the Bonapartist ladies were cutting away the stitches that held the *fleurs-de-lys* in place,
and burning them in the grates.

Meanwhile, downstairs other activities were taking
place to the sound of happy laughter. Footmen were
laying up long tables, chefs and scullions preparing a
great banquet, and butlers getting up from the cellars
hundreds of bottles of wine to put in the great silver
coolers, already half-full of ice.

Again Roger went out into the square. Several hours
had passed since news of Napoleon's bloodless victory at
Melun had come in, so he was expected to arrive at any
moment. The bourgeoisie had donned the tricolour
cockade, and were now reassured. They had no love for
Napoleon, but his coming meant that their lives and
property were safe. There would be no revolution; the
groups of *sans culottes* had broken up and slunk away
back to the slums where generations of them had lived
in misery, no better off under Napoleon than they had
been under Louis XVI. Now and then, when a coach
appeared, there came a burst of cheering as the crowd
assumed that the vehicle was bringing the Emperor,
but each time they proved mistaken.

The wait seemed endless, dusk fell and a chill wind
sprang up. Still no advance guard appeared heralding

the approach of the Emperor. Wet, cold and disappointed, many people went home, but a few hundred
lingered on, Roger among them. At about half past
eight he was again standing near the gates of the
Tuileries when, by the light of the lamps, he recognized
Lavalette coming toward him. Roger called a greeting,
then asked:

'Has something gone amiss? He should have been
here hours ago.'

Lavalette took him by the arm. '*Non, mon ami*, all is
well. But there are so many people crowding the roads
to welcome him that he can be driven only at a walking
pace. And I have just received a courier, with the news
that, to avoid further obstruction, he is going round
Paris, so he will enter from the north instead of the
south. He will be here shortly now, though.'

They went into the palace and at the bottom of the
grand staircase were cheerfully hailed by Marat, Duke
de Bassano, Savary, Admiral Decrès, who had been
Napoleon's Minister of Marine, and a dozen other of
his paladins. All of them, and hundreds of other
officers now crowding the stairs and galleries, were in
full-dress uniform, and many were accompanied by
their wives, also in Court dress.

At nine o'clock a great commotion could be heard
out in the courtyard. The doors were thrown open,
there were deafening shouts of '*Vive l'Empereur*', then
Napoleon was carried in on the shoulders of his Guards
and surrounded by his adherents, Bertrand and Drouot,
who had accompanied him from Elba, Caulaincourt,
Lefebvre, Flahaut, Mouton and others who had ridden
out to meet him at Essonnes.

The inrush from the courtyard and mass of people
inside who pressed forward to greet Napoleon caused a
solid jam on the wide staircase. His face was chalk-

white, and he was in danger of being crushed. Breathlessly, he gasped:

'*Mes enfants!* You are suffocating me.'

'For God's sake, put yourself in front of him,' Caulaincourt shouted to Lavalette.

Clinging to one of the banisters, Lavalette backed his way up the stairs, shielding the Emperor until he reached the top. There, scores more people fought to kiss his hands, his arms and the hem of his grey coat. Only with great difficulty was he got to the throne room where his step-daughter Hortense and his brother Joseph's wife, the ex-Queen of Spain, waited to greet him.

He had made the journey from Cannes to Paris in half the time it took a normal traveller, and made good his boast that he would be back in Paris on his son's birthday, the 20th March.

16

An Emperor in Chains

In the midst of the uproar, to everyone's amazement Fouché, Duc d'Otranto, was announced. For many years, after the Emperor and rivalled only by Talleyrand, he had been the most powerful man in France; but he had twice been caught out conspiring against Napoleon, and for a long time had lived in compulsory retirement; so his reappearance at this moment was a gesture of incredible audacity.

His ups and downs in life had been quite extraordinary. During the Revolution he had been the reddest of Jacobins, become a pro-consul under Robespierre and was responsible for the massacre of the Liberals at Lyons. With the reaction under the Directory, he had narrowly escaped the guillotine, and scraped a miserable living in hiding as a pig farmer. Somehow he had managed to raise a little capital, and in a few years made a fortune as an army contractor; then, miraculously, become Minister of Police. In that post, under Bonaparte, he had organized a vast network of spies all over Europe and through them had, with indefatigable industry, compiled thousands of dossiers containing the secrets of every person of importance. These had enabled him to blackmail the highest men and women in the whole of the Napoleonic Empire to act in accordance with his wishes, and he had nipped a score of conspiracies in the bud. But, believing that France needed peace, in 1810 he had entered into secret negotiations with England, behind Napoleon's back, and, his agent having been caught, he had got off lightly by being exiled to his country estates. On Napoleon's abdication he had returned to Paris, and entered into friendly relations with the Bourbons. Now he again blandly offered his services to his old master.

Half an hour later Roger came upon the redoubtable Fouché standing alone at one of the tall windows, quietly observing the drunken revelry of the soldiers and their women in the courtyard below. The two of them had first chanced to meet before the Revolution, when Fouché was still a lay brother of the Oratorian Fathers, and Roger still in his teens. It was then that Fouché had learnt that Roger was the son of an English Admiral; but, for his own reasons, he had always kept that fact to himself. Their first encounter had caused them to become enemies for many years, but on Napoleon's return from Egypt, it had suited Talleyrand and Fouché—who were as oil and water—to combine forces, in order to make Bonaparte First Consul. Roger had played a part in that conspiracy and, from that time onward, he and Fouché had buried the hatchet; so he now approached him with a friendly smile and said:

'*Monsieur le Duc,* pray accept my congratulations on your courage. I know of no other man who would have voluntarily come here tonight, knowing there to be a good chance that he would spend what remains of it in prison.'

Fouché never looked anyone straight in the face, and his own had always been as pale as that of a corpse. He averted his fish-like eyes, but there was the bare suggestion of a smile on his lips as he replied:

'*Merci, mon cher Comte,* but it required no courage. I had only to whisper to him that, within a matter of days, he would be assassinated unless he made me again his Minister of Police.'

Roger raised his eyebrows. 'But I thought he had already given that post to Savary.'

'Oh, the Duc de Rovigo.' Fouché snuffled, having been cursed with a perpetual cold. 'He was only barely competent to run the police while Napoleon was the all-powerful Emperor, but in a situation such as the present one, only I am capable of protecting him; and he knows it. Having gained the kudos of taking over, Savary will be only too pleased to be relieved of the job. He has too many Royalist friends that he would be reluctant to prosecute.'

'You imply that he is hedging his bet against the possibility of Napoleon being overcome by the Allies, and Louis put back on the throne?' Roger asked, fishing for Fouché's opinion, which he knew from their past relations would be an honest one to him.

'Of course, as is everyone here, except for the bone-headed Generals.'

'Yet you have needlessly put yourself forward, and are again become a leading Bonapartist.'

' 'Tis due to my insistent urge to be at the centre of things, and so in a position to save France from our Corsican maniac. Time and again Talleyrand and I have attempted to rid the country of him, and he's had cause enough to have us shot. But, as far as both of us are concerned, he is bewitched and acts like a fool. Last time it was Talleyrand who succeeded in pulling him down. This time, unless he has me killed at the last moment, it will be me, and within three months we'll be finished with him for good.'

It was four o'clock in the morning when Roger got

to bed and, before he dropped off to sleep, he thought again of his conversation with Fouché. Clearly, in spite of the tremendous ovation Napoleon had received at the Tuileries that night, his fortunes were still very much in the balance. Talleyrand would be doing his utmost to persuade the Allies to declare war on him, and Fouché would be working in secret for his over-throw. Only if he carried out his declared intention of becoming a pacifist liberal ruler did he stand any chance of survival. So once more Roger contemplated leaving Paris while he still had the chance to do so. But that meant abandoning his only prospect of a secure and happy future. Again he decided to gamble everything by hitching his wagon to Napoleon's star.

A few hours later he crossed the Rubicon by having his trunk brought down from the attics, putting on the old uniform it contained, and sallying forth to attend a parade, which the Emperor had ordered for midday, of the troops that had returned to Paris. Later, as they were returning to the Tuileries, Napoleon beckoned him up and said:

'Lavalette has told me how it was you who suggested seizing the Hôtel des Postes. I am very pleased with you and confirm the promise I made you in Elba. The uniform you are wearing is in a sad state. When you order a new one, have the badges of a General of Brigade put on it.'

In the throne room the Ministers Napoleon had appointed that morning had all assembled. Most of them had been reinstalled in their old offices: Marat at the Foreign Office, Decrès the Marine, Gaudin Finance, Marshal Davout had been given the War Office, and Carnot had been persuaded to become the Minister of the Interior.

The last was a great triumph for the Emperor's new

policy of representing himself as a constitutional monarch, subject to the will of the people. Before the Revolution Carnot had been an officer of Engineers. From the beginning an ardent Republican, he had been chosen in '91 as a member of the Legislative Assembly, and had voted for the death of Louis XVI. But in charge of the War Department, he had performed prodigies, not only in welding the rabble of the cities into resolute soldiers but even, on one occasion, leading them to victory in person, while dressed as a civilian. Within a year he had raised seven armies that succeeded in defending the frontiers of France from the trained troops of the Allied monarchs, and he had become known as 'the organizer of victories'.

During the Terror he had been a member of the dread Committee of Public Safety, but had taken no part in its bloody decrees, continuing to concern himself only with the needs of the Army. Later he had served the Directory and then Bonaparte, but resigned from both offices when he found they were departing from the true principles of 'liberty, equality, fraternity', and for some years voluntarily exiled himself in Switzerland. He had most strongly opposed Napoleon elevating himself to Emperor, and all his wars of aggression. But now, persuaded that Napoleon's forced abdication and exile had entirely altered his outlook he had agreed to enter his Ministry. By doing so, his example, as a man of unquestionable integrity, would bring over the Liberals who had the power to prevent the mob from attempting another revolution.

For some days the position in the provinces remained uncertain. The King was at Lille with Marshals Mortier, Marmont and Macdonald, and a considerable body of Royalists. Marshal St. Cyr had declared for the King in Orléans. Marshal Victor had put down a

I

mutiny in favour of Bonaparte, and was said to be advancing on Paris. The Duc de Bourbon commanded a force in Angers. The Duc d'Angoulême was rallying the Royalist forces in the south and his Duchess held Bordeaux.

But matters soon clarified themselves in favour of Napoleon. The troops of Marshals Victor, Oudinot and St. Cyr all revolted against them. Marshal Suchet brought over his divisions in Alsace, the Duc d'Angoulême's men had gone over to General Grouchy, and General Clausel drove the Duchess from Bordeaux. Brittany and Poitou both declared for the Emperor. Excelmans' advance on Lille caused Marmont to fear that the troops there might revolt and join him; so, on the Marshal's advice, the King retired to Ostend. Meanwhile, in Marseilles Marshal Masséna had played a cunning game, keeping the white flag flying, but sending troops in pursuit of Napoleon only belatedly; then, when he learned that he had reached Paris, he simply abandoned his command and went into retirement. Thus, in a short time the Emperor had re-established his rule over practically the whole of France.

Yet, during those last days of March, he received most unwelcome news from beyond his frontiers. Immediately on reaching Paris he had written most affectionately to his wife, asking her to rejoin him and share his throne, now that he was back in France, and to bring with her the little King of Rome, whom he loved so dearly. Then, even before there had been time for him to receive a reply, intelligence arrived from Vienna that Marie Louise had formally renounced the title of Empress and severed her relationship with him for good. Depressed by memories of the Tuileries, now not to be renewed, he moved to the smaller Palace Elysée.

Marie Louise's repudiation of him was not only a great blow to him personally, but damaged him in the eyes of many people, for it disclosed that his statements about having the goodwill of Austria had no foundation. Still worse, it was followed by the news that, on the 15th, Austria had signed a new Treaty of Alliance with Prussia, Russia and Britain, and published a Declaration which ran:

'Bonaparte, having broken the agreement by which he was established on the island of Elba, has destroyed the sole legal title to his existence. By landing in France he has become a disturber of the peace of the world, a public enemy and an outlaw.'

The Treaty stipulated that, should it prove necessary to re-establish Louis XVIII on his throne, each of the four Powers would provide one hundred and fifty thousand men, and with these six hundred thousand troops crush the usurper once and for all.

Disturbing as this was to his Ministers and the people of France generally, Napoleon displayed great skill in reassuring them. He pointed out quite truthfully that the declaration of hostility was no matter for immediate concern, because the Powers were in no position to implement their threat. All of them were war-weary and incapable of putting considerable forces in the field. Those of Russia were many hundred miles distant, those of Austria fully employed in again taking over the northern Italian States, those of Prussia employed in taking over the Saxon and Rhineland territories she had acquired by the peace treaty of the previous year, and the flower of the British army had been sent to the United States, in an endeavour to put a favourable end to the war with the Americans that had broken out in 1812. Moreover, all three Continental Powers were on the verge of bankruptcy, so a renewal of the war could be undertaken only by subsidies from Britain; and, with her own very heavy commitments, she would be most loath to provide them.

Further, as he had planned, he proceeded to do his utmost to sow dissension among the Allies; and to this end, on reoccupying the Tuileries, he had come upon one weapon that he believed would prove invaluable. In the King's hasty flight from the palace he had left behind a number of State documents. Among them was a copy of the secret treaty signed, just before Roger left Vienna for Elba, by Austria and Britain, to go to war with Russia and Prussia should they forcibly assert their claims to Poland and Saxony. Feeling confident that evidence of this piece of backstairs diplomacy would revive the Czar's enmity to Austria, Napoleon sent it to him.

He then replied to the Allies' declaration of hostility by issuing a manifesto, justifying his return to France. He maintained that it was the Allies who had broken the treaty. They had bound themselves to continue the rewards he had given to his army and faithful followers; to allow the members of his family to remain in possession of all their property, movable and immovable; to protect his person on his way into exile; to make over to the Empress Marie Louise the Duchies of Parma and Placentia; to allow her and his son to join him in Elba; to provide a suitable establishment for his stepson Eugène de Beauharnais; to provide the members of his family with an income of two million five hundred francs a year, and himself with an income of two million. Yet they had broken every one of these promises. His soldiers and returned prisoners of war had been left to starve, the estates of his family had been confiscated and their possessions stolen, his wife had been deprived of the promised duchies, he had been denied her company and that of his son, and not one sou of income had been paid either to him or any member of his family.

This justification was widely circulated, and he sent copies to all the Allied Sovereigns. In addition he wrote in his own hand to each of them, stating that mature consideration had decided him definitely to forgo all thought of future aggression against any other country, no longer to rule as a despot but as a constitutional monarch, and that his sole desire was to ensure the peace and prosperity of the people of France.

On learning this, Roger's hopes that he might enjoy a happy future with Georgina visiting him at St. Maxime rose considerably, for he felt that Napoleon had produced a strong case for having returned to France, and an assurance of his pacific intentions which it would be difficult for the Allies to ignore. But an event occurred which seriously jeopardized these prospects.

Murat had left his Kingdom of Naples to participate in Napoleon's Russian campaign of 1812. He had left it again the following year to command the cavalry against the Allies in Germany. But, after the Emperor's defeat at the battle of Leipzig, he had decided that Napoleon was finished, so had abandoned the Army and returned for good to his own kingdom. Then, while the Emperor was fighting his final battles on the soil of France, Murat had definitely deserted his cause and, on January 11th, 1814, made a treaty to aid France's enemies.

As Roger knew, at the Conference of Vienna the future of the Kingdom of Naples had been one of the principal bones of contention. Ferdinand, as the King of the Two Sicilies, had sent representatives from Palermo—which he had made his capital since being driven out of Naples by the French—to demand the restoration of his old dominion on the mainland. As he was a Bourbon, his claim had been strongly supported by his relatives, the Kings of France and Spain. This had placed Austria and Britain in a very awkward situation; for, although they both favoured the principle of legitimacy, to prevent Eugène de Beauharnais—then Napoleon's Viceroy in Italy—from sending troops to assist his stepfather in France, they had made a treaty with Murat, whereby if he would send his thirty thousand Neapolitans to attack Eugène, they would maintain him on his throne.

So far the matter had remained unsettled, but Murat's representatives in Vienna had led him to believe that the decision would be given against him, and that he might soon be deposed. Before going to Elba Pauline had spent some time in Naples. No doubt largely owing to her, Napoleon forgave Murat his treachery, and they had opened a friendly correspondence. This, coupled with Murat's fear of losing his throne, led to far-reaching results.

Immediately he learned that Napoleon had landed in France, having great faith in his brother-in-law's abilities, he wrote assuring him of his support, then set about initiating a plan he had long cherished secretly. Previously to Napoleon's conquest of Italy, it had been split up into numerous independent states, most of which were subservient to Austria. They were run on mediaeval lines, which meant no voice in their government for the well-to-do and virtual slavery for the peasants. Napoleon had not only made northern and central Italy into one kingdom, but had given people of all classes the rights and liberties gained by the French through their Revolution. Everyone hated the Austrians and their local tyrants who had recently returned. Murat saw his chance in this. He anticipated Garibaldi by half a century and proclaimed his intention of uniting the whole of Italy under a liberal monarchy. On March 20th, at Ancona, he called on all Italians to rally to him and declared war on Austria.

Napoleon heard this news with consternation and fury. He had been using his utmost endeavours to persuade his old enemies that he had become a reformed character, and was now a man of peace who no longer had any thought other than for the welfare of his people. And here was his impetuous fool of a brother-in-law ruining everything. Without even a word of warning, he had broken the peace and Europe was again plunged in war.

Outside France the 'justification' made little impact, and the Allied Sovereigns ignored Napoleon's letters. The Prince Regent returned unopened the letter addressed to him.

Whether the Emperor's approaches would have been received more favourably had his brother-in-law not acted so rashly remains in question, but it is extremely doubtful. In the British Parliament the Whigs, led by Whitbread, protested most vigorously against a reopening of the war. But they were greatly outnumbered by the Tories and Lord Grenville, speaking in the House, expressed the opinion of the vast majority of knowledgeable people. After stating that by the violation of the Treaty of Paris, the Allies were now actually at war with Bonaparte, and that it was not a question of whether we should make war, but whether we should conclude a peace, he added:

'No reasonable man could confide in the security to be found in a treaty with Bonaparte . . . Speaking of the security or insecurity of treaties, he should not attempt a statement of how many violations Bonaparte had been guilty, but he would ask anyone to show him one country during the last ten or twelve years which had sought peace or safety by treaty with him that had not found itself visited with the highest aggravations of the very evils it had sought to ward off.'

That was the essence of the matter. He had lied so often and so flagrantly that no-one would now accept his protestations that he desired only peace. Moreover, since they dared not trust his word, had they agreed to make a peace with him they would have had to maintain large armies and navies for many years, in order to be in a position to protect themselves should he break the treaty.

Yet there remained a powerful counterweight to this rooted distrust and animosity among the ruling classes of his enemies. The Congress of Vienna had put the clock back a quarter of a century by reimposing autocracy on a great part of Europe, and repartitioned it in a way that caused intense resentment in many countries. Belgium was now a part of Holland and ruled by a Dutch King; part of Saxony was subject to Prussia, northern Italy again to Austria; many of the small Rhineland States had been given to alien rulers; the States of the Church, in middle Italy, had been returned to the Pope and Russia dominated Poland. Of all this Napoleon was well aware, and that as the creator of his Legal Code which gave equal justice to all classes, given successful campaigns, he would be welcomed by many million people.

Napoleon also believed that it would be many months before an Allied army could be sent against him. Russia's ability to mobilize was notoriously slow; Prussia was handicapped by having to garrison and police the great new territories she had acquired; the British were incapable of putting a really formidable army in the field, and Austria was now fully engaged by the war Murat had forced on her in Italy.

In the meantime, the Council of State had sent an address to the Emperor, making it plain that though he might use that title the sovereignty of France now rested with the people. They then called on him to guarantee by proclamations to the Army and the nation all the liberal principles and rights which had been won by the Revolution.

To comply was most strongly against his inclinations, but he had already come to realize that, although his return had been accepted by the majority of the population, they had no intention of allowing him to enjoy again the despotic powers he had gradually built up from the time when he had become First Consul; so he replied with deceptive meekness that his only desire was to serve the people. Then, as a sop to liberal opinion, he decreed the abolition of the slave trade which he had formerly flatly refused to consider.

Shortly afterwards, Carnot raised the question of education, pointing out that there were two million children in France who did not receive even primary schooling, and that this must be rectified. To do so would entail a very considerable sum of money, and Napoleon needed every cent he could raise to increase the size of his army; but, again, he did not feel himself strong enough to oppose this socialist measure, so made the best of things by agreeing with apparent enthusiasm.

Money was a problem as, unlike the old days, he could no longer demand huge indemnities and subsidies from countries he had conquered, and he had had to forgo the hated *droits réunis,* which the Bourbons had promised to abolish but then gone back on their word. He was further greatly irritated by having to abolish the censorship and submit to a free Press which now criticized his every action.

He saw Roger daily and did not disguise from him the fact that he was bitterly disappointed by the results of his return. In the past he had ridden roughshod over everybody, and treated even the Senate with open contempt. Now he was no more than a figurehead, and dependent on retaining the good will of a group of men who were determined that his powers should be limited to those of a constitutional monarch.

In the meantime three of his brothers had returned to Paris: the indolent Joseph, the scatter-brained Jerome and, most unexpectedly, Lucien. The last was a most unprepossessing person, with long, gangling limbs, but a first-class brain. He had played a major part in getting Napoleon made First Consul; had then become a Minister, and abused his powers shamefully. Having amassed a great fortune, his socialist principles had reasserted themselves to the point of violently opposing Napoleon making himself Emperor, quarrelling with him and, in 1804, taking himself off to Rome.

Presumably it was Napoleon's widely publicized statement that he now intended to reign as a constitutional monarch that had induced Lucien to return after his long residence abroad. As he had always been regarded as a dyed-in-the-wool Republican, Napoleon was pleased to have his support as evidence of his assumed new radical outlook, and planned to get him made President of the Lower House of the Assembly which was now being summoned. But once more he had to submit to a snub from the group that was keeping him in Power. Instead of Lucien, they elected Lanjuinas, an honest, fearless representative of the old Republicans.

The only happiness Napoleon now enjoyed was

reviewing his troops and, highly conscious that he dared waste no time in preparing to resist the attack still threatened by the Allies, he worked daily with Davout. Apart from the half-dozen Marshals who had remained loyal to Louis and were now with him at Ghent, the Emperor was sadly missing others of his old paladins. Augereau, who had betrayed him, had gone into retirement, as also had Masséna, Berthier, Oudinot, Moncey and Jourdan. He had not yet fully forgiven Ney for his past treachery, so left him with his command at Besançon. Suchet guarded the Alps and Brune commanded for him in the south. So he had with him only Davout at the War Office and Soult, whom he had made his Chief of Staff.

The strength of the Army had also been greatly reduced by the Bourbons, and it was essential to build it up again. Junior officers who had been forced into retirement were volunteering to rejoin by the hundred, but he needed privates, so one day he announced to his Council, 'I must have an immediate levy of three hundred thousand men.'

'That is impossible,' said Carnot. 'The conscription laws will no longer be obeyed merely by your order.'

'What?' exclaimed Napoleon. 'Am I no longer Emperor?'

'Yes, Sire. But with restrictions and limits.'

Giving way to a paroxysm of rage, the Emperor jumped up and strode out of the room.

This was by no means the last humiliation Napoleon was to suffer. It was proposed in Council that he should give up his title and assume that of *Generalissimo* or President of the Republic. Lucien Bonaparte was to become Minister of the Interior, and Carnot to replace Davout as Minister of War. The last, and Admiral Decrès so furiously opposed this that, after giving way,

Napoleon suddenly reversed his decision; but compromised by agreeing to give the nation a more liberal constitution.

This was drawn up as 'An Additional Act to the Constitution of the Empire'. Its principal concessions were that no tax could be imposed, no loan raised, no levy of men made for the Army, except by consent of the Chamber of Deputies; all acts of government must be signed by the Minister of the Department; judges were to be irremovable for life; all trials were to be held in public, and no person could be arrested, prosecuted, imprisoned or exiled except according to the forms prescribed by the laws.

This new piece of legislation was offered to the French people for acceptance or rejection by a referendum. The Army and Marine were also given the right to register their opinion and this, being contrary to all precedent, caused much resentment among the public. The result was for acceptance by a large majority, but it was remarked that less than half the people who were entitled to vote exercised that right and, on balance, the Additional Act did Napoleon far more harm than good. While it pleased the Liberals, the masses were disappointed, because it was much less radical than they had been led to expect, and the devoted Bonapartists were greatly dismayed that the resolute Emperor of the old days should now have shown such weakness.

The result of the plebiscite was announced, and the Emperor publicly signed the Act before a great concourse of troops and people assembled on May 26th on the Champs de Mars. Afterwards, all the Senators and Deputies renewed their oath of allegiance to him, and he presented eagles to the standard bearers of the Imperial Guard.

The emotions of the crowd were so aroused by this splendid spectacle that they gave the Emperor a tremendous ovation, but their enthusiasm for him was far from deepseated. Ten days earlier, the Royalists in La Vendée had again taken up arms, and civil war had broken out in Brittany; but it was another international war that the people were now dreading. Their memories of their sufferings in the previous year were still vivid. The occupying forces of barbarian Cossacks and jack-booted Prussians had treated them with great brutality. Thousands of French girls and women had been raped, the furniture in countless homes either wantonly smashed up or stolen. And if that happened again, it would have been caused by Napoleon's return; for it was not against the French people that the Allies threatened to renew the war, but against the Emperor personally. It had even been suggested to him that, to save the nation, he should voluntarily retire again into exile, but he kept assuring them that their fears of another war were groundless.

During these weeks between the beginning of April and the end of May, Napoleon's efforts to divide the Allies or come to some arrangement with them were unceasing. He even wrote to his father-in-law, offering to abdicate in favour of his son, with Marie Louise as Regent; but this offer was rejected.

Meanwhile, the Allies were making their preparations to renew the conflict. A Russian army was on the march southward, the Prussians were massing on the Rhine, and the English were sending troops to Belgium. Murat's attempt to raise the Italian people against their Austrian masters and his impetuous attack had, at first, met with spectacular success. With eight thousand men he had invaded the Papal States and in turn captured Rome, Florence and Bologna. But, when he reached the line of the Po, his fortunes turned. By then the Austrians had mustered a considerable army of dependable troops. The Neapolitans made poor soldiers. They were checked at Emilia, then forced back to Tolentino and there, on May 3rd, utterly defeated. As Murat retreated, he could not rally even ten thousand men to defend his capital. On the 15th of the month he was forced to disguise himself and flee from Naples by sea. So Austria was again master of Italy, and now free to send her best troops to join those of her allies.

For some time past, Roger had reluctantly abandoned all hope that Napoleon would be allowed to retain his throne without fighting for it; but, like most of his fellow officers, he thought it unlikely that the campaign would open before the autumn. It was obvious that none of the Allies would be stupid enough to attack France separately, and several months must elapse before all four of the Great Powers could possibly concentrate in mass, either on the Rhine or in Switzerland.

This delay before the fighting started would be invaluable to Napoleon, as it would give him the time to build up a formidable army again. The Bourbons had reduced it to two hundred thousand men. The Emperor's call for volunteers had already brought forward eighty-five thousand old soldiers, most ex-prisoners of war, and in September the annual levy was due which, with the further volunteers who were coming in daily, should bring his army up to four hundred thousand.

Some twenty-five per cent of these would, admittedly, be raw recruits, but they could be spread evenly among the seasoned regiments and would soon model their conduct on that of the N.C.O.s and other old soldiers. Moreover, there was the National Guard. All citizens between twenty and sixty years of age were required to serve in it. Since April, Napoleon had decreed that a great part of it should be mobilized, and it was estimated that by midsummer two hundred and fifty thousand would be available. He planned to use these for garrisoning his own fortresses; and in the new campaign, unlike those previous to 1814, he would not have to deplete his forces in the field by garrisoning fortresses on the far side of the Rhine and in Italy, or holding down Spain.

The Allies meanwhile would be preparing to invade France. They had declared that they would raise six hundred thousand men for the purpose. But it was certain that Britain would not be able to contribute her one hundred and fifty thousand, so it seemed probable that the Allied army would not exceed half a million men. That would give them a superiority over Napoleon of five to four. But against that they would, as had always been the case, be hampered by divided command and opposed to the greatest military genius of the age. Therefore, Roger thought it highly probable that, in the autumn campaign, Napoleon had a very good chance not only of holding his enemies at bay, but of forcing them to come to terms with him.

Personally he was not unduly concerned that he would again have to participate in a series of battles. As he was not a regimental soldier, he never had to take part in cavalry charges, nor hold a place in an infantry square to resist one. His sole duty was to take his turn with the other A.D.C.s in carrying orders at a gallop across the field from the Emperor to corps or divisional commanders. He had had horses shot under him, but only twice had been severely wounded. That might happen again, or he might be killed by a stray bullet or cannon-ball. He might, too, have to use his sword in an encounter with a Prussian, Austrian or Russian, but it had never greatly troubled his conscience that he had maimed or killed foreign soldiers in order to maintain his false identity as Colonel le Comte de Breuc, and so be of great service to his own country.

It was on June 1st that all his assumptions about the coming conflict were suddenly shattered. He was on duty in the anteroom outside the big salon in the Elysée, where Napoleon held his conferences. The door opened, and General Rapp, now a Corps Commander, emerged. In the Russian campaign, Rapp had occupied Roger's new position as A.D.C.-in-Chief, so they knew each other well. Smiling at him, the General said:

'Well, Breuc, our master has just been disclosing to the Council the strategy he means to adopt. He has decided to wait no longer, but eliminate one of our enemies before the others can take the field. We'll be off to war next week, and are going into Belgium to drive the English into the sea.'

17

The Die is Cast

FOR once Roger lost control of his features. His mouth dropped open and he stood there aghast at the idea that he would be called on to fight his fellow countrymen. Throughout all the campaigns in which he had accompanied Napoleon, the Emperor had never been personally opposed by a British army, so never before had Roger been faced with such a situation.

Rapp stared at him for a moment, then asked, 'What's the matter, man? Aren't you glad we'll be leaving Paris and free at last from these damn' niggling Deputies?'

It was impossible for Roger to give the real reason for the shock he had received. Quickly pulling himself together, he replied, 'Naturally I am. But I was so amazed at what you told me. To take such a decision the Emperor must have gone out of his mind.'

'Oh, it entails a big risk, I grant you that, and several people argued against it. But there's a lot to be said for taking the initiative.'

'What, with an army of fewer than three hundred thousand, half of which will have to be left behind for one reason or another?'

'Not as many as that. We have only one frontier adjacent to enemy territory—Prussia's new province along the Rhine. It is of no great length, and hundreds of miles from Prussia proper, so we haven't much to fear from that quarter.'

'It will need at least a division to guard it, though. Then we'll have to leave others to prevent the Spaniards from taking it into their heads to cross the Pyrenees, and the Austrians launching an attack from Nice. There is also the coast. To leave that open would be to invite a British landing. And we have the best part of twenty thousand men tied up in La Vendée.'

'True; but Soult has taken all that into consideration.

'How is he shaping as Chief of Staff?'

'No-one could equal that sour big-head Berthier at the job, but Soult has more brains than most of the Marshals. Anyway, he says he can put one hundred and twenty-five thousand men into the field, and secret orders for troop movements are being sent out tonight.'

'What is the latest intelligence about Allied forces in Belgium?'

'The milord Wellington is in command, but since he arrived there early in April it is not thought that he has succeeded in building up his English to more than thirty thousand. Of course, he has Hanoverians, Brunswickers and Nassauers under him as well. Then there are the Dutch-Belgian troops of this new state created for the Dutchman now called King William. Together they total perhaps one hundred thousand, but they'll need twenty thousand to garrison Antwerp, Ostend and other fortresses, so we should considerably outnumber them. That was one of the Emperor's strongest arguments for striking now. We should be able to put the weakest of the four allies out of the game before any of the others can come to his assistance.'

'You forget the Prussians. They must have at least one corps on the Rhine.'

'They have. But will they dare risk their necks before

their main army can come to its support? I doubt it.'

'If they do, we'll be in an unholy mess. The frontier of Rhenish Prussia is no more than a hundred miles from Brussels, and almost due east of it. Should the Prussians get early intelligence of the Emperor's intentions and decide to act, they will be in a perfect position to outflank him.'

The General shrugged. 'I have already agreed there is some risk entailed, but for the chance of disposing altogether of the English it is worth taking. A decisive victory over them would give the others pause. Austria is bitterly resentful of Prussia's recent aggrandisement. With the milord Wellington's army out of the way, we should be able to smash Prussia. That would delight the Austrians, so they might well leave Prussia to her fate. Besides, think of the political advantages of this move.'

'Political advantages?' Roger repeated vaguely, his mind still mainly occupied with his personal problem.

'Why, yes. Where are your wits today, Breuc? How would you rate our master's present popularity?'

'It has never been lower. The people were delighted to be rid of the Bourbons, and expected miracles of Napoleon; but he's in no position to perform them. The nation is now split into half a dozen factions, only one of which is wholeheartedly for the Emperor.'

'Exactly. And what is the time-honoured way for a government that is unpopular to unite a nation behind it? To go to war, *mon ami* To go to war.'

Roger nodded. 'That would certainly put an end to the discontent in the Army. It's just what all the old "moustaches" have been longing for. They spent so many years of their lives looting and raping that they will cheer themselves hoarse at the thought of having the old days back again. It would bring back to the

Emperor the support of many other people, too. But not the majority. They were led to believe that he was on good terms with Austria and England, but they are now undeceived and dreading France again being occupied by the Allies.'

'You are wrong again. That would be the case if the Emperor had waited until the autumn. They would then have had real cause to fear that we should be overwhelmed by the massed armies of our enemies. But for us to go into Belgium now is a very different matter. Belgium was for so long a part of France. Its people are of the same blood as ourselves. Against their will they have been shamefully given to the Dutch. This will be a war of liberation, to free them and regain our old frontier on the Scheldt. Believe me, the nation will be behind the Emperor to a man.'

Giving Roger a friendly slap on the shoulder, Rapp added, 'But I've a host of things to do, so I must go now. *Adieu, mon ami.* We'll soon be seeing a lot of each other in Flanders.'

Left to himself Roger wrestled with this new problem that faced him. He felt that, now Napoleon intended to reopen hostilities himself by attacking the British, the probability was that the three other Allies would immediately hasten their preparations to the utmost, in the hope of falling on the aggressor while he was still engaged in Belgium. If they succeeded, that would certainly mean the end for Napoleon. In any case, Roger's first thought had been that he ought to slip out of Paris that night and make his way to Brussels as swiftly as possible, in order to warn Wellington of the impending invasion.

On the other hand, Rapp's belief that the Austrians would back out of aiding the Prussians, and so bring about the collapse of the whole Coalition, could not be ignored. If matters went that way, Napoleon would keep his throne, and Roger, if he remained with him, retain both his honours and the marvellous prospect of having Georgina to live with him at St. Maxime— all of which he would certainly lose if he set out for Belgium that night.

In spite of his earlier decisions that, if things went well with the Emperor, he would live in France in future, Roger's patriotism had never wavered, and in this new crisis he had every intention of serving his own country to the utmost of his ability. But the question now arose of how best to do so. As yet he could only warn Wellington of Napoleon's general intention, and there were plenty of other people in Paris who would shortly be in a position to do that. Many Royalists had remained in the capital, and obviously a number of them would be in constant communication with King Louis, who was now in Ghent, and he would pass on all the information he received to Wellington.

The thing that would be of real value to the Duke would be knowledge of the Emperor's strength and the dispositions he would make for his attack. For the moment Roger was ignorant of these, but he would be certain to learn them by the time the French army reached the Belgian frontier. Then, therefore, and not now, would be the time to quit Napoleon and make for the British headquarters.

For this reason Roger decided on a policy which had served him well on numerous previous occasions. Until the time was ripe, he would maintain an attitude of masterly inactivity.

During the week that followed, Roger and the rest of the Emperor's entourage were overwhelmed with work. Baron Méneval, Napoleon's *Chef de Cabinet*, was red-eyed from lack of sleep. Marshal Soult dictated despatches to the Commanders of formations until his voice was hoarse, and his temper frayed to ribbons. The A.D.C.s were constantly on the run with verbal instructions thought too dangerous to put on paper, to Napoleon's most trusted adherents. All over France regiments were on the march, the majority in a northerly direction; but the ultimate intention of all these movements was kept strictly secret by the senior officers who alone were entrusted with it.

Early in June, an event occurred which, had Napoleon acted differently, might have changed the fate of Europe. He received a letter from his brother-in-law, Murat. Having fled in disguise by sea from Naples, the ex-King had landed at Toulon on May 19th, and he wrote offering his sword to his former master.

Although Murat was a vain, boastful blockhead, the fact remained that he was, without exception, the finest cavalry leader in the world. He had a genius for assessing the lie of the land on a battlefield, for distances that horses could cover at speed, according to their degree of freshness, and of timing for when he should give the order to charge. In the flamboyant uniforms he had designed for himself, huge plumes waving from his busby, smothered in jewels and armed only with his gold Marshal's baton he had, on innumerable occasions, led charges that had overwhelmed masses of enemy infantry and massed batteries of guns. But Napoleon, convinced that had it not been for Murat's impetuous invasion of the Papal States peace could have been kept and the Allies would have refrained from combining again against France, angrily and stupidly refused the services of this great paladin to whom he owed so many of his victories.

On June 7th, in great state the Emperor opened the first session of the newly-elected Chambers of Peers and

Deputies. Having gained their goodwill by speaking enthusiastically of the new constitution, he went on to announce a piece of news that, most fortunately for his purpose, had just come to hand. The French frigate *Melpomène* had been attacked and captured in the Mediterranean, after sustaining terrible casualties, by an English 74-gun ship-of-the-line. Great indignation was expressed by the Assembly, and it enabled Napoleon to make a rousing appeal to their patriotism. Pointing out that France was surrounded by enemies, he begged them not to waste their energies in party disputes, but to unite and support him in such measures as he felt necessary to take in defence of the nation against the monarchies who would deprive the people of their liberties.

Early the following day another piece of news came in, which again could have changed the history of Europe, had Napoleon acted differently. On June 4th the Chouans in La Vendée had suffered a disastrous defeat at St. Giles, near Nantes, and their brave leader, la Rochejaquelein, had been killed. Against them the Emperor had sent two divisions and a brigade of the Imperial Guard. Had he recalled them immediately, it would have given him the better part of another twenty thousand men for his Belgian campaign; but, probably fearing that the revolt had not been completely stamped out, he failed to take the risk of doing so.

Having appointed a Council of Regency, with his brother Joseph as its President, he gave a small dinner party for his family on the evening of the 11th.

At four o'clock in the morning of the 12th an imposing cavalcade had assembled outside the Tuileries. Before the broad steps of the palace stood Napoleon's travelling berlin. It was drawn by eight mettlesome horses; the coachman, postillions and outriders were clad in rich liveries. Behind it were row upon row of mounted officers in a great variety of splendid uniforms edged with gold lace. A light breeze ruffled the ruches of white feathers adorning the cocked hats of some and gently swayed the tall plumes rising from the busbies of others. Scores of flambeaux lit the scene, glinting on helmets, sword hilts, sabre tassels, epaulettes, spurs and the medals that decorated the breast of every one of them.

The Emperor came down the broad steps accompanied by Caulaincourt and Méneval. A fanfare of trumpets sounded. Everyone came rigidly to attention. No sooner had Napoleon and his companions settled themselves in the big coach than it set off at a fast trot.

As A.D.C.-in-Chief, Roger rode in the first rank of officers who followed. All hope of maintaining peace was now at an end. Fate had decreed that yet once more he must play a part in Napoleon's wars.

18

Roger's Greatest Coup

DRIVEN at high speed, in twelve hours the Emperor was at Laon and on the 14th reached Beaumont, on the French frontier, where it projected most deeply into Belgium.

With great skill he had succeeded in moving his main army up to positions between Valenciennes and Thionville, without alarming the enemy, and he now contracted it to a front of thirty-five miles, centring on Beaumont. Rapp had been detached with the 5th Corps, numbering twenty thousand men, to face the Rhine, and the Emperor had under his own hand five others: the 1st commanded by Count d'Erlon, the 2nd by Reille, the 3rd by Vandamme, the 4th by Gérard and the 6th by Count Lobau. No Marshal led a corps, as Soult was Chief of Staff; Grouchy, only recently made a Marshal, had been given the cavalry.

Yet the bravest of Napoleon's old companions was, after all, destined to play a big part in the campaign. The Emperor had ordered up the troops from Besançon, but he had not yet forgiven Ney for promising Louis XVIII to bring the invader from Elba back to Paris in an iron cage. Sadly, dressed in civilian clothes, Ney followed his troops to Beaumont in a hired trap. There, Napoleon saw him standing forlornly outside an inn. An emotional reconciliation immediately took

place. The Emperor then gave him command of fifty
thousand men—the 1st and 2nd Corps, ten regiments
of cavalry and seventy-two guns—which amounted to
nearly half the available troops.

However lacking Napoleon's army may otherwise
have been in renowned leaders of his past campaigns,
and small as it was compared to the legions half a
million strong that he had mustered in 1812 and 1813,
it was one of the finest he had ever commanded. In his
Russian and German campaigns at least half his
troops had been forced levies from countries he had
conquered, and a high percentage of the French had
been boys in their teens, recently conscripted. With
him now he had no divisions of Prussians or Austrians
who, if things went badly, might desert him; no Saxons
or Italians who could not be relied on to continue
fighting if they found themselves out-numbered, and
no youngsters who had had no more than a few weeks'
training on a barrack square. All his troops with
very few exceptions, were French and tough, tireless
men who had soldiered with him through many
campaigns.

Since his return to France he had been very skilful
also in refurbishing his own image. So successful had
he been that the majority of people had come to
believe that he had never really suffered defeat in his
last campaign. That was only a lie put about by the
Bourbons. The truth was that he had been betrayed by
his Marshals and in particular by Marmont, Duke de
Ragusa, who had surrendered Paris. This version of
the events leading up to his abdication had become so
generally accepted that the word *ragusa* had been
adopted into the French language as synonymous with
traitor. In consequence his veterans had complete confidence in his genius, and thought of him only as the

man who had led them to victory at Wagram, Austerlitz, Eylau, Friedland and the battle of the Pyramids.
Wherever he came in sight he was again greeted with
deafening shouts of '*Vive l'Empereur*'.

A further advantage he had in this campaign was
that the Belgians looked upon themselves as French,
and ever since his return to Paris had been praying that
he would come to liberate them from the hated Dutch.
In consequence, while there were many Belgian spies
working for him across the frontier and constantly
sending in reports of the strength and position of enemy
troop formations, Belgians who corresponded with
friends in France and so learned from them that
French troops were marching toward the frontier,
kept this information to themselves.

The upshot of this was, as Roger learned to his consternation, that the Emperor was extremely well
informed about the situation of Wellington's forces,
whereas, since they were spread over a front of nearly
fifty miles between Mons and Ghent and showed no
sign of concentrating, it was evident that they were
still unaware that Belgium was about to be invaded.

Greatly worried by this, Roger now blamed himself
for not having left Paris secretly at the beginning of
June, in order to warn Wellington of Napoleon's intentions; but it had never for a moment occurred to
him that Royalist intelligence in Paris was so inefficient
that word of the Emperor's preparations for war would
not have been sent to Louis XVIII. Possibly it had, but
de Blacas and the other fools in Ghent had been so
wrapped up in their own egotistic intrigues that they
had neglected to pass it on to the British or Dutch. In
any case, now that Napoleon's army was concentrated
on the frontier Roger felt certain, knowing him so well,
that he would lose no time in launching his offensive;

so any warning to Wellington would now come too late to be of any value. In consequence, he decided to remain in Beaumont and hope that, during the next few days, another opportunity of serving his country would arise.

Napoleon's information about the Prussian army was by no means so good. Unlike the Belgians, the population in the Rhine provinces was almost entirely pro-German, and Prussia proper was bitterly anti-French; so it was next to impossible to secure accurate intelligence about the numbers of troops still under arms there. It was, however, known that General Ziethen had a corps about thirty thousand strong, extended over the sixty miles between Liège and Charleroi; so if the Emperor drove straight ahead from Beaumont in the direction of Brussels and the Prussians decided to come immediately to the assistance of their Anglo-Dutch allies, Napoleon's flank would be exposed to attack from Charleroi.

He dared not risk that, and the only alternative was to open war against Prussia at the same time as he invaded Belgium. By striking at Ziethen's corps at once with greatly superior numbers, he considered he could swiftly overwhelm it, then fall on Wellington's army and destroy it before the Prussians had time to bring up their main army from Prussia.

Roger's assumption that Napoleon, having succeeded in concentrating his army on the frontier unknown to his enemies, would lose not a moment of this advantage but strike immediately, proved correct. At dawn on the morning of June 15th the French army prepared to cross the frontier and throw itself upon the centre of the Allied line where the ends of the two armies were adjacent but under different commands.

That morning the Emperor had cause for both sorrow

and rejoicing. He learned that Marshal Berthier, Prince de Neufchâtel and Prince de Wagram, who for so many years had been his Chief of Staff, and with brilliant precision arranged the deployment of his troops before battle, was no more. After joining his family in Bamberg and seeing enemy soldiers marching through the street toward the frontier of France, he had been so stricken with remorse at having deserted his old master that he had committed suicide by throwing himself out of a window.

The other news, brought by fast courier from Paris, was that overnight the Emperor had once more become the national hero. Within twenty-four hours of leaving the capital, it had become generally known that he was about to wage a 'war of liberation' by invading Belgium. The French had long looked on Belgium as part of France, and its severance from France the previous year had been more bitterly resented than any other article in the Treaty of Paris. He was swift to realize how much this sudden upsurge of popular feeling meant for him. Given a victorious campaign, he would be able to knock off the shackles with which the Jacobins and Liberals had confined him. Once more the autocrat, he could dissolve that hated Assembly of Deputies, as he had already told his intimates he intended to do at the first favourable opportunity.

However, he was unable to open the battle as early as he had hoped, because the corps of Vandamme and Gérard, with which he intended to attack the Prussians —while those of Reille and d'Erlon under Ney advanced against Wellington—were both late in coming up into position. An accident had befallen the single officer sent by Soult with orders to Vandamme to march at 2 a.m., and Gérard was delayed by one of his Generals, an old Vendéean named Bourmont, suddenly deciding to desert and take a number of his officers with him. But, once the assault was launched, Napoleon's seventy-eight thousand French easily drove back Ziethen's thirty thousand Prussians. The bridges across the Sambre were forced, the Emperor himself directed the capture of Charleroi and, by evening, Grouchy's cavalry corps had driven the Prussians back to Gilly.

The results of the day were highly satisfactory to Napoleon, as he was confident that he had succeeded in his objective of driving a wedge between Ziethen and Wellington. But what he did not know was that the Prussian forces in that area were far larger than he had supposed. Their army of the Rhine consisted of not one but four corps. Those of Perch and Thielmann were at Namur and Ciney, no great distance to the east, and that of Von Bülow further off at Liège. Ziethen, too, was far from finished. His rear guard battalions had been badly mauled by the French cavalry but, apart from that, he had succeeded in making an orderly withdrawal. Another factor, only belatedly known to the Emperor, was that the redoubtable Blücher had hastened to the scene and taken command in person.

This last piece of information did not perturb Napoleon. Although he had spent eighteen hours in the saddle that day and was very tired, he was in the highest spirits and displayed contempt for his adversaries, declaring that he admired Blücher's courage, but thought him a poor General, and that he considered Wellington both incapable and unwise.

Soult, who had fought against Wellington in Spain, was bold enough to say that he disagreed, and that the Emperor might have cause to change his mind when he was opposed in person to the Duke.

At that the Emperor sneered, 'Oh, naturally you are afraid of him, because he defeated you time after time.'

So confident was Napoleon that he had everything
well in hand that he sent a despatch from Charleroi
to Ney, early on the morning of the 16th, stating that
he intended to attack the Prussians again at Sombref if
they had not already retreated further, and clear the
road as far as Gembloux, while Ney was to advance
through Quatre Bras and halt two leagues beyond it.
They would then unite and march on Brussels. He also
sent orders to Grouchy to continue his advance past
Sombref, so as to fall on the retreating enemy's left wing.

It was close on eleven o'clock before the Emperor
reached Fleurus and, to his annoyance, he found
Grouchy still there; but the Marshal excused himself
by reporting that the village of Ligny, which lay ahead,
was strongly held by the enemy. Napoleon then went
up to the top of the windmill to survey their position for
himself.

A shallow valley of corn fields separated the two
villages. On the further slope, beyond Ligny, stood two
smaller villages: Bry and Sombref, between which were
ranged Ziethen's infantry. Another, nearer village, St.
Amand, lay to the left on higher ground, and through
Ligny itself ran a stream with high banks. But Napoleon could not see this or anything of the village except
the roofs, as it was concealed in a hollow. He was therefore ignorant of the fact that the buildings were packed
with troops, and that behind the opposite slope Blücher
had brought up the corps of Perch. Owing to Gérard's
delay in arriving with his corps, the Emperor was
unable to open the battle until two o'clock. The time
lost enabled Thielmann's corps also to come up; so,
while Napoleon believed himself to be opposed to
twenty thousand Prussians at the most, he was now out-
numbered, for Blücher's force had been raised to
eighty-seven thousand.

Ney had also met with delay in getting his troops up to Quatre Bras, so was unable to open his attack until two o'clock, and this loss of the morning by both French forces enabled Blücher and Wellington to meet.

The Duke had undoubtedly been caught napping, as he was still at supper at an impromptu dance given by the Duchess of Richmond in Brussels, when the news was brought to him that the French had crossed the frontier. After sending urgent orders to concentrate his army, he rode to Quatre Bras, arriving at ten o'clock that morning. Finding no sign of imminent action there, he sent off a despatch to Blücher, then followed it himself at the gallop to Bussy, where the two commanders held a hasty conference. Blücher asked the Duke to send support to him at Ligny, but Wellington could only promise to come to his aid if he was not attacked himself. He then returned with all speed to Quatre Bras, in time to direct operations against Ney.

It was not until the battle of Ligny was about to begin that masses of infantry pouring over the far slope behind Ziethen's battalions caused Napoleon to realize that he was opposed to far greater numbers than he had expected; but, still confident of victory, he launched Vandamme's corps against the village of St. Amand and that of Gérard against Ligny, while Grouchy's cavalry protected the French right flank.

The fighting was ferocious in both villages. Gérard's leading companies were mown down by volleys from the Prussians who held Ligny. Then the French artillery opened fire with devastating effect; hundreds of cannon-balls smashed in roofs and walls and started fires that threw up flames and great clouds of smoke. Gérard attacked again and this time his men reached the houses. Innumerable hand-to-hand conflicts took place in them. At length the Prussians were driven out and over the stream, but reinforcements stiffened the resistance, so that the French could not force their way across the water.

Vandamme's troops stormed St. Amand, but could not proceed further. At the expense of his centre, Blücher sent regiment after regiment to hold the high ground there. The heat of the burning houses, in addition to the scorching sun of a midsummer day, was almost unbearable. Thousands of men were locked in deadly combat as the long line, half obscured by smoke, swayed back and forth.

Roger remained with the Emperor and the rest of his staff up in the mill, as there were no special orders to be sent to the corps or divisional commanders. They were all doing their utmost to break through the Prussian line. The battle had been raging for just over an hour when Roger heard Napoleon mutter:

'If only I hadn't let Ney have d'Erlon. Had I his corps here, I'd have the Prussians on the run.'

For a few minutes the significance of the remark was not fully grasped by Roger, then he suddenly realized the possibility it offered. Quietly he slipped away and down into the lane. Running to the place where his charger had been stabled, he mounted and left Ligny at the gallop. Quatre Bras lay to the north-west, about six miles away. Heading in that direction, he rode all out, as though he was hoping to win a steeplechase. As he drew nearer to Quatre Bras, the sounds of gun-fire coming from that direction told him, as he had supposed, that a battle was raging there between Ney and Wellington. But he saw nothing of it, other than drifting smoke partly obscuring the blue sky, because some two miles from Quatre Bras he came upon French troops lying about on the grass, and learned that they

K

belonged to d'Erlon's corps. Five minutes later he
found the Corps Commander, whom he knew well.

Pulling up his steaming horse, he saluted d'Erlon and
asked in surprise, 'Why are you here, Count? I expected to find you in the thick of the battle.'

D'Erlon smiled. 'You had best ask the Marshal.
He ordered me to keep my corps here in reserve.'

Wiping the sweat from his forehead, Roger said
quickly, 'Thank God for that! I'll not have to ask you
to break off an action and perhaps leave him in difficulties. I've come from the Emperor. Old Blücher has
sprung a surprise on us by bringing up two extra corps.
The fighting at Ligny is terrific, and to break the
Prussians the Emperor needs more troops. His orders
are that you should bring your corps to Fleurus.'

'What!' exclaimed d'Erlon. 'March my corps to
Fleurus! I cannot do that. The Emperor placed me
under Marshal Ney.'

'I am aware of that, General; but this order super-
sedes that one.'

'But Wellington must be bringing up fresh troops.
The Marshal may need me at any moment to reinforce
him.'

'That cannot be helped. The Emperor needs your
corps urgently.'

'I appreciate that. But if I withdraw it from here,
that might cause Ney to lose his battle.'

'It is a risk that must be taken, Count. The battle at
Ligny is all-important. The Prussians are fighting most
doggedly, and it has emerged that their forces there are
greater than ours.'

'Have you a written order for me from the Emperor?'

Roger drew himself up and replied haughtily, 'Count,
you must be aware that as A.D.C.-in-Chief to the
Emperor, I do not need to bring you one.'

Slowly, d'Erlon nodded. 'That is true. Very well, then.'

Turning to an adjutant who stood near, he raised his hand. A moment later the bugles rang out, men scattered for half a mile round came to their feet and quickly fell into formation. A groom brought forward d'Erlon's horse, he mounted it and, with Roger beside him, set off at marching pace in the direction of Fleurus.

'Do you know, Count, how the Marshal's battle is going?' Roger asked.

'Well, I think,' d'Erlon replied, 'he opened it with Reille's corps only, because mine had much further to march, so was far behind and my men needed rest. From walking wounded who have come back I've a fair idea about what has been happening. There were only about seven thousand Dutch facing Ney to start with. Under their Prince of Orange they made a stout stand, but were soon driven from a farm called Bemioncourt, which formed the key position. Then Wellington himself appeared on the scene, with a division of English infantry and a Dutch-Belgian brigade. Our people could see the Duke quite clearly, up on a hill on the far side of the crossroads. The Marshal's artillery made mincemeat of the Dutch gunners, but I'm told that the English division was General Picton's, and they fought like devils. The last I heard, though, was that they were being driven back and cut up by our cavalry.'

As they rode on d'Erlon wished to take a route that would have brought his corps behind Ligny, and so out-flanked the Prussians; but Roger insisted that the Emperor would wish that it should come up behind Fleurus, to act as a reserve. D'Erlon, knowing how much store Napoleon set on using his own judgement in the timing of bringing a reserve into action and the direction in which it should be sent, reluctantly agreed. So it was past five o'clock before the corps got into its new position, a mile or so to the south-west of Fleurus.

When the Count had selected a spot shaded by some trees for himself and his staff, to await further orders, Roger rode on to Ligny to let the Emperor know that d'Erlon's corps was at his disposal. On reaching the mill he found everyone there tense, and the Emperor in a quandary how he should next direct the battle.

His hope had been that Ney, after dealing with the Anglo-Dutch, would swing his army in a right wheel to envelop the Prussians' right wing and rear. So important had this move become when the full strength of the Prussians had been realized that, at 3.15, Soult had sent off a despatch to Ney, the concluding phrase of which had read: *The Prussian army is lost if you act with vigour. The fate of France is in your hands.*

Yet still there was no news from Ney, nor sign of his army approaching on the north-western horizon. Blücher's troops still held on to their position on the slope just beyond St. Amand, but to enable them to do so he had had to weaken his centre. News reached Napoleon that Lobau's corps, which had been the most distant on the previous day, was at last coming up behind Fleurus. Now that he would have this as a reserve, he decided to send in the Imperial Guard to smash through the centre of the Prussians.

Just as he was about to give the order, one of Vandamme's *aides-de-camp* came galloping up to the mill to report that his General had sighted a great mass of troops, from twenty to thirty thousand strong, coming from the north-west and heading toward the rear of Fleurus.

This filled the Emperor and his staff with instant consternation. They jumped to the conclusion that, just as the Prussians had proved to be in much greater strength than expected, so Wellington, too, had after all not been caught napping, but had brought his whole army against Ney, defeated him and was now about to attack the French at Fleurus from the rear.

While Napoleon and Soult were still anxiously discussing how to deal with this new threat, Roger arrived to report that he had brought d'Erlon's corps up to within a mile behind the village. The Emperor stared at him in mingled relief and astonishment, then burst out:

'So they are the mass sighted by Vandamme. But how dare you act as you have done! I gave you no order to take d'Erlon's corps away from Ney.'

Roger was ready for that and, simulating surprise, cried indignantly:

'Sire, you did so in effect. It was soon after three o'clock, when you first realized that we were faced with far greater numbers of the enemy than we had expected. I heard you say, "If only I hadn't let Ney have d'Erlon. Had I his corps here, I'd have the Prussians on the run." Naturally, I didn't lose an instant, but galloped off to get it for you.'

The Emperor's face lightened for a moment and he said, 'As I inspired your impulse, I can hardly blame you.' Then he frowned again. 'But what in the devil's name is it doing behind Fleurus? It ought to be up on the left of our line, outflanking the enemy. Why the hell did you not lead it there?'

Again Roger protested, 'Sire, I would not be guilty of such impertinence as to attempt to direct your battles. I have simply brought up the corps you required. It is for you to decide how you mean to use it.'

'*Mon Dieu!*' exclaimed the exasperated Emperor. 'I've not a glibber man than you in my whole army.

But it's true that I do not permit decisions to be made for me. Get back now as fast as you can to d'Erlon. Tell him to advance with all speed past Vandamme's corps, then encircle the Prussians who are still holding out behind St. Amand.'

For some time past the sky had been clouding over, and the atmosphere had become terribly oppressive. Suddenly the storm burst. Great crashes of thunder drowned the sound of the guns, forked lightning streaked the black sky in a dozen places, the rain streamed down in torrents, hiding from sight the trampled cornfields in the valley that were now half covered with dead and wounded.

Within a few minutes of Roger leaving the mill his uniform was sodden and by the time he had mounted his horse he was soaked to the skin. Nothing could have suited him better, and he was filled with elation, for he had succeeded in accomplishing the great coup he had devised—to use Napoleon's muttered words as an excuse to deprive Ney of half the army with which he was attacking the British.

Doing this was, he knew, hard on Blücher, but he had done what he could to mitigate its value against the Prussians by bringing it up well behind Fleurus instead of direct to the field of battle. And now the terrible storm would further minimize its usefulness, by increasing the time needed for him to get back to d'Erlon and that which must elapse before the Count could bring his corps into action.

The blackness of the clouds was such that the summer evening had become almost as dark as night. Nearby streams were overflowing their banks, and the country lanes swiftly turning into mud. He nearly came to grief on a tree that, struck by lightning, had fallen across the road. It was a good twenty minutes after leaving the mill before he reached the place where he had left d'Erlon.

To his amazement d'Erlon was no longer there, neither were any of his men. The only signs that they ever had been there were some pieces of soaked paper and a few empty bottles, evidently thrown away after some of them had had a snack.

For some ten minutes Roger scouted round the area, peering ahead through the downpour, but d'Erlon and his corps had completely disappeared. Greatly puzzled, he rode back to Fleurus to report to the Emperor.

By the time he reached the mill the rain had lessened. While he had been absent, the situation had greatly altered. Regardless of the storm, the Emperor had launched the Imperial Guard against the Prussian centre, and they had broken through it. He had then left the mill to supervise in person a charge by Milhaud's cuirassiers against St. Amand. That, too, had proved successful. Blücher's army was now cut in half and his regiments were retiring toward Bry and Sombref. Between the two villages the Prussian cavalry made several charges, but they were repelled by Gérard's men and Grouchy's squadrons. For another hour or more the battle continued to rage by the evening light, but by nightfall Blücher's army was in full retreat toward Wavre.

Later that night the Comte de Flahaut, sent by Ney, arrived at the Emperor's headquarters, and the mystery of the disappearance of d'Erlon's corps was explained. When the Marshal had sent for him to act as support in the battle he had learned to his fury that the Emperor had ordered the corps to Ligny. He had at once despatched an A.D.C. after it, to inform d'Erlon that he needed his corps most urgently, and that d'Erlon was under his orders. Feeling that the Emperor did not appear to have any immediate need of him, whereas Ney had, d'Erlon had marched his corps back to Quatre Bras. But it had arrived there too late to go into action.

At Quatre Bras Ney had had the better of it, and forced Wellington to retire toward Genappe; but if Ney had had d'Erlon's corps with him he could have followed up with it and gained a complete victory.

So Roger had done far better than he had ever hoped. Not only had he saved his own countrymen from a severe defeat, but he had also kept d'Erlon's twenty thousand men out of both battles and they had not fired a single shot that day.

19

Battle and Chance Encounter

THERE ensued an acrimonious discussion between de
Flahaut and Napoleon. The Count described his
Marshal's fury at the Emperor having withdrawn
d'Erlon from his command and so deprived him of a
great victory. Napoleon retaliated by demanding why
Ney had failed to carry out his orders to occupy the
heights beyond Quatre Bras on the night of the 15th,
and failed to open his battle the following day before
2 p.m. Flahaut protested that, contrary to the information given by Soult to Ney—that the latter would meet
with no opposition—when his cavalry vedettes reached
the heights they found them already occupied by
enemy troops under Prince Bernard of Saxe-Weimar;
so he had naturally given his weary men a night's rest
by halting them at Fresnes. His delay in attacking had
been caused by two factors: firstly, he had only Reille's
corps with him, d'Erlon having that morning advanced
no further than Thuin; secondly, while preparing to
attack on the 16th, he had learned that Prussian
columns were marching westward from Sombref, a
movement he had feared might cut his line of communications at Fresnes. Hence his delay, until reassured by further information later in the day, that
his rear was not endangered.

Meanwhile Roger learned from Flahaut's A.D.C.

what had taken place at Quatre Bras. That offic
entirely supported his Marshal, and added that, as
Commander, Ney had been terribly handicapped b
the fact that he had taken over only two days pr
viously, so a staff had had to be got together for hi
hurriedly, some of whom he did not know and othe
who did not know one another.

The position behind Quatre Bras had greatly favou
ed the Allies, as the height was flanked on the left b
Bassu wood, so it was not until Reille had pressed hon
his attack that the weakness of the enemy was realize
Wellington had then arrived with English and Dutc
troops. They had beaten off Reille, and Ney had ha
to resort to using the whole of his artillery on them.
had caused terrific havoc in the Allied ranks, enablir
Reille to attack again. But by then a second Britis
division and the Brunswickers were entering the battl
and gave Wellington superiority of numbers. D'Erlon
corps could have turned the tide, but he had disap
peared. As a last resort Ney had launched Kelle
mann's heavy cavalry, and it had saved the day fo
the French. Both armies had fought with great stul
bornness, and were terribly mauled. By nightfall th
battle had ended in stalemate, Ney withdrawing
Fresnes and Wellington retiring up the Brussels roa
toward Genappe.

On the following morning, the 17th, Napoleon drov
to St. Amand, mounted his horse there and rode ov
the battlefield. It was an appalling sight. The ruine
villages were positively choked with bodies, the Lign
stream was full of them and dead and wounded la
scattered thickly all over both slopes of the shallo
valley. It was later established that the battle had co
the French eleven thousand casualties and the Prussiar
fourteen thousand.

Having given orders to several officers that the enemy wounded were to be cared for equally with the French, Napoleon dismounted and was subject to one of those strange periods that had affected him in recent years. In spite of the fact that the last of the Prussian troops were only just disappearing over the horizon in the neighbourhood of Sombref, where presumably they had fallen asleep from exhaustion, the Emperor, instead of giving orders for an immediate pursuit of Blücher's army, entered into a long discussion with Grouchy, Gérard and other senior officers about the political situation in Paris.

While they listened with obvious restlessness, the thoughts of Roger, who was standing in the background, had turned to a very different subject. As he gazed round on the thousands of dead and dying, his mind was occupied with the phenomena of death.

From the first time he had heard, many, many years before, of the theory of reincarnation from his friend Droopy Ned, one of whose hobbies was the study of Eastern religions, he had accepted it as the only logical belief. The Christian doctrine, derived from the Jews, that the dead were judged on a single life, tried by a god in the form of a huge man, and awarded either a pleasant residence above the clouds for eternity or sent to roast in hell's flames for ever, was manifestly absurd.

How could one agree that a man who had led a saintly life but, provoked beyond bearing, committed a murder, deserved to be tortured for all time; or that a man who had been guilty of consistent meanness and sadism deserved perpetual bliss because he had given his life for a friend? What of those who had been born half-witted, deformed, or the children of criminal parents who brought them up to follow evil ways?

When he had first mentioned the subject to Georgina,

he found that she was as firm a believer in reincarnation as he was. From her gipsy mother she had inherited psychic powers, and on several occasions had, without seeking them, received communications from the spirits of people who had been dead many years. Two of them had told her that, after a long period of rest, they were about to return to earth in new bodies, to pay off debts they had incurred in former incarnations, and learn new lessons for their future advancement.

From their youth onward, he and Georgina had discussed the subject many times. Both of them were convinced that the bond between them had been forged by having known each other intimately in several previous incarnations, that death could part them only for a little while, and they would be drawn together again in other bodies in incarnations yet to come.

While Napoleon continued to abuse the Jacobins and Liberals who had so greatly curbed his powers since his return, Roger gazed, almost in a trance, at one dead soldier after another, speculating on what the future might hold in store for them. Would the Prussian Captain with a bully's brutal-looking jaw return to serve under a harsh taskmaster; would the boy drummer with the fine, broad forehead become a judge; would the French Colonel with the many decorations again become a soldier and win still greater honours; would the private with the beautiful, long eyelashes perhaps be a woman in his next incarnation?

At last, after wasting half the morning in riding round the battlefield and talking with officers who dared not disagree with him, Napoleon was suddenly recalled to the fact that, although on the previous day he had won a splendid victory, he had not yet finally defeated his enemies.

One of Ney's A.D.C.s arrived at the gallop. Breathlessly he informed the Emperor that Wellington was again occupying the high ground beyond Quatre Bras, and that Excelmans scouts had reported Prussian cavalry to be occupying Gembloux. Napoleon was furious, as he had early that morning sent an order to Ney to press hard on the British. Now he decided to take over from Ney and attack them himself.

He was completely satisfied that the Prussians had been so badly mauled that they would be incapable of causing him any serious trouble for several days to come; but considerable numbers of them had got away, and it was important that they be prevented from joining the British. It seemed a sound assumption that Blücher's shattered corps would have retreated eastward to fall back on von Bülow's still intact corps at Liège; so, to prevent their attempting to move toward Wellington, the Emperor ordered Marshal Grouchy with his cavalry, and Vandamme and Gérard's now battered corps in support, to advance on Gembloux and drive the Prussians still further east. Early that morning Count Lobau's corps had come up to Fleurus and, with these fresh troops, Napoleon himself set off for Quatre Bras.

It was just as they were about to leave that they learned from the interrogation of a wounded Prussian officer that Blücher had narrowly escaped being killed or captured on the previous day. The gallant old Field Marshal had led one of the last charges in person. His horse had been shot under him, he fell, was rendered incapable of getting to his feet, and his own horsemen had been driven back by the French cuirassiers. He had been saved by his adjutant, Nostitz, who had flung himself down beside him and covered him with a cloak. As senior Prussian officers, unlike the French, wore very plain uniforms, the French took no special notice of them neither when pressing home their charge nor while trotting back afterwards. So Nostitz was able to rescue his badly bruised chief.

At about two o'clock, the Emperor was approaching Quatre Bras. To his fury he found that Ney was still only skirmishing with the British, so he left his carriage, mounted his white horse and urged his cavalry up the road at a gallop. Wellington, up on the heights, evidently sighted this new force coming up from the direction of Ligny, and decided to retire. Ney had also seen it and went to greet Napoleon, who yelled at him, 'You have ruined France!', then ordered him to attack with all his forces.

As the two French armies advanced and Napoleon threw in his formidable cavalry, another terrible thunder storm broke. Again the rain came down in torrents, turning the corn into sodden, tangled masses that hampered both the French advance and the British withdrawal. To save themselves from the French horse, the Allies retreated as swiftly as they could, choking the narrow street of Genappe and its bridge.

Beyond it, to save the British rear from slaughter, Lord Uxbridge, who commanded the cavalry, sent in the 7th Hussars against the leading French squadrons, which were the mounted units of the Imperial Guard. In all such cavalry encounters the French had the advantage, because they were equipped with steel corselets, whereas the British were unarmoured and could not use their sabres effectively against the bodies of their opponents. In this case, too, the Hussars, being light cavalry, were at a further disadvantage. The French had the better of it, cut them up, scattered

hem and renewed the pursuit in the pouring rain.
But on the slope Uxbridge had the heavy Household
cavalry. He launched them against the French, and
his time the British checked and drove back Napoleon's
inest horsemen.

The action saved the Allies' retreat from becoming
a rout, but the French still came on, and fighting con-
inued till twilight fell, horses and men plunging and
lithering on ground that had been churned into a sea
of mud. But Wellington succeeded in drawing off the
greater part of his army in good order along the road
o Waterloo, then turned at bay on the high ground
n front of the village. Napoleon, arriving on the rise
acing it at 6.30 p.m., ordered a strong force to charge
he slope, but the British artillery tore great lanes
hrough the weary French, and the Emperor was
orced to accept that all chance of destroying his
nemy that day had gone.

It was an appalling night. The storm continued for
everal hours. The troops were soaked to the skin,
heir knapsacks saturated. Wherever they moved,
hey squelched and floundered. Both armies bivouacked
s best they could where they had halted, the Allies
n the slope of Mont St. Jean, the French in the shallow
alley, their centre being the village of Planchenoit.
The Emperor made his headquarters at Caillou farm,
but slept in a tent pitched in a wood about a mile
urther forward. At one o'clock he awoke, went right
p to the front and walked about with General
Bertrand among his men, constantly asking groups of
hem if they had heard any sounds of the enemy
eating a further retreat. That they should do so was
is one fear, as he felt confident that, having seriously
rippled the Prussians, he would defeat Wellington
ext day and enter Brussels before nightfall.

Meanwhile, Roger and others at headquarters had learned through British and Dutch prisoners further particulars of Ney's first attack on Quatre Bras. In the early stages of the battle it had looked as though the Allies would be overwhelmed by the far greater numbers of French. But a battalion of Highlanders in square had resisted charge after charge by Lancers until it was almost annihilated. The Dutch King's son, the Prince of Orange, had been captured, but his Belgians had rallied and rescued him, although only at the price of being cut to pieces shortly afterwards. It was General Picton's division of veterans who had fought in the Peninsula, that had saved the day by holding their ground hour after hour with dogged courage. In the Bossu wood there had been terrible slaughter, and the French were within an ace of capturing it when the British Guards reached the battlefield. They had marched for twelve hours without a halt long enough to have a meal; yet, in spite of hunger and fatigue, they had driven the French back down the hill. But then Napoleon had arrived on the scene, turned the tide of battle and chased the Allies back past Genappe.

The Allies had sustained one great tragedy in the loss of the Duke of Brunswick. In 1809 he had organized an unsuccessful revolt in his own country against Napoleon's occupying forces, but led his Brunswickers, fighting the whole way, across Germany until they could be taken off by the British Navy. In England they had been formed into the King's German Legion and sent to fight under Wellington in the Peninsula, then returned to Germany in 1813, where they had assisted in the defeat of Napoleon at Leipzig. At Quatre Bras, early in the battle, the Duke received a severe wound, but had it bound up and returned to

lead his men in further charges. Later he received two
slight wounds and another serious one, but still fought
on until struck in the chest by a bullet and killed.

At last the dawn of the 18th broke and, now satisfied
that the Allies intended to give battle, the Emperor
returned to his headquarters. There he found a
despatch which had been sent off by Grouchy at 10 p.m.
the previous night. The Marshal reported from
Gembloux that some Prussian regiments had retired
toward Wavre, but the greater part of them, under
Blücher, had fallen back in the direction of Liège,
and he intended to pursue them; but, if necessary,
he would turn west to prevent any Prussians there
from joining Wellington.

Grouchy had proved himself an excellent cavalry
leader, but had had no experience of handling an
army, and his despatch was not entirely clear. But he
had twenty-one thousand men under him, so Napoleon
felt confident that he would have no difficulty in
keeping the Prussians busy. He then gave Soult
instructions for a reply. However, that also, as had
been the case with several of the Marshal Duke of
Dalmatia's despatches during this campaign, was not
altogether clear. For six years in Seville he had ruled
as the uncrowned King of southern Spain, amassed a
fabulous collection of paintings from castles, churches
and palaces, and enjoyed scores of lovely women.
Roger well remembered Soult's beautiful young
mistress-in-chief who had worn the uniform of a
Captain of Hussars, so that she could accompany
him on reconnaissances. That was Soult's *métier*,
and he was a highly competent General in the field.
But, as a Chief of Staff, he was a very poor substitute
for Berthier. In this case, the orders he sent to Grouchy
were that he must move toward Wavre to keep the

Prussians there occupied, but on no account must he lose touch with Blücher's main body.

The Emperor was in high good humour at breakfast, and remarked, 'The enemy's army outnumbers ours by more than a fourth; nevertheless, we have ninety chances out of a hundred in our favour.'

He was wrong about numbers, for he had seventy-four thousand veterans against Wellington's sixty-seven thousand men, only twenty-four thousand of whom were British, the others being Hanoverians, Nassauers, Brunswickers and Dutch Belgians; so the odds on Napoleon being the victor were even greater than his boast. However, Wellington had one great advantage. At Ligny the French had been able to see the whole of Blücher's army, right back to Sombref; whereas here, at Waterloo, the bulk of the Allied forces lay concealed behind the ridge of Mont St. Jean, so Napoleon's artillery could not bring direct fire upon them until they emerged over the crest, nor judge the number of the Duke's reserves.

It was obvious that the Allies did not intend to give up their advantageous position by opening the attack, so it was for Napoleon to make the first move. Owing to the terrible downpour on the previous night, the ground was still so sodden that any movements by artillery would be greatly hampered by mud. For that reason the Emperor decided to give time for the soil to dry, and did not order his troops to take up their positions until 11 a.m. His intention was to smash right through the Allied centre by a tremendous frontal attack, and his army was massed on a very narrow front in three lines. The first consisted of Reille's corps on the left and d'Erlon's on the right, both flanked by cavalry on the outer wings. The second line consisted of Count Lobau's corps, and the

third of the Imperial Guard, thirteen thousand
strong, again flanked by two thousand cavalry on either
side.

Wellington had put twelve brigades into his front
line, only six of which were British. His position formed
an L. In the middle of the long sector stood the farm of
La Haye Sainte, at the junction stood the château of
Hougoumont, both of which were strongly fortified.
On his right the short section of the L ran back to the
village of Merbraine, as a precaution against that
flank being turned. On his left flank there were two
small farms—Papelotte and La Haye—also fortified,
and the protection of a large wood named Bois de
Paris. It was from this side, too, that he expected the
support of some Prussian units, which had been
promised him in a despatch he had received that
morning from Blücher. The bulk of his army lay
concealed behind the crest.

At 11.30, the French artillery opened fire, and Reille
led the first attack on Hougoumont. The château had a
walled garden and orchard in front of and to the east of
it and a small wood on the west. The walls were loop-
holed and the place was garrisoned by two battalions
of the British Guards, plus a Dutch unit under the
Prince of Orange. Again and again Reille hurled his
divisions against it; again and again they were repelled.
At last they succeeded in capturing the coppice and
the orchard, and the dead were piled high against
the walls; but they could not penetrate the garden,
farm buildings or house.

Costly and determined as this attack was, it was
only a diversion. The main assault was to be delivered
half a mile to the east, where the road from Genappe
cut straight through the centre of the battlefield, across
Mont St. Jean towards Waterloo. There, covered by a

battery of eighty guns, d'Erlon's corps was drawn up
in four great columns, each consisting of eight battalions.

Senior officers who had fought in Spain were aware
of the stout resistance that could be put up by the
British double line against attack by columns, and
Soult warned the Emperor of it. Napoleon replied
with a sneer.:

'You were beaten by Wellington, so you think he is
a great General. But I tell you that Wellington is a bad
General, and the English will merely be a breakfast
for us.'

Reille, too, declared that against the English
frontal attack was rarely successful, and urged the
Emperor instead to attempt to outflank them. But he
would not listen.

Just as he was about to give the order to attack,
a large body of troops was sighted in the far distance,
about six miles to the north-east, on the heights of
Chapelle St. Lambert. Several of the Emperor's
staff believed them to be Grouchy's army but, as the
Marshal had reported that a number of Prussian units
had retreated to Wavre, Napoleon decided that these
must be they. However, they were several miles away,
and he took the view that by the time they could come
up he would already have won his battle; so, at 1.30
p.m., he launched d'Erlon's thirty-two battalions
against the Allied centre.

At the sight of this vast mass of enemy infantry
marching steadily up the slope toward them, the
Dutch-Belgian brigade panicked and fled; but Picton's
two British brigades stood fast. The French, now
handicapped by their own depth, could barely return
the fire poured upon the heads and sides of their
columns, yet they marched on and, with cheers of

triumph, reached the crest of the slope. To save the hard-pressed infantry, Lord Uxbridge sent in Ponsonby's Union Brigade, consisting of the 1st Royal Dragoons, the Scots Greys and the Inniskillings. Their charge stampeded the massed French columns, and they were driven pell-mell back into the valley. The Gordons had been one of the regiments in the line greatly reduced in numbers. Those who remained grabbed at the stirrup-leathers of the Scots Greys as they galloped by, and these two famous regiments, shouting 'Scotland for ever', together hurled themselves on the fleeing French.

In this immortal action several thousand French were killed or wounded, and three thousand taken prisoner. But the cheering British were too rash, and carried their charge too far. Napoleon launched his cavalry on both their flanks; a thousand of them were killed and the remainder barely escaped. This action also proved most costly to Wellington, for both Picton and Ponsonby, two of his best Generals, were killed in it.

By this time, the Prussians, as Napoleon had rightly believed, were seen entering the Bois de Paris in considerable numbers, and it was learned from scouts that they were men of von Bülow's corps which, unknown to Napoleon, had marched direct from Liège to join Wellington. Moreover, a despatch had just come in from Grouchy, sent off at 11 a.m., showing that on receiving Soult's somewhat contradictory orders, he had given first priority to pursuing what he believed to be the main body of the Prussians east; whereas, in fact, as it had recently been learnt, Blücher and the majority of his troops had retired on Wavre, so were not many miles distant and in an excellent position to support von Bülow.

In the circumstances, Napoleon's wisest course would have been to break off the battle. But that would have meant throwing away the successes of Ligny and Quatre Bras, by which he had driven a wedge between the Allies. Given another day and he would have to face them fully united; whereas if he could destroy Wellington's army this afternoon, he would as good as have brought his whole campaign to a victorious conclusion. It was his confidence that he could do so that decided him.

At 3.30 he sent orders to Lobau for his corps, and to two brigades of reserve cavalry, to deploy eastward in order to halt von Bülow's advance. He then put Ney in command of his front line, and charged him with renewing the attack. Several units of Reille's corps hurled themselves on Hougoumont, and others of d'Erlon's on La Haye Sainte. Further ghastly carnage ensued, and up to a thousand dead and dying lay round both buildings, but the French could not take either, neither could they succeed in forcing the Allies back over the crest of the slope.

By 4 p.m., Ney realized that his infantry attack had failed, so he ordered Milhaud's two divisions of cuirassiers to charge the British line between the château and the farm. At the approach of this five-thousand-strong phalanx of horsemen, the fifteen British and Hanoverian battalions formed square to save themselves from annihilation. The French cavalry attacked them furiously, then raced past them and drove the Allied gunners from their guns. Returning, they again attacked the squares, but a deadly musketry fire from them threw the squadrons into disorder. The Duke then called up his cavalry reserve. Its charge drove the French back down the slope. Yet that was only the first of Milhaud's attacks, several of which

Ney led in person. At intervals, each time they were driven back, the French opened fire with their cannon on the British squares, and did terrible execution.

Meanwhile, von Bülow's troops were approaching through the wood on Napoleon's right. At about 4.30 their advance guards emerged from it; by five o'clock the Prussian guns opened up and their infantry launched their first attack. Blücher's troops at Wavre could have been sent in hours earlier; but it later transpired that this long delay was due to Blucher's Chief of Staff, Gneisenau, who greatly distrusted Wellington and did not believe he really meant to stand and fight. He had arranged for von Bülow's corps, which had to come all the way from Liège, to go in first, because it was fresh and thirty thousand strong, so would be better able to resist an attack if left in the air by the British than the other corps that had been mauled at Ligny.

Count Lobau's corps was the weakest in the French army, having only ten thousand men; but he deployed them skilfully at right angles to the main French front, with the farm of Planchenoit as a bastion on his extreme left, and stoutly defended his position against three times his numbers.

During this time the main battle on the crest of the hill continued with unabated fury. After an hour of charges, although the British squares were sadly depleted Milhaud had failed to break a single one of them, and his squadrons were in hopeless disorder. In desperation, Ney called up the reserve of heavy cavalry, that of the Guard and Kellermann's two divisions—another five thousand horsemen. For another hour the bloody slaughter of men and horses went on without a moment's interval. The French charged at the squares, were met by volleys that brought down the leading lines and forced those behind to separate. They galloped on between the squares right to the rear of the Allies' position, re-formed and charged again. To relieve the strain on the dwindling squares, the Duke threw in all his cavalry except the two brigades of Vivian and Vandeleur on his extreme left rear and, at every opportunity, reinforced the squares with his reserves of infantry, until he had none left.

During this ceaseless mêlée of cheering, cursing, screaming men sabering and bayoneting one another on the hill-top, von Bülow's Prussians had stormed Planchenoit, but somehow Lobau managed to keep his line intact, and drove off the far greater numbers that were hurled at his weak corps. Then, at six o'clock, Napoleon sent four battalions of the Young Guard to his assistance, and they retook the farm.

At about the same hour, Ney at last decided that his cavalry had been so terribly decimated by the British musketry that they were no longer strong enough to succeed in breaking the squares, so he drew them off. But during those two terrible hours the corps of Reille and d'Erlon, although greatly reduced by their assaults earlier in the day, had had time to rest and recover. So, now on foot, Ney again led the French infantry up the slope to the attack.

After all these hours, the French now achieved their first real success. All day the German legion, holding La Haye Sainte in the centre of the line, had beaten back infantry attacks or suffered bombardment by artillery, but they had now run out of ammunition. With the utmost gallantry they continued to fight on with their bayonets and swords, but they were over-whelmed by d'Erlon's men. The few survivors were driven out, and the Allies had lost their key position.

Reille also came near success when his men attacked

Hougoumont. Some of them actually managed to get up on to the roof of the château, but they were killed by the British Guards who had held the place all day until it became a shambles of dead and dying.

Roger could not know that it was Charles's regiment, the Coldstream Guards, who were hanging on so grimly to the château, but he thought it certain that Georgina's son would have been recalled from his long leave, and be somewhere in the battle; so he thought of him many times that day, and prayed fervently that he would not be killed or seriously wounded.

The battle had been very different from that at Ligny. There the Prussian line had formed a convex curve which could be viewed by the Emperor from the mill at Fleurus from end to end as though in an amphitheatre. Throughout the conflict the line had only bent here and there until it finally broke in the centre; so Napoleon had had no need to send orders to his corps and divisional commanders to alter their line of attack. Here, he could not see the whole battle from one position. For most of the day he was at the house of Lacoste, only a few hundred yards short of the inn of La Belle Alliance, which formed the centre of his front, immediately opposite La Haye Sainte; but several times he rode over to an observatory opposite to and at no great distance from Hougoumont. From the first sighting of the Prussians, he had also had to alter the disposition of numerous units.

In consequence his A.D.C.s had been in the saddle for a great part of the time since the battle opened. Several of them had been killed or severely wounded, others had minor wounds or musket balls through their clothing. Roger had been lucky to get off so far with only a gash in his left shoulder and his hat shot away. But he had had a horse shot under him, so was covered from head to foot in mud, as also were nearly all the troops who had been engaged in the fighting.

It was close on 6.30 and Ney still attacking the Allies with the corps of Reille and d'Erlon when, in the parlour of Lacoste's little house, the Emperor beckoned Roger over, pointed to a map that was spread out on the table and said:

'The Prussians are pressing us hard on our right flank now and Ziethen's corps has come up behind von Bülow's, so we may have to give way in that quarter. Should we do so, I shall forgo further frontal attacks and redeploy my army westward. With luck we could then outflank the British and drive them back on to the Prussians. But success would depend on the strength of the Allies on our left. If they have further reserves concealed behind the hill that side of the village of St. Jean, such a move would be too dangerous. I wish you to ride out right round our left flank, and up to the crossroads at Le Mesnil. From the high ground you will be able to assess my chances of encircling Wellington. Off with you now. Take no unnecessary risks, and rejoin me as speedily as you can.'

Roger saluted, ran from the room and mounted a horse which looked fairly fresh. No mission could have pleased him more, for to Le Mesnil and back entailed an eight-mile ride, and that would keep him out of the battle for the best part of an hour. On either side of the road were massed battalion after battalion of the Imperial Guard, Napoleon's grand reserve which had not yet fired a shot. As Roger cantered along in front of those to the west of the headquarters, they were sitting about smoking and playing cards. He passed the observatory on their left flank, crossed the main road leading from Nivelles to Mont St. Jean, at the hamlet of Mon Plaisir and, now that he was well out of sight, reduced his pace to an easy trot as he proceeded up a lane leading north. At the next cross-roads he turned north-west and reached the village of Braine l'Alleud, passed through it and headed north again to another crossroad near which there stood a windmill on high ground.

As he approached it he saw a solitary figure, in civilian clothes and a low-crowned top-hat, sitting on a bank watching the battle through a large telescope. At the sound of his horse's hooves, the man lowered his telescope and looked at him. To Roger's amazement the man was Nathan Rothschild. Reining in his horse, he exclaimed:

'What in the world are you doing here?'

It was the Rothschild who, meeting him in Vienna, had led to his discovering that Mary was forging drafts on his account at Hoare's; but Roger had first met him many years earlier in Frankfurt, before he and two brothers had established branches of their banking house in London, Paris and Vienna. The eldest brother, too, who had remained in Frankfurt had, in 1813, enabled Roger to escape across the Rhine from the Prussians who were after him. In the years between, the Rothschilds had created the most powerful financial house in Europe.

Standing up, Nathan politely raised his hat and replied, 'I am equally surprised to see you, Lord Kildonan. I had no idea that you had become a soldier.'

Roger smiled. 'You may recall, Sir, that when in '95 I came to your father's house to request a loan of a million francs on behalf of the British Treasury, I was on a secret mission. In a sense I am again so employed, hence my uniform. But to come upon you in Belgium greatly surprises me.'

'I dared not remain in London, dependent on rumours about the result of this campaign. Too much depends on it. I felt that I must come myself, in order to be an eye-witness of the outcome. As you must know, my House has always supported Britain against the tyranny of Bonaparte. We have many millions invested in the British Funds. Their worth depends upon which side emerges victorious from this ghastly conflict raging there below us. If Wellington wins through, Rothschild's will be saved. If not, we may be near bankrupted overnight.'

'I understand your anxiety.' Roger patted his horse's neck. 'But what I do not see is how your witnessing the battle can affect whether the Funds rise or fall on 'Change in London when the news comes through.'

Rothschild gave a faint smile and gestured over his shoulder. 'My lord, behind the mill there is a sunken road. Waiting for me there is a light carriage drawn by eight horses. From here to Ostend is no more than seventy miles. There I have a racing yacht ready to take me across the Channel. Given a fair wind, I'll be in London by tomorrow morning. If Bonaparte defeats the Duke, as I much fear he may, since he has not yet thrown his mighty Imperial Guard into the battle, I'll be the first to reach London with the news. That will enable me to sell a great part of my British Funds before they fall, and thus save my House from ruin.'

'Sir,' laughed Roger. 'Had I still a hat, I'd take it off to you for showing such enterprise. As it is, I can only wish you good luck, and pray that on your reaching London you'll have good cause to buy more British Funds, instead of selling them.'

With a wave, he cantered on, crossed the sunken road and passed a spinney in which he glimpsed the movement of men in blue Dutch-Belgian uniforms. But the spinney was small, so he knew that it could only be an outpost. Riding on for another mile, he reached the hamlet of Le Mesnil. From the eastern outskirts he could see the houses of Mont St. Jean behind the high ground on which the conflict was raging, and the main road to Brussels up to the point where it entered the forest of Soignes. Not a single unit of the Allies was to be seen. Ambulances and walking wounded moved in a steady stream away from the battlefield; but clearly, on the east side of Mont St. Jean, Wellington had already thrown all the reserves he had into the battle.

Halting there, for the hundredth time since he had left Elba with Napoleon, Roger speculated on what the future might hold for him. He was terribly conscious that he had become a plaything of Fate, and that his future would be settled by the outcome of the battle being fought at that moment. If victory went to Napoleon he would, within a few days, turn on and destroy what remained of the Prussians. With two out of the four Allies defeated and new units being formed in France daily to reinforce his army, he would have no need to fear the Austrians. They and the Russians might well climb down and agree a peace. So, if Roger returned to Paris with Napoleon there would be a very good chance of his being able to carry out his cherished plan of retiring to St. Maxime and having his adored Georgina come there to stay with him.

But in no case could he aid the Emperor to defeat Wellington. So he must ride back and make a false report—that the Duke still had a massive reserve behind his right flank—and thus prevent any possibility of Napoleon attempting to outflank him.

If the Allies did win, then all prospect of St. Maxime with Georgina would be gone. The Anglo-Prussian army, supported by Austria and Prussia, would again invade France and occupy Paris. They would restore the Bourbons, and all the officers who had rallied to Napoleon would be proscribed. Having accompanied him from Elba, Roger would be high on the list. Talleyrand, who was known to be now at Ghent with Louis XVIII, would see to it that no harm came to him and get him safely away; but there would be no place for him in France, and England was barred to him. He could hope for nothing. Exile with only a pittance would be his lot.

With a sigh he turned his mount about, to ride back to the Emperor and tell him that his only choice was to continue his frontal attacks or break off the battle.

Between Le Mesnil and the windmill there lay a shallow valley. As Roger walked his horse down the slope, the battle became hidden from him; then, as he trotted over the far rise, the whole panorama was again spread before him. On a front of three miles along the slope of Mont St. Jean, the terrible conflict was still raging. The boom of cannon and roar of exploding shells made a continuous thunder, through which could be heard the sharper crack of volleys of musketry. A haze of smoke extended over the whole field, but only in places totally obscured the lines and groups of struggling infantry and charging horsemen. From well behind the mount, right down the slope to past La Belle Alliance and for over a mile on each side of it the ground was littered with fallen soldiers in uniforms of red, blue, green and black all mingled together. In some places they lay in heaps,

and scattered among the dead and dying men were
thousands of still or writhing horses.

Yet, as Roger topped the rise and this awful spectacle of frightful carnage again came into view, his
attention was immediately distracted by trouble
only fifty yards ahead of him. Below in the sunken
road stood Rothschild's light carriage, but only two
of the horses remained harnessed to it. The traces of
the other six had been unfastened, and the horses
were being led away by Dutch-Belgian soldiers—
evidently those he had glimpsed twenty minutes earlier
as he passed the copse. Rothschild stood on the bank,
waving his arms and cursing with impotent fury,
while a mounted officer in a red uniform looked on,
laughing.

Roger hesitated only a moment. There were half a
dozen Dutch-Belgians, but he could not stand by and
see his friend the banker robbed in this way, which
could prove his ruin. The red uniform of the mounted
officer made it as good as certain that he was British.
Spurring his horse into a canter, Roger rode up behind
him and shouted:

'Hi! You can't do this. You've no right to steal
that gentleman's horses.'

The officer swung round and stared at him. Roger
went as white as chalk, and his blue eyes suddenly
blazed with anger. Fate had brought him face to
face with his life-long enemy, the man he hated so
intensely that he had sworn to kill—George Gunston.

20

Threat of Final Ruin

As Roger's gaze was riveted on Gunston's reddish, fleshy face, a score of memories flashed through his mind: the way in which Gunston had tormented him at school; the fights forced on him when he had refused to comply with the bigger lad's demands, although it was asking for a drubbing; how, a few years later, he had nearly been robbed of his first great coup by Gunston's stupidity; lovely, young Clarissa's death, due to Gunston's tardiness; the months he had spent in Guildford Gaol as the result of the drunken brawl following Gunston's attempt to force Georgina; the brutal trick he had played on Mary in Lisbon. On account of any one of the three women Roger would have called him out, and had long since made up his mind that Gunston should pay with his life for having, through his negligence, robbed Clarissa of hers.

Whipping out his sword, Roger cried, 'You brute! I've got you now! Draw and defend yourself, or I'll slice your head from your body.'

Instead of drawing, Gunston backed his horse away. He had suddenly taken in the fact that, in spite of the mud with which Roger's uniform was covered, it was French. His eyes opening wide, he exclaimed:

'God's blood! I knew you for a traitor when I saw

you sneak out from Talleyrand's palace in Vienna. Now you avow it by openly fighting for Bonaparte.'

'I am no traitor,' Roger retorted hotly. 'Now that I am about to kill you, you may as well know the truth. I went there at the Duke's behest, and have long been a British secret agent. But you'll not live to blab that.'

Gunston's loose mouth broke into an evil grin. 'A likely tale! Were it even true, the fact that you're wearing the uniform of a French General of Brigade is good enough to sign your death warrant.'

Rothschild jumped down from the bank in which he was standing, ran forward and cried. 'Lord Kildonan speaks the truth. I have known him a score of years and can vouch for it.'

Swivelling round, Gunston snarled at him, 'Why the hell should I believe you? You're taking his part because I've commandeered your horses for my men. Keep out of this, or 'twill be the worse for you.'

Urging his mount forward again, Roger cried, 'Mr. Rothschild shall have his horses back. I'll see to that. And what, I'd like to know, is a British Brigadier doing away from the battle?'

Flushing, Gunston again pulled away and retorted, 'I was given command of the Dutch-Belgian cavalry. Some of my men were unhorsed and ran off. I had to get them back.'

'What?' Roger sneered. 'You command a brigade, yet left it to recover half a dozen deserters? I ne'er heard so feeble an excuse to cover cowardice. Come now. No more of this. Show your steel and defend yourself if you can.' Spurring his horse, he made for Gunston.

'Stop!' Gunston shouted. 'Stop, you fool! If you dare make a pass at me, I'll order my men to shoot you down.'

L

In the heat of the moment Roger had thought only
of his chance to settle accounts once and for all with
his enemy of a lifetime. He had not given a glance at
Gunston's men who, still holding Rothschild's horses,
stood there staring at the two quarrelling officers. Now
he realized that, to attack Gunston, meant they would
fire at and kill him. Yet what had he to live for? Only
the chance that Napoleon might win the battle, win
another against Blücher, then make his peace with
Austria and Russia. Otherwise, Georgina lost for good,
and a dreary future with little money, at some embassy
abroad. In a flash his mind was made up. Gunston
weighed thirteen stone, and had strong muscular arms,
so was a redoubtable antagonist, but Roger knew
himself to be a better swordsman, with swifter reactions.
Given a few minutes, if he escaped the Dutch-Belgians'
first bullets, he believed he could kill Gunston—although
it might, seconds later, cost him his own life. Raising
his sword high, he slashed at Gunston's head.

Gunston ducked the cut, rowelled his horse so that it
reared, whipped out his sword and, at the same moment,
shouted to his men in French, 'Fire at him. Fire!'

As the horse's hooves struck the ground, Roger
lunged. Gunston succeeded in parrying the thrust.
Roger knew that it would take the men a minute or
more to load and prime their muskets. Again he
slashed at Gunston's head. Time being all-important,
he had struck too swiftly, and his sword only glanced
off Gunston's epaulette. He lunged in turn, but Roger
swerved aside. As he did so, he caught a swift glimpse
of the men. Only one of them had moved and had his
musket raised. The others, holding the horses, had
remained quite still, their eyes riveted upon the combat.
As Roger swerved, Gunston lunged at him yet again.
Their swords clashed and Gunston's slid harmlessly

under Roger's arm. Swiftly he turned his horse, in order to bring himself on Gunston's left. As he did so it brought him face to face with the soldier aiming at him. A tongue of flame spurted from the barrel of the musket, followed by its crash. But the bullet whistled high overhead. Out of the corner of his eye Roger glimpsed the act that had caused it to do so. One of the other men had knocked the musket up. Instantly his heart leapt with new hope. The Dutch-Belgians had entered the battle against Napoleon with great reluctance. They were pro-French and five of them at least wanted to see their British officer killed.

His elation was short-lived. Gunston thrust again. Roger bore down his blade, but it plunged into his horse's neck. Blood spurted from the wound, the animal gave a loud neigh and sank to its knees. Just in time Roger disengaged his feet from the stirrups. But he was now unhorsed. A moment before, with the Dutch-Belgians neutral, he had believed he had Gunston at his mercy. Now his enemy had the advantage.

As Roger pulled his left foot across the saddle of his dying horse, Gunston gave a cry of triumph and slashed furiously at his head. Before regaining his balance, Roger stumbled. The stumble saved him. Gunston's blade scythed over his head, but so closely that it grazed the scalp, severing a tuft of hair. Again Gunston's sword sliced down. To escape the slash, Roger flung himself forward. His face came into violent contact with the front of Gunston's thigh, and the point of his half-raised sword pierced Gunston's calf. With a yelp of pain he reined back a few yards. For a moment the two adversaries glared at each other. Both of them were now panting; Gunston's forehead was beaded with sweat, and blood was running from Roger's nose.

Gunston raised his sword high, spurred his horse and

charged in, hoping the animal would hurl Roger to
the ground. But one of Roger's greatest assets as a
swordsman was his agility. He stood still until the
last moment, then leapt aside. The horse's head flashed
past him, but he was just not quick enough to avoid
Gunston's blade. Lifting his sword had been a feint.
As he charged, he brought it down for a swift thrust
and it entered Roger's left side. Yet at the same second
Roger, too, had lunged. His blade slithered over Gunston's saddle and buried its point in his groin. Roger's
gasp of pain was drowned by Gunston's howl of agony.
He threw back his head, dropped his sword, slumped
sideways and rolled from the saddle.

His right foot was caught in the stirrup. The horse
galloped on, dragging him behind it. After covering
thirty yards it came to a halt. Roger could not judge
if the wound he had inflicted had been mortal. Determined to make certain, he went after his enemy at a
staggering run. Gunston was lying on his back,
smothered in mud and blood, and groaning loudly.
At the sound of Roger's running footsteps he made a
great effort and raised himself on one elbow. His free
hand went to his sash and jerked a pistol from it. Roger
was still ten feet away. Gunston's eyes were half-
closed, and as he took aim his hand wavered, but at
such close range he could hardly miss. For a moment
Roger feared that his opponent would prove the victor
after all. Rallying his strength in a last attempt to save
himself, he leapt forward. Before Gunston could press
the trigger, Roger's sword swished down. The slash
caught Gunston across the face, slicing through his
nose and one cheek. His hand still held the pistol, but
he dropped it at the moment when Roger struck again.
His second slash went home a few inches lower down.
The blade descended on Gunston's Adam's apple,

making a ghastly gash that nearly severed his head from his body. Sweating, panting, his free hand pressed to his wounded side, Roger sank down beside his dead enemy.

Two minutes later, Rothschild, his postillions and the Dutch-Belgians were crowding round him. They got his arm out of his jacket and cut away his blood-stained shirt. Fortunately, Gunston's sword had not cut deeply into his side. The wound was about six inches long, but shallow. It had glanced off a rib and, although painful, had done him no serious damage. Two of the soldiers produced field dressings, staunched the flow of blood and wound a bandage round his body.

Having thanked them in French, he got to his feet and went on, 'Now, *Messieurs,* about the horses of the English gentleman. You know well that you have no right to them. You must re-harness them to his carriage. Then, if you take my advice, you will make off as quickly as you can to your homes.'

The man who had fired at Roger demurred. 'If we are to go swiftly, General, we must take the horses. Or better still, the carriage, for riding bareback can be mightily unpleasant after a mile or two.'

'I must have my horses and carriage,' Rothschild burst out. 'I must! It is imperative.'

'You shall,' said Roger, 'or, if you do not, only five of them will ride in it.' As he spoke, he stooped, snatched the pistol from beside Gunston's hand and pointed it at the man who had spoken. 'Hands up!' he snapped, 'or you'll be as dead as the British officer behind me.'

Caught off his guard, the man's jaw dropped and he obeyed. But it was a ticklish situation. The soldiers had all left their muskets behind them, down on the road-side. But if they rushed him, he would be able to shoot

only one of them. Rothschild would come to his help
he felt sure, so might the postillions. However, they
were Belgians, so they might not. The odds were that
they would remain neutral.

As the soldiers hesitated, he slowly moved the pistol
from side to side, covering each of them in turn, then
said, 'Come now. I am grateful to you men for having
looked to my wound, but I cannot stand by and see
my friend robbed.'

Rothschild then intervened. Unbuttoning his coat
he revealed on one hip a leather satchel, attached to a
belt round his waist. Opening the flap he thrust his
hand in and produced a handful of gold pieces. 'Do
as the officer bids you,' he said, 'and I'll give each of
you two of these to help you on your way.'

Roger drew a sharp breath. Instantly he realized
that the gesture had been extremely rash and could
increase their danger. At the sight of the gold the men's
eyes opened wide. Rothschild had taken only a dozen
or so coins from his great purse, but its bulk showed
that it contained two or three hundred. To these
poor men such a sum would be a small fortune, so
they might be tempted to attack the banker for it.

Next moment Roger's fears were realized. The man
who had been speaking to him jumped forward and
snatched at the weighty satchel. The pistol Roger was
holding was single-barrelled, so had only one bullet
in it. If he used his one shot only to wound that would
lead to a general scrimmage. Having seen the gold,
the postillions would side with the soldiers, to get a
share of the loot. Rothschild and he had not a chance
against so many men. And they would not only be
overpowered, but killed, and buried as a precaution
by the attackers against their crime being traced to
them. Loath as he was to do the logical thing, he knew

he had no alternative. The pistol cracked. The bullet struck the man who had snatched at the satchel in the side of the head. His skull splintered and gushed blood. Without a sound he dropped dead.

The others gaped, paralysed with horror at the sight of their comrade killed in cold blood. But Roger was not looking at them. Swivelling round, he dropped the pistol and grabbed the sword he had let fall as he had slumped down beside the dead Gunston. A sickening pain stabbed his side, and he went white to the lips. But turning again to face the soldiers, he croaked:

'Come on, now! The . . . the next one of you to make trouble will taste cold steel.'

They were still aghast at his ruthlessness. By the glare in his blue eyes they knew he meant what he said. Cowed, they turned away and began to walk down to the road. When they had covered a dozen yards, Roger sighed with relief, turned again and walked back to Gunston's charger, which stood nibbling the grass not far from its master's body. Sheathing his sword, Roger raised his hand to the saddle holster. The pistol Gunston had pulled from his sash had been only a pocket weapon carried for emergencies. As Roger expected, the holster held a big, long-barrelled pistol. Taking it out, he made certain it was loaded, then hooked his left arm through the bridle of the horse and followed the little group down the slope.

He saw that Rothschild had run ahead and dived into his carriage. Next minute he emerged with a pistol in each hand and shouted to the soldiers, 'Keep away from your muskets, or I'll fire.'

Again Roger drew a breath of relief, for he had feared that, on reaching the road, the men would grab their firearms and, as he approached, shoot him down. But now any chance of doing so was denied them.

Scared and sullen they filed off along the road, leaving the postillions to collect the horses and re-harness them to the carriage.

Waving aside Rothschild's effusive thanks, Roger smiled and said, 'It was the least I could do. Two years ago your brother saved me from being imprisoned by the Prussians, and it was you who warned me in Vienna that my wife was playing ducks and drakes with my fortune.'

'Did she succeed in robbing you of a really crippling sum?' the banker asked.

Roger nodded. 'Before I could get back to England and stop her, she had got hold of the greater part of my lifetime's savings; so I am now little better than a pauper. God forbid that Napoleon should win this battle; but if he does, and manages to keep his throne, I'll be well enough off. I have property in France and, since he still believes me to be his man, he'll see to it that I'll lack for nothing. But if he goes under, I'll be left high and dry.'

'The battle!' exclaimed Rothschild. 'I must see how it goes.' Pulling his long telescope from his pocket, he swung round and ran up the bank on the far side of the road. Roger called to one of the postillions to tie Gunston's horse to a fence in front of the mill, got out his glass, followed the banker and sat down beside him.

Roger's fight with Gunston, the affray with the Dutch-Belgians and re-harnessing the horses to the carriage had occupied no more than fifteen minutes. The guns still thundered and muskets flashed, but between the clouds of smoke they could see that, apart from the hundreds of dead and wounded, the valley was now empty. A thin line of red coats still held the crest of the hill; so Ney's last charges had failed. The survivors of the Chasseurs, Hussars and Lancers he had led earlier could be seen milling about in disorder right back between Mon Plaisir and the Observatory. The château of Hougoumont had been set on fire by the shells from the French guns, and was now a flaming ruin, from which a few British Guardsmen were staggering.

Taking out his watch, Roger saw that the time was 7.15. At that moment the sound of distant bugles came to them through the smoke-laden air. In the neighbourhood of La Belle Alliance the whole French front suddenly moved forward, and Roger gave a gasp.

'He's sending in the Guard! Oh, God help us! Those devils fought at Marengo, Jena, Wagram, Austerlitz. Hardly one of them but has the Legion of Honour. It is his grand reserve. I never thought he'd risk it. He wouldn't even at Borodino. He must be desperate. But it's all or nothing with him now. And he's right. Reduced in numbers as our poor fellows are, and having fought for hours on end, how can they possibly stand up against ten thousand veterans who have been lying smoking their pipes all day?'

Leaving two battalions in Planchenoit and five in Rossome as a last reserve, Napoleon led forward the other nine in hollow squares, to La Haye Sainte and there handed over to Ney, who led them at a slight angle toward the Allied front, a little to the west of burning Hougoumont.

Rothschild did not say a word. Their telescopes glued to their eyes, they sat side by side watching the extraordinary spectacle. With the precision of troops on parade, the Imperial Guard marched across the valley, appearing as one huge column seventy men abreast. As they advanced, every French gun still serviceable opened up a murderous fire on the Allied line. The remnants of the corps of Reille and d'Erlon were forming up in the valley, to support the Guard, but Milhaud's cavalry still milled round between Mon Plaisir and the Observatory in hopeless disorder. Ney, at the head of the Guard, had his horse shot down but, jumping clear of it, the indomitable Marshal waved his sword and continued to lead the attack on foot.

On the Allied side, General Maitland had succeeded in partly sheltering his brigade behind a low bank. Wellington could be picked out astride his horse on the crest of Mont St. Jean, just behind the centre of the British line. A little to his rear were his staff: twenty strong that morning, now reduced to three. He made a gesture and obviously gave an order. The infantry went down on their knees, then lay flat, evidently so that they were less exposed to the bullets of the enemy.

Imperturbably the massed squares of the Guard, each over one thousand strong, marched up the slope, their standards topped by golden eagles held aloft, their bands stimulating them with martial music. A quarter of a mile behind them, now right forward in front of La Belle Alliance, Napoleon could be spotted by his white horse. His staff, too, had dwindled to a mere handful of mounted men.

As the Guard breasted the rise, the leading ranks fired a volley, but those behind could not yet use their muskets. It was followed by a terrific crash. The whole British line, a full mile long, had fired simultaneously. The heads of the column, which had now split into two, came to a sudden halt. Their front ranks withered away as though cut down by huge scythes. Hundreds of them died or fell wounded at the same instant. Rank after rank stumbled, pitched forward, or backward, slumped down or lurched sideways. But the halt was only momentary. Undismayed, the ranks behind pressed on, stumbling over the sprawling bodies of their comrades. Colborne skilfully wheeled his regiment so as to enable it to fire into the flank of the nearest column. Scores more Frenchmen staggered and collapsed. But there were thousands still uninjured. Ignoring the fallen, the Guard continued its desperate endeavour to advance. Now, though, they were hampered by the piles of bodies immediately in front of them. With splendid courage, they scrambled forward over the mounds of corpses. Yet another volley from the Allies, and hundreds more went down. The broken ranks forming the heads of the columns wavered. At last their magnificent discipline failed them. Some fell on their knees to take cover behind the masses of fallen, others turned to run. Through his telescope Roger saw the Duke take off his cocked hat and wave it. As he did so he shouted:

'Up, Guards, and at them!'

The long, thin line of Redcoats came to their feet. Cheering wildly, with fixed bayonets they charged down the slope into the stricken, bewildered mass of French. Not even half the Imperial Guard had yet been in action, but they panicked. Rank after rank dissolved into a ragged, close-pressed horde of men fleeing for their lives. A great cry went up that rang in fear or triumph across the whole battlefield:

'*La Garde recule!* The Guard gives way! The Guard has broken!'

Roger jumped to his feet and, his glass still held to his eye, exclaimed, 'The day is ours! We've won! God bless the Duke. He's snatched victory after all!' But when he turned, Rothschild had already gone. He was jumping into his carriage. A moment later, his horses at the gallop, he was on his way to Ostend.

With a laugh, Roger sat down and again surveyed

the incredibly exciting spectacle. Several battalions of
the Old Guard were still in the valley, but the helter-
skelter retreat of those in front threw them into hopeless confusion. They, too, took to their heels, stamped-
ing in turn all that was left of Rielle's and d'Erlon's
corps, which had just re-formed. On the far right the
Duke had loosed his last reserves, the British cavalry
brigades of Vivian and Vandeleur. Yelling, their
swords held high, they charged down the slope on the
east side of Mont St. Jean, sabering the panic-stricken
French as they ran. Count Lobau's men had fought
most gallantly, keeping the Prussians at bay all through
the long, hot afternoon, but now their left wing gave
way. The Young Guard hung on to Planchenoit almost
until the end; but Zeithen's cavalry broke through
between it and the remnants of d'Erlon's corps, joined
up with the British at La Belle Alliance and drove all
before them.

In vain Cambronne endeavoured to stop the rout of
his never-before-defeated regiment, by yelling, 'Turn,
men! Turn! The Guard dies, but it never surrenders.'
In vain Ney, who had had three horses shot under him
that day, waved a broken sword above his head and
yelled, 'Cowards! Stand fast and see how a Marshal of
the Empire can die!'

Prayers and threats alike were useless; the Guard,
Reille's, d'Erlon's and Lobau's men, Milhaud's cavalry
and the French gunners became inextricably mixed,
fleeing in terror as the British cavalry cut them down
and the Prussian Uhlans drove lances into their backs.

The battalions of the Guard that Napoleon had retained in the rear formed square, to resist the onrush of
their terrified countrymen. Wellington, wishing to
spare them, sent an officer galloping to call on them to
surrender. But the foremost three squares refused,

stood firm and were annihilated almost to a man. The other two, with the Emperor in the centre of one of them, were now the only French troops still in formation left on the battlefield. They had been far back, near Rossome, and succeeded in getting away. The British infantry, nearly every one of whom had received minor wounds during the long day's fighting, had been finally exhausted by their charge down the slope. It was beyond all question that they had the whole French army on the run but they themselves could run no farther. Sweating, gasping, aching in every limb, they halted near Rossome, leaving the pursuit to the cavalry.

Squadron after squadron of Blücher's dragoons and Uhlans were emerging from the wood near Planche-noit. Their hatred of the French knew no limit, and now was their hour of revenge for all they had suffered during the years that Prussia had been subject to Napoleon. They took no prisoners, laughed at all pleas for mercy, and the French rout became a massacre.

By 8.30 there was not a French soldier on his feet left in sight. For the last time, in the evening light, Roger swept his glass over the battlefield. For more than two miles across, and two miles in depth, from the slope behind Mont St. Jean right down to the Emperor's first headquarters at Caillou, there was scarcely a yard of space between dead or moaning men, stricken horses and overturned gun carriages. All that was left of Hougoumont, La Haye Sainte and La Belle Alliance were red, smouldering ruins. In the courtyard of the last, Wellington and Blücher met by accident. The tough old German embraced the Duke, tears of joy running down his furrowed cheeks.

Closing his telescope, Roger crossed the road, mounted Gunston's charger and rode north to Le

Mesnil. As his side hurt him and he now had no cause
to hurry, he proceeded only at a walk. At Le Mesnil he
turned east and, by the time he reached the village of
Waterloo, full darkness had fallen.

As he had supposed, before the battle Wellington had
made his headquarters in the village. Going there he
enquired for the Duke and learned that he had just
returned. The officer to whom Roger spoke was wearing civilian clothes covered with mud and blood. Like
a number of others, on leaving the Duchess of Richmond's dance he had had no time to change into
uniform. Seeing that Roger was dressed as a French
officer, he looked very surprised, but when Roger
announced himself as General Comte de Breuc, the
A.D.C. assumed that he wished to surrender to the
C.-in-C. in person, and said he would ask if the Duke
would receive him.

After a wait of half an hour, Roger was shown in.
Wellington was alone and had just finished writing a
despatch. Looking up he said, 'I hardly expected to
see you here, my lord. And in a French uniform, too!
I hope you've not been killing some of our countrymen.'

Roger shook his head, 'Nay, Your Grace, I managed
to get away from Napoleon halfway through the battle.
Permit me to offer you my heartiest congratulations
upon your magnificent victory.'

'I thank you. But it was a damned close-run thing!
And due to the courage of those thieving, drunken,
scallywags of mine, putting up such a stout resistance.
Tell me now; how come you to be here?'

'I arrived in Elba only the day before Napoleon left
it, so could not avoid becoming involved and having
to accompany him.'

'Elba. Of course, I recall now that I sent you there

from Vienna. 'Tis regrettable, though, that having been with him all this time you were unable to send me any information that might have been of assistance.'

With no evidence to support his claim to having diverted d'Erlon's corps at Quatre Bras, Roger did not care to mention it, so merely said, 'Since Napoleon kept me with him as his A.D.C.-in-Chief, it was not possible. But I did all I could to hamper him. And I can give you a report on the state of things in Paris.'

'Good, good! That will be useful. I see, though, that you are wounded.'

'Not seriously, Your Grace. But I must have the wound properly attended to as soon as possible, lest it becomes infected.'

'Of course. But every surgeon we have for miles round is dealing with urgent cases. Can you ride as far as Brussels? 'Tis some ten miles.'

'Walking my horse, I can manage that.'

'Very well. I'll give you a chit to one of the temporary hospitals we have set up there. And my orders are that the French are to be cared for equally with the British and Germans. Our Hanoverians and Brunswickers fought splendidly. So, too, did some of the Dutch-Belgians; but a whole brigade of Flemish that I had posted up at Braine l'Alleud deserted without firing a shot.' As the Duke spoke, he tinkled a bell on his desk. One of his adjutants came in, and he told him to write a note stating that the Comte de Breuc was to be treated with every consideration. Ten minutes later, Roger was on his way to Brussels.

It was a nightmare journey. The highway through the forest of Soignes was one long procession of ambulances, carts and carriages that had been brought from Brussels, and mounted or unmounted men, all of whom had arms, legs or heads swathed in blood-stained bandages. The only sounds were the rumbling of wheels, the clop of horses' hooves, and the groans of the wounded.

Drooping with fatigue and loss of blood, Roger entered the city in the early hours of the morning. Lanterns and flambeaux lighting the main streets revealed a macabre spectacle. They were jammed with vehicles and wounded in every variety of uniform. Slowly Roger edged his way through the press and, as he was still wearing a French uniform, he was at last directed to a Belgian hospital. It was a large private mansion which had been taken over, and was already crowded. But on showing the Duke's chit, he was found a truckle bed, from which the corpse of a man who had died had just been removed, in a third-floor room occupied by three other officers.

Full daylight had come before a Belgian doctor came to examine him. His long ride from the mill had inflamed the wound and, having dressed it, the doctor said he must remain there for the best part of a week before he would be fit to be moved.

During the next few days, people coming and going brought in particulars of the French army's ignominious flight. By the light of the moon, Gneisenau himself had led his Prussian horsemen all night in their pitiless pursuit. At Genappe, Napoleon had striven to check his routed army, but the narrow bridge there was choked with men despairing of their lives. The sound of the enemy's bugles only a quarter of a mile away, compelled him to leave the carriage from which he was shouting appeals to his troops. He had to mount a horse and narrowly escaped capture as only with difficulty was a way made for him across the crowded bridge. At Quatre Bras he again endeavoured to rally a few hundred of his fear-maddened men, but before he could do so he was chased over the battlefield of the previous two days, still littered with the corpses of men and horses. Seven times he had attempted to stem the human tide, but it was hopeless. Next morning he reached Charleroi, spent and weeping. Some ten thousand men, most of whom had thrown away their arms, were all that were left of the great host he had sent into battle, and they struggled back in little groups across the Sambre into France.

Wellington's army had lost thirteen thousand men, more than half of whom had been from his original twenty-four thousand British. The Prussians had lost some six thousand, the French every one of their two hundred and fifty guns, thirty thousand dead or wounded, seven thousand taken prisoner and many thousands more had deserted.

As Roger lay in bed, he had ample time to think about his future. The Emperor still had Grouchy's command of some twenty-one thousand men, and Rapp's small corps further east, but they must already have suffered heavy casualties from the Prussians and by now be being driven back toward Paris. Napoleon could not possibly form another army of sufficient strength to defeat the Austrians who were already massing on the Rhine, and the Russians who were fast approaching it; so he was finished.

That meant that Roger, too, was finished so far as living in France was concerned. Within a few weeks, the war would be over, so there would be no more secret missions for him to undertake; even had he been willing to undertake them. And he was not. For the best part of twenty years he had served Pitt, risking his life many times, but being generously paid for it. By 1809 he had decided that he could not expect his luck to last indefinitely, so made up his mind to retire. But fate had not allowed him to. He had become involved in the Peninsular War; later, out of patriotism, he had allowed himself to be persuaded to undertake a diplomatic mission to Sweden, and that had led, first to his being caught up in Napoleon's retreat from Moscow, then being carried off to the United States, who were at war with the British in Canada; in 1813 a private obligation had again forced him to go to Spain and Germany; lastly, Mary's insane jealousy had compelled him to ask Castlereagh for employment that had taken him to Vienna, Elba and Waterloo.

In the old days he had had abundant initiative and stamina, but they had gradually declined. On the 8th January last he had reached the age of forty-six. He was now middle-aged and tired; so no longer fitted for anything but a peaceful occupation. If that were not enough, he had worn out the valuable dual identity he had built up as de Breuc in France and Brook in England. Too many people now knew them to be the same man.

Sadly he considered his resources. During his years as a secret agent he had put by a very considerable sum, and that had been nearly doubled by the money his father had left him. But Mary had robbed him of all but a fraction of it, and sold his family home, Grove Place, into the bargain. No doubt she had managed to salt most of the money away somewhere; but the fact remained that it was gone and by the time he had caught up with her only something under five thousand pounds had been left of his fortune. He had drawn one thousand pounds before going to Vienna. Most of that had gone there, and on his journey to Elba, and neither Castlereagh nor Wellington had paid him anything. He had, however, managed to recoup himself in Paris by drawing money due to him from Napoleon's Treasury, and had in his money belt gold and bills of exchange amounting to about one thousand two hundred pounds. With what remained in Hoare's bank that gave him again five thousand pounds. From that, in safe securities, he could hope for an income of not much more than two hundred pounds per annum. Even with the salary from some minor diplomatic post on the Continent, he would have no more than a pittance compared to the rate at which he had been living for many years; and to sponge on Georgina, her boy Charles or Droopy Ned, he would not even consider. It was a miserable prospect.

Suddenly a thought came to him. As Thatched House Lodge was a grace and favour residence, that had been safe from Mary's clutches, and the contents must be worth a great deal of money. All his life he had loved beautiful things. He had bought Chippendale and Adam furniture, silk Persian rugs, fine china and Venetian glass. Then there was the Queen Anne silver and a fine collection of miniatures which his father had left him. The paintings too, which Georgina had given him—several by the great artists Gainsborough and Reynolds, who had been her rival tutors when she was in her twenties—by now must have become valuable.

The thought of parting with his treasures greatly distressed him. But he would have to live abroad, and if he sold everything, that should bring him at least twenty thousand pounds. With the five thousand he already had, even at three per cent that would give him an income of seven hundred and fifty pounds a year. And on that, plus a few hundred as salary, he could live quite comfortably. Much cheered, he drifted off to sleep.

On the morning of his fifth day in hospital he was brought a large, heavily-sealed packet. Opening it he found it contained a letter from Wellington, and an envelope containing another letter. That from the Duke ran:

My dear Lord Kildonan,

We had been much puzzled by the withdrawal of the Comte d'Erlon's corps from Quatre Bras. The interrogation of a prisoner who was one of Bonaparte's A.D.C.s has now revealed the reason, and I can only suppose that you were too modest to tell me of it when we last met. It now emerges that, during the battle of Ligny, you heard Bonaparte mutter that he wished he had not given d'Erlon's corps to Ney. Without receiving any direct order, you took it on yourself to dash off to Quatre Bras and bring d'Erlon's corps to Fleurus, thus keeping it out of the battle.

For this service neither I nor your country can render you sufficient thanks. Had Ney been able to throw d'Erlon's corps in at the critical juncture, we would undoubtedly have been driven from the field in confusion, and it is very doubtful if my army would then have been able to make a stand at Waterloo.

I had not forgotten the imputation made by Brigadier General Gunston in Vienna, on seeing you leave Talleyrand's house, poorly clad, early one morning—that you were in the pay of the French—and I had intended to take some step to clear you of this imputation. Now I propose to do this by procuring for you a Knighthood in the Most Noble Order of the Bath and, in the citation, have it stated that the award is in recognition of your acting for me while in Vienna as a most valuable contact with the French.

I trust your wound is healing well and that by now you are near recovered. With this I enclose a letter for you that I received some days ago in Brussels; but I did not then know your whereabouts, so was unable to forward it. And on the night of the battle my mind was so occupied that I forgot to give it to you. My apologies.

I have the honour to be, Your Lordship's, etc., etc.

Roger was naturally delighted, for such a citation might well secure for him a better post as a diplomat than he had previously had any reason to hope for.

On opening the enclosed letter, he found it was from Droopy Ned. It was dated June 10th; with it was a news sheet cutting, and the letter read:

My dear Roger,

I fear this brings bad news for you. But I am in hopes that, as you were with His Grace of Wellington in Vienna, you are with him still or that he will know your whereabouts, and that this will reach you in time for you to return to England to prevent another dastardly act by your wife.

By the enclosed cutting from The Chronicle, *you will see that she has advertised the sale by public auction of the contents of Thatched House Lodge . . .*

21

Sold Out

ROGER was appalled and, for a few minutes, utterly stricken by this threat to a reasonably pleasant future which he thought he had solved.

During the pas two days he had been congratulating himself. To sell his treasures had only recently occurred to him; but, having once decided to do so, he had thought of other assets he had at Thatched House Lodge. There were his coach and four, which he used when going to evening parties in London, the carriage in which Mary had driven out in the daytime, three other horses, including his beautiful bay mare, for which he had paid three hundred guineas. There were the rare jade carvings he had brought back from India, two fine suits of armour inlaid with gold tracery which he had bought in Spain, his collection of weapons acquired in a dozen countries, the charming models of six ships of war, in each of which his father, the Admiral, had served at one time or another, and the beautiful tapestry work on which his mother had spent so many hours.

Looking through the advertisement from *The Chronicle* that Droopy Ned had sent him, he sighed as he saw other items: his fine cellar of wines, linen, garden tools, kitchen and dairy implements, saddlery, steel fire irons, mattresses and silk bedspreads. He had at first only guessed at the price his special treasures might fetch, and clearly the whole contents of the house would bring in a much greater sum, especially as the sale had taken place at the height of the London season and scores of wealthy people would have driven out to Richmond, in the hope of picking up bargains. Instead of twenty thousand pounds, the contents of the house should bring in thirty thousand, and instead of putting it in the Funds, he could have asked Rothschild to invest it for him; so even if he failed to secure a post thirty-five thousand pounds would have brought him an income of anything up to fifteen hundred a year.

Obviously Mary had again forged his signature when giving the auctioneer instructions to sell. Although she had already robbed him of many thousands, she meant to have the last penny from him. How could anyone be capable of such malice? But it must be demoniac possession, not malice, for in Portugal, Russia and America she had adored him. While he had been absent all those months on the Continent in 1813–14 and she had taken to drink, it must have opened her mind to evil forces. Brooding on the fact that it was on Georgina's account that he had gone abroad must have built up this intense jealousy. Then, actually coming upon them naked in bed together had proved the last straw; her brain had given way to the devilish impulse to destroy them.

Now, with all his possessions, valuable and trivial, gone, his resources were again reduced to five thousand pounds. Even if he invested it with Rothschild, who could probably get him five per cent, his income now would be no more than a miserable two hundred and fifty pounds.

Again he looked at the advertisement. Right at the bottom it read: *Can be viewed 26th, 27th and 28th. Sale*

Friday, 30th June. Staring at it, he gasped, 'God be praised!' Droopy's letter had reached him in time. It was only the 23rd, so he could easily be in London well before the 30th, and stop the sale. Nevertheless, he meant to take no chances. His wound was healing well. If he took care not to over-exert himself, there was no reason why he should not leave Brussels that evening.

Having examined him, the doctor agreed. So in the afternoon he went out, bought himself a suit of civilian clothes and sold Gunston's charger, which brought him the equivalent of another seventy-four pounds. He then hired a coach and was driven the thirty miles to Ghent, where he slept the night.

King Louis and his Court of exiles were still there; so the following morning, Roger enquired for Talleyrand, then went to the mansion in which the Prince had installed himself. He received Roger with delight and limped forward from behind his desk to shake his hand, congratulating him on having come safely through the past few months of uncertainty and renewed war. Then he sent for wine, and they sat down to talk.

Roger told of his journey to Elba and of accompanying the Emperor right up until Waterloo. Then Talleyrand gave him particulars of the development of the campaign and of the reports he had received from his spies in Paris. Napoleon had succeeded in rallying all that remained of his army at Laon, then hastened to Paris, where he arrived, physically exhausted, on the 21st. However, he had pulled himself together sufficiently to send for his Ministers and tell them he meant to carry on the war by a *levée en masse,* with which he would defend the capital. According to report, a furious disagreement had ensued, and it remained to be seen if he would succeed in getting his way.

Meanwhile, on the 18th, Grouchy had come upon

Thielmann's corps, defeated it, driven it across the Dyle and would no doubt have pursued him; but, on the following morning, he had learned of his Emperor's catastrophe at Waterloo and that Blücher was now in a position to cut him off. With good generalship he had promptly retired on Namur, fought a successful rear-guard action there, then got his army safely away up the valley of the Meuse into France. The Austrians had completed their concentration on the Rhine, so Rapp's corps would shortly be overwhelmed, and one hundred thousand Russians were on the march westward.

It was obvious, therefore, that Napoleon's situation was now hopeless. Even if the government in Paris agreed to his ordering a *levée en masse*, the greater part of it would consist of cripples and youngsters fresh from school, whom there would be no time to train. Such a force, with the limited number of veterans that remained to him, handicapped by a great shortage of cavalry and artillery, could not possibly resist the mighty army with which the Allies would invade France. It could now be only a matter of weeks before they were again in Paris.

Neither Roger nor Talleyrand was the least doubtful about the outcome of the war, but the question which did cause the latter very great concern was what would happen afterwards.

Once Napoleon was dead, or again sent into exile, what would the future hold for France? Obviously that would be dictated by the victorious Allies. Last time, owing largely to the British and the Czar, the peace terms had been very generous. But, having been put to great exertions and enormous expense to mobilize their armies again, they could not be expected to let France off so lightly this time. It was probable that they would impose a huge indemnity, and that France would have to suffer occupation by foreign troops for many years, until it was paid.

Also, last time Talleyrand had been in Paris. By his skilful arguments he had persuaded the Allied sovereigns that the principle of 'legitimacy' was the proper policy to pursue in establishing a new government for the conquered country, and so brought about the Bourbon restoration. But nobody could maintain that their rule had brought happiness to the majority of their subjects. On the contrary, they had brought back many of the old abuses of power, disbanded a great part of the Army and left thousands of France's heroes to beg their bread, reimposed the hated taboos favoured by the Church, and had flagrantly broken many of the promises they had made when signing the peace treaty. Could it be expected that they would be welcomed back?

And this time Talleyrand would not be in the capital to give a lead, persuade, bribe or overawe the old die-hards of the Revolution who had always hated monarchy. But they were there. With the *noblesse* again in exile, and the Bonapartists proscribed, the Deputies left in the Chambers would have a free hand in forming a different type of government and persuade the Allies that they represented the 'will of the people'. That, in a year or so, might lead to another Terror.

Knowing so well Talleyrand's great love for France, Roger felt the deepest sympathy for his anxiety. But he could do no more than express his earnest hope that matters might not go so badly. Then, having refused an invitation to stay on to dinner, he said he must be on his way and by evening he completed his journey to Ostend.

As Wellington's headquarters had been in Brussels,

there was no lack of ships crossing back and forth, and the following day Roger took passage in a ship that landed him at Dover on the morning of the 26th. Having four days still in hand before the sale, it occurred to him that, in view of all the ill Mary had done him, it would give him some little pleasure to tell her personally how, by having arrived in England in time, he could thwart her last wicked intent. So after breakfasting at an inn, he hired a fast post-chaise and, instead of driving to London, had it take him the seventy miles to Brighton. There he spent the night at the Old Ship Inn.

Thinking it unlikely that Mary would be up before ten o'clock at the earliest, he did not make his call at the fine house she had bought, then so cunningly made over to her partner, Mrs. Vidall, until eleven o'clock. On enquiring for Mary, he learned that she was no longer there, and had left some weeks earlier. He realized then that she would probably have returned to Thatched House Lodge to make arrangements for the sale; but it was also possible that she was staying at some hotel in London, so he asked to see Mrs. Vidall.

He was shown upstairs to the room in the front of the house where he had last seen Mary. After a few minutes the raddled old harridan, her hair not yet dressed, and wearing a chamber robe, waddled in. To his enquiry she replied:

'Your wife? No, she's not here, neither do I care a devil's halfpenny where she's gone. We threw her out at the beginning of the month.'

'What!' Roger exclaimed. 'But she owned this house, if not legally, by a partnership arrangement she made with you.'

The old woman leered at him. 'She did until she signed away her share in the partnership to me in

April. To begin with, being a Countess, she was an
asset to the house, but her drinking so heavy led to her
making scenes that upset the customers. I let her stay
on the last two months only so that she'd gamble away
all that was left of her money.'

'All? But, damn it, woman, she had thousands!'

'Bless you, don't I know it? 'Twas the luckiest day
of my life when she first crossed my doorstep. You
should have seen the stakes the little ninny put up. The
bucks who lose fortunes at White's and Almack's come
here to play when they're down in Brighton. They took
her on and had the lot off her.'

At White's Roger had seen members stake up to five
thousand guineas on the turn of a single card or, in the
early hours of the morning, when desperate, endeavour
to recover their losses by pledging even their country
houses. If Mary, drunk and obsessed with gambling,
had played against such men, he could no longer
doubt that she had squandered his fortune in less than
a year. Sourly he said:

'No doubt you helped her lose her money, and took a
handsome cut out of her losses.'

The blowsy gaming-house keeper only laughed and
sneered, 'What if I did? There's naught that you can
do about it.'

Roger knew only too well that she was right. With
an oath, he turned and marched out of the room.

That afternoon he took the coach to London, and
arrived at Amesbury House a little before eight o'clock.
Droopy was at home and, as Roger was shown in to
him, cried happily, 'So my letter reached you. Thank
God for that! 'Tis only the 27th, and the sale is not
until the 30th. You've still ample time to see the auctioneers and have it called off.'

Embracing him, Roger replied, 'Yes, Ned. Bless you

for letting me know what was afoot. I've thought
things over, though. I don't mean to see the auctioneers. They won't pay the money over until my property
has been sold. And I'm broke to the wide, so I mean to
let the sale take place and will claim the proceeds
afterwards.'

'No, no! You must not do that.' Droopy's tone was
shocked. 'I've money; near a six-figure income. Ample
for both of us. I wouldn't miss several thousand a year.
You must look on me as your banker for any sum you
like.'

Roger smiled, but shook his head. ' 'Tis truly generous of you, old friend, but I could not accept. I've
always stood on my own feet, and I mean to continue so.
I'll manage somehow.'

Droopy frowned. 'Roger, act not like a fool. If you
have scruples, we'll come to some arrangement. I have
it! I'll appoint you my agent. You can live at Normanrood and keep an eye on my rents, but come to London
whenever you wish. You know well that you will always be welcome here.'

Again Roger shook his head. 'No, Ned. I could not
do that. You'll recall my reason for last going abroad.
That insane wife of mine has sworn that she will kill
Georgina, even if she hangs for it, unless I remain out
of England. I had thought of appealing to Castlereagh.
I am confident he could find me some diplomatic post
in Spain, Italy or the Netherlands. But with the money
from the sale of the contents of Thatched House Lodge,
I'll have ample for my needs.'

'So be it then,' Droopy nodded. 'Since you are determined to sell, I'll attend the sale and buy such items
as I know you to treasure most. And those, I insist, you
must accept as a present.'

'I would think myself churlish to refuse. I'd like

above all the paintings Georgina did herself and gave me. But we must agree a limit on what you spend. Let us say five hundred pounds. That would be a most handsome gift. But I warn you, pieces to a greater value than that I'll refuse to accept.'

'When you have been out there tomorrow, let me have a list of things you would particularly like to retain; then, should they exceed that sum I'll keep those over it to give you as Christmas presents.'

'Dear Ned, you are the very kindest of men. But I'll not be going out there tomorrow. 'Tis the last of the three view days, so the house will be swarming with people. Thursday has clearly been set aside for the auctioneers' men to rearrange everything ready for the sale on Friday. So I'll go the day after tomorrow, as I think the odds are that Mary is there, and I'll be able to get her on her own.'

Droopy had been going out to sup with friends, but made no mention of that, in order to spend the evening with Roger, and sent out a running footman with a note cancelling his engagement. Over the meal Roger gave an account of his journey to Elba, the months he had spent with Napoleon, and the Waterloo campaign. Droopy then gave him the latest news from France. Fighting was still going on outside Paris, but the Chambers had ruled that, as the Allies had declared their war to be not against France but against Napoleon in person, he should be deprived of his authority, and they had demanded that he should abdicate. Whether he would do so, or use such troops as he had to continue to assert his will, was not yet known.

As they were about to go to their bedrooms, Droopy asked, 'Have you heard of the amazing coup that Rothschild made on the result of Waterloo?'

In giving Droopy an account of the battle, Roger had made no mention of having met Rothschild, nor of having killed Gunston. Now he said, 'So his initiative and the fatigue he must have sustained were well rewarded. I encountered him on a hill top, observing the battle, and when the Imperial Guard broke, he dashed off in a light carriage he had waiting. At that pace, over those roads, I marvel he had an unbroken bone left in his body by the time he reached Ostend.'

Droopy laughed. 'Had he had to spend six months in hospital afterwards, it would still have been worth it. Here in London, knowing that the Duke had such a mixed force under him and part of that unreliable, against Napoleon's veterans, every one was most pessimistic. The Funds fell sharply. Then, when the news came through of Blücher's defeat at Ligny and the Duke's at Quatre Bras, they positively plunged. The following morning Rothschild appeared on 'Change and leant against a pillar there, looking like death. All who saw him took it that his pigeon post had brought him early news of an even more disastrous defeat of the Allies, and he was ruined. But in fact he was the only man in London who as yet knew that Napoleon was finished. While his people openly unloaded his shares to any takers they could find, a score of secret nominees were buying up for him every share they could lay their hands on. That evening news of the Duke's victory became public and the Funds went up sky-high. 'Tis said he made a million.'

'A million!' Roger echoed. 'A million in a day! Fantastic! Then at least I can count on him investing for me at good interest such money as I can save from the wreck of my fortunes. But tell me, how fares Georgina? Is she well?'

'She is not in England.'

'What! Gone abroad at the height of the season! Why, and where?'

'To Vienna. She left London last week. 'Twas on the Saturday if my memory serves me. She took Charles and Susan with her. But why they should choose to go travelling abroad when it is high summer here is more than I can say.'

'I can,' Roger said with obvious annoyance. 'She has returned there to resume an affair she was having just before old Kew died, with the handsome Archduke John. They first met some years back when she was Baroness von Haugwitz and living in her husband's castle on the Rhine. She and the Archduke took a great fancy to each other then; and both must have remembered the other with much pleasure, for it was he who asked her to come to Vienna at the time of the Congress. As a widower he was free to make frequent rendezvous with her, although no scandal attached to their friendship. No doubt it is to prevent tongues wagging, now that Vienna is no longer thronged with half the nobility in Europe, that she has taken the young people, on the pretence of showing them that lovely city.'

Droopy laughed. 'Poor Roger. 'Tis obvious that the Archduke put your nose out of joint. But be not too concerned. Apart from that with yourself, Georgina's affairs have never lasted any great length of time. I'll wager that within a few months she will have tired of His Highness. The thing that matters is that, Georgina being abroad, you need have no fear that Mary may harm her; so you can remain here with a quiet mind for a while.'

'You're right on both counts, Ned, and I am much relieved. With an ample income of over a thousand a year, things will not be too bad. When Georgina tires

of her royal beau, no doubt she'll be willing to pay me
lengthy visits. I'm beginning to look on my enforced
exile much more cheerfully.'

Next morning, being anxious that Mary should not
chance to learn prematurely of his return to England,
instead of going out with Droopy, Roger spent several
hours endeavouring to interest himself in some of the
books in his host's fine library.

At four o'clock Droopy returned waving a copy of
The Chronicle and crying that it contained news of
interest. Spreading the paper out, he pointed to an
announcement inserted by the auctioneers. They
apologized to such of their clients as had been out to
view the contents of Thatched House Lodge, as the
sale was now cancelled, the properties having been
sold *en bloc* by private treaty.

'I am also told,' Droopy said, 'when I spoke of it this
afternoon to some of our friends at White's, that the
same notice appeared in yesterday's *Chronicle*; but I
missed it. How, think you, will this affect your chance
of making Mary hand over the money she is to receive
from it?'

Roger shrugged his shoulders and replied, 'I see no
reason to suppose this will make any difference. The
auctioneers will receive the money just the same, and
my thought was to force Mary into writing a letter instructing them to pay it into my account.'

After a moment Droopy said with a frown, 'I pray
you will succeed in that, but 'tis by no means certain.
The sale is now accomplished. There is at least a possibility that Mary may have already claimed the money
from the auctioneers; and, if so, made off with it.'

'Hell's bells!' Roger exclaimed. 'Dam'me, should
that be so 'twill prove my final ruin. I'll be left with
no more than five thousand pounds. There will be

M

nought for it but having to beg a minor diplomatic post from Castlereagh, as I had planned to do before it occurred to me that I could sell the contents of Thatched House Lodge.'

'You would be wise then to lose no time in waiting on him. Any day he may be off to Vienna, now that Napoleon is all but defeated, to confer again with our allies.'

'You are right, Ned. I'll to the Foreign Office now to secure myself a sheet anchor. Pray God that the auctioneers still have the cash, or that I'll succeed in forcing Mary to hand it over. In that case I'll be well enough off to travel, or settle in any city on the Continent I may choose. But, should she have pipped me at the post, being accredited to one of our larger embassies would at least enable me to lead a not unpleasant life.'

Droopy nodded. ' 'Tis to be hoped that your luck will be in tomorrow. But 'twould be wise, if you can see Castlereagh this evening, to think of yourself as though you had already seen Mary and could expect nothing from her. Your request will then have a greater effect on him.'

With this sound advice in mind, Roger hurried off to the Foreign Office and sent his name up to the Minister. After a wait of three-quarters of an hour, Castlereagh received him very pleasantly, listened to an abbreviated account of Roger's doings since he had left Vienna, then gave him the intelligence he had received up till that morning.

Apparently, on reaching Paris Napoleon had declared that he meant to dismiss the Chambers and assume absolute power. But the wily Fouché had persuaded him that the Deputies, although restless, could be won over; so the Emperor's prospects would be better with their backing than if he made open enemies of them. Instead of acting at once, as he had intended, Napoleon said he would sleep on it. His hesitation proved his undoing. The Chambers had time to meet, and passed a measure proposed by Lafayette—that they should continue in perpetual session and that anyone who attempted to dissolve them should be arrested for high treason. They had then called out the National Guard for their protection and formed a Provisional Government with Fouché and Carnot as its leading members.

Roger smiled. 'If Fouché is now at the head of affairs, Napoleon is finished.'

'Yes. Only this morning I received a despatch stating that the Chambers had sent him word declaring his deposition. He agreed to abdicate in favour of his son, and on the 25th left the Tuileries to retire to his private property at Malmaison.'

'And what prospects think you, my lord, have the Bourbons of achieving a second restoration?'

'They are now better than we had at first supposed,' Castlereagh replied. 'And we favour it, for it is reasonable to assume they will have learnt their lesson and grant a more liberal constitution, by which they would abide. If the people will accept them, that would mean a stable France, and we regard that as of the first importance. Immediately after Waterloo the Duke wrote to King Louis, urging him to issue a proclamation promising an amnesty to all who had taken up arms against him, and to re-enter France with the least possible delay. On the day Bonaparte abdicated the King crossed the frontier at Château Cambresis and was well received in Cambrai. The south has always been Royalist, and in the west La Vendée can be counted on to support him.'

Roger then made his request for employment.

Castlereagh raised an eyebrow. 'I recall, my lord, your making a similar request to me last August. It led to my taking you on my staff for the Congress of Vienna. But now, only loose ends have to be tied up, and there is no similar employment that I can offer to a man of your abilities.'

With a rueful smile, Roger said, 'My lord, at that time I wished only to get away from England. Since going to Vienna I have had the misfortune to sustain serious financial losses, so I am in sore need of some post which will supplement my income, for 'tis now reduced to a mere pittance.'

Having expressed his sympathy, Castlereagh said, 'I had always supposed you, my lord, to be a man of considerable wealth. It was for that reason I did not offer you any financial recompense when you accompanied me to Vienna, thinking that some honour might better suit the case. But if you are in need, I will willingly see to it that you receive a grant from the Treasury. However, over twenty years of war have proved incredibly costly, and our trade nearly brought to ruin, so I fear it could not be for any really substantial sum. Say, perhaps, a thousand pounds?'

'I would be most grateful for that. However, my request to your Lordship is for a permanent post, perhaps in the Diplomatic Service.'

Castlereagh shook his head. 'With your exceptional knowledge of affairs, few men could better represent Britain abroad as a Minister, or even an Ambassador. But I fear that is out of the question. It would be entirely contrary to precedent to deprive a *diplomat de carrière* of his chances of promotion by appointing someone who has not spent his life in the Service. Perhaps, though, we might find you some sinecure in England. I will speak of the matter to Lord Liverpool.'

As Roger could not disclose Mary's threat to murder Georgina, he replied:

'Unfortunately, a wound I received at Marengo has so afflicted my right lung that I am unfitted to winter in England. But I had no idea of aiming so high. I had in mind some quite minor post.'

'My dear Kildonan, you are not the man to run errands for people you would count your inferiors. You would be miserable in such a situation. At least you must have some position of responsibility, and be your own master. Besides, it would be embarrassing for one of our envoys to have as an underling a man of your distinction. I could of course . . . but no.'

'What was your lordship about to suggest?'

'A Consulship. But such an offer is beneath your dignity to accept.'

Roger smiled. 'You mean because I am an Earl. But beggars cannot be choosers. I can think of a dozen Jacobite Peers who went into exile with the Pretender and, their estates having been confiscated, would have jumped at such a post had they been eligible for it. Think, too, of the French who sought refuge here, owing to the Revolution. Many Counts and Marquises earned their living for years as dancing and fencing masters, or even as barbers. If you could procure me a post as Consul in some city where the winters are mild, I would be grateful.'

'So be it, then,' Castlereagh shrugged unhappily. 'I would that I could do more for you. Within a few days I will let you know what I have to offer.'

As Roger walked back to Amesbury House, he was far from happy at the result of his interview. He knew that Castlereagh had been right in his objections to securing him a minor post in an embassy; but it would at least have enabled him to reside in some capital where his name would be a passport to the best society. Now, should he fail to secure the money from the sale, the best he could hope for was to live in some port such as Genoa, Oporto, Malaga or Cadiz and spend his time assisting merchants in their business. The salary, too, of a Consul would not be more than a hundred or so a year.

It was with this in mind, and in a great state of anxiety that on the following morning Roger rode out to Richmond on one of Droopy's horses. It was a lovely summer day and, as he trotted over the greensward towards Thatched House Lodge, thoughts of other lovely days there ran through his mind: those during the first two years when he had been married to Susan's mother, living a life of leisure in the days before the name of Napoleon Bonaparte had been known to anyone except a few hundred people in Corsica and officers and men in the French Army; those in more recent years when he had had Susan as a lovely young teenager staying with him; times when Georgina, Droopy Ned and other friends had been his guests for a few nights; of the days when he had held garden parties for his neighbours and there had been games and laughter and abundance of peach-*bola*; Mary's delight when he had brought her as his wife to be mistress of his charming home. How utterly tragic that drink should have led to her becoming so possessed by evil that, down at Newmarket, she had actually fired a pistol, with murderous intent, at Georgina's face.

Outside the gate there still stood a board advertising the sale and listing the most valuable contents of the house. But across it there was now a broad strip of white paper, bearing in thick brush strokes the one word, 'Cancelled'.

No-one was about. As usual in fine summer weather the front door stood open. Tying his mount to the railing he walked up the path and into the house. No sound disturbed the warm silence, except for a faint swish of someone sweeping with a broom in the kitchen quarters. He looked in Mary's little parlour, the drawing room, his library and the dining room. It had occurred to him that, the sale having been cancelled, she might have left the house and he would have difficulty in tracing her. But it was equally possible that she was, as he had found her on his last visit, upstairs in her room, lying in bed, drinking.

He went up unhurriedly, took a deep breath and opened the door of their bedroom. Mary was there, but not in bed. Clad only in a soiled chamber robe, she was half reclining on a *chaise-longue*, from which there was a pleasant view out of the window across the park. On a small table by her side stood a glass and a decanter of port; but it was nearly full, so evidently she had only recently started her day's potations.

Her hands lay idle in her lap. Sitting up with a start, she exclaimed, 'Why, dam'me, if it's not my husband!'

With a grim smile, he replied, 'It is, madam. But I shall not burden you with my presence long. I have come here only to call you to account for having sold my property and to rectify the matter.'

'Indeed,' she sneered. 'And how, pray, do you propose to do that?'

'Very simply. Obviously, believing me to be abroad and so hear naught of it, you forged a letter in my writing asking you to sell the contents of this house and pay the proceeds into some bank where you have opened an account since you began to rob me.'

'Your guess is right, my lord, and the devil's own

work I had to pen a whole letter in your hand which
would be above suspicion. But I succeeded. The auctioneers raised not an eyebrow when I produced it to
them. They were so pleased at the thought of their
fat commission that they nearly kissed me.'

'Having stolen the greater part of my fortune, you
did not scruple to rob me of my last possessions?'

'Lud, no! Why should I, after the scurvy way in
which you threw me aside to pleasure your whore, the
Duchess. Besides, I had to have the money. That
treacherous bawd, Emily Vidall, outsmarted me and
threw me from the house near penniless.'

'I have been to Brighton and seen her. That she is as
crooked as a corkscrew I've not a doubt, and should be
rotting in some gaol. But had you not become a sot,
even the cleverest of crooks could hardly have swindled
you out of that house, the jewels you bought and many
thousands of pounds besides, without your being able
to seek legal redress on some plea or other. However,
that is now beside the point. I intend at least to secure
the money paid for the contents of this house. You will
sit down at your bureau and write a letter to the auctioneers, instructing them . . .'

'To pay the money to you?' Mary broke in with a
laugh. ' 'Twould be useless. They have already paid
me. Since the sale was by private treaty, I was taking
no chances of the buyer backing out at the last moment
and, having cancelled the auction, have all to do again;
so I insisted on immediate payment.'

'Who was the buyer?'

'I've not a notion. He insisted on remaining anony-
mous as far as I was concerned. But he must have known
this house and its contents well, and been determined
to have your treasures. The auctioneers estimated that,
sold by auction, they would have fetched anything

from twenty-five to thirty thousand pounds. I asked thirty-five to start with. There followed a fortnight's haggling, and on Saturday last I said I would settle for thirty-two thousand. By Tuesday the auctioneer's draft was in my bank.'

'You did well, then. And from what you said a while back, the auctioneers settled promptly, so the money is now in your bank.'

Mary took a swig of port and nodded. 'I received the draft on Tuesday.'

'Very well then. Instead of writing to the auctioneers you will write to your bank, instructing them to pay the amount received into my account at Hoare's.'

'You stupid oaf. Is it likely I'd so oblige you? And you cannot make me.'

Roger made no reply. Turning his back, he walked into his dressing room, took a key from a hollowed-out, leather-bound book on the bottom shelf of a dwarf bookcase there, and unlocked a small wall cupboard. From it he took a nearly full bottle of yellow pills. Returning to the bedroom with the bottle in his hand, he said quietly:

'I think I can persuade you. The choice is a simple one. Either you write that letter, or you will not leave this room alive.'

Mary started up, her eyes popping and ran a hand through her dishevelled hair. 'You don't mean that?' she gasped. 'You'd not murder me! You dare not! You'd swing for it.'

His smile was grim. 'No, Mary, you are mistaken there. It will appear that you died by your own hand. And, seeing the state to which you have brought yourself, no-one will be surprised that you decided to end your life.' Opening his hand, he showed her the bottle and went on:

'These pills are opium, compounded with another substance which is more dangerous. The latter kills pain almost at once, the opium induces sleep. Two can be taken without risk, four would possibly cause death, and six would certainly prove fatal. Unless you do as I bid you, I shall give you ten, then leave the open bottle by your bedside.' As he was speaking he uncorked the bottle, shook out a pill and put it in one waistcoat pocket, then recorked the bottle and put that in the other.

Mary had come to her feet. She opened her mouth to shout for help, but he was too quick for her. The pills were actually plain opium, and he knew that in any case he could not bring himself to kill her; but he hoped to scare her into writing the letter, and had no scruples in preventing her from bringing anyone to her assistance. His fist shot out and struck her hard in the stomach.

Instead of a cry only a gasp came from her mouth, and she doubled up. Seizing her by the hair, with his left hand he threw her backwards on to the bed. An instant later, his left hand went up to her nose and gripped it firmly. His right hand went to his waistcoat pocket and he took out the pill. After a moment she was compelled to open her mouth to breathe. Still holding her nose he pushed the pill into her mouth, then put his hand over it until she was forced to swallow.

Standing up, he smiled grimly down on her and said, 'There! That is an earnest of my intent. Attempt to cry out and I'll again drive the breath from your body and administer a second pill. Now will you write?'

Still panting for breath, she came to her feet, helped herself from the decanter to another large glass of port, drank it straight down and hiccuped.

Muttering, 'Damn you for a swine! May perdition take you,' she stumbled to her bureau, on which there were pens, ink and a sand-sifter. Having taken from a drawer a piece of paper embossed with the Kildonan crest, she pulled from a pigeon hole a letter with a heavy seal which had been slit open at the top. Holding it out to him, she said:

'I knew not where this would find you, so kept it here. Recognizing the writing as that of your whore, I naturally opened it. I scarce thought, though, that I'd have the pleasure of giving it to you in person. Read it while I'm doing as you bade me.'

Snatching it angrily, Roger took the letter from the envelope and carried it to the window to read it in a better light. It was dated June 23rd and read:

Roger, my heart,

I gather that your wife has been living in Brighton for some time. I therefore assume there will be only servants at your home, and your dear old Dan Izzard more likely than anyone else I can think of to have your address abroad, so be able to forward this to you.

Although we have been life-long lovers, it is clearly Fate's decree that we should never marry. When you were at last prepared to give up your activities on the Continent and settle down, I waited for your return in vain: then, believing the report that you were dead, and not caring what became of me, I married my old Duke. After his stroke the surgeons made a wrong prognosis and declared he might well live another dozen years. As I could be with you only infrequently, it seemed good sense to both of us that you should marry again. Alas, that your choice should have fallen on Mary, who showed such delightful promise, but has turned out to be a most wicked shrew. As you must have heard, Kew died last December, much sooner than expected, and I became free again; but you are still tied to Mary and as you are over twenty years her senior, she may well outlive you.

Therefore, my dear love, I feel you will not hold it against me that I have now decided to combine ambition, which has ever been part of my nature, with true affection. The Emperor, with less reluctance than we might have expected has, in view of my rank and a personal liking for me, given his consent. Tomorrow I am leaving for Vienna to marry my dear Archduke John . . .

Roger gave a cry of anguish and dropped the letter. Mary had been covertly watching him. The second his cry rang out, she sprang to her feet and ran from the room.

In that moment a great blackness surged through Roger's mind. With appalling clarity he realized what Georgina's letter meant for him. Gone now were those consoling possibilities that, although he must live abroad, she would at least come out for visits to share the winter sunshine with him. Even had she married an ordinary nobleman that might somehow have been managed, for she could have brought her husband with her and, with the one exception of Charles's father, she had never been faithful to her husbands as far as he was concerned, any more than he had been to his wives. But for her to marry an Archduke made such meetings impossible. She could not cozen the brother of a reigning Emperor to take her for a holiday to the South of France. And, even if he paid visits at long intervals to Vienna, he would never be able to see her in private. She would be the mistress of a great household, with ladies-in-waiting always in attendance, her comings and goings dictated by etiquette and no more able to carry on an amorous intrigue than could a prisoner in a cell. He had been stricken in a way that had never occurred to him to be possible. He had lost his beloved Georgina. Lost her for ever.

These searing thoughts raced through his mind in less than a minute—thirty seconds perhaps. He was vaguely conscious of Mary's footsteps as she fled, but did not even turn his head. She and the money he had been endeavouring to extort from her mattered little now.

He was brought back to the present by a cry and two loud thumps, one after the other. They could mean only one thing. That last long draught of port had made Mary unsteady on legs long unused to taking any exercise. She must have tripped and fallen down the stairs. Walking quickly out on to the landing, he saw that he had guessed correctly. Mary lay, a twisted, unmoving body, at the bottom of the flight. His housekeeper, Mrs. Muffet, was bending over her. Quickly she took Mary by the shoulders and lifted her a little. Her eyes were open, but she made no sound, and her head fell limply sideways.

Mrs. Muffet caught the sound of Roger's footsteps. Looking up, she exclaimed:

'Oh, your lordship. I'd no idea you had come home.' Then after a moment, she added, 'I was passing through the hall. Hearing her ladyship running, I wondered why. I saw her bump against the newel post and slip, then she lost her balance. She . . . she's broken her neck. Oh, my! The poor lady's dead.'

Together they carried Mary's body upstairs, laid it on the bed and turned the top of the sheet down over her face. In a hoarse voice, Roger said, 'Mrs. Muffet, find Dan, please. Tell him what has happened, then he is to ride over to Dr. MacTavish and bring him here as soon as possible.'

She had begun to cry, but bobbed him a curtsey and hurried from the room.

For a few minutes he stood looking down at Mary's body. They had had some happy times together, but after all she had done to him during the past year, he could feel no real grief at her death.

As he turned away, his eyes fell on Georgina's letter, where it had fluttered to the floor. Picking it up he read on from where he had left off. It consisted of assurances she had made him many times before—that he was the only man who ever had, or would really count in her life, and of deep regrets that Fate had come between them in the person of Mary, thus making it impossible for them to spend their later years together in sweet companionship and tranquillity. She added that she was taking Charles and Susan with her to Vienna for the marriage, and that they meant to buy a house there, so that they could come out to be with her for a few weeks two or three times a year, yet be much more free than if they stayed as her guests in the Archducal Palace. They would, of course, be most happy for him to accompany and stay with them whenever he was able to do so. And she counted upon his doing that, because it was unthinkable that their life-long bond should be completely severed. Perhaps he could come out with them for Christmas. In fact, she would not take no for an answer.

He gave a deep sigh. It was at least some consolation that she had no thought of separating herself from him for ever. But such visits to Vienna could lead only to bitter frustration. He would see her and again delight in her wit and laughter; but even when she spent afternoons or evenings at the house of Charles and Susan, she would have to be accompanied by a lady-in-waiting. Circumstances would never allow them even half an hour alone together. Only too well he knew the rigorous etiquette with which the members of the Imperial family were hedged about.

Slowly he read the letter through again. His eye lit

upon the phrase . . . '*I became free again but you were still tied to Mary*'. Its implication came home to him in a flash. Mary was dead. Georgina had left for Vienna only on Saturday. If he set off immediately he might yet overtake her before she reached the Austrian capital. Overtake her, persuade her to give up the Archduke and marry him instead.

In two strides he reached Mary's bureau and snatched up the letter he had forced her to write to her bank which would give him thirty-odd thousand pounds. As his eye scanned it, his heart missed a beat. Instead of a letter to her bank, she had scrawled:

You poor fool. I drew the money out on Wednesday in one-hundred pound notes to guard against any chance of your hearing about the sale and coming to claim the money. I've hidden it, and in a place where you will never find it.

Closing his eyes, he put a hand to his head. That demon-possessed, malicious bitch had pipped him on the post. She had had only the previous day in which to hide the money, so he should be able to find it, even if it meant pulling the house to pieces and digging up the whole garden. But such a search would take weeks, perhaps months. And he dared not lose even a day if he were to catch up with Georgina before she reached Vienna. He was again reduced to a beggarly income of two or three hundred a year. How could he go cap in hand to Georgina and propose that, instead of marrying her Archduke, they should marry and he would live on her? His pride made that unthinkable.

He could tell her that he had something like thirty thousand pounds here at Thatched House Lodge—if he could find it. But he might fail to do so. There was always the chance that Mary had buried the money the previous night in one of the many coppices in the great park. No, Fate had yet again stymied him.

On going downstairs he found Mrs. Muffet waiting for him in the hall. She asked tentatively if he would like her to prepare a meal for him. He did not feel he could eat anything, so he declined her offer with a word of thanks, and went into the dining room. There he helped himself to a stiff brandy and water, carried it into his library and sat there moodily for the best part of an hour.

Inevitably his thoughts centered on Mary. Even to get the money, which would again have made him independent, he would never have dreamed of killing her. And now she was dead no threat or trick could lead to her disclosing where she had hidden it.

For her own sake he felt that Fate had been kind in ending her life so swiftly and painlessly. Even with the thousands from the sale of the contents of the house what could the future have held for her? As a dipso-maniac she would have gone from bad to worse. Within a year or two at most delirium tremens would have set in. Having no relatives or friends to take care of her she would have ended up as a pathetic creature in a madhouse.

When he thought of the change that had come over her tears came to his eyes. He recalled her sweetness and gaiety when she had first fallen so desperately in love with him in Lisbon; her splendid courage during the terrible retreat from Moscow; and how utterly shattered he had felt when he had feared her dead after her fall from a high cliff into the St. Lawrence river. Her degeneration in less than two years from a gay and pretty girl into a blowsy, vicious slut, whose brain had become addled by drink, was utterly tragic. Yet he had to be honest with himself and face the fact that it was his conduct that had driven her to drink. His love for Georgina was his very life and nothing on earth could have induced him to give her up. Even so, he felt terribly conscious of his guilt and raised his bowed head only when Dan knocked on the door and announced Dr. MacTavish.

They went upstairs together. The doctor's examination was brief. He confirmed that Mary's neck was broken, and said she must have died almost instantly. Then, giving Roger a curious glance, he asked, 'Was there any witness to the accident?'

The question suddenly brought home to Roger that the doctor and numerous other people must be aware that, for a long time past, his relations with Mary had been strained, and they had been living apart. It could well be thought that, on his unannounced return, they had had a violent quarrel and he had thrown her down the stairs. He then realised how fortunate he was that Mrs. Muffet had been passing through the hall and had seen Mary trip and fall; so he was able to allay any suspicions the doctor might have had.

MacTavish said he would notify the undertaker in Richmond about her ladyship's death, have a woman sent to lay her out, and make the other necessary arrangements. Roger then saw him downstairs, mount his horse and ride away.

Now feeling that he ought to eat something before he set off back to London, he went into the kitchen and asked Mrs. Muffet to bring him some cheese and biscuits in the library. As he sat down, his eye fell on a pile of letters at one end of his desk. There were not many, as he had spent so much of his time on the Continent that few people wrote to him at Thatched House Lodge. To kill time while Mrs. Muffet prepared his snack, he began opening them, having turned the pile upside down to look first at the ones which had been there longest. There were several appeals for charity and invitations to long-past entertainments, a begging letter from an old school friend who had fallen on hard times, and one from the local parson asking for a donation to repair the church belfry. Then, when he opened the very last letter, he saw that it was from Nathan Rothschild. It was dated only two days earlier and read:

My dear Lord Kildonan,

I trust that, as a result of the Emperor's complete defeat, by this time you will have returned to your home and that this missive will reach you safely.

Your lordship's courage, resource against odds and un-hesitating determination to rescue an acquaintance in dire straits, when you came upon me overlooking the field of Waterloo, constitute an episode that I shall recall with grati-tude as long as I live.

Your gallant action enabled me to save my House from ruin, and I pray you never to forget that, at any time or any place in which the House of Rothschild can be of service to you, that service will, in accordance with instructions I have sent out, be most willingly given.

By now you may have heard that, being the first to arrive in London aware of the result of the battle, enabled me to make a very considerable sum. In fact our final figures show that we profited by over one million pounds.

Such service as you rendered me and mine cannot be fully paid for by a remuneration in hard cash; because, had you not cowed and outwitted those Dutch-Belgians, they might well have taken my life, in order to prevent my identifying them later as thieves. But I can at least send you a normal com-mission of ten per cent on my successful transaction, and I beg that you will accept the enclosed draft on my House for £100,000.

I have the honour to be your lordship's, etc., etc.

Roger's mouth fell open and he jumped to his feet. One hundred thousand pounds! He was rich again—richer than he had ever been before.

Running from the room he collided with Mrs. Muffet bringing his plate of cheese and biscuits. Pushing past her he cried, 'I have business in London that brooks not a moment's delay. You will be hearing from me.'

A moment later he had mounted his horse and was heading for the park gates. His mind was in a whirl.

Would he be able to overtake Georgina before she reached Vienna? And—if he succeeded—would she forgo her Archduke to marry him?

22

Race Against Time

SHORTLY after two o'clock Roger was back in London. Riding straight to Hoare's Bank in the Strand, he saw the junior partner with whom he usually dealt and, without one word of explanation, paid that miraculous golden draft into his deposit account. Acknowledging the young man's amazement only with a happy smile, he ran out, remounted his horse and, ten minutes later, had made his way through the crowded streets to Amesbury House.

Thankfully he learned that 'Droopy had not yet gone out, and was in his library. Crossing the hall in half a dozen strides, Roger entered the room waving his hat, his face aglow.

Peering at him with his short-sighted eyes, Droopy smiled and exclaimed, 'Hell's bells, man! What's to do? Has someone left you a fortune?'

'Yes, Ned! Yes! A hundred thousand pounds. Believe it or not, 'tis true. A draft on Rothschild's Bank for that sum, in recognition of the million I enabled him to make after Waterloo.'

Suddenly Roger's smile faded, and he went on gravely, 'But I've other news. Mary is dead. I was endeavouring to extract from her the money she received from the sale of my goods and chattels, when she gave me the slip, fell down the stairs and broke her neck. And yet more news. At Thatched House Lodge I found a letter from Georgina. It explains why she left London at the height of the season. She is on her way to Vienna to marry the Archduke John. In this I need your help, Ned, and urgently.'

'Dear Roger, you have but to ask and aught that I can do . . .'

'I mean to follow and overtake her if I can. I failed to prise the money for the contents of the house out of Mary; so when she broke her neck I was still as poor as a church mouse. Her death made me again a free man, but I could not possibly have brought myself to beg Georgina to take me as her husband instead of the Archduke. To ask her to give up such high estate and live as a Consul's wife in some foreign port was unthinkable. Neither could I support the thought of living on her and becoming known to everyone as a parasite. Then, an hour later, I opened Rothschild's letter. In a second his splendid generosity made me rich again, and no fortune hunter if I asked Georgina's hand.'

Droopy frowned. ' 'Tis all of nine hundred miles 'twixt London and Vienna, but she left here on Saturday and today is Thursday. She must be halfway there by now. I sadly doubt your being able to overtake her before she reaches the Austrian capital, and once she has joined the Archduke she will be fully committed.'

'I know it, Ned, and do I catch her first 'tis no guarantee I can persuade her to change her mind. This affair of hers with the Archduke John is no new thing and they are much attached to each other. I've had her love since we were boy and girl, but many times circumstances have compelled us to spend years apart, and in the meantime ambition to achieve rank and power have played a great part in her life. To ask her to forgo becoming an Imperial Highness is no light matter. As I've never ceased to be her lover, all the odds are she'll expect me to be content to continue in that role on such occasions as we can meet discreetly. But I've long wanted her most desperately for my own, so I'll not leave this slender chance untried. To secure it I'll have to travel more swiftly than I have ever done before. By tonight I must be in Dover. Will you lend me a light vehicle and your fastest horses?'

'You shall have of my best, and there are few better in London Town. I think a chaise I recently bought would be best for you. It has the newly-invented form of springs, so is comfortable to travel in even when driven at full speed, and several of my stable boys are trained postillions. You can send them back from Dover, but I pray you have the chaise shipped over with you. 'Tis all Lombard Street to a china orange against your being able to hire a vehicle in Calais as well suited to your purpose.'

'Bless you, Ned. Now, there is one other matter. Mary's funeral must take place within the next few days. Despite her villainous conduct towards me this past year, I would that I could pay my last respects to her; but in the circumstances that is impossible. I pray you, go down to Richmond and take charge of things there for me. Have a notice of her death and funeral put in *The Chronicle,* send flowers and attend the service yourself, for I fear few others than the servants will. Mary had no relatives other than a Canon in the north and his family. 'Twas he who succeeded to the title, and such little money as there was after the death of Mary's father. Perhaps, too, you will write the Canon a line, telling him that I am abroad. You will find his address in a book in the right-hand drawer of the desk table in my library at Thatched House Lodge.'

Droopy nodded his beaky head. 'All this shall be done. How stand you for money?'

'Thanks, I have ample. I drew the equivalent of twelve hundred pounds from Napoleon's paymaster before leaving Paris; mostly in bills of exchange, and have the greater part of it still. If you'll forgive me, I'll go now to my room, change into suitable clothes and pack a few things. Then I'll be off.'

Twenty minutes later, when Roger came downstairs carrying his valise, he found that Droopy had given all the necessary orders. He was standing behind the table in the library on which stood a dust-encrusted bottle and two glasses. The wine was a dry old *Arbois Vin de Paille* from the Jura.

'I chose this as a stirrup cup for you,' Droopy smiled, 'because it was the favourite wine of Henri of Navarre, a most wise and courageous king and the most successful of all royal lovers. May its association with him give you strength and success.'

For ten minutes they lingered over the glorious golden wine. Then a footman came in to announce that the chaise was at the door. Raising his second glass, Droopy said, 'I've had a picnic basket packed for you and sent a galloper ahead to have relays of horses ready for you every ten miles or so along the Dover road. Here's to your fortune in the mad chase you are about to undertake. May you catch her and win her.'

'A thousand thanks, Ned. You are a friend indeed.' Roger tossed off the wine remaining in his glass and they hurried out through the hall to the courtyard. A final handshake, and Roger jumped into the chaise. It had a deep back seat, wide enough to sleep on, with ample pillows and rugs. There were windows on either side, another instead of a box in front, and it was drawn by four fine horses. As it rattled over the cobbles and into Arlington Street, Roger waved and just caught Droopy's shout:

'God be with you.'

The postillions had been told not to spare the horses. Once clear of the traffic, they put them into a gallop. The Kentish fields of fruit and hop poles flashed by on either side. The relays of horses were standing ready outside the post-houses. For mile after mile the light chaise rocked from side to side. By half past six Roger was in Dover.

He had himself driven straight down to the harbour. The sum he offered to be taken immediately across the Channel soon produced a bearded skipper who owned a fast craft. Roger tipped the two exhausted postillions with the lavishness of the proverbial lord, and, at the sight of a fistful of crowns, willing hands loaded the carriage on to the deck and secured it there. The sky was overcast, but the wind not unfavourable, and in the early hours of the morning he was set ashore at Calais.

The bearded skipper sent his men to collect some down-and-outs, who were sleeping rough in wharfside sheds, to help unload the chaise. Meanwhile, Roger walked quickly to the best hostelry in the town, at which he had several times spent a night or two, and roused the landlord. A bargain was soon struck, which secured the best post horses available, and two reliable postillions. The landlord came out and bellowed to his stable hands, who were sleeping up in a loft. Putting on their clothes, some set about getting the horses ready, while others went to get the carriage from the quay. As the sun came up on Friday, the 30th, Roger was on his way to St. Omar.

At the hostelry in Calais, he had had no more than a

mug of coffee l: :ed with brandy, as during the crossing
he had supped well off the contents of the picnic
basket provided by Droopy. While doing so, he had
spread out a map on the cabin table, and made some
calculations.

As Georgina had left London on the previous Saturday, it was as good as certain that she would have
spent the night at Dover, and not crossed until Sunday,
so he had gained a day on her. From Calais to Vienna
was some eight hundred miles. She and the St. Ermins
would be sure to travel in a large, comfortable berlin
drawn by four horses. Such vehicles when used by
Napoleon with six horses and stopping only for relays,
could cover great distances in twenty-four hours. But
Georgina's party would not sleep in theirs. They would
spend the nights at good hostelries in the big cities
through which they passed and, as such travel was
fatiguing, the odds were that they would not cover more
than seventy miles a day.

If Roger's assumption was correct, that meant she
would be at least eleven days on the road, and reach
Vienna on July 6th or 7th. But this was the fifth or
perhaps sixth day since she had left Calais, so she must
already have accomplished half her journey. That was
unless, as the young people with her would pass through
cities they had never before visited, the party might stop
off here and there for a day to see the sights. On the
other hand, Georgina might take advantage of the long
summer days to drive greater distances. If so, she could
reach Vienna by July 4th. Once there, she would be
publicly received by the Archduke as his bride-to-be,
and Roger's slender chance of persuading her to forgo
this illustrious marriage would be reduced to next to
nil.

For him also to reach Vienna by the 4th meant that

he would have to cover one hundred and forty miles a day. As he intended to sleep in his carriage and drive through the nights, he thought he could manage that; and even have a good chance of catching up with Georgina while she was still a hundred miles or more from the Austrian capital. But five or six days in almost constant movement would prove terribly exhausting, and travelling fast meant risking accidents. Grimly he realized that only an iron determination, coupled with good luck, would enable him to achieve his objective.

Long experience of travel across Europe had taught him the wisdom of keeping to main highways, for to take short cuts along by-roads often resulted in infuriating hold-ups owing to unreported avalanches or swollen rivers that local ferries were unable to cross. So, when he reached St. Omar and the road veered north-east to Cassel, he had to go some ten miles out of his way until it turned south-east to Lille. There, while his horses were being changed for the second time, he bought some cold food and bottles of wine. At the hostelry he enquired if Georgina and her party had halted there on the previous Monday or Tuesday, but none of the stable hands recalled their having done so.

From Lille the way led on to Tournai and shortly before they entered that city it began to rain. To Roger's fury he had to have the hood of the chaise put up, with a resultant loss of speed, and he had to shelter miserably under the shiny leather apron. It was still raining when they reached Namur, where he warmed himself up with a hot grog, and the rain continued all through the night until, early in the morning of Saturday, they entered Liège. He had spent a miserable night crouching under the covers on half-soaked cushions, but at least he had the satisfaction of knowing that, in the twenty-four hours since he had left Calais, they had covered one hundred and ninety-two miles—a considerably greater distance than he had hoped for.

Again on the Saturday, Droopy's light chaise performed wonders. The main road took them thirty miles north-east of Aachen, but from there ran eastwards to Düren, then south-east to Coblenz on the Rhine. On and off it continued to rain, and the river was in spate, but they made splendid going on the level road that wound along the bank of the river and later along that beside the Maine. When Roger awoke from a doze, by the early light of Sunday morning he knew that, when they reached Frankfurt, they would have done over two hundred miles in the previous twenty-four hours.

But, alas, his delight at this splendid progress was suddenly dashed. On coming round a corner, the chaise narrowly escaped running straight into the back of a slow-moving market cart. Swerving their horses violently, the postillions prevented a serious smash-up but the wheels of the two vehicles scraped harshly together.

A moment later Roger realized to his fury that one of the chaise wheels was wobbling, so was liable to come off at any moment. He was forced to tell his men to reduce the pace to a walk and could console himself only with the fact that they were already in the outskirts of Frankfurt, so it would not be long before they came upon a wheelwright.

A few people were already on their way to early Mass, and a citizen in his best broadcloth directed them to the house of a wheelwright, who willingly opened his shop for them; but it took well over an hour to repair the damage. In the meantime Roger walked on to one of the best inns, ordered breakfast for himself and made his usual enquiry, whenever he changed horses, about Georgina. For the first time he got a satisfactory answer. The landlord remembered her party well; two lovely ladies and a handsome young gentleman, English and of the highest rank, also a maid. They had slept there on Thursday night and left on the Friday morning about nine o'clock, in a great, yellow coach.

This news perturbed Roger greatly. In spite of the good milage he had made, Georgina was still a full three days ahead of him, and there were fewer than four hundred miles now to Vienna. Her nine o'clock start showed that she was travelling for longer hours than he expected, and covering nearer one hundred miles a day than seventy—no doubt because the weather was so miserable that there could be no pleasure in strolling about the cities, and she was anxious to get her journey over as quickly as possible.

As soon as he was told that his carriage was outside, the horses changed and ready to start, he settled his score and walked out of the inn. As he did so, an officer wearing the uniform of a Saxon Hussar was dismounting from a steaming horse, which suggested that he was riding all-out with despatches. At the second glance, Roger recognized him as a Captain who had been attached to Napoleon's staff at Dresden, before the battle of Leipzig, when he had been with the Emperor as an A.D.C. Recognition was mutual, and greeting him politely Roger said in French:

'It looks as if you have come from the front. How goes the campaign?'

Having known him as Colonel Comte de Breuc, the Captain eyed him dubiously for a moment, until Roger added, 'Like many others, after Napoleon's abdication I went over to the Bourbons.'

The Captain then smiled and replied, 'Very well for

us. It may not be over for a month or two yet, though.
The Prussians are nearing Paris. On the 29th they
reached Argenteuil, and 'tis said that Prince Blücher
sent a flying column ahead to seize a bridge over the
Seine near Malmaison, in the hope of capturing the
Emperor, who had been living in retirement there since
the Chambers deposed him. But Blücher's plan was
foiled by Marshal Davout. What a stout-hearted man
that is! He had the bridges across the Seine destroyed
and swears that he will defend Paris to the last man
unless the Allies agree to spare the city. We have many
friends in it who let us know what is going on. Davout
has summoned every garrison in west, central and
southern France to concentrate on the Loire. He reckons
that he can still put one hundred thousand men into
the field, and, as a General, he is second only to
Napoleon. He will prove a tough nut to crack unless
we give him reasonable terms.'

'And what of the Emperor?'

'He has gone. It is now Fouché who rules in Paris.
On the night of the 29th he sent Napoleon an order to
leave the capital, and he went. It is not known whither,
but 'tis said he hopes to be granted asylum in either
England or the United States. If he is caught by the
Prussians, though, he will receive no mercy. Blücher
has sworn to hang him.'

Roger would greatly have liked to discuss the situation further; but the knowledge that Georgina was
travelling much faster than he had expected filled him
with dismay. He now felt that unless he was to lose his
chance of catching up with her, he must not waste a
second; so, with a wave of his hand, he jumped into
his carriage and the postillions at once put the horses
into a trot.

As he drove toward Würzburg, his thoughts were still

on the news he had received. Much as he disliked
Davout personally, he had a great admiration for him.
The previous year, when Napoleon's Empire had
crumbled about him and he had been compelled to
abdicate, Davout, Marshal Prince d'Eckmühl, Duc
d'Aurstädt, had still been holding out in Hamburg;
and now, although his master had fled, he was still
defying France's enemies.

How intriguing it was, too, to think that both
Napoleon's greatest servants—without whose help it is
unlikely that he could ever have been able to create his
Empire, extending from the Baltic to the toe of Italy—
should have turned against him when they felt he was
putting his personal ambition before the welfare of
France and, each in turn, brought him down. Men so
utterly different in every way—first the exquisite,
epicurean, licentious aristocrat, Prince Maurice de
Talleyrand, and now the corpse-like, slovenly, murderous, puritanical revolutionary, Joseph Fouché.

Although Roger knew that he should rejoice at the
ex-Emperor's final defeat, he could not help feeling a
little sad for him. He had always admired Napoleon's
courage, humour, great generosity and loyalty to old
friends, and he had spent so long in his company that
he had become really intimate with him. With nos-
talgic thoughts of his own youth, Roger recalled those
evenings long ago at Malmaison, when General Bonaparte, as he was then, had been wonderful company,
joined in playing blind-man's-buff, or had all but one
of the candles put out and told ghost stories to frighten
the ladies.

But there was his other side. He was foul-mouthed,
an habitual liar, utterly unscrupulous, so greedy for
glory that he always claimed battles really won by his
Marshals as victories of his own; and above all, for

his personal aggrandisement, he had caused greater numbers of his fellow beings to die before their time, or suffer in a hundred ways, than any other man in recorded history.

The fact that, after the Revolution, he had brought order out of chaos to France, his regal patronage of the sciences and arts and the great Code of Law that he had created, could not compensate for a fraction of the misery he had caused.

Roger did not think that Britain would give him asylum, and that if he did succeed in reaching the United States, the Allies would demand that he be handed over to them. This time he would be given no miniature kingdom from which he might escape and yet again bring about the futile slaughter of countless unfortunate soldiers. Unless old Blücher caught and hanged him, he would spend the remainder of his life as a prisoner, probably in the Azores or, perhaps, on St. Helena, which had also been suggested.

It rained again nearly all day, although not so heavily, and by offering most lavish sums for milage covered to each pair of postillions who took over with every relay of horses, Roger made very satisfactory progress through Würzburg to Nürnburg. That evening, at the inn where he pulled up, he learned that Georgina's party had spent the whole of Saturday there, on account of a weakened axle, and left on the Sunday morning, so he felt wonderfully elated, as they were now only a day and a night ahead of him. In high spirits he drove on towards Regensburg.

But his elation was not destined to last. Some eighteen miles short of the city misfortune struck him a savage blow. Without warning, the mended wheel gave way. The chaise lurched, and Roger was woken by being thrown violently sideways, then forward. By thrusting out his hands, he managed to save his face, and the postillions succeeded in halting the horses quickly. But it was about four o'clock in the morning, and they were passing through forest country, where dwellings were few and far between.

Roger learned from the postillions that they had driven through a good-sized village about three miles back, and that some two miles ahead of them lay another; but that was only a hamlet, so there was a much better chance of there being a man competent to mend the wheel in the former than in the latter. Cursing, Roger set off back along the road between the dripping trees, with one postillion, leaving the other to look after the horses and his valise.

When they reached the village after a three-mile tramp through the mud, the dwellings were still in darkness, but they succeeded in finding the local blacksmith's and roused the smith from his sleep. A generous offer from Roger induced the man to agree to come out and mend the wheel, and a quarter of an hour drifted by while he dressed and collected his tools. He was an uncouth fellow, and possessed neither a trap nor a horse, adding that no-one in the village owned any vehicle other than farm carts; so the three of them had to trudge the three miles back to the carriage. For the best part of half an hour the blacksmith tinkered with the wheel; then, to Roger's fury, sullenly declared that he could not refix it so that it would be really safe.

By then it was seven o'clock and raining again. Tired, wet and bitterly frustrated, Roger strove to control his anger, for he could not leave Droopy's fine carriage abandoned there in the ditch. Much as he begrudged the money, he had to pay the surly blacksmith handsomely to have it collected and stored until someone could be sent to mend it properly and arrange for its return to London.

With his two postillions he then set off for the hamlet. There, enquiries soon disclosed that there also no transport was available other than farm wagons and cart-horses. Neither was there for miles round a big house where something speedier might have been procured. So a wagon it had to be.

In spite of Roger's urging, the peasant who drove them could not get his big cart-horse into more than an amble now and again, so it was getting on for one o'clock before they reached the centre of Regensburg. In nearly thirty hours, Roger had covered only one hundred and seventeen miles, so the odds were that, instead of gaining on Georgina, she was still further ahead of him than she had been the previous morning.

For several hours past he had been hoping that, once in Regensburg, he would quickly be able to secure a good vehicle and fast horses with which to make up this lost time. But he again met with infuriating disappointment. It transpired that a wedding of importance was being celebrated in the city that day, and the landlord of the inn at which Roger had been set down had hired out both the carriages and a coach that he owned. An ostler was sent out to try the other inns, in search of a speedy vehicle, either for hire or sale. Roger took the opportunity to have his cloak dried and ate a hearty hot meal, but after an hour he began to fume with impatience at the ostler's failure to return. At length the man came back, but he had been able to secure only a small coach drawn by a single horse. Seething with rage, Roger was torn between delaying further in the hope of finding something better, or continuing his pursuit of Georgina at a pace that would probably be less than that of her coach. Deciding that

N

any progress toward Vienna was better than none at all, he urged the coachman to do his utmost, and jumped into the coach, but it was close on three o'clock by the time he was clear of Regensburg.

With only one horse and a heavier vehicle, he could now travel at only a third of the speed he had attained when in Droopy's chaise; and, as they followed the road on the south side of the Danube, he suffered agonies as the horse had to be walked up every hill and often far from steep slopes. During the afternoon and evening, every time the horse was changed he enquired about quicker means of transport, but none was available. It was midnight before he had covered the sixty-eight miles to Passau, and from there it was only one hundred and fifty miles to Vienna.

He had driven the six hundred and fifty miles from Calais, because he could not possibly have got as far as he had in the time had he ridden, for he would have been compelled to break his journey several times and lose precious hours in sleep; but now he decided that his only chance lay in taking to horse. Paying off the coachman, he picked the best mount among those in the stable of the inn where the coach had pulled up, had his valise strapped to the back of the saddle, and headed for Linz. Having ridden the forty-five miles during the night, he dismounted in the stable yard of the post-house there, to change his horse, at five o'clock on the Wednesday morning.

After rousing an ostler, he made his usual enquiry about Georgina's party, and learned that they had eaten there at about four o'clock on the previous afternoon, then driven on. These tidings filled him with a surge of new hope. There were still over one hundred miles to go to Vienna, and it was certain that Georgina would put up somewhere on the way for the night; so he might catch her yet. Eagerly he asked the man the most likely town in which she would next break her journey, and he replied, 'Probably Amstetten, as that is about three hours drive from here.'

Beaming with delight, Roger realized that he could easily reach Amstetten in a couple of hours, and so be there when they came down to breakfast. It so happened that at that moment a sleepy stable lad, making his way to the privy, passed near them, and caught what they were saying. Halting, he said, 'The party in the yellow coach won't be going that far, *mein Herr*. The coachman asked me how far Enns castle was up the river, so they must be biding there this night.'

'Enns?' Roger repeated quickly. 'How far is that?'

'Twenty-five kilometres, or thereabouts,' the lad replied. 'Place takes its name from a small river running, into the Danube. Town's some three kilometres up it, an' the Archduke's castle a kilometre or so further on.'

'The Archduke's castle!' Roger repeated, aghast. It had instantly recurred to him that, on Georgina's previous visit to Vienna, the Archduke had planned to ride out to meet her. Evidently that is what he had now done, and received her at the castle the previous evening as his future bride.

In an agony of distress, Roger absorbed the full implications of the turn—so disastrous for him—that events had taken. All those hundreds of miles swaying in unending discomfort while being driven at high speed in Droopy's chaise, gold and silver coins by the score given to postillions, ostlers and others to hasten the pace at which he could cross Europe, close on a week without a single hour of proper sleep—only in the end to prove a waste of money and endurance.

Only two minutes earlier he had exulted in the belief that within another few hours he would have Georgina in his arms and might persuade her to become his wife. Suddenly a few words from a stable boy had destroyed that hope utterly. Georgina was already with her Archduke. She would have been formally received by him, with royal pomp and ceremony as his fiancée, so was now fully committed to become his wife.

23

Do You Remember?

AFTER a moment Roger said wearily to the man who had just saddled a fresh horse for him, 'I'll not ride on after all. Instead, I'll go into the inn and take some refreshment.'

Dawn had not yet come, and the dark rain clouds shut out what would have been first light. But the ostler roused a potman who lit candles for Roger in the deserted parlour of the inn. The man also took his long cloak, so that it could be set to dry before the kitchen fire, as soon as that was lit. Morosely silent, Roger sat slumped in an easy chair, his long legs spread out in front of him, and his hands thrust deep in his breeches pockets. When the potman asked if he would not like a hot drink to warm him up, he merely nodded. Ten minutes later he was brought a big tankard of *brantwein* and water, flavoured with mint.

As he sipped the steaming brew, he wondered if it would be a good idea to go to bed in the inn and get drunk. When he had learnt that Amanda had died in giving birth to Susan, he had done that and remained drunk for a week. He had done so again on returning to England in 1810, expecting to marry Georgina only to learn that, believing him dead, she had married old Kew. This was just such another occasion.

Having drained the tankard, he sent for another and

got through half of it while still brooding bitterly on his misfortune. Then, quite suddenly, the thought came to him that he was behaving like a selfish fool. Georgina had believed him tied to Mary indefinitely, and that as he was so many years older than she was there could be little chance of his regaining his freedom. Therefore, now that Georgina's Duke was dead, she could not be blamed for rejecting a solitary widow's lot and instead marrying again—this time a companionable man for whom she felt affection. Moreover, her beauty, charm and high intelligence had brought a royal lover to his knees, no less than the brother of an Emperor.

Every friend she had ever had must be showering her with congratulations. Why then should he, Roger, stand aside and play the churl? Her marriage to other men, or his to other women, had never marred their friendship. Instead, although she would know his feelings, his proper role was to hide them and congratulate her most heartily on her great good fortune. Having come so far to find her, instead of returning angry and broken-hearted, he must put a brave face on his misfortune, ride the few miles which were now all that separated them, accompany her to Vienna and appear delighted to have got there in time to be present at her wedding.

It was now past six o'clock. The whole house was astir and the maids busy in the kitchen. Abandoning what remained of his second tankard, he shaved, washed and tidied himself in the closet, then ordered breakfast. Over the meal he took his time, as Enns Castle was less than two hours' ride away, and he thought it unlikely that Georgina and her friends would come downstairs before about nine o'clock. Refreshed by his rest and meal, his mind now calmer than it had been for days and cheered by the rightness of the decision he had made, at half past seven he set out on the final stage of his long journey.

The road continued alongside the broad Danube. Owing to the recent heavy rains, the river was very swollen and in several places had overflowed its banks, flooding large areas of fields. On reaching the tributary and turning right toward the town, he saw that the Enns was also in spate and that the lower lands on both sides of it had become sheets of water. The town itself was small, having only one street of gabled houses along the river, with three turnings off it that petered out after a few hundred yards, into hilly country.

On breasting a slight rise half a mile beyond the town, he had his first view of the castle. It was an imposing pile, rising from a shallow valley, with the clusters of irregular turrets and spires usual in Germanic *schloss*. As he came nearer, he saw that from the river side of the road that passed below it, there ran a short, high causeway leading to a one-storey pavilion built on piles in the river, and now only just above the level of the rushing stream.

It was a type of 'folly' popular at that period with noblemen whose great houses were adjacent to rivers or lakes. As they were never permanently occupied, and servants could be sent back to the mainland when no longer required, they made an excellent setting in which to entertain a pretty mistress. In some cases they were fitted up as casinos, in which the host and his friends gambled far into the night; in others, they were simply used as places in which a family could be served with a meal as a pleasant change from the gloomier setting of a baronial dining hall.

As Roger looked at the little pleasure house, he thought how delightful it would be there on a sunny evening, and that even now, in spite of the rain, to sit

for a while behind the broad main windows would not
be unattractive, on account of the view of the surging
river. A few hundred yards above it there was a dam
with, beside it, a weir over which the water was
cascading, the floods having turned it into a foaming
waterfall.

Turning off the road, Roger trotted up the slope that
led to the great doorway of the castle. It faced toward
the little town, and it was evident that, from the upper
windows on that side of the lofty pile, a fine view could
be obtained over the roofs, of the Danube curving away
into the distance. As he jerked down the iron bell pull
beside the lofty door, Roger wondered for a moment
if he should ask for Georgina or the Archduke. When
last they had met, the Archduke had been quite pleasant to him, but he knew of Roger's old association with
Georgina, so it was possible that he might, now he and
Georgina were engaged, resent the unannounced
appearance of her former lover. So when the door was
opened by a footman, he gave his name and asked for
the Duchess of Kew.

The man called to a boy who was standing nearby to
take Roger's horse, then bowed him into a spacious
hall, and referred him to a soberly-clad major-domo.
In reply to Roger's repeated inquiry, the senior servant
told him that the *gnädigefrau Herzogin* was still up in her
suite, but the *Graff von St. Ermins* and his lady were in
the orangery, and went off to announce him.

Two minutes later Susan came running from a nearby passage. Throwing her arms round Roger's neck,
she cried, 'Oh, Papa, what a wonderful surprise! How
lovely to see you and know that you are safe and sound.'

Charles was behind her: tall, handsome, smiling. As
they shook hands, Roger said, 'You have no idea how
relieved I was when I learned from your Uncle Ned

that you had accompanied your mother on this journey.
I had greatly feared you might have been killed or
seriously wounded at Waterloo.'

'I was mightily peeved that I missed the battle,'
Charles replied. 'But I suppose I should really count
myself lucky. When I was out riding toward the end of
April, my mare put a hoof down a rabbit hole, I sailed
over her head, and had a nasty fall. Broke my right
arm, and badly at that. So when the regiment crossed
to Belgium a few weeks later, my arm was still in splints,
and I was left behind in charge of the depot.'

'Where . . . where is the Archduke?' Roger nerved
himself to ask.

'Oh, he's not here yet,' Susan said, with a shake of
her reddish-gold curls. 'The weather has been so
atrocious that instead of loitering to see the sights in
some of the cities through which we passed, we decided
to get our journey over as soon as possible. We arrived
a whole day—a day and a night rather—sooner than
we were expected. So he'll not be here until midday
tomorrow.'

Roger went quite pale, and for a moment his heart
stood still. Although Georgina was under the Archduke's roof, she had not yet seen him, and so had not
publicly accepted him as her fiancé. Fate, after all,
had given Roger this last slender chance of persuading
her to change her mind before she was fully committed.
Swallowing hard, he said to Susan:

'I . . . I gather that Georgina is not yet down. Run
upstairs, darling. Let her know that I'm here, and that
I've driven like Jehu these past few days, in the hope
of catching up with her before she reached Vienna.'

Charles shook his head. 'No running upstairs for my
lady wife these days.' Then, with a laugh, he waved a
hand toward Susan's stomach.

It was only then that Roger realized that her full skirt did not altogether conceal the fact that she was pregnant. With a cry of delight, he took her more gently in his arms and kissed her, exclaiming:

'You darling girl! So you're going to make me a grandfather. How truly marvellous! And, indeed, you must not run. It was naughty of you just now even to have run out to greet me. We must all take the very greatest care of you.'

'I'll go up to Mama,' Charles said, 'and tell her of your arrival. She will, I know, be overjoyed to hear that you have come all this way to be present at her wedding.'

Roger had recovered sufficiently to take that unconsciously nasty jab without changing his expression; but he thought it well to let Georgina have his news at once so that, instead of springing it upon her, she might have time to think about it before she saw him. So he said to Charles, 'Would you also tell her that my wife is dead?'

'Oh, dear!' Susan opened wide her fine blue eyes. 'Poor Mary. I . . . I'm sorry.'

'You have no need to be,' Roger told her gently. 'She died suddenly and almost painlessly. She had become a confirmed drunkard, so had she lived on, in time she would have suffered greatly for many months. Perhaps, too, in a lunatic asylum, for in one way at least she was already insane.'

'Poor woman,' Charles muttered. Then he added, 'I'll tell Mama. And, no doubt, she will come down; although, being greatly tired from our journey, she had meant to spend the day in bed.'

Roger gave a faint laugh. 'Tired, did you say? I'm more than that. I'm utterly exhausted. I've made the journey from London in a little under a week. I've not spent a single hour in bed, and I'm black, blue and aching in every limb after being bumped about in fast-driven conveyances. I could lie down here on the floor and fall sound asleep within a minute.'

'Why don't you then?' asked Charles. 'Not on the floor, of course, but I'll order a room to be got ready. 'Twill not take more than ten minutes.'

For a moment Roger considered the suggestion. In his present state, his mind half-numbed with fatigue, he was in no condition to plead his best with Georgina. After a few hours' sleep he would be able to put up a far better showing. The best time of all would be when they had dined, laughed together again and renewed the physical attraction for each other that always exercised its spell when they had been separated for some months.

'Very well,' he agreed. 'Give my message and my love to your mother, and have a bed made ready for me. At what time do we dine?'

'Six o'clock. And we are having dinner down in the little pavilion on the river. There is a kitchen there, and all one may require. From that level the view of the rushing water and the foaming weir must be most spectacular. It was Mama's idea when she saw the place on our arrival here yesterday evening, and she made enquiries about it. I'll have you called at five o'clock.'

Twenty minutes later Roger was in bed and so sound asleep that it would have taken an earthquake to rouse him. When he was shaken awake by Charles some six hours later, he saw that his valise had been unpacked and the fine clothes in it laid out. After shaving he dressed in them and went downstairs, to find Georgina sitting with the St. Ermins in a small, richly-furnished drawing room.

Standing up as he came in, she smiled and said, 'I

can hardly bid you welcome to my castle, Roger dear, but the welcome is no whit the less for that.' Then she kissed him on both cheeks.

The butler served little glasses of *Baratch*, a dry Hungarian spirit distilled from apricots, and for a while they talked of their respective journeys, the almost ceaseless rain, the inches-deep mud into which one stepped every time one left a vehicle, and the awful bumping over bad stretches of road.

Then, putting on their cloaks and escorted by footmen holding large, carriage umbrellas over them, they made their way down the incline and across the causeway to the charming little pavilion. For a few minutes they were thrilled by the sight of the swirling river rushing only a foot or so below the floor on which they stood, the clouds of spray rising from the foam of the waterfall that the weir had become, and the solid sheet of water that now overlapped the dam itself falling like a curtain of liquid glass. Then they sat down to dine.

Over the meal Roger told of the life he had found Napoleon leading on Elba, of how he had been carried off by him on that amazing, unopposed march to Paris, and of the campaign that had ended at Waterloo. Then he described his swift return to England on receiving word from Droopy that Mary had put the contents of Thatched House Lodge up for auction, only to find that she had already sold them by private treaty. Briefly he gave an account of their meeting and how she had met her death, yet cheated him in the end by having hidden the money she had received for his property.

'Oh, poor Papa!' exclaimed Susan. 'But the money must be either in the house or near it, so the odds are that you'll find it after a while.'

He nodded. 'Let's hope so, but 'tis the loss of my things that grieves me far more. Some of them I greatly treasured, particularly a portrait of Georgina by Gainsborough, and several of her own paintings that she gave me.'

Georgina smiled at him. 'Dear Roger, you shall have them back, and more, I promise you. Immediately I heard about the sale, I guessed it to be another of Mary's disgraceful measures to bring about your ruin, so I had an agent get in touch with the auctioneers. I instructed him, though, not to reveal my identity; lest, should Mary learn of it, she might refuse to sell to me, out of malice. The negotiations took some time, since I was determined she should not get one penny more out of me than I was forced to pay. They were still haggling when I left London: but I had given my agent orders to close the deal before the sale, whatever it might cost.'

His mouth a little open, Roger stared at her. 'That then is why the public auction was not called off till the Tuesday. And 'twas you who had bought the whole contents of the place by private treaty. To prevent their being distributed among scores of people was indeed a truly generous gesture. And it cost you thirty-two thousand. Well, thank God, I'm now in a position to reimburse you and buy the lot back.'

Georgina stared at him in surprise. 'But . . . but from what you said, I gathered that by this sale Mary had robbed you of nearly every penny you possessed.'

Roger laughed. 'I thought that, too, for an hour or so after she had broken her neck. Then I opened a letter that had been waiting for me there. It referred to an incident I have not yet told you about which occurred during the battle of Waterloo.' He then described his meeting with Rothschild and the astounding generosity of the banker resulting from it. As he finished, he added: 'And, of course, I'll gladly repay you for having bought all my treasures.'

Georgina shook her head. 'I could not be more glad for you, but I'll let you do no such thing. Brides may give as well as receive wedding presents, and I mean to make them a present to you.'

By this time they had finished their dessert and the servants had cleared away. Waving aside Roger's thanks, Georgina said to the two young people, 'My darlings, I feel sure Roger has some other things to say to me, so leave us now. Have an early night. Happy dreams to you both.'

Smiling, the other two stood up. There were kisses all round, then Charles and Susan left the room and were followed by the last servant over the causeway. Meanwhile, Roger and Georgina remained seated, facing each other across the table. After a moment's silence Georgina said:

'Dearest Roger. Mary now being dead and you once more in possession of a handsome fortune, I know what you have followed me to say. But do not say it. My mind is already made up.'

Her expression was so firm that the words he had been preparing to say died on his lips. He could only mutter, 'You . . . you really mean that?'

'I do. And nothing anyone could say will change it.'

For many years Roger had known Georgina's strong will, and that her decisions were irrevocable. Things had turned out as he had feared they might when he had learnt at Linz that she had reached the Archduke's castle before he could catch up with her. He now felt there was nothing he could do but accept defeat gracefully; so, with a smile, he said:

'I only hope that your decision will mean great happiness for you.'

'It will,' she declared confidently. 'As you know, I am now forty-seven. I no longer crave new beaux, adventure and excitement. I've had a marvellous life, and lived every day to the full. So, too, have you—the Right Honourable the Earl of Kildonan, General Count de Breuc, Commander of the Legion of Honour, Chevalier of the Order of St. Anne of Russia, of the Crossed Swords of Sweden and of the Star and Crescent of Turkey. 'Tis a fabulous career.'

'True enough,' he nodded. 'And you may add to that Knight of the Bath, for the Duke has promised me the Order. How little I thought to rise so high on that day long ago when, in the room at the top of Sway Tower, you seduced me.'

'Damn you, Roger! I've always maintained it was the other way about, though I'll admit now that I led you on. As for me, I've done none too badly, but I was always ambitious.'

'You were indeed. Do you remember boasting to me on that day we first made love that you would be a Duchess before your hair turned grey?'

'I do indeed. But 'twas a near thing; and although it still appears to be blue-black, for some years past I've had to have it tinted.'

'No matter. You are no whit less lovely than when you were in your early thirties; and as a bedfellow you have, if it be possible, improved with the years. What hundreds of wonderful nights we've passed in each other's arms. Do you remember that night on which we agreed that you should marry Charles's father, and I would marry Amanda? Then we slept together.'

Georgina roared with laughter. 'Could I ever forget it? What would those poor dears have thought of us had they ever known? But we played fair with them afterwards, and never let them guess that in secret our love for each other never ceased to exceed the love either of us could give them. And, as it proved, those were the only truly happy marriages we ever made. Is it not wonderful, too, that through them the blood of both of us is about to animate the heart of a mutual grandchild?'

'Nothing could give me greater joy. Let's hope that Charles's father and Amanda may now be overlooking us, be aware of that and share our delight. Though 'tis possible that one or both of them may by this time have become reincarnated.'

'I doubt that,' Georgina shook her head. 'According to such few contacts with the beyond as I have been granted, and to the pundits of the East, our holidays from the trials and tribulations of life down here average two hundred years. Talking of this, though, I do not envy your Mary her next incarnation. Her wickedness toward you has accumulated to a mighty heavy score she'll have to pay off.'

Roger made a gesture of dissent. 'Not necessarily. Her last years were desperately unhappy. It may be she was then paying for unhappiness she had inflicted on someone else in a former life. I, too, am not guiltless as far as she is concerned, for her suffering was due to my putting my own happiness before the vows I took when I married her.'

'No, Roger. There I do not agree. Moral obligations differ with races and communities. Those of an Asiatic potentate, a Negro living in a jungle and an Elder of the Scottish Kirk have no more resemblance than red, blue and yellow. In England and other places people in puritan communities may kick over the traces from time to time, but they have been brought up to

regard themselves as guilty sinners on having broken
their marriage vows. Whereas, with the aristocracy a
different code has long been the rule. Both sexes while
still young became aware that, though they may hope
for a period of married bliss, 'tis no more than normal
that, later, husbands and wives should indulge in
peccadillos. Mary's misfortune was that she had the
mind of a bourgeoise, whereas you acted only in
accordance with the code accepted by your caste.'

'You comfort me somewhat.' Roger smiled. 'May
the Lords of Light not punish us too severely for our
many infidelities to those to whom the Christian Church
would have bound us indefinitely, however much we
came to regret having gone to the altar with them. I
wonder, though, what roles you and I will next be
called upon to play.'

' 'Tis believed we are tenuously linked in groups, so
perhaps I'll be your father.' Georgina laughed, 'If so,
I warn you that I have ever believed that to spare the
rod is to spoil the child.'

'The bond between us is so strong that we might be
born twin sisters.'

'That would be pleasant, yet put an unwelcome
prohibition on certain of our activities. I'd prefer even
to be a maiden aunt who dotes on you.'

Roger grinned. 'My aunt you might be—but a
maiden, no.'

They were silent for a moment, then Roger resumed,
'Recalling our marriages. The worst we ever made were
yours to von Haugwitz and mine to Lisala. Behind the
façade of her great beauty she was a most evil woman,
and as a man your husband was her equal. 'Twas a
miracle that we escaped their plot to kill us both, and
that instead they should have received their just deserts.
Do you remember how astonished we were as we sat

on that vine-covered terrace beside the Moselle and learned that they were both dead?'

'Lud, yes! And the joy I felt at knowing myself to be free of that bisexual brute. I must have been mad to marry him, but he was devilish good-looking, intelligent, and could be most amusing at times. It must have been reaction after having had poor, unexciting Mr. Beefy for a husband.'

'Your sugar king. Yes, he was a simple, honest fellow; although, like many of his kind, he was ignorant concerning all great issues, so enraged me when he laid down the law about foreign affairs.'

'He was my devoted slave, and I had a great fondness for him. It was long before I could forgive you for having brought about his death.'

'Oh, come, Georgina! You know well it was a tragic accident. I had snatched up a sword to use it on that lecherous oaf, Gunston, for having attempted you. Beefy should have done so himself, but he lacked the guts. Instead, the pacific-minded fool sought to separate us. 'Twas no fault of mine that he received my thrust. The case of Humphrey Etheridge was very different. Finding us in bed together was excuse enough for his rage, but he should have behaved like a gentleman and called me out, not attempted to strike you across the face with his riding whip. Even so, I have ever had upon my conscience that the terrific blow I landed with my fist upon his heart should have brought about an apoplexy.'

'You need not have. 'Twas the heavy scent bottle I threw at the same moment catching him on the temple that killed him; and I felt no regrets about his death. By the time you first returned from France he lived only to ride to hounds by day and punish the port at night. I had Stillwaters, and had become Milady

Etheridge. It was for that I really married him, but I was bored to tears and, had you not reappeared on the scene, I'd have taken some other lover.'

He smiled. 'You could not have given me a more ardent welcome. Do you remember those weeks I spent as your guest at Stillwaters, before Humphrey found us out?'

'Could I ever forget them! We were both scarce in our twenties, and had roused in each other fires that neither of us could quench.'

'Ah, that waiting until I could safely cross your boudoir from the bedroom you had given me, to yours, seemed interminable. And the nights were never long enough.'

'We made up for that, though, nearly every day; and in the oddest places. I'll ne'er forget how scared I was that one of the gardeners would come upon us, yet could not bring myself to refuse you when you insisted on having me in the boiler house.'

'I felt as though the end of the world had come when I had to go abroad again after you first became a widow.'

' 'Twas as well you did, for your having been in Russia enabled you to save me from being hanged for Humphrey's death.'

'True, and my securing the means to do so brought about the fall from which my first wife died.'

'You did not love her, though. I forget her name, but you always spoke of her afterwards as "that little Russian bitch".'

'It was Natasha Andreovna, and a bitch she was. Piping hot one day and icily malicious the next. I'd never have dreamt of marrying her had not the Czarina Catherina forced me to as the lesser evil than being sent to Siberia.'

'Catherine the Great! What a wonderful list we could make between us of the people we have known. For you, Napoleon and all his Marshals . . .'

Roger laughed. 'Do not forget his sister, the beautiful Princess Pauline. Stap me, but she was a riot to go to bed with.'

'Better than myself?'

'How can you even suggest it?'

'I thank you, Sir; but from the Princess's reputation you flatter me. 'Tis said she even lured her brother into committing incest with her.'

'I do not believe that. But she'd have proved a marvellous asset to a whore-house, for she could keep half a dozen lovers satisfied, yet con all of them into believing her to be his mistress alone.'

'I'd find no pleasure in performing the physical act unless I were also mentally drawn to the man, and no woman can have a deep feeling for so many men at one time. But to continue with our list. You have known nearly every crowned head in Europe, and Pitt, Talleyrand, Metternich, Nelson, Emma Hamilton, Sir Sidney Smith, Castlereagh, Fouché, Sir John Moore, the Duke, Carnot, Barras, Mirabeau, Robespierre, Danton, Marie Antoinette, and I know not who else.'

'Ah! That last name! How it recalls my first years in France while I was still in my teens.'

' 'Twas during that time you had that long, desperate passion for young Athénaïs de Rochambeau. Do you remember how, on your return to London, I consoled you for having lost her?'

'Indeed I do. Never shall I forget that first night we spent together in your studio. But I had not lost Athénaïs, for I had never had her then. When I first came upon her, and she saved me from Fouché by letting me hide in her coach, she was but a lovely child of fifteen, and during the four years that followed I thought of her only as an angel come down to earth.'

'Angel or not,' Georgina rallied him, 'you found her warm enough flesh and blood when you met her again a few years later, during the Revolution.'

'Yes, she was working with the Royalists in La Vendée, and refused to leave France when I begged her to let me get her away to England. But the very night we again came face to face she eagerly became my mistress. And what joy we had of each other for a few short weeks. The grief I felt was near unbearable when, after a brief absence from Paris, I learned that her lovely head had fallen into the bloody basket of the guillotine.'

'Oh, that ghastly Revolution! And you, unscrupulous devil that you are, to gain your ends with the Terrorists incited the mob to hang my poor Don Diego from a lamp post.'

'Nay. 'Twas but an act of justice. Politics were only a side issue in the matter. I would have killed him anyway. And you were in part to blame for his death. You encouraged him to become your lover, and 'twas in the hope that you would marry him were he free that he murdered his wife. I played only the part of an unofficial executioner.'

'So you told me afterwards. But your case against me is a poor one, since she was clearly already being unfaithful to him—and with you. I greatly doubt if you would have gone to such extremes against the poor fellow had it not been for your love for her.'

'My dear, in that you are wrong. 'Tis true that I was attracted to Isabella, for she was intelligent far above the average, in addition to her Spanish dark good looks. But she was a prude by nature, and I pursued her more out of a determination to make her submit to me than from genuine passion. As it was, I succeeded only after she had married, and then found her poor sport in bed. So her death meant no more to me than the loss of a friend. Yet, in the long run, that unpleasant business turned out all for the best; because, with Don Diego out of the way, your thoughts soon turned more favourably to Charles St. Ermins, and you became his Countess.'

'True, and apart from those brief periods you and I were able to spend together, dear Charles gave me the the happiest years of my whole life.'

'Moreover, he raised you from being merely a Baronet's wife to the status of a great lady.'

Georgina shrugged. 'With Stillwaters and ample money, I had already made myself that. There were few people of importance whom I did not already entertain: a score of Princes and Ambassadors, Fox, Sheridan, Beau Brummel, Canning, Portland, Addington, Gainsborough, Reynolds—and I had the pick of the handsomest and wittiest men in London as my lovers. Though, unlike yourself, I can count few heads outside Britain, since I have travelled only in Europe, and the West Indies.'

For a moment Roger was silent, then he said, 'The terrifying experiences we met with on our voyage to the Caribbean recalls to me that sweet chit, Clarissa. Although she was so young and, as Amanda's cousin, had been taken by her on the voyage with us, she did her damnedest to seduce me that night she and I were lost together in the forest.'

'At least that testifies to her good taste,' Georgina laughed. 'And, knowing you as I do, it amazes me that for once you observed your marriage vows and repulsed her. She got you in the end, though, after Amanda's death. What a minx she was, becoming a

stowaway in the ship in which you sailed to India as a
result of your duel with Malderini.'

'Yes. During the voyage I had to pass her off as my
boy servant. Her passion for me was insatiable, and I
came to love her dearly. For a while in Calcutta we
lived most joyously, and I would have married her
had not Fate decreed the poor sweet's death.'

'You certainly did not waste your time during your
travels in the East. There was, I recall, a Sultan's
daughter that at one time you designed to marry. I
forget her name.'

'Zanthé—and I would have, had not Napoleon
whisked his entourage back to France without warning.
Eastern women have a great advantage over Western
ladies when it comes to making love, for they are
taught from their teens a hundred ways of raising a
man's desire again and again. But Zanthé's amorous
accomplishments apart, I twice owed my life to her. In
Syria she saved me from a most hideous death, then
nursed me through the plague on our way back to
Egypt.'

'Syria! Egypt! Where is there that you have not
been? You have lived in near every country in Europe,
and visited Africa, Brazil, the United States, Canada,
Turkey and Persia. I envy you your travels.'

'They had their fascinating side, but were far from
an unmixed blessing. Apart from the many battles in
which I had to risk my life and was several times
wounded, I was caught up in a revolution in Turkey,
in Africa I narrowly escaped being eaten by cannibals,
and in Persia I met Lisala who brought more pain and
grief upon me than any other woman in my life—except
perhaps for Mary—and I'd never have married Mary
had I not by chance come upon her again in Russia.
No, my dear, you are far more to be envied for having

spent most of your life in England—especially England as she has been during this past half-century.'

'Why that particular period? You seem to forget that during the greater part of it we were at war.'

'The war made little difference to the world of rank and fashion in which you were, and still are, a reigning beauty. In the years through which we have lived, England achieved a greater degree of intellect, art and elegance than any other country since the fall of Rome. Under a monarchy, the powers of which are curtailed by a strong and, in many cases, gifted nobility, we enjoy true individual liberty and protection from becoming the victims of the uneducated masses—as proved the case in France. Our morals were our own affair, and we could do as we would without others pulling long faces. But I see a new spirit abroad for which I do not care. The increase in industrial under-takings has brought discontent among the poorer people; individualism and eccentricity are now frowned upon, and this new century is bringing in a hypo-critical puritanism among the upper classes. The days when men carried swords at night, and wore tricorne hats were more to my liking than these times in which they carry umbrellas and wear stove-pipe headgear.'

Georgina nodded, and her dark curls glinted in the candlelight. 'In that I do agree. Men were then not afraid to fight a duel on some pretext, although in fact from resentment at a slur put on a woman they loved; and false prudery now oft makes conversation insipid. The fashions, too, are designed to convey it. How prim and dowdy girls look nowadays in these new bonnets, compared to those great cartwheel hats bedecked with ostrich feathers that I used to wear.'

'Yes. We dressed like peacocks then, and lived to love, fight, laugh and play merry hell all round the town. Those were the days, and we'll not see their like again. But we have been blessed to have been born in our age, and in having such wonderful experiences to look back upon. 'Tis right now that we should settle down to a quiet life. I doubt, though, if you can expect a life of true relaxation with your Archduke.'

'Archduke?' Georgina echoed, her big eyes opening wide. 'Roger, you fool! I'll find it hard to tell John tomorrow; but 'tis you, not him that I am going to marry.'

For a moment Roger was struck dumb, as a great surge of joy ran through him, and she went on quickly: 'I told you a while ago that I had made up my mind and nothing anyone could say would induce me to change it. I made it up the moment Charles told me that Mary was dead, and you had near killed yourself pursuing me. There could be but one reason for that, and I near fainted from sheer happiness.'

His hands were quivering as he stretched them out across the table, caught hers and, almost hysterical with joy exclaimed: 'You mean it? You really mean that you'd give up the splendour that could be yours for a quiet life with me?'

Georgina smiled her bewitching smile. 'Have you ever known me say a thing I did not mean? Where shall we make our home? I am so attached to Stillwaters that I should be loath to leave it permanently; but if you'd prefer the cosiness of Thatched House Lodge to my great mansion I could be happy with you there.'

'No, no, beloved. Stillwaters is equally dear to me. That must be our country home, but I'll keep Thatched House Lodge on and we would go there for a few nights occasionally.'

She nodded. 'Such an arrangement would be perfect. I shall no longer have Kew House in Piccadilly as that naturally goes to my old Duke's heir. But whenever we are up half the night at a ball in London we can always stay with Charles and Susan in Berkeley Square.'

'True. I wonder how long we shall continue to enjoy dancing till dawn.'

'For a few years yet. But just now and then; for I've near had my fill of it. I only pray, though, that we do not outlive our physical well-being. To become blind or deaf, or suffer the other inflictions of old age does not bear thinking upon.'

'We may be spared such penalties. 'Tis said that those beloved by the gods die young, and they have favoured us above most mortals.'

'They have indeed; and should they maintain their kindness when they call one of us, whenever that may be, they will ordain that the other shall not long survive the first to go.'

Roger nodded his agreement. Then, after a moment's silence, he said, 'We do become too serious, and have made no mention of your other residence. Now and then, for old times' sake, we must laugh and love the whole night through in your studio out in Kensington, where you have so oft transported me to paradise.'

She gave a happy sigh. 'What memories we share! How well I recall that night on which I challenged you to drink more champagne than myself, with the result that finally we both fell out of bed.'

'Ah! And that on which you slipped cantharides into my soup, and were well paid out for it by my attentions being so unremitting that you were too exhausted to get up next day.'

'Enough, dear Roger; enough I pray. I'll never deny myself to you but there will be other joys. Now that all is at last set fair for a prolonged peace we'll be able to travel on the Continent together. We must, too, visit again your little château at St. Maxime. Do you remember how we spent the New Year's Day of 1810 there?'

Roger laughed. 'How could I forget. And do you remember . . .?'

Georgina did not hear the remainder of his sentence. At that moment his words, the pattering of the rain on the roof and the rushing of the river beneath them were drowned by a thunderous roar. They both sprang to their feet and ran to the big window. In the falling dusk, a terrifying sight met their eyes. The dam had burst, and a towering foam-tipped wave, fifty feet high, was racing towards them. Inevitably it must sweep away the frail little pavilion like a house of cards—and everything in it.

As he threw his arm about her, she cried, 'Oh, Roger, my love, there is no escape! We are about to die! This is the end!'

'Nay, dear heart,' he answered firmly. ' 'Tis no more than a passing to a new beginning.'

The Roger Brook Saga

THE LAUNCHING OF ROGER BROOK

1783-1787. Roger runs away from home and his first love, Georgina Thursby, then sails with a smuggler to France. In turn, he becomes assistant to a travelling quack doctor, a lawyer's clerk and secretary to a Marquis, with whose daughter, Athénaïs, he falls in love. Versailles in its heyday. To save Athénaïs from an hateful marriage he fights a duel; then learns a diplomatic secret that may cause war. His desperate flight with a price on his head back to England.

THE SHADOW OF TYBURN TREE

1787-1789. Roger's love for Georgina, now Lady Etheredge, is renewed. They are surprised in bed by her husband, who is killed. Roger enters Mr. Pitt's service as a secret agent. He is sent on missions to the Courts of Denmark and Sweden. The war between Sweden and Russia over Finland. In St. Petersburg Catherine the Great endeavours to ensnare Roger. On his return home he finds that Georgina is about to be tried for the murder of her husband.

THE RISING STORM

1789-1792. Roger sent to France by Pitt. The Court at Fontainebleau. His mission to the Grand Duke of Tuscany, accompanied by Isabelle d'Aranda. Kidnapped. The opening scenes of the French Revolution. The taking of the Bastille. The King and Queen brought to Paris by the mob.

Roger's mission to Naples. He joins Isabella at the Court of Spain. Her fate and that of her husband. The affair of Nootka Sound. Pact made by Georgina and Roger when in bed together—she to marry the Earl of St. Ermins and he Amanda Godfrey.

THE MAN WHO KILLED THE KING

1793-1794. Roger sent back to France by Pitt. 'Bring me the Dauphin, Mr. Brook, and I will pay you £100,000.' The storming of the Tuileries by the mob. Roger disguised as a *sans culotte* becomes a Revolutionary Commissioner. His attempts to rescue the Royal Family from the Temple. The Great Terror. Sent by Robespierre to Brittany. The trial of Athénaïs. The King and Queen guillotined. Roger traces the Dauphin.

THE DARK SECRET OF JOSEPHINE

1794-1796. Roger sails for the West Indies with Amanda, Georgina and Charles St. Ermins. Captured by buccaneers. Escape to Haiti; Josephine's girlhood. Roger recalled. The Revolutionary War. Roger sent to Prince de Condé, then to General Pichegru to bribe him to come over to the Royalists. Paris under the Directory. At the siege of Toulon Roger meets Bonaparte, then only a Captain of Artillery. Later he plays decisive part in marriage of Napoleon and Josephine.

THE RAPE OF VENICE

1796-1798. A duel causes Roger to leave England. His ship is wrecked off Zanzibar. He succeeds in reaching India; his desperate adventures there. Return via Egypt to Venice where he falls foul of the 'Council of Ten'. Bonaparte there after his first victorious campaign in Italy. Josephine saves Roger and Napoleon takes him on his Staff. Conspiracy to assassinate Napoleon foiled by Roger.

THE SULTAN'S DAUGHTER

1798–1799. Roger accompanies Bonaparte to Egypt as an A.D.C. Battle of the Pyramids. He gets away to Naples. Nelson and Emma Hamilton. Roger sent to Sir Sidney Smith at siege of Acre. Rejoins French in retreat to Egypt. Battle of the Nile. Returns to France with Bonaparte. Conspires with Talleyrand and Fouché. Napoleon's bid for supreme power—the *coup d'état* of 18th Brumaire.

THE WANTON PRINCESS

1800–1805. Roger crosses the Alps with Napoleon and is wounded at Marengo. He gets back to England and is sent by Pitt to St. Petersburg; the murder of the Czar Paul I. Recognized as an Englishman, to save his alibi, Roger covers the seventeen hundred miles to Paris in fourteen days. Napoleon makes himself Emperor and his sister, Pauline, a Princess. Roger's love affair with her and his return to England, where he is imprisoned for homicide. His escape to France and mission to Spain. Trafalgar.

EVIL IN A MASK

1806–1809. Roger wounded at Eylau and captured by the Russians. His missions to Turkey and Persia. Return via Spain to Lisbon, now threatened by the French. Carried off with Portuguese Royal Family escaping to Brazil. Back in Europe at the Conference of Erfurt he again meets Georgina, now Baroness von Haugwitz. Both narrowly escape death in a castle on the Rhine.

THE RAVISHING OF LADY MARY WARE

1809–1812. Sent to Hamburg by Napoleon, Roger is arrested by the Prussians and condemned to death. His escape to England and visit to Lisbon during the Peninsular

War. His missions for Wellington to Marshals Masséna and Soult, then capture by bandits. Escape, return to England. Sent as secret envoy to Bernadotte, Crown Prince of Sweden; thence to the Czar Alexander in St. Petersburg. Rejoins Napoleon. The terrible retreat from Moscow in 1812.

THE IRISH WITCH

1812–1814. Roger unwillingly carried to New York. The Anglo-American war of 1812. With the help of Red Indians he escapes to Canada and so home. Meanwhile his daughter by Amanda, Susan, and Georgina's son Charles, who are in love, have become involved with the New Hell Fire Club. The witch who runs it has designs on Charles's great fortune, but he joins Wellington's Staff in Spain. Roger learns that he has been taken prisoner and, to secure his release, rejoins Napoleon. The battle of the Nations. The witch lures Susan to Ireland. Napoleon again defeated in France, abdicates. Roger goes in search of Susan who is about to be sacrificed in a Black Mass on Walpurgis Night.

DESPERATE MEASURES

1814–1815

All volumes can be obtained, or will be published, separately in the clothbound, black and gilt Lymington (collectors) Edition or in Arrow paperbacks.

Dennis Wheatley's work has been published in:

BELGIUM
BRAZIL
CZECHOSLOVAKIA
DENMARK
FINLAND
FRANCE
GERMANY
HOLLAND
HUNGARY
ITALY
MEXICO
NORWAY
POLAND
PORTUGAL
RUMANIA
SPAIN
SWEDEN
SWITZERLAND
TURKEY
THE UNITED STATES
YUGOSLAVIA

also in

ARABIC
ARMENIAN
FLEMISH
HINDI
MALTESE
RUSSIAN
SERBIAN
SLOVENE
THULU